LIVING OFF THE GRID

A Collection of Short Stories
and Words of Love New and Revisited

Volume III

By JB Evans

Copyright © 2024 **JBE Publishing**

All rights reserved. No part of this publication may be reproduced, distributed, or transmitted in any form or by any means, including photocopying, recording, or other electronic or mechanical methods, without the prior written permission of the publisher, except in the case of brief quotations embodied in critical reviews and certain other noncommercial uses permitted by copyright law. For permission requests, write to the publisher, addressed "Attention: Book Rights and Permission," at the address below.

Published in the United States of America

ISBN 979-8-89395-668-9 (SC)
ISBN 979-8-89395-666-5 (HC)
ISBN 979-8-89395-667-2 (Ebook)

Library of Congress Control Number: 2024922479

JBE Publishing
222 West 6th Street
Suite 400, San Pedro, CA, 90731
www.stellarliterary.com

Order Information and Rights Permission:

Quantity sales. Special discounts might be available on quantity purchases by corporations, associations, and others. For details, contact the publisher at the address above.

For Book Rights Adaptation and other Rights Permission. Call us at toll-free 1-888-945-8513 or send us an email at admin@stellarliterary.com.

Author

As a writer I used letters to form words. Then I use the words to lead you down a path of emotion. I write short stories of love. Think about that?

Do I pull from my experiences and try to transfer them to you? Or maybe I try to think how your heart dealt with your feelings of love. Or maybe a blend of both. I pull on heart strings. I pull you into the story. Not everyone with every story. But the readers tell me when a real connection is made. That story had a special meaning. It pulled just the right string.

The love a mother has for her child. A couple sharing wine and holding hands. The soft words mixed with strong feelings. The pair who grew old together. Their love tested by the fire of time. The one who sits alone. Their other half no longer there. A smile still forms. The feelings still live in the heart. Just as strong as the day first felt. Things are different now. Love still so strong, a strength that will never weaken.

So, I write. I use the letters to form the words. I take your heart and walk a path of make believe. And when we reach the end, all I hope for is that you smile and say "I enjoyed that"! And hopefully you look forward to the next one.

Acknowledgements

The following people did the work so I could publish:

    My Daughter: April Cooper

    My friend: Corrie Cabral

    My brother-in-law: Dick Speed

John Fleck: He planted the seed and encouraged me to do this project.

Audrey Muffoletto: who came up with a "short cut" to cut the work in half.

Rebecca Dixon: For making sure the story contents were correct.

My sister Beth: She demanded to be in the acknowledgements.

To Stellar Literary Press and Media for their support.

And last: To Office Depot in Beaumont Texas. The staff assisted me in every way.

                Thanks to Everyone!!!

Contents

Chapter 1

Story 1 "The Proposal" 1
Story 2 "Friends Come When You Need Them Most" 3
Story 3 "Your choice in how you live" 5
Story 4 "Loss is not fully understood by the very young" 6
Story 5 "The Honor Protected" 7
Story 6 "The Love between mother and son" 9
Story 7 "The Doctor finds himself" 10
Story 8 "Teacher" 11
Story 9 "Ageing" 13
Story 10 "Letter to GOD" 15
Story 11 "The Word Friend Makes Me Smile" 16
Story 12 "Life is Sometimes Unfair" 17
Story 13 "We All Grow Up" 18
Story 14 "What We Just Don't Know" 20
Story 15 "Know Love Takes Work" 21
Story 16 "Unselfish Service" 22
Story 17 "Things Slowly Change" 24
Story 18 "Express Yourself" 25
Story 19 "Sometimes you just need to believe" 26
Story 20 "The Love of a Wife" 28
Story 21 "Hugs" 30
Story 22 "Miracle of Passion" 31
Story 23 "The Special Evening" 32
Story 24 "Final Days" 34
Story 25 "Christmas" 35
Story 26 "A Kind Man in the Park" 36
Story 27 "A Kitten named 'Cotton'" 39
Story 28 "What is Beautiful?" 41
Story 29 "How Generations Change" 42
Story 30 "When a Friend becomes Family" 43
Story 31 "I want to be a Fireman" 45
Story 32 "The Memories Held in A House" 46

Story 33 "Falling in Love is not always something you control" 48
Story 34 "Dreams" 49
Story 35 "A Friend Named Hope" 51
Story 36 "Becoming a Man" 53
Story 37 "The Old Man and the Boy" 54
Story 38 "Never Blame the Innocent" 56
Story 39 "He's Along Now" 57
Story 40 "The Speed of Love" 58
Story 41 "Seeing Life Through Clearer Eyes" 60
Story 42 "Love Lost" 62
Story 43 "Still in Love" 63
Story 44 "Life Never Ends" 65
Story 45 "The Square Peg" 66
Story 46 "The Image Reflected" 68
Story 47 "We Are Always Watched Over" 69
Story 48 "Family Lost then Found" 71
Story 49 "Fatherhood" 72
Story 50 "Secrets" 74
Story 51 "How much Love can you give your Pet?" 76
Story 52 "Save Our Planet" 78
Story 53 "Attitudes" 80
Story 54 "Parenting" 81
Story 55 "The Love of Brothers" 83
Story 56 "Always a Dancer" 85
Story 57 "Can We Change" 86
Story 58 "The Man Never Seen" 87
Story 59 "Her First Love" 89
Story 60 "He Saw His Mother's Love" 91
Story 61 "Timing" 92
Story 62 "The Value of Love" 93
Story 63 "A Woman So Special" 95
Story 64 "Letter to Santa" 96
Story 65 "First Kiss" 97
Story 66 "None of us Die Alone" 99
Story 67 "What a Mother Sees" 100
Story 68 "Blessings" 102
Story 69 "Dreams" 104
Story 70 "A Daughter Returned" 105
Story 71 "Friendships Sometimes Changes the Odds" 107
Story 72 "A Fathers Love" 109
Story 73 "You're Fishing for a Dinner Date" 111

Story 74 "We All Can Change" 113
Story 75 "The Beauty Your Eyes See" 115
Story 76 "Be the Example for Good" 116
Story 77 "The Pressure of Not Disappointing Your Parents" 117
Story 78 "Trust" 119
Story 79 "Time Never Rest" 120
Story 80 "ABCs to Relationships" 121
Story 81 "Depression" 122
Story 82 "When Paths Cross" 123
Story 83 "The Loss of a Dear Friend" 125
Story 84 "Life" 127
Story 85 "Just Separated" 128
Story 86 "Being Together" 129
Story 87 "The Heart Knows Best" 130
Story 88 "Potential" 131
Story 89 "Final Words" 133
Story 90 "The Wonder of Ageing" 135
Story 91 "Hours Left" 136
Story 92 "Dark Clouds" 137
Story 93 "We All Need What We Don't Ask For Sometimes" 139
Story 94 "What you Teach, They Learn" 141
Story 95 "I can't explain it" 143
Story 96 "The Romance of Holding Hands" 144
Story 97 "Love" 145
Story 98 "Giving is the Reward" 146
Story 99 "True Love" 147
Story 100 "David and Mary" 148
Story 101 "The Road of Life" 150
Story 102 "In my Fathers Image" 151
Story 103 "Morning Coffee" 152
Story 104 "Letters of Love" 154
Story 105 "Marriage" 156
Story 106 "A Letter to GOD" 158
Story 107 "Life in between" 159
Story 108 "He wouldn't give up" 161

Chapter 2

Story 1 "Remembered Stories"... 163
Story 2 "We Should Never Lose on Love".. 165
Story 3 "Guarding Angles"... 166
Story 4 "People of the streets".. 167
Story 5 "A New Dad"... 168
Story 6 "Young couples in love".. 171
Story 7 "Coffee in bed"... 172
Story 8 Growing Up is Not a Cake Walk".. 174
Story 9 "Love that doesn't die"... 175
Story 10 "The road to Manhood"... 176
Story 11 "My Destiny"... 178
Story 12 "The influence of a bird"... 180
Story 13 "Why I Love your Mother".. 182
Story 14 "Enduring Love"... 183
Story 15 "Aging".. 184
Story 16 "The Final Walk".. 186
Story 17 "Always Keep Them Close".. 188
Story 18 "Who We Are".. 190
Story 19 "Growing Up".. 192
Story 20 "Living Alone".. 193
Story 21 "Family".. 195
Story 22 "Letters of Love"... 197
Story 23 "The wonders of Aging"... 199
Story 24 "She Met Sam"... 200
Story 25 "What is your Happiness".. 201
Story 26 "You're The One Who Chooses"... 203
Story 27 "Remembered How"... 204
Story 28 "The Journal"... 205
Story 29 "The Power of Caring".. 206
Story 30 "The Love of a Son".. 208
Story 31 "Strength"... 210
Story 32 "Getting Through"... 211
Story 33 "What is Life".. 213
Story 34 "Friendships"... 215
Story 35 "When It's Important, Don't Accept a No"........................... 217
Story 36 "You Touch Lives".. 218
Story 37 "My Beautiful Flower".. 220
Story 38 "Believe In Angels"... 221
Story 39 "The danger of speed"... 222

Story 40 "Life and Stories of Love" 223
Story 41 "Churches" 225
Story 42 "Reunions with Purpose" 226
Story 43 "I Love You Dad" 228
Story 44 "The Power of Love" 229
Story 45 "Years of Friendship" 231
Story 46 "The Changes of Life" 232
Story 47 "When Love Matures" 233
Story 48 "Ever Changing" 234
Story 49 "Do you enjoy being in Love" 235
Story 50 "Memories – They Remain Raw Longer Than Wounds" 236
Story 51 "Time and its affects" 237
Story 52 "If I died tonight" 238
Story 53 "The Loving of Pets" 239
Story 54 "Memories make experience" 241
Story 55 "Neutrality" 242
Story 56 "Love Your Pet Equal to Their Love for You" 243
Story 57 "Children in the park" 245
Story 58 "After Life" 247
Story 59 "I See Beauty Everywhere" 248
Story 60 "Let's go fishing today" 249
Story 61 "The neighbor's boy" 251
Story 62 "The Unexplained" 253
Story 63 "What are you thankful for?" 255
Story 64 "Maturing" 257
Story 65 "Daddy's Love" 258
Story 66 "My magic window" 260
Story 67 "The Thief" 261
Story 68 "One More Time" 263
Story 69 "The Classics" 264
Story 70 "You are always cared for" 265
Story 71 "He Wants Her for His Wife" 267
Story 72 "We Choose" 269
Story 73 "Under Orders" 270
Story 74 "Keep The Fire Burning" 271
Story 75 "A Stranger today, a Mother forever" 272
Story 76 "Separation" 274
Story 77 "When We Move On" 275
Story 78 "We just love dogs, you can't help it" 276
Story 79 "Repairing a loss" 278
Story 80 "A Prayer to His Father" 280

Story 81 "Paths cross and cross again" 281
Story 82 "You make your life" 283
Story 83 "Morning Coffee" 284
Story 84 "You make your life" 286
Story 85 "Call me Teacher" 287
Story 86 "Never Refuse to Help Someone in Need" 289
Story 87 "The feelings of Love" 290
Story 88 "The Song of a Bird" 291
Story 89 "A Father and His Daughter" 293
Story 90 "The Picture Box" 294
Story 91 "I wanted you to know" 296
Story 92 "Make Time for Your Child" 297
Story 93 "Habits of Dogs" 299
Story 94 "You Never Die" 300
Story 95 "Compassion Can Come from Anywhere" 301
Story 96 "I'm 27,375 Sunsets Old" 303
Story 97 "I Hold His Hand" 304
Story 98 "Into The Wild" 305
Story 99 "What We Love" 307
Story 100 "I needed to remember" 308
Story 101 "We All Live for A Reason" 309
Story 102 "Valentine's Day" 310
Story 103 "I Want To Remember" 311
Story 104 "You Can Always Help" 312
Story 105 "She Needed Help" 313
Story 106 "Smiles" 315
Story 107 "The Love of A Pet" 317
Story 108 "Enjoy Each other" 319

Chapter 3

Story 1   "Responsibility to your family is utmost" 321
Story 2 "Finding Love in a Crowd" 323
Story 3 "It's hard for love to leave sometimes" 324
Story 4 "The Bond of Friendship" 325
Story 5 "Chance meeting" 327
Story 6 "Love is a choice" 329
Story 7 "While he forgets" 331
Story 8 "Your Weakness Can Sometimes Be Your Strength" 333
Story 9 "I was granted my wish" 335
Story 10 "The Journey" 336

Story 11 "Sometimes Your Life is Chosen" 338
Story 12 "A Bible on the bed" 340
Story 13 "Pictures in a box" 342
Story 14 "It's You Who Makes Your Future, Not Your Surroundings".. 344
Story 15 "Show your Love" 345
Story 16 "Family" 346
Story 17 "Courage" 349
Story 18 "Umba" 350
Story 19 "Early Mornings" 355
Story 20 "Senses" 357
Story 21 "Nothing remains the same" 359
Story 22 "The strong and the weak" 360
Story 23 "Happiness is always just around the corner" 361
Story 24 "Respect this life" 363
Story 25 "Revenge" 364
Story 26 "Greatness" 366
Story 27 "He can find your smile" 367
Story 28 "Unending Love" 369
Story 29 "No Matter What, You Can Always Do Something" 370
Story 30 "Inseparable" 372
Story 31 "The Friendship of two boys" 373
Story 32 "Asking For Help" 375
Story 33 "Good in everyone" 376
Story 34 "A Prayer answered" 378
Story 35 "Strange Events" 379
Story 36 "The strength of my love for you" 381
Story 37 "The value of a child" 382
Story 38 "How Commitment is Defined" 384
Story 39 "A bottle of pills" 385
Story 40 "Change isn't a bad thing" 387
Story 41 "A Beautiful Dream" 389
Story 42 "The Power of Hope" 390
Story 43 "The Power of a Prayer" 391
Story 44 "Happiness is Sometimes Hidden" 392
Story 45 "Time is only so long" 393
Story 46 "Mother Nature" 395
Story 47 "Introductions" 396
Story 48 "Brave Parents" 397
Story 49 "Kindness" 398
Story 50 "Different Lives; Common Happiness" 399
Story 51 "I'm my father's son" 400

Story 52 "That inner voice" 402
Story 53 "Sometimes the One You Love Will Fade" 403
Story 54 "Don't grow old alone" 404
Story 55 "The sacrifice of love" 406
Story 56 "The Honor Protected" 407
Story 57 "We're here for a reason" 409
Story 58 "Our Pets" 410
Story 59 "We Can All Look the Same, Yet Be Very Different" 412
Story 60 "We are all unique" 414
Story 61 "Together Always" 415
Story 62 "The Orphan" 416
Story 63 "How old are you" 418
Story 64 "What the young believe" 420
Story 65 "She Just Wanted to be a Nun" 421
Story 66 "Together Forever" 423
Story 67 "Another day together" 424
Story 68 "To Earth I Return" 425
Story 69 "He saved her life" 427
Story 70 "How fast things can change" 429
Story 71 "Sometimes There is No Map for the Road We Find Ourselves On" 431
Story 72 "I've loved her for so long" 432
Story 73 "Friendships can weather storms" 433
Story 74 "The Responsibility of Being the Oldest" 435
Story 75 "Peace and Happiness" 437
Story 76 "I Love" 439
Story 77 "I See Great Things" 440
Story 78 "Never get to comfortable" 441
Story 79 "The only child" 442
Story 80 "Friends can be strangers" 444
Story 81 "Be the example" 446
Story 82 "He crossed over to save his father" 447
Story 83 "Aged Friendships" 449
Story 84 "A love story" 451
Story 85 "Conversation with Dad" 452
Story 86 "People Can Be Very Different" 453
Story 87 "A Grandmothers Love" 455
Story 88 "Not a bad life" 456
Story 89 "Always Have Something Nice to Say" 457
Story 90 "Starting Over" 458
Story 91 "The Deepest Love" 459

Story 92 "The Perfect Date" 460
Story 93 "How I Go" 462
Story 94 "My Quite Time" 463
Story 95 "Just The Possibility of Losing Your Special Love" 464
Story 96 "Always Smiling" 465
Story 97 "This I will do"... 466
Story 98 "Protectors Come in Many Forms"....................................... 467
Story 99 "A Father Forever"... 468
Story 100 "Leaving the Nest"... 470
Story 101 "Never Allow Anger to be a Wedge" 472
Story 102 "All the Reasons I Love You" 473
Story 103 "The good in Life"... 474
Story 104 "We Never Know the Full Story"....................................... 475
Story 105 "From Kindness comes Beauty" 476
Story 106 "The Passage of Time"... 478
Story 107 "Complicated Love"... 479
Story 108 "Tipping the Scale" 480
Story 109 "I still Kiss him good night" 481
Story 110 "A New Dawn"... 482
Story 111 "Happiness is never that far away" 483
Story 112 "The Beauty of a Flower" 484
Story 113 "Marriage"... 485
Story 114 "My Special Person"... 486
Story 115 "Be Careful of What You Ask Your Grandkids to do" 488
Story 116 "Living Of Grid"... 490

Chapter 1

Story 1
"The Proposal"

There was a man with a lot of years under his belt. He was in love and had been seeing a special woman for over a year. He now wanted to marry her. So, this was how he asked.

He set up a table and lights in the backyard, since it was going to be a beautiful fall evening. He ordered food, so there would be no kitchen time. Soft music played. He then drove to pick her up. He had told her to dress up for a special night. He walked her to the car, opened the door, and told her how lovely she looked tonight. It made her blush a little. He held her hand as he drove. It felt so soft.

He reached his house and quickly moved around, opening her door again. Together, they walked to the backyard. She was very impressed with what he had done. But she had no idea of his plans. They drank a glass of wine and spoke softly. He couldn't believe how beautiful she was tonight. His heart was pounding.

They ate their meal, even danced a few times. Then he knew it was time to ask for her hand. He stood up, walked to her side, and got on one knee.

"My love, I want to be with you every day. I want to wake up by your side and tell you I love you every morning. You are so beautiful and have such a caring heart. It's bold of me to think you might answer my question with a yes. Your eyes still have the sparkle of your youth. I'll be there when you need me and never leave your side. You are my beautiful flower.

"Marry me. Make me the happiest man on earth. I know you love me. I see it all the time. Do this for me. Will you marry me? Will you let me put this ring on your finger? Will you be my wife?"

Her eyes filled with tears. She said, "Yes, I will marry you. We will tell each other our love every day. You are truly my best friend. I know you will make a wonderful husband. I want to spend the rest of my life with only you." With that, he stood up with her and slipped the ring on her finger. They sealed their promise with a kiss.

People can fall in love at any age. Don't keep it pinned up inside. Let the other one knows.

Story 2

"Friends Come When You Need Them Most"

An old man fell and broke his hip. So, in the hospital he went.

Now on a good day he wasn't pleasant. So, under these conditions he was a total jerk. Each and every day he yelled at the staff. No one wanted to work with him. Then entered Nancy. She was going to take none of his abuse. In fact, she was willing to dish it out.

The first week was a battle of strong wills. No one was sure who won that round. The second week he slapped her. She looked him dead in the eyes and slapped back. Her slap would make Will Smith look like a sissy. Then she added "if you give out anger, you get anger back! I'm your nurse. You will not treat me with disrespect. Learn that!"

He could feel the sting on his cheek. But in some strange way he did just that. He gained respect for her that morning. Slowly his days became much calmer. He looked forward to seeing her. One day she shows up with a wheelchair. He looks and says, "no way." She placed both hands on her hips and gave him the look of, don't start that shit with me today, I'm not in the mood. With time he was moved to a different area of the hospital for rehab. He was assigned a different nurse. His position? Hell no. Get Nancy in here, now. He argued for days. Finally, he had the director come to his room. "I'll make this easy. How large of a donation to this hospital will it take to have Nancy assigned to me starting today?" Nancy showed up that afternoon.

Nancy was no longer his nurse. She was his friend. And friends he didn't have many of. Really just one. She left the hospital and became his personal attendant. She got him reconnected with his family, which was no easy task. His life had gone through a total reshape. All for the better.

Finally, he called her in to talk with him. When she entered the room all his family was there. She was a little confused.

"Nancy, you have returned me to happiness. Me and my family are so very thankful. You have been added to the will. I've hired a new caretaker. You will supervise her work. You can keep your room or we'll buy you a home. Your choice, you're family now. No one will protest the will. Thank you for everything."

When he passed on, she sat with the family. And they included her in all family events. Her unique way of handling his anger was just what he needed. She thinks of him daily and smiles when she looks back. He was her friend also.

Story 3
"Your choice in how you live"

We all have a path we will walk in life. I believe there is no choice in this.

We see and do things that shape us into the people we will be in life. If we learn respect, then we will be respectful to others. If we learn generosity, we will be generous to the less fortunate. If we're taught to work and be a part of the society, we will be great citizens.

This lifestyle is under attack. Why work? Let me take what's yours. Let the government pay me to play all day. I want free food. I want free housing. I want money mailed to me. And if I need more, I'll just steal it.

So, what about the ones who don't buy into such a path? People who take pride in being a contributing citizen. Why are they looked down upon? Men just want to be men. Women want to be women. Why mix the two? If you do I guess that's your business. Just don't push it on me. I'm walking my path. And I'm both happy and content with my decisions. You walk your path and I'll walk mine. You don't answer to me and the reverse.

I won't judge you. Live your life. I could care less what picture is on a can of beer. If you're a believer you'll be held in judgement at the end of life. Till then live-in harmony. There are jerks out there for sure. And they're on both sides of the fence. Let them battle it out between themselves.

Walk your chosen path in peace. Take pride in a good life. And seek out other like-minded people for you friends. Surround yourself with all that is good. And there is plenty of good out there. Look closer.

Story 4
"Loss is not fully understood by the very young"

A small girl asks her father, "Where exactly is Mother?"

The father stops what he's doing, gets down on a knee, and says, "She's in heaven."

"But where is heaven? People talk about it, but where is it?"

The father picks her up, goes to a chair, and holds her close.

The girl says, "I know it's not in the sky. That's silly. So where?"

The dad kisses her forehead and says, "Heaven is in your heart. Your mother is there. She's always with you. Always by your side. But because of heaven, she's in my heart also. She protects us from harm every day. She watches out for you and me and keeps us safe. That's her job now."

"Why did she die? Why did she leave us? I miss her."

The father hugs her a little tighter. "God wanted her to be with him. He needed another angel. Your mother was very special. You … we were lucky to have had her for the time we did."

A tear rolls down her cheek. "But I miss her so much. I cry at night."

A small pain goes through the father's heart. He kisses her again. "Never cry alone in bed. From now on, come to me, and we'll miss Mom together."

Dad is gone now. I will always remember that night. He made me feel so safe. So, loved. He lives in my heart now. I hold my child. I hum to her as she sleeps in my arms. I hope one day she'll ask me, "Where is heaven?" And for a short time, I'll be my father. I'll give his words to her. I'll hold her tight and make her feel safe like my father did me. I miss him so.

Story 5

"The Honor Protected"

There was a quarterback and a virgin, their paths crossed.

The football player had his way with the girls at school. He really showed little respect. Then one day he noticed a pretty young girl who wasn't interested in him. So, he told his friends he would "bed" her in less than two weeks. And so, his pursuit began. What he didn't expect was her confidence and morals. She cut him off at every approach.

Finally, she had him listen to her. "I'm saving myself for the man I marry. I will pick him more than he will pick me. I have standards, standards you have long lost. I'm after a marriage that will last till death. Not some weak fun in the backseat of your dad's car. So go on your way and let me be."

But his pursuit of her didn't go unnoticed.

Another girl became very jealous. She wanted to destroy her. She placed drugs in her locker and turned her in. And sure, enough the drugs were found. It was looking bad.

She sat in a chair across from the principal with police on each side of her. She was about to be taken in when the door opened. There stood the quarterback. He entered the room. "What is this about?" Asked the principal.

"I'm here to confess what was said. I placed the drugs in her locker because I knew she would never be suspected. I didn't want them found on me. I set her up."

She looked up to his eyes. She could see he was lying. A quick-thinking policeman asked him what they found. His story quickly fell apart.

"Why would you try to help this girl?" He sat down and began to speak. "I had a chance to talk with her once. In that short time, I saw my weakness and her strength. She has more character than all of us combined. She is innocent. On that I'll stake my life. I don't know who did this to her, but I will stand my ground, it was me."

"Your life would be ruined!"

"What about hers?" he asked. "What's happening is not justice. I'll stand for her innocence. And I will not back down!" In the end she was released.

Out of the blue he got a call. It was her. "You once asked me out. Is that still there? Just for a coke and ice cream. But we could talk."

"Yes, it's still there. And I'll treat you with all the respect you deserve. Trust me."

Years later they had children together. And to this day their love for each other grows stronger.

Story 6
"The Love between mother and son"

A mother holds the hand of her son. All the worry has taken its toll on her. She has no power in the outcome soon to come.

The son looks up at her. "Can you hold me"? All the wires, all the tubes, she looks down and with a heavy smile says "yes". She lies by his side being ever so careful and pulls him to her heart. How am I to give up? Tears stream down her cheeks.

A nurse enters the room. With full panic she says she can't do that. Their eyes meet. The nurse lowers her head and says she's sorry. I'll give ya'll privacy. "Everyone will knock before they enter." She quietly leaves.

"Am I going to die?" The mother gives him a loving squeeze. "I'm not sure. This is how we lost your father. He lived to sixty-two. But if you do, he'll be there to hold your hand." She hears a soft knock on the door. People enter and tell her it's time for him to go with them.

The boy lived to the age of sixty-seven. He remembers that day in the hospital as if it was yesterday. He cared for his mother the rest of her days. Never married to stop this pain for others.

We are always faced with different challenges. Some much heavier than others. But we work out the answers. We find the balance to adjust to. People are stronger than we think. And sometimes the children are the strongest of all.

Story 7
"The Doctor finds himself"

There was a doctor. His life was basically chosen for him. He came from a long line of family members in the medical profession. His father was a doctor. So, he was pushed into medical school. His grades and accomplishments were above average. He finished near the top of his class. Major hospitals wanted his skills. His dad basically chose for him. Pushed directly to the emergency room. He saved many lives. But he could not save them all.

This was very hard on him. After his shift, he would walk to the hospital chapel. There he would pray and shed tears for the ones who didn't live. He would question his skills. That person had a family, and he would have to tell them their family member wasn't going to join them. He felt so inadequate. He blamed himself. He didn't lose many, but even one was hard on him.

One day, he had finished his prayer for a young boy who had been in an accident. He had arrived too late. He was too far gone. But this boy hit him very hard. His eyes were closed, and tears streamed down his cheeks.

He felt a hand on his. He looked over to see a woman. Her face was full of understanding and comfort. She said, "Don't be so hard on yourself. God calls some of the people home, and no skill could stop his word. What you do is honorable. The fact you're here speaks of your caring heart. You did your best with my son. God had other plans for him. Thank you for caring so much." She hugged him and went back to her family.

Suddenly he understood. He was a good doctor. A very good and caring doctor. He walked with a new self-strength. He went to save another life.

Story 8

"Teacher"

When you look into the mirror, what do you see?

I see age. Experience. I see the wrinkles earned in life. The skin thin now, the body tattered. I see a teacher. A teacher for the young. I see my children, my brothers and sisters. I see my father and mother.

I know so much yet so little. The eyes of the very young trust me. They feel secure. My hands are still strong, but a baby will sleep on my soft shoulders. I tell them stories of my youth. They hang on every word. I watch them grow. One day the first born finds love and starts a family of their own. They show their love, their respect. My place in their hearts is without question. Time marches on.

Soon I don't move around as much. They proudly show me their children. I get the credit for starting it all. I do my best to share as much as possible. I'm still a teacher. I relish my role. I nap way too easily. I dress a little warmer. I don't talk as much; I eat smaller portions. I look so different. I won't own a dog any longer, it's too hard on me when I outlive them. And then one day it's my turn and I begin to pass myself.

I'm propped up with soft pillows. A child holds my hand. My grip is so fragile now. I know I must go; my stay is over. I fall asleep for my last time. Tears are shed.

My son steps up and tells the small ones not to worry. He will fill my shoes. He says "call me teacher."

Story 9

"Ageing"

Growing to a ripe old age is not without its dark side.

You make friends as you live your life. Family surrounds you. The people you see time and time again on the screens. Friends of friends. You connect with so many people. So where is the flaw?

You watch them pass. The "less healthy" go before you. I've seen so many. Many of them pay for the sins of their youth too early. Their weight. Their bad habits. The list goes on and on. None of us will live forever. But a few will outlive many in their circle. Diseases take some. Accidents take their share. Old age itself will claim who ever last the longest.

So, what do we do? I say enjoy your life. What ever time you have left, enjoy it. Mend those fences. Stop the bad habits that kill. Is smoking really that great? You are willing to give up ten years of your life for such a trivial pleasure?

The older you get the harder it gets. Just getting out of bed you will start making sounds you never made before. You don't see as well. Hearing is harder. Doctors are good friends. But each year you add another year to your tally. There is a tremendous pleasure in adding so many years. Everything changes. And whether you like it or not you will change also.

Know you will lose friends, family, and old acquaintances. It's the natural order. Do your part to add the years to your tally. Happiness will never abandon you. You need to never be guilty of abandoning the happiness you're entitled to. Remember, you must change with the changes that become part of your life. Stay active. Too much chair time isn't good.

Your time will come. Don't rush it. Enjoy all that surrounds you. But no matter how long I live, I'll never enjoy raw onions!!!

Story 10
"Letter to GOD"

A small girl writes a pleading letter to GOD.

I know I'm small. I also know I'm not smart about a lot of things. But you took my father back to heaven. I miss him. I cry, and I see my mother cry. Could you not loan him to us for just one day? So much was never said. We aren't asking you to change your mind. Just let us talk to him. Please.

The mother comes into the room and sees her daughter crying. She reads the note. She picks her up and holds her tight. Then she says, "Darling, we can talk to your father every day. He's in the room right now. He can hear all your words. He can even put his strong arms around you for comfort. It's different now. But he never leaves your side. He'll wait on the other side for us to join him one day. He'll be the first one you see. All of our loved ones are there waiting for us to reunite one day. I know you're sad, so am I, but I know he's here in another way."

"So, dry your tears and finish your letter to him. I'll bring you an envelope to put it in. Your father will read it and be very proud of you. He'll talk to you. It may be in your dreams. It might just be a memory he doesn't want you to lose."

"Your father is not gone. Have faith in that, and I love you so much. We'll go for a walk when you're done and mail your letter to him. Just put heaven on the outside. I'm sure he's excited and waiting for it."

Story 11
"The Word Friend Makes Me Smile"

Friendship; a word, or a commitment, or both?

We pick and choose people we want in our inner circle. But what do we expect of them? Being honest with us? There when we need help, if possible? Telling us about a problem before they tell others? Trust!

We are all different, and so are the boundaries we establish.

I feel we most want companionship with people who won't judge. We all walk a path not so straight. We do and they do. But our friendship is not based on judging the other but accepting them. Some people say they don't make friends easily. It might just be acceptance. If you burn your trust you're removed from the inner circle. Can you ever return? It's not that easy. You basically, start all over. But now you carry a mark. With time, and a lot of work you'll be forgiven. You were once a friend!

Find the value you label a friend. Know yourself. Know them. Have friends who are there till death. You don't have to talk or visit daily. Visit when too much time has passed. And an occasional call if the visit is not that possible.

We all need friends. Don't take advantage or be the victim. Strike the balance.

Friends are fantastic!

Story 12
"Life is Sometimes Unfair"

The boy just stared at him. Finally, he spoke. Do you not see you're a pillar of strength for many? Everyone will die. It's just life. But think of the people who knew your story and saw your strength. Think about the strength you gave them. GOD didn't take you because he had a purpose for you. You were a beacon of light for the ones who needed a light in their life. You shared your strength weather you were aware of it or not. Your story is so moving. I look at you and feel nothing but respect. My name is David, and in the time, you have left I would like to be here with you. I'll be your family now.

The old man spoke the stories of his life to David. Burt grew weaker each day. He passed with David holding his hand.

David carried the memories of his stories the rest of his life. He had no parents. They died when he was young. But an old man named Sam became his father replacement. Sam really did become his family that day. And in that short time, he loved that old man as if he was his father all his life. And to this day he feels his father's strength was passed on to him.

Story 13

"We All Grow Up"

I woke up one day to find my life had changed. We all start out kind of the same. You're given a room in a big house; your food is prepared each day. You're driven around town; all your clothes are picked out and paid for. Life is pretty sweet. Then you wake up one day, and your life has changed. You have to clean your room now. You're forced to get up early to go to school. You have homework. It's now your job to mow the yard. To help around the house. No choice. And it doesn't stop there. One day, you wake up, and sure enough, your life is different.

Now you're in the military. Discipline and responsibility are drilled into you daily. You are no longer a child. You have entered adulthood. Now you worry about sleeping. You get up and realize your world has changed again. You have to go to work. You're married and have children. They are so expensive. How did your parents do it? All of their needs trump yours. A car, college, weddings, their first home. All you seem to do is bring the money in the front door only to push it out the back. And then one day, you wake up, and your world is different. You have grandchildren. Your children now want to pay for your needs. They check up on you. They now worry about you. Your life has changed. You go to sleep.

Now you walk with an unsteady gait. You look back on all the mornings you noticed the changes. You smile. Your grandchildren now drive. Your children struggle with the dollars now. But you, well, you're retired. You're now the babysitter. The children's best friend. You're so much wiser now. So experienced. You smile even bigger. You live on so much less. Not really a problem. You need so much less.

You get into the recliner you got as a gift, close your eyes for that daily nap, and know you can ask for any task to be done while you sleep, and it will happen. You smile in your sleep.

Story 14
"What We Just Don't Know"

If I only knew then.

You left when I least expected it. You were just going for eggs. And I lost you that morning.

If only I knew.

I wouldn't have allowed you to leave. We had a beautiful life to look forward to. A family to start. We were looking at a larger home, I had no idea. I don't think I told you I loved you for the last time. Took that last kiss. Felt your arms around me for our last hug.

I would give up everything we ever had for your return. I would give up our meeting for the first time. Our first kiss, everything.

If only I knew then.

Now my life has fully changed. Sorrow overwhelms me. My last vision of you will be in a casket. Who should have to endure such things? I want you back. What can I do? Why is there nothing I can do? I've lost the love of my life.

If only I knew, I could have intervened.

I asked her for breakfast. It was because of me she left that morning. Left never to return. My guilt is overwhelming. I can barely look at her parents. They don't blame me.

If only I knew!

Shower the ones you love with affection each and every day. Speak your soft words to them. Make them smile. Be sure they know they're loved. It can all change. Change so quickly it can cause you to lose your balance. After reading this go to your loved ones and shower them with hugs and kisses.

You never know!

Story 15
"Know Love Takes Work"

He met her at the fair. The dance night.

She stole his heart, something he couldn't change. As they danced close, she laid her head on his chest. Slow dancing was her biggest thrill. She always kept her eyes closed. Taking in the full experience of the dance.

They dated for a couple of years. Then got engaged. They both respected each other. The relationship was special to say the least. They did fun things together. He wanted more time with her. So one day he knelt before her. She said yes, but made him promise to always take her slow dancing.

Their love for each other never lessened. Years passed. Grandchildren came into the picture. Music would play and they would slow dance in the living room. The grandchildren taking their turns, as did their parents when small. Time continued on.

Age will always take its toll. The bones stiffen. Balance not as steady. The love was strong. But the dances would have to stop. She looks up at this man whose strong arms had held her so many times. "I'm going to play my favorite song for a last dance. I want to close my eyes and live our first dance once more. I want to hear your heart beat. I want it to end with a long kiss. You've been a perfect husband and father, thank you for allowing us to age together. For loving me the way you did. I'm not leaving yet but I wanted to say this to you. The music is starting. Let me close my eyes and listen to you breathing so much in love".

She rest her head on his chest and closes her eyes. He smiles and moves ever so careful. It was her last dance. Their love still flourished for many years. Love is a beautiful thing. Everlasting under the right environment.

Know love take work. But with tender gardening, worth every minute of it.

Story 16

"Unselfish Service"

There was a family on vacation—the baby, the dog, the grandpa, and the rest. They were having a great time.

They came to a lookout point and decided to pull over and take a few pictures. All was going well; grandpa was getting the baby out. Once on the ground, the baby wanted to run. As grandpa reached for the baby's hand, he tripped on a loose rock. This allowed the baby to run free. And he was running straight for the edge.

Once everyone realized what was happening, the baby tumbled over the ledge. The screaming started immediately. Everyone rushed to the ledge and saw the small boy about twenty feet down. The men and then the women tried to move down to the baby. All they did was allow more dirt and rocks to rain down on the child, moving closer to the ledge.

Panic was overtaking the group. He was just right there, and they couldn't reach him. He slid a little closer to the ledge. Then, out of nowhere, the dog lunged past. He spread out all four legs and slid to the baby. He got a mouthful of the baby's clothes. The family dog was going to save the family member. Slowly, he turned around. He was not a huge dog, so the trip up was very difficult for him. He would make it up a couple of feet, then slide back one.

The mother made eye contact with her dog, Rex, and could see the stress in his face. He was losing. So, they made a human ladder and lowered one of the boys down. "Just grab Mike anywhere." About eight inches separated them. The boy couldn't be lowered anymore, so it was up to Rex. Their eyes met once more, and Rex said goodbye. He gave one last lunge and gave his all. The boy grabbed the baby's clothes, and Rex let go. Over the edge, he fell, looking at his family one last time.

The mother understood why Rex let go. He couldn't risk the boy losing his grip on little Mike. He gave his life to save his small friend. Everyone was incredibly happy but also incredibly sad. Eventually, the point was renamed "Rex's Point" in honor of the dog. A dog so loyal he willingly gave his life to save a family member.

Just like Rex, our veterans give up their lives to protect their loved ones, to keep our nation great, and to die for strangers, if necessary. Honor them! Keep them in your prayers. We want any and all soldiers to return safely. But we know they all won't. Guess what—they know that too. Yet they go and sacrifice themselves, if that is what it takes. Always honor them! Not all are willing to go so far. They go out for love of their country and their families.

Story 17
"Things Slowly Change"

She was in the waiting room so excited! It was going to be her first granddaughter. Finally, the great news came. And what a beautiful child she was.

The grandmother would get to work and find out the baby had thrown up on her back. How cute is that. All the memories of younger days. Always willing to take her grandchild for the weekend. Rocking her at night while she cries. Feedings, all the required responsibilities. The months slide by.

Now while still in love, the mother's role comes first. Grandmother has plans for the weekend. No babysitting right now. Chasing her around the house makes her too tired. Hire someone if needed. I'm busy. Now it's come to weekend visits. Fun still, of course. That lisp when talking so cute. Baking cookies together, the new grandson in a bouncer by them. Changing diapers has somehow changed. There is no way all of this came from this child. A grown man can't produce this much. And the smell, what climbed up his butt and died?

Being sick isn't just crying any longer. Now supper is sprayed all over the floor, and that's if you're lucky. Sometimes the event has you throwing up as well. I think in the car is the worst. After they're gone, you are still driving with that new scent thanks to them.

They do grow up. Now the empty house longs for that noise. The calls have become less frequent. Cleaning up after them wasn't that bad really. What you wouldn't do to have a little more of what you were complaining about then.

So where does this road lead? You sit in that hospital again. Waiting on your first great grandchild. Looking forward to your time with this small little boy. All the difficult times long forgotten. You can hardly wait.

Story 18
"Express Yourself"

How many times have you ever said "I just didn't know what to say"? Or maybe "how to say it" more likely.

Sometimes we want to speak our feelings. Sounds so simple. A problem of the ages. We may lack the confidence. Possibly fear a rejection. An embarrassment we don't want to face. We want to tell our feelings but how? We can speak the words. How do you arrange them so your feelings are felt?

Sure, we can all say that a flower is pretty. Can you describe its smell? Can you pick and choose the words that they can close their eyes and smell it also? When a couple marries. They write words to promise the other a lifetime of "feelings of love". Those words flow from the heart. Heard by all, but felt so strongly by the couple. Your desire to say your feelings are so important you'll allow no mistakes. Those pieces of paper are kept forever. Read many times over. The feelings are relived. A rejuvenation of your love that day. It warms the heart.

We all have feelings to express. Never fear putting pen to paper. Words of love and kindness are needed right now. For yourself. For the ones you love. And for the world we live in!!! Make hearts smile.

Story 19
"Sometimes you just need to believe"

A family was at the hospital checking in on a family member who broke his arm.

With them was a four-year-old girl who decided to walk into the hall. She turned and went down the hallway. No one noticed she had even left. As she walked, she heard crying. She came to a door and saw two grown-ups bent over a bed. She was far too young to understand their grief. She walked in and asked if the girl had a booboo. The parents turned in surprise.

The small girl walked over to the mother and put her arms up to be picked up. The mother quickly lifted the small child. "Is that your baby?"

"Yes," she answered.

"She's pretty. I want to be pretty like that one day."

Tears flowed from the mother, and she hugged the little girl.

"What's her name?"

"Nancy," she answered.

"That's a nice name. I'm Sherri."

"Where are your parents?" they asked.

"Down the hall," she answered. "I sneaked away," she said with a smile. "I knew I was needed here." She looked at the mother. "Everything will be fine for you. Just have faith."

The mother was in shock. How could such a small child say such a statement? "I hope you're right. I need a miracle today for my daughter."

The little girl slipped to the floor and started walking away. "Keep your faith. You're being watched." The little girl walked out the door. She stopped and looked back at the mother.

"I'm needed elsewhere. She'll be fine."

With time, she asked her daughter if she would like to be a big sister. (She was pregnant again with another girl). "We'll name her Sherri."

Story 20

"The Love of a Wife"

A man wanted to climb a mountain. He had no experience in this arena.

His wife begged him not to do this. At least take someone with him. He always came back it was a personal quest. Something he must do alone. There are no towers, I can't reach you by phone or you me. He was headstrong, nothing she could say would change anything. So he kissed her goodbye and left.

The journey went without a hitch. It took three days but he made it to the summit. He took pictures and pitched a tent. He would spend the night there. But things didn't go as planned. In the night the wind picked up. A major wind. He woke to his tent almost ready to fly into the air. And him inside. He quickly threw all he could in his backpack and moved to the door. The shift in weight was all it took. The tent started to roll with him inside. He slammed against a rock and lost consciousness. When he awoke pain was the number one feeling. Both his leg and arm was broken.

His head was bleeding and he felt like he was in a plastic bag. It was then he realized he was hanging in his tent. He cuts a small hole to pier out. He was hanging from a cliff. The tent had snagged on a rock and that was all that saved him. The wind had blown him over the edge. And to make things worse, he was in a crevice.

Anyone looking for him would never see him. He was facing a slow death.

He wouldn't listen to his wife. Someone he loved so dearly. Someone who cared and loved him just as much. No way to move with two broke limbs. He would wait for the end to come. Days passed. And he slowly lost consciousness. He dreamed. He could hear his wife asking him to return to her. Come back for the sake of the family. He could feel his daughter hold his hand. In its own strange way, it was a form of heaven to him. His last encounter with the ones he loved. Then he hears a voice he doesn't recognize. She's asking people to leave so he can rest. He fights to open his eyes. When he does the bright light blinds him for a moment. There stands his wife and daughter. He was alive, but how?

His wife confesses she sewed a tracker into his backpack. Once his movement stopped, she connected authorities. It was her who saved his life. He squeezed her hand. I vow to you from this day forward all major decisions, we make together... A promise he kept.

Marriage is a union of two. Equal partnership. And just being the male doesn't automatically make you the most qualified.

Story 21
"Hugs"

I saw a post about the value of a hug. I had to think about that.

I've known people who say they are a hugger. They give out hugs like crazy. A dime a dozen. And there are those who sit in sadness and say they need a hug. That hug has a very different value. It's for a comfort needed at that time. Time will move much slower and the squeeze tighter.

Lovers separated. They will hug and kiss when reunited. A silent form of communication is spoken with both parties that was heard very clearly. To hug your child, your parent, family, is a different hug entirely.

So how many hug types are there? And what does each one express? We hug pets. Heck we'll even hug a gift. We will hug strangers. We have invisible hugs for memories. A clear hug that you are the only one who sees and feels it.

Can we live without hugs? I don't really think so. They are too ingrained in us as a people. A mother daughter talk where the mother speaks of her desire to hug her late husband. Mentally they both hug him. For a moment he's in that room. All because of a desire to have one last hug.

So how many different hugs are out there? Probably more than I can find in this short story. But a really nice feeling knowing they are waiting to be found.

Story 22
"Miracle of Passion"

A small boy was playing in the yard. He got new toys this morning, and he was having fun. His new ball got away from him and rolled into the street. He ran to get it back, and that was when it happened. He could see himself in a bed. All the wires attached to him. All the small lights blinking. What was happening?

Then a lady took his hand. She seemed to have a soft glow about her. Her hand felt warm. "Am I dying?"

She looked down and smiled. "Not today. No one anywhere will die today. Jesus is making a miracle. Not the weak or the strong. Not the good or the evil. The believers or the nonbelievers. No one dies this day. To him, you are all humankind. It is the people of this world who divide themselves. They want to be with people like themselves. The good want to be with other good people. And unfortunately, the evil surround themselves with other even more evil people. So, on his day of his birth, he will save everyone. This will be noticed by the people of this land. There are many of us holding the hands of the injured. You are being healed as we speak. How will this be explained? Who will become a believer today? Your free will is going to allow the conclusion you choose to accept. But with others, their eyes will open. Jesus is speaking to all humankind this day. I think they will have no choice but to listen. So, close your eyes and rest. You will remember this as a dream. But you will remember. All of the injured will. All of you will be believers and spread your story. Humankind will move closer to God this day. The day of his birth."

Story 23

"The Special Evening"

It was the morning before, and he had so much to do. So up early.

The wife was returning this afternoon. He had three days to work all the details out. He wanted this to be so very special. Not even one detail could be overlooked. He had been planning this for weeks. The big day was tomorrow, and he was excited.

They met two years ago and fell in love almost overnight. Dated for a year and a half then married. They were so in love with each other. And the love blossomed from there. He was probably spending too much on this day, but it was to be so very special. A memory to always look back on with a smile. A nice hotel, a once-a-year dinner, and a night of dancing. Champagne of course. Chilled and placed in the room. Yellow roses, her favorite. A gift for her to look upon and remember tonight. He could barely contain his excitement. He even had a box to put the phones away and out of reach. No stone unturned.

After she came home and rested, he told her they were going on a date and to start getting ready. This she was very pleased with. Once ready he waited. And to her surprise a limo parks outside their door. He looks to her with a big smile and full of pride and says "take my arm and let me show you, my love."

Their night together was a memory for life. It was their first Valentine's Day as a married couple. One he made sure she would never forget.

Happiness isn't the money spent. It's the love shown. No, he never spent that much again on a date. He didn't have to. Her heart was his. But Valentine's Day was always special for them, even if sitting by a warm fire in the living room.

Tomorrow is a big day. Make it special!

Story 24
"Final Days"

What happens inside of you when you're told your days are ending?

Our mortality we're born with. Time, we take for granted. No cares at all until that news is delivered. Instead of years, you now have days, weeks, or months. My how your thinking changes. You are now reliving your life. Seeing all you did right, and some things not so right. Heaven and hell never seemed so real. Is everything in order? Can you leave and not burden the ones you love so much? Time has taken on a great value. Much more valuable than diamonds or gold.

Even your eyes talk to you now. You see and question. So many questions. You don't want to leave, but just like four cars at a four way stop. It's your turn now, and you must go.

Acceptance finally seeps in. Your understanding of life and death clearer now. The anger or disappointment turns into a mist. It leaves. Now what? What needs to be done before you go? Those are the priorities now. Contact with family and old friends seem important now. No time to waste. Fences need mending. Apologies given. No anger any longer, just reality. Does it really matter if they were the one in the wrong? Let it lie. If only I had two more years I could repair so much. Two years I had and wasted. No do overs.

All of us need to look at our lives as if our time was up.

What would you do?

Story 25
"Christmas"

The girl goes into her grandmother's house. She is somewhat confused. "I was next door at Judy's house. They must have a hundred presents under their tree. We have four. Why?"

The grandmother gets her a cookie and some milk and asks her to sit at the table and hear her out.

"Depending on the age, the gifts vary. Your mother may get one expensive gift that costs more than all of yours. She doesn't need or want much. Christmas is for the young mainly. You outgrow things. Clothes and toys. So, replacing them is a strategy. If you've grown a lot over the year, you'll probably get more clothes. If you've been getting them all along, then maybe an older variety of gifts. There is only you and your brother. Judy has a larger family. Plus, her cousins have Christmas there every year. You can be sure not all those gifts are for Judy and her brother. Her cousins are probably bringing their gifts over for Christmas morning. Please try to understand, Christmas is not about gifts. It's a coming together of the family. A showing of love. Remembering the birth of Jesus. Everyone eats together and enjoys the company of all. As you grow older, you'll understand better. Now help me bake a pie for our Christmas dinner. And you'll get to open a gift early. I got you something special to wear tomorrow. You're growing so fast!"

Story 26

"A Kind Man in the Park"

A man was on a bench in the park. He had his tablet and was doing drawings of formal gowns.

He looks up to see a small boy staring at him.

"Hi, I'm Robert. What's your name?"

"I'm David, where is your mother?"

"Oh, she'll find me she always does. Are you married?" That question caught him by surprise.

"No. Why do you ask?"

"Well, my mom needs a boyfriend, and you look like a good one."

"Well, thank you, but is that your mother coming this way?"

"Yep!"

"We won't tell her you asked me that. It will be our secret. BTW what is her name?"

"Sandra," he says.

The mother comes in and scolds him for sneaking off. "Sandra, he's a delightful boy. No harm done."

"He told you my name? What else?"

"Just small talk between boys. I would like to buy him a scoop of ice cream, would you like a coffee?"

She looks him over. He looks harmless. "Sure."

He puts on his coat and hat. She looks at him with a little concern.

"Don't worry, I slipped away from the office and don't want to be seen. I'm not a threat of any kind."

They had a great coffee and spent a couple of hours just talking. When they got up to go their separate ways the boy asked, "will we see you again?"

He smiles and answers, "it's up to your mother."

She makes eye contact and studies him for a moment. Smiles and answers him, "that would be nice."

He gets her number. They have a couple more dates. Then he tells her he has something to say.

"I haven't been completely honest about himself. I own a very high-end gown boutique. I would like to take you to a dinner at my favorite restaurant. I want you to go to this address and they will pick out a gown for you. And please no questions yet, we'll talk over dinner."

Very confused she agreed. She went to the boutique and was greeted by a very chic woman.

"You must be Sandra. Mr. Davis has left clear instructions for us. Let's get started. Bring her a glass of champagne."

She was looked over and never asked for a size. Gown after gown was shown. She tried on two and picked out one.

"I could never afford such a dress and in no way would I allow Dan to buy this for me."

"Mr. Davis owns this boutique. You will wear it on consignment. Please allow him to do this, he has a grand dinner planned for you both. He's really a good man."

So, at around four her doorbell rings. A team of ladies are at her door.

"May I help?"

"We're your makeup group. Mr. Davis sent us. We're to assist you this evening. Let's get started." When seven arrived, the doorbell chimed. She answers. There stands Dan in a tux. And a limo parked in front.

"You look absolutely gorgeous. Are you ready? We have reservations."

"Yes, I'm ready and you have a lot of explaining to do. What is up?"

So, as they drove, he talked.

"I have money. Lots of money. But what I didn't have was someone who cared just for me. Someone who would love me because of the person I am. I want to show you that man. I'm asking that you and Robert allow me to be part of your lives. And when you see me for who I am, understand how your life will change. Both you and Robert, then, if accepted, I'm going to ask for your hand. I've already fallen in love with you. And I see you love me also. I want to build on that if you agree. We have dinner reservations. We have hours to talk, take my hand and let's start this wonderful evening."

Story 27

"A Kitten named 'Cotton'"

She was only four years old. But she no longer enjoyed her dolls.

"Mom, they just lay there. I have to do everything. It's not fun anymore". So, the mother thought. "How about we go to the animal shelter and find you a kitten? It's alive, loving, and will grow, and constantly be changing. What do you think?"

"Really!!! Let's go". "You must understand that this kitten will be a best friend to you. Its care will be your job. I'll help any time you ask. But the kitten will be yours. It will be here for years. Are you sure you want this?" And with all the sincerity a four-year-old could muster she says "thank you mommy".

Off they go. They look at plenty of kittens. Till finally they find the one. She named it Cotton because it was pure white. An innocent friendship between a cat and a little girl began. Soon they were inseparable.

Cotton helped her through the good and bad times. Cotton slept in her bed with her. Anywhere she sat the cat was there. Cotton lived an old life. Almost eighteen years. Her passing was a major hurt for the girl now woman. It seemed Cotton was always by her side. No longer. So now what? She was engaged now. Making plans for a modest wedding. A part of her heart was in tears. At such a powerful time she was sad.

Her future husband stepped up. "Your heart will be asked to share its love. Me, our children, our families, the world we live in. I'm sure you could find a little room for a small kitten. With our first child, let's give that baby a special friend. I think it's something that would please you." "Can we get it when our baby turns four"? "If that would please you, of course. We have a wedding to plan. Let's get busy". He gives her a hug and a kiss.

We experience many things in life. The impact our pets have on us is probably one of the deepest. The love exchanged, true and innocent. Treat them well. They are a best friend.

Story 28
"What is Beautiful?"

A daughter asks her mother, "What is beautiful?"

The mother looks at her and says, "Such a big question from such a small girl. Let me see if I can answer you. You are beautiful. Beautiful is the day I first held you in my arms. Your father is beautiful. Isn't he handsome? Men are handsome". Colors can be a beautiful sight, but they can also be bright and vibrant. Beautiful is one of the special words. It wants to be used a lot.

"Nature, science, everyday things, sounds, sights—beauty is all around us. Music is beauty. The sounds take you to places in your heart. The news will show us bad things. But there are beautiful people there. They are not the news, yet they are there. There are many people out there with a beautiful soul. You just have to look a little harder. They can be easily found".

"Take the time to share an image of something beautiful. A flower, a bird, something to make them smile. Something beautiful to start their day. They'll appreciate that. Show others you have a beautiful heart, and they will show you theirs".

"Our world is a very beautiful place. Never lose sight of that. It's full of beautiful people, beautiful countries, and beautiful sights. There is a saying: stop to smell the flowers. And flowers can be so beautiful. Slow down. You'll see that one day."

"So, you think you know beautiful now? Did I do well?"

"Mom, I think you are beautiful."

Story 29
"How Generations Change"

He sits in his favorite outdoor chair. His cat in his lap. The afternoon sun feels good on his face. The cat is quite content also. Some young boys come walking by. He remembers his days of youth. Running around barefooted, not a care of any kind really. Just being a kid. He helped his dad with the work around the house. No pay, just doing what's expected of him. He had to grow up to find out his parents were abusing him. Wasn't that way then. Young men took pride in helping the family. They never took his money. He gave it to them. Some days it was his money that put food on the table. He could look around the table and see his help in action. Those were days long past.

Now he wonders what the boys walking the sidewalk would think. Would they even understand? Parents raise their children differently today. Everyone is allowed to walk their own road. To this day he still takes pride in the work he did to help. He's in his twilight. His days are numbered. Today is a warm sunny day. Love still fills his heart. He hopes the boys grow up to be good men. Great providers. They have plenty of time to see the bigger picture. Today I guess you just let them be boys.

It's Sunday. Time to visit his wife. Talk with her for a while. If only she could talk back. Fresh flowers and a note of love. He sure misses her. They'll see each other again probably soon. But today on this gorgeous afternoon all he wants is her company. To speak soft words. That's the day he wants.

Story 30

"When a Friend becomes Family"

At what point does a friend become family?

Is it because you've known them since their earliest years? Sounds more like friendship to me. They know you and almost all the other family members. Does that qualify? Maybe they come to family reunions as an expected guest? When is that threshold crossed? When do they become family? A hard question without an easy answer.

Would they place themselves between you and harm with no concern of their own safety? Your dog will do that. Not every family member will do that and yet they are still family. Would they die for you to keep you safe? As I said, your dog will do that.

To be labeled as family is an honor. A brother or sister from another mother or father, but full acceptance by the family. Does that not make you feel special? So, what if you fall in love with one of the family? Do you now reject your family ties? How will it affect the rest? Do you see each other in secret? When do you both bring it out? I really don't see a problem there. The family would probably be happy for you both. You are an honorary member. And everyone wants the happiness you both deserve. You actually solidify your title as a family member.

    Anything good is almost never a bad thing. Live your life right. And when you step on thin ice, well be careful!

Story 31
"I want to be a Fireman"

A father and his son were sitting together when his dad said, "You're sixteen now. Do you know what you want to do as a grown-up?"

The boy looked up and said, "Dad, I've always known. I want to be part of a team of firefighters."

The father's head snapped back a little in surprise. "Really?" His mind went into the past. And yes, his son had said he wanted to be a fireman. But Dad had taken it the same as if his son had said, "I want to be Superman." They talked.

"When I was small, I thought the firetruck was the coolest car in the world. The lights, all the sounds, all the neat gadgets. I've never lost that love. I know all the guys at the station on Fourth Street. I help wash the truck sometimes and get to ride it when it has to be moved."

The father looked down at his boy and felt guilt. *Am I a good father if I did not know all of this? Have I paid so little attention that I'm in the dark?* The father asked if he realized the responsibility and lifestyle of firefighters. "At any time, day or night, you're on call. Your home life is not average. And your wife requires a tremendous amount of understanding and the willingness of sacrifice. And you will be putting your life on the line for strangers. On any given day, you may not come home. You realize all of this?"

The son smiled and said he'd been talking to the men there for years. They told him of his life to come. But he still wanted to be part of the team, their firefighter family. The father looked down at his son with great pride. In his eyes, he was no longer a boy.

"OK, so we need to make a plan. A road to get you there. Let's talk to the fire chief. We'll talk to the college counselor. I'll help you live your dream. I'm proud of my son!"

Story 32

"The Memories Held in A House"

The new life has begun. He can look around and see things in their designated places. But absolutely nothing is the same. He lives by himself now. His wife is no longer with him. GOD asked her to be with HIM. He needed her, her help, and her contribution to heaven. As a believer he doesn't question. Sadness fills his heart anyway. He misses her so much already.

They say time will heal the deep cut in his heart. Maybe so. But it won't be any time soon. His children said he should sell the house and move in with one of them. Living there will be very hard for him.

What they fail to understand is I get to see her each and every day. Standing at the sink. Smiling behind a load of laundry needing to be folded. I took that time for granted. I should have been by her side helping. We would have talked. I know that for sure. Now my chance is gone. Gone forever. My memories will comfort me. I can see her napping in her chair. I can almost feel her touch. The softness of her cheek. I've kissed that cheek a thousand times. If only I could have just one more.

Sell this house. Not ever! I'm still with her here. She's still with me. We'll still grow old together. Just in a different way. I still talk to her. Share my feelings. That might sound silly. I close my eyes and she comes to me. I'm not losing my mind; I'm pulling up memories. It's all I have now. I smile all the time. She can still make me laugh. I can almost hear her speak. Ask me questions. No, I'll never leave this house. We'll grow old together.

Her closet will go unchanged. Her pillowcase never washed. It has a place of honor next to me while I sleep. I can roll over and see her sleeping. I do miss her so much, but I don't question. Yes, tears do come. They will never fully leave. My life has changed.

We have many difficulties in our lives. How we handle them is critical to our well-being. If you stay strong, you will see that light in the darkness. Move toward it. Never stay in the dark. Your happiness is in the light.

Story 33
"Falling in Love is not always something you control"

There was a young man not wanting love. His life was planned out, and love would come later when better prepared for it.

Things don't always go as planned. He meets Sherri. She stole his heart the moment he laid eyes on her. Love took its course. A few years went by, then he knelt at her feet and asked her to spend the rest of her life with him. There are so many twist and turns in life.

They had a little girl together. It wasn't easy on Sherri and one child was all she could have with him. She felt disappointed she couldn't give him a son also. Not to worry, if I want a son bad enough we'll adopt one. Till then I have a beautiful daughter to help raise. The years passed.

Their years together were filled with love. Love for each other and love for their growing family. They had grandchildren now. Such a wonderful gift. He moved much slower now. He could see his story was ending. Caring for the needs of his wife filled his days now. She still gets her coffee in bed. Propped up with pillows, one cube of ice always there. He knows what she likes.

He has long talks with his daughter. Her care if he should leave first. Plenty of dollars set aside for her. SHE WAS HIS FIRST LOVE. It never wavered.

If you're lucky enough to find that perfect love, feel blessed. Sharing love is very simple. The well of soft feelings never runs dry. Problems come and go. A loving couple can weather any storm. It will carry you through all the deep water.

Story 34
"Dreams"

There was a single man who would have repeat dreams. What made this so unusual was that it was always the same girl. These dreams went on for years. Never disturbing, he actually enjoyed them. His life was so busy he had no time-—or made no time—to date. He had one of these dreams about every month or so.

He was embarrassed to say anything about his dreams. So, he kept them private, to himself. With time, they became more frequent. He could never get her name, or he would wake up. So, he just stopped trying. As I said, he enjoyed his dreams when they came. He figured it was his way to deal with never dating. They would hold hands and walk along a lake or maybe the beach. Their conversations were always pleasant. He figured this was what love was like. He would wake up in such a good mood, and a smile never left his face.

One day, he met a lady who claimed she could read his palm. Out of curiosity, he agreed. She took his hand palm up and looked. Her head pulled back. "The woman you will marry is trying to make contact with you. She's been staying in your dreams so as not to lose you. Look at me and tell me I'm wrong!"

This shook him up some. "What do I do?"

"Is there a place you meet more often than not? Think."

"Why, yes, there is."

"Find that place, and you will find her."

In his next dream, he took mental notes. He did research. He found the place. A bench by the lake. Then one day, a woman walked toward him. It was her. There was no mistake. It was the woman in his dreams. How should he handle this, not wanting to scare her off but wanting her full attention? So, when she got directly in front, he said, "Do you have the correct time?"

They made eye contact. He saw her study him. "Yes, it's three seventeen." She looked harder. She said, "Do you mind if I sit for a minute? I need a short rest."

The rest of the story you can fill in yourself.

Story 35

"A Friend Named Hope"

We all have problems in life. And yes, some take a heavy toll. Here's a story of one.

A mother had a child the age of seven. This child was overactive. He was never at rest. The mother was always in a state of stress. One day out of frustration she voiced to herself she wishes she had waited to have a child. Words she soon came to regret.

The boy became ill, so ill it took his life. The words were always in her head. Her guilt consumed her. She couldn't stop the feelings this was all her doing. With time her guilt was too much for her and she took her life.

This left a father and husband who lost his whole family all within a year dealing with his losses. It wasn't his fault. He could not go back in time to change anything. He had no choice but to accept it all. He turned to church. He said prayers to himself. With time he began to heal. His life came back to him. His pain was leaving.

We all have our brick walls we have to face at times. Some seem so tall and thick we feel there is nothing we can do. Never lose your hope. Hope is the one friend that never leaves you. With hope your life will return.

Story 36
"Becoming a Man"

The father now has his son. He was so proud of him. He took him everywhere.

As the years passed, the boy changed. Always arguing, never wanting to do what he was told. He believed that at age fifteen he was a man now. He no longer needed to listen to his parents. So, he left home.

With time he got a girl pregnant. He was growing up to the mature side of life. He had a family now. Hadn't seen or spoken to his parents in years. Slowly he began to understand what his father was trying to teach. He was too embarrassed to call. Didn't really know a number any longer. Time continued on.

He finally talked with his wife and asked to go meet them. The past needed to be fixed. They needed to know they had a granddaughter. He went home. What he found was his parents, both of them, were gone. Both had gotten very sick and died. His parents had left everything to him. Their only child. He was told where they were buried.

He goes alone to find them. At their grave he speaks. Looking up he says his father had wisdom. A wisdom he didn't want to listen to. It was him who wanted to be right, not his father. He made him work, work he didn't want to do. But that had built his character. He was a very reliable worker, a valued employee. And as strange as it sounds he made him a good father and husband for his family.

Too late he figured out his father's wisdom. And he couldn't look him in the eye and say "thank you". No shaking his hand or a father-son hug. All too late for any of that. And all because he thought he was a man no longer needing parents. Now he knows how wrong he was.

Growing up isn't easy. Especially the teen age years. You wake up one day and the parents are just memories. It's their teachings you'll remember. That road map to grow by. But they will be gone. Be the example for your children to admire. Be the child a parent can show great pride in.

It's the way things should be!

Story 37

"The Old Man and the Boy"

An old man was walking the sidewalk. He was bent, using a cane, and wore a hat and long coat. He spotted a chair, so he sat for a minute. That was when he heard "That's my chair."

He looked to see a small boy. "May I sit for a minute?"

The boy looked him over and then said, "Sure." He sat down on the ground and said, "I see you come by almost every day. You don't have a car?"

"Well, my health is not so good. My doctor said I need to walk. Where do you live?"

"Oh, just up the street a ways."

They visited for a few minutes until the mother called the little man in. "I've told you not to talk to strangers."

"I know, but he's nice. And pretty old. I like him."

So, the friendship began. The old man told him stories. The boy made him smile. Seems they both needed each other's company. One day, the old man gave him a gift. It was a billfold with a ten-dollar bill in it.

"Never spend that money. It's there for an emergency." Then he showed him his. "Always be prepared for an emergency."

The days passed, and his stays got longer. They truly enjoyed each other's company. The mother even started bringing him a glass of water when he sat. "You know, Mom, he kind of reminds me of Dad. I know he's a lot older, but he always makes time for me. He doesn't mind talking to me. I think he likes it."

"He does," the mother answered.

Then the day came when he didn't show.

The mother and boy went looking for him. They talked to neighbors and found out where he lived. They knocked on his door. A neighbor spoke up. "He's no longer there. He passed away. Died while on his walk." The mother and especially the boy were devastated. Tears flowed.

"Do you know where he is now?"

"He had no family I know of. Try the morgue."

They found where he had been. "We shipped the body to Chicago. He had a bigwig son there. That's all I know."

They left. "Mom, I never even got to tell him bye. When Dad died, I got to tell him. But not Mr. Daniel. I told him in a prayer last night, but I don't know if he heard me."

The mother took him in her arms and held him tight. "He heard you. I promise you that."

The years went by. The boy grew up. He never forgot his friend Mr. Daniel. He realized he was a son to him because his own son had drifted away. A lesson he learned and never forgot. A family member is not always blood. Everyone should realize that.

Story 38
"Never Blame the Innocent"

A young girl was jerked from the street. She was brutally raped many times then left for dead. She recovered in a hospital. But her mental scars ran deep. Weeks later she found out she was pregnant.

The pressure to abort the child was tremendous. She kept telling herself if she killed this baby was, she any less of a monster? She was mentally hurt but alive. The child was without fault in this. She had the child. He deserved life.

At the age of nine he asked "should I hate my father for what happened to you? Do you?"

She looks down at him and this is what she said:

"Hate will destroy even the strongest ones. You can't find happiness in a world of hate. So, the answer for you is no! He will answer to a higher court one day, if not already. But look at you. I love you so much. You have been a real blessing in my life. I am so thankful for you. Thankful for the love you return back to me. There are those out there who fight for the right to kill the unborn. I have no answer for them either. I don't understand them, and they don't understand me. But in the end, we will all be judged."

She raised him to respect people. To know and understand morals. To be a man to look up to. They went to church every Sunday. She did her best with him. He made her proud. What more could a mother ask of her child?

With time she was laid to rest. He married and had children of his own. Our world was a little better because of him. A child who was given life over abortion. An innocent child who grew up to be an example of what's good and right.

He was a life, not a choice.

Story 39
"He's Along Now"

He stayed in bed till almost eight o'clock. The sun was up and it was time to get moving. But sadness consumed his thoughts.

You see this was his first morning to wake up to an empty house. For so many years it was him who was up early and made coffee. He would gather fresh flowers from the garden and place them on the table outside. A small but very appreciated gift. All her favorite ones of course. He loved her so much. She no longer sleeps by his side. He'll have to visit her where she rest now. Bringing her that first batch of flowers will hurt his heart. He feels the pain already.

His kids want him to sell the house and move in with one of them. With time maybe. Right now he couldn't leave. Too many memories to keep them together still. No, he won't leave yet. He looks over and sees her cup. A tear fills his eye. He'll place it in a place of honor. His life must move on. Things are different now. An adjustment to be made. She would want that for him. Even from above she wants his happiness. And he knows that.

He needs to make a store run. Buying for one now. That must change! He'll go by the pound. He's sure there is a dog needing company also. The kind of friend he needs right now. He'll make that stop. A brown pup he can care for. That makes him smile. The first smile in weeks.

Yes that's what he needs. Time to get dressed and get on the road. A friend is waiting for him.

Story 40
"The Speed of Love"

A small girl sat on the bed with her arm in a cast. She was alone.

She had taken a terrible fall and, at the least, broke her arm. She was in a ward with several other beds with children. She watched as different parents came and went as they checked on their child. Not even the staff from the orphanage checked on her; she was truly alone. She would spend several days there for observation. At night, she would cry, but she didn't want anyone to know.

After a couple of days, the lady came in as usual to give her fresh sheets. She asked why she cried at night. Was she in pain? The girl was shocked. "How would you know that?"

The lady sat on the edge of the bed, placed her hand on the child, and said, "I change the sheets. I see the stains of tears. Do you have pain?"

Her eyes filled with tears. "No," she said. "I'm alone, and I guess I'm lonely."

The lady smiled and gave her a hug. "Not after today," she said and walked away.

The next day, she returned. She wasn't wearing the hospital uniform. And she carried a small package with a bow on top. "I brought you something."

With excitement, she opened the gift. It was a frilly bed shirt for her. With wide eyes, she said, "It's beautiful."

"Well, I thought you might want something a little nicer."

"Can I wear it now?"

"Sure. Let me help."

So, the quiet little girl got a caring friend, and she realized she didn't even know her name. "What's your name?" she asked.

"Kathy," she answered with a smile. "My name is Kathy, and I know you are Susan." Kathy spent the day with her. As she left, she stopped by the nurse's station and asked when Susan would be leaving.

The nurse looked both ways, then whispered, "It might be never. She has some serious internal injuries. Surgery is being scheduled as we speak. I saw the concerns on the doctor's face. She took a really bad fall."

Kathy came back the next day. But the bed was empty. She hurried to the station to find out Susan had taken a turn for the worse and had been rushed into surgery. Kathy had worked at the hospital long enough to know this was very serious. She immediately hurried to the floor where Susan was.

As she arrived, she went to a nonpublic area to sit. Just moments later, a small body was wheeled past, covered in a white sheet. Her whole body went limp. She was overwhelmed with emotion. She had grown up as an orphan herself. She clearly understood what the small child had felt. Now she was gone. But not alone. She sat and cried. She sobbed tears for little Susan. A concerned nurse came to her side. "What's wrong?"

She wiped the tears away and said it was over the loss of the orphaned girl. "I had no idea I could love someone so quickly. I wasn't able to change her life."

The nurse hugged her and whispered in her ear, "Susan's surgery is wrapping up now. She's going to be fine."

Five years have passed since then. Susan now calls Kathy "Mom." She gets all the love and attention she needs now. She will never be alone, and her new mother makes sure of that.

Story 41
"Seeing Life Through Clearer Eyes"

There was a bitter man. Never felt life dealt him the cards he deserved. So, he received a visitor in the night.

If you ever saw the Christmas show it's kind of like that, yet different. He woke up in the night to find a woman sitting by his side. She looks down and says "enough of your bickering! I'll show you real misery! You will feel the pain of the innocent. Now go back to sleep!"

He awakes in pain. Heavy pain. He's in a hospital, but in a third world country. He tries to speak but can't. He needs attention but has no way to attract someone for help. Tears roll from his eyes. He can see others. All the moaning, all the cries for help. Doctors and nurses moving from bed to bed. They declare the man next to him dead. The body was quickly replaced. Finally, they get to him.

The doctor tells him they have no medicine for his condition. "We're not a large American hospital, we have so little. If the pain becomes too great, we can inject you and end it all. It's the best we can do, sorry."

He thinks of his life. How he would like to be in his house that he hated so much. He always felt sick, how he would invite those feelings over what he has now. They come and force a liquid down his throat.

"It will make you sleep. You'll forget about the pain for a while."

He dreams of walking in the summer heat. Feeling it on his face. In proper doses it's not that bad. How he hated it back then. He sees how he had wasted all of his good feelings. Tossed them to the curb. He only saw and felt the negative things in his life. And he could see how they really didn't exist outside of his head. Such a waste of a good life. He had so much. Now he was to die alone in pain. Alone with no friends or family. The pain wakes him up. He moans and that is noticed by the doctor.

He bends over him and says "there is no hope for you, and we need your bed. You'll feel nothing. I hope you led a gracious life," and he pushes in the fluid. He awakes.

He's in his bed. Everything was so real. The pain, the conditions. All so real. Devine Intervention gave him a second chance. Nothing in his life has changed but him. He takes out his phone and dials a number.

"Son? It's your dad. I know we haven't talked in years; will you allow me to change that? Can I take you and your family to dinner tonight so we can talk? I see things better. I was a fool. Please accept."

Appreciation for what we have is the way to happiness. Longing for what we don't is cancer. As you go through life smile at your accomplishments. Know you tried your best, but you don't get all you want. That's life for all of us.

Story 42
"Love Lost"

What happens when the one you love moves on from you?

He truly was in love with her. The center of his universe. But still needed to grow more. I guess a little scared of the full commitment, not wanting to take that last step. Could have been his ego, who knows? But what she deserved he fell short. Now he occasionally sees her, married to another. Looks happy now.

You live alone. But that is because you are still in love with her. There is no anger. She gave you your chance. It just slipped through your fingers. So what now? How do you move on? Do you even want to? Why can't you shake this place in your heart? So you go about your life. A friend to other women. Not wanting to love again. Not unhappy. Just not married to her yourself.

Our paths in life lead us many places. Our control of the destination isn't always recognized. And when it's finally recognized, well you missed the turn. No way to circle back now. You just continue your way on your path. Disappointed you weren't more aware of the signs. Listened closer. Your fault entirely. So now what?

Do you find some lame reason to call? Just to hear her again. That sweet voice. Or just stand on the sidelines. Not wanting to complicate anything, no awkward situation. Just a longing to sit and visit once more.

This is your life now. The one you accepted. There are still untraveled roads ahead. You'll wear your walking shoes again. Just not right now. You don't feel ready yet.

Story 43

"Still in Love"

Just like clockwork, he shows up every Valentine's Day with flowers and a card.

I've been here eighty years, and he had already been coming. I'm not sure how long. We're just told to leave the area and give him privacy. I think it was a car crash. He must have really loved her.

He gets out of his car. Breathes a long sigh. And makes his way to the grave. He gently replaces the dried stems with fresh, colorful flowers. He places his card in the box he placed there to keep them out of the elements. He takes his time to find the perfect card. He writes his special note to her, seals it, and leaves it in the box. She'll read it from another place. He's sure of that.

He sits on a bench provided for him, looks down, and begins talking. "My little bird, you know my love for you has never faltered. I miss you so much. But I've come this time to ask permission. Permission to love again. I will not replace you in my heart, just share the space with another.

I've fallen in love again. She is so special. I smile more. She makes me laugh. My time with her is beyond value. I also know you want me to love again. To open my heart once more. I want it to be to her. I want to feel right about this. I'm asking for your permission."

Right then, a small bird lands on the stone. It looks him over. Stares. It spends a minute or two, then moves to a branch of a nearby tree. His eyes tear up. He knows it's just a bird, but to him, it's an approval.

Story 44
"Life Never Ends"

A father has been feeling bad for a while now. The time to see the doctor finally came.

He was asked to come in and bring his wife. As nervous as they were, they hoped for the best. But that was not to be. The news was bad. He only had weeks and he would feel worse every day. He would receive medication for his pain, and he needed to get his affairs in order while he could.

News like this will totally change the way you see life. The summer nights weren't so hot any longer. They became beautiful. Cherished. He would hold his wife; he loved her so. They discussed all the arrangements, the tears flowed. Family and friends came from far and wide. Goodbye can be a difficult word. Feelings laid out for all to see. Time is short when it's slipping away. He feels his weakness overtaking his once strong body. If only another week. Or maybe just a few more days. Anything.

He takes more meds now. It's harder to keep his focus. He doesn't want to take them, but he really doesn't have a choice. His time is short now. His eyes are closed more often. He hears the sounds of the people talking. He wants to say something, he just can't. Someone is holding his hand. Speaking soft words. He can feel the love. Then he hears a voice. Clear and strong.

"Dan, it's time to go. We have a journey to take. Say your goodbyes, they'll feel it in their hearts. You'll be with your family again later. I just need to prepare you for your next existence. A wonderful new time awaits you. Walk with me."

Story 45

"The Square Peg"

Why do women cry so much and a man so little? An old question with a thousand answers.

Women were gifted with a compassion in which there is no equal. Their understanding of things so much deeper. The ability to emotionally repair a bad situation. Men lack those qualities. They're too busy forcing the round peg into the square hole. And believe me they will do it. The damage is irrelevant. It's the goal that matters.

His son hurts himself and the response is "boy get up we have work to do". While the mother goes down on one knee to check things out. A full inspection and a Band-Aid if necessary. Both full of unconditional love, but two separate ways to handle it. The women knows it's necessary to step in and the man just looks at her and asks "WHAT"?

Man and woman are the two sides of the balance. They need each other to survive. The woman will shed tears because her heart aches. The man will show anger and have no idea why? If he is a man, a true man, he'll accept her wisdom. Not really question. Just huff a little as if to say he was the right one. That's part of his uncontrolled ego. He knows!

So, both need the other. The circle can't be completed without acceptance. Women have the compassion and understanding. And men, well they are the experts at getting round pegs to fit in a square hole.

Story 46
"The Image Reflected"

We've watched it from a very young age, this ever-evolving image.

It's different with everyone. Some look too much, and others not enough. We stand back and tilt our heads, or we move in close and try to see what is not there. Sometimes we don't want to accept what we see. But it never lies. It can pick up every detail and miss nothing. This would seem impressive in any other surroundings; we only wish we could do as well.

We visit this image and inspect for the slightest change. As funny as it might sound, we sometimes take pictures. Why? Because of the truth it shares. I don't know. Evolution affects everything. And this is no different. At one time, water was our only source. Then a polished metal that only the rich or powerful could claim. But the drive to own this technology pushes us still. To keep track of details, this technology is in every room in your home. Handheld, large and heavy, and everything in between. By law, it has to go with you as you travel. But no one complains. In fact, it's welcomed.

We must be able to see our reflections. To check on our looks. Oh, the vanities we have. Without our mirrors, we are a lost world. We don't want to be told of our flaws. We want to find them ourselves and fix them if possible. We want people to think we wake up this perfect!

We've watched our image change since as far back as we can remember. The evolution of our self. Are you satisfied with what you see?

Story 47
"We Are Always Watched Over"

My sixth sense told me something wasn't right.

But I kept walking. I look down at my arm and see the bone. I'm hurt and hurt bad. But I kept walking. I look behind and see a smoking car. I've had an accident. I hear traffic but no one is stopping. I'm getting dizzy. If I don't make the road, I die where I fall. I dropped to one knee.

Then I feel a hand on my shoulder. "Allow me to help," its a small boy. "Put your hand on my shoulder and stand."

"I can't, I don't have the strength."

"Do this or you will die."

So, he mustered his strength and stood again. One step at a time. "Keep moving. We're going to make it." They get to the road, and he sinks to the ground. The last thing he hears is "you'll be safe now dad, thank you for allowing me to help."

He wakes up in the hospital. His wife by his side. He's still sedated but waking up. "Where is the boy?"

"Who?"

"The boy who saved me?"

"There was no boy. You were by yourself. The sight has been swept, just your car and your footprints leaving."

He looks at his wife. "I think I was with Bobby. I'm sure I saw him."

"John, it's the medication. We lost Bobby three years ago. Just rest."

"I remember it so well, he was there."

"Just get more sleep."

A nurse walks in and gives him a sleep aid. He closes his eyes and sleeps again. The nurse hands her a package. "This is the personal belongings of his. They were removed when he was admitted." As the nurse turns to leave, she pours the contents on a table. In astonishment she quickly says "Wait! You took these things from him?"

"Yes, I'm the one who collected them."

"This chain and cross, where did it come from?"

"He was wearing it." And she leaves.

She doesn't know what to think. What to believe. Their son was buried with that chain and cross around his neck. How could her husband come into possession of it? She sits down and takes his hand. She'll wait to hear what he has to say about what happened. How could that chain get around his neck? What did he experience? Whatever he has to say, she'll believe him.

Story 48
"Family Lost then Found"

The phone rings. A man picked it up. Hello?

"This is your son Bill. Can you talk?" He answers, "Sorry wrong number. I have no son named Bill." "As a matter of fact you do, it's me, and I think I can give you the proof." Intrigued he says "speak".

"You once loved a girl named Nancy Davis. You two ere lovers. You left for the military and ya'll lost contact. Nancy was my mother. When you left she was pregnant. She never told you about me. You married while away. You didn't know. She had no anger toward you that was by her fault. And she told me to neve have anger either." There was a long silence.

"Where is Nancy now?" "Gone. She got very sick and died." "What do you want?" "Almost nothing. I just want to meet you. I want to meet my father. I will walk in, share a coffee with you then leave. I don't want to cause any problems for you. You'll never have to see me ever again." "Are you asking for a blood test?" "No. When you see me you will agree or not. Mom always said I look like you. I've never even seen a picture of you. Once you married, she got rid of them. I just want to meet you and shake your hand." Long silence again.

"Bill I want to meet you too. I loved Nancy with all my heart at one time. It's just things happen. Let's have that coffee and see where this goes. If you are mine, and at this time I have no reason not to think that's possible, we will make up for lost time. You have family to meet. And I'm sure they will want to meet and accept you. They will understand."

Story 49

"Fatherhood"

Father's Day. Once a father, what changes? Do you become more tolerant? Maybe more responsible? How does it affect a man? This is my opinion. You look into a mirror and see both pride and fear. Your wife is an adult. That child is so small, so helpless. You now care for something that totally depends on you as a provider. It's not your new dog or cat. You and your wife created this life. You know what her responsibilities are. Let's look at yours.

You must love that child more than your own life. There is no more showing up late for work and putting your job in jeopardy. Saying, "This job sucks," and just walking off. You consider a second job to be an even better provider. You now help out even more. It's your obligation. You're now required to be an even better husband. You were forced to grow up even faster. Now you look at what you want and think, *What does my family need? I can go without.*

Happy Father's Day to all of you dads and future dads. Save now. Their college days are ahead of you. Their education is a part of your new responsibility. Best of luck with everything.

Story 50
"Secrets"

It was a cool spring day. You might say the stars were in alignment. A soon to be mother is on her way to the hospital.

"Hurry" she says, "I'm close."

Soon she was on a gurney going into delivery. Everything kind of blurred for a few minutes then she hears the crying of a baby. The nurse hands the child to her mother. A tiny girl is placed on her chest. Tears flow and emotions run high. The doctor whispers in her ear, "comfort her, but know there is an issue. We'll discuss it later. Her health is fine. Show her love."

The mother and child are moved to a room. She looks the baby over and can't see anything out of the ordinary. The doctor will come later and explain.

When he does come, he takes her hand and tells the new mother that there are problems with her legs. She will never walk. But her health is fine, and she will grow up just fine. The mother looks down and smiles. "If that's GOD'S will, I won't question it."

And so, the years pass. She's now seven. Adjusting just fine. Well-liked by all. Her grandfather comes in one day with an arm full of supplies. He said more was in the car. He bought her everything she needed to learn to paint. Even tapes explaining all she needs to know. This changed her life. Gave her a focus she didn't know she needed. Her talent with paint excelled. She majored in art and went on to be an illustration giant. Everyone wanted her talents. From the outside looking in she seemed to be on top of the world.

She was lonely. Her work kept her isolated. Then one day she receives an e-mail. It's from a man, around her age. He tells her of how talented she is. And if she doesn't mind, he will talk to her about her illustrations. She quickly agrees. A friendship begins to grow. She doesn't want to tell him she is wheelchair bound. So, she avoided mentioning it.

Their friendship lasted for many years. They exchanged pictures of their smiling faces but never went farther than that. Then one day he tells her he's in the hospital and things aren't good. He wants to talk with her every day if she doesn't object.

That wasn't good enough for her. She flies to his location. Finally, she wheels herself to his room. She looks up to see the name. David James. A nurse walks up to her. "Are you here to see David? If you want, we can place him in his wheelchair and push you both outside. The sun will do him good."

"If he is so weak, I'm not sure that's good."

"David has no legs. He's been in a wheelchair since birth. You didn't know that? He'll be fine."

Amy was in a state of shock. He never mentioned it. And just like her, he must have been embarrassed to let the other know.

"Do me a favor. Let me touch up my makeup then push me back." Once returned she took a deep breath and entered the room.

Never think you're not good enough for someone. Till you get to know them, you don't know their insecurities. The loss hurts both.

Story 51
"How much Love can you give your Pet?"

He found this unwanted puppy by the side of the road. He was near death. Against better judgment, he picked him up.

He carried him to a vet. Found out it would be fairly expensive to save him. This small dog left for dead. Not a friend in the world. It struck a nerve. He paid to save his life. And starting that day they were inseparable. He named him Thunder as kind of a joke.

They were together for ten years, he would walk him in the neighborhood in the evening. One day a pack of dogs came running at him, and they meant harm. He looked around for an escape to find none. His thoughts went to "so this is how I go". There would be no way to survive such an attack from so many dogs bent on taking him down.

Then out of nowhere Thunder shot past. He ran straight into the pack. Thunder was a big dog but the odds were totally against him. Blood and fur flew everywhere. The man found a bat in the yard and joined the fight. By the retreat of the remaining dogs the man was bleeding from his arms and legs. Thunder lay dying.

The man ran and got his car, scooped up Thunder and raced to the vet. Once there they required aid to stop their bleeding. He tells the vet to please save his dog. A medical team showed up and wants to take him to the hospital. Absolutely not. My dog is dying in there and I won't leave him.

The vet comes to him and says "he's torn up too bad". "He needs to be put down". "No! You will go back in there and try to save him". "This will cost you thousands and he probably won't make it". "That dog just saved my life. Go back in!!!"

Jump ahead three months. Thunder lays on a bed built special for him. He's missing one leg but recovering well. Now it's the man who follows his dog everywhere. All he wants to do is please Thunder. He doesn't care about the money spent. His dog was willing to die to protect him. He did save his life. They saved each other.

Our pets become family. Not really meant to be but it can't be stopped. The devotion of a pet needs to be returned to that animal. And Thunder was a pampered pet the rest of his days. His ashes will be mixed with his beloved family and buried with them.

Story 52

"Save Our Planet"

I didn't see the forest because the trees were in the way!

Old saying but so true. We are always looking for things that, when found, were right there in the open. Our focus was spread too thin. It could almost not qualify as focus.

Mother Nature is all around us. Flowers so small they are hardly noticed. Trees so lush and green they just blend in. Their uniqueness unnoticed. They have a job in our welfare. We need them. Yet we cut them down for any purpose that suits us. It's said we don't need to go to Mars. We need to focus on our planet. We have the ability to balance everything. We need not give up much. Just our total disrespect to the planet.

Our oceans have been contaminated with plastic. Countries with corrupt governments don't care about the environment. Power and money are their motivations. You can't blame their people because they have no choice.

Our carbon footprint is a serious subject, yet our officials have the largest ones. They preach, and none of it applies to them. Power and money.

So out here, I cut and plant. I thin, which gives a better forest. I'm lucky to be here. I want to protect it.

Story 53
"Attitudes"

What kind of person are you on an absolutely gorgeous day? Does the day define you? Are you different depending on whether the sun is out or not? Some are controlled by this. Others stand in defiance. You have the ability to pick your attitude for that day. And sure, you can't be 100% positive each and every day. Some factors do drive your feelings. The death of a loved one. A major medical situation. A headache. So how strike the balance?

I think you must take control of your feelings. Your mother ever tell you "you better straighten up in the same pair of shoes you got mad in." She's telling you that you are in control. To not allow your emotions to place you in a bad place. So just like the one who puts on extra unwanted pounds, you have to exercise and monitor food intake to get back in shape. No, it's not easy. But you can win. Keep your emotions in check. Know you're not perfect, but not a jerk either. Strive for the better you. If 100% is not possible, settle for 70%, maybe even 40% slowly take control of how you feel. Much more than not, it's a personal choice.

Story 54

"Parenting"

He lacked manners, this child of the new era. Never could be properly disciplined. So he developed an attitude early. He would yell at his parents, show disrespect, and pretty much tell them what he would do and not do.

This went on in his life. His friends were no better. So trouble followed them around like a bad smell. No respect for the law, whatever they wanted they took. But nothing will last forever. One day they were on the receiving end. Another group of older boys wanted their shoes and jackets. A fight ensued. One of the boys got killed. The natural path for this kind of lifestyle.

But in prison there was discipline. Something he wasn't used to. Both from the guards and the inmates. During a rioting episode he was killed. He didn't fit in on the outside and didn't fit in on the inside.

So what is the lesson to take away?

You must as parents be the example for your children. Involve yourselves early in their lives. Teach good and bad. Take them to church. That's one of the most responsible things you can do for them. Encourage their leadership skills. Both the boys and the girls. If you stand with them in a court room, you'll one day stand at their grave.

As parents, take the control back. It is you who will guide them. Not strangers. It is you who must make the calls. Strangers don't love your child!!! Your children are just a way to force change you don't want. Start now!!!

Story 55

"The Love of Brothers"

There were two twin boys who were very close. While one worked and studied hard, the other just wanted to play. The good brother did all he could to help the other but to no avail. One went to college, and the other joined a gang.

The good one studied criminal law enforcement. He wanted to understand how he might help his brother. Upon graduation, he was assigned to the unit that went after the *baddest* of the bad. He didn't know where his brother was, but he knew he was somewhere in the city.

Then, a lead came in. A gang was using an old building as their lair. Everyone was called in on it. The building was surrounded, and everyone was told to come out with hands up. The bullets began to fly. People were dying on both sides. The good brother, David, slipped in a window. He slowly moved toward the gunfire. And he came face-to-face with himself. Both had guns drawn. One or both would die that day.

David told him to put his gun down. "You can't do anything to stop me from firing. David, I'm a killer; you are not. Move aside and let me leave."

"I can't do that. Don't make me fire, please!"

"I know Mom and Dad loved you more. You were the better son. Just move aside and let me go."

"I can't!" A shot rang out, and then a second. David watched his brother fall. He ran to him.

The brother said, "I'm the killer, but I couldn't kill you. Don't feel bad about this. You are the one who should live. Not me. I couldn't go to prison." David held him as he slipped away. He looked back to where he stood. The bullet was three feet above his head. His brother had sacrificed himself.

He went to the funeral in uniform. Just him and his wife. From there, he turned in his gun and badge. He quit law enforcement that day. A piece of him died, and to this day, he asks, "How can twin brothers turn out so differently?" No family member should be in a position to kill any family. He carried the weight of his decision till the day he died.

Story 56
"Always a Dancer"

A small girl watched her mother dance.

They lived alone. So, she danced alone. As the girl grew older, she danced with her mother. And in time with her new father-in-law. Dance became her passion. And so, the training for her future began.

She had dance lessons, and she excelled. When the time for college came, she asked if she could be trained in New York? The mother borrowed money and sent her to the school of her choice. There she excelled even farther. Very soon she was on full scholarships. She was watched by every scout in the dance field.

Finally, she was asked to dance to a song and would be paid very handsomely. She quickly became in demand. Agents were demanding to represent her. She told them no. Her mother was her agent and money would go to no one else. They tried to block her from performing. She was just too talented. She danced for years. Finally, the day came when she was too aged for the work. She retired as a very wealthy dancer.

While out shopping one day a young teenage girl approached her. "I recognize you," she said. "My hope is to one day be as good as you."

Looking down she said, "my days of glory have passed, I now dance for me." The girl looked up in adoration and said, "let me dance with you."

A friendship developed between the two. The dancer now had a daughter to share her talents with. No, she was not hers, but she could believe so. And the girl, well she was trained by the best dancer on the planet.

With time she passed on. She left everything to the loved friend. Included was a training facility. And her request to keep her name alive by showing other hopefuls how to bring their talents to the stage. This is now one of the most prestigious studios in New York. Can you name it?

Story 57
"Can We Change"

They lived in the country. Far removed from the rest.

Each day the mother would go for a walk down a trail in the woods. With her walked her three-year-old daughter. The day started out as most but quickly changed. They were always accompanied by the family dog. Her name was Grace. A medium size animal. Full of spirit and love for her family. The only family she knew.

On this walk the mother kept hearing something following them. The dog was on edge about something. And then it happened. A cougar stepped into the trail. A big one, and it wanted the child.

The mother was without any defense at all. Never needed anything till then. She snatched her daughter up knowing she might die that day. That's when Grace moved to the front. All of her hair was bristled up. She would defend her family in a battle she couldn't win.

Grace was the one to attack first. As fierce as any warrior she lunged at the cougar. The fight was on. Fur and blood went everywhere. The mother was horrified by what she saw. But she kept moving backwards. Finally she ran. The safety of her child was the most important thing.

She came back with her husband and a gun. They found Grace. Alive yet not to survive. So badly injured. So gently they picked her up and brought her back. Tended her wounds as made her last hours as comfortable as possible. She was buried under a large oak in the yard. A small fence around the grave. She gave her life for the only family she had. There is so much honor in that.

We need to see everyone as an extended family. Separation is not needed right now. I hope change is in the wind. I hope we can come closer together as a Nation. We can always hope. Let's make change one small step at a time.

Story 58

"The Man Never Seen"

There was this creepy old guy who lived deep in the woods. He had three dogs and three cats. A sprinkle of chickens and ducks. Really weird guy. He would spend his days splitting wood and listening to music. In the summer, it was cutting grass and building areas of shade for him and his flowers. Who does that and can be called normal?

Occasionally, he snuck to town, unseen by anyone but a lady who worked the streets. He had a lake, and he purchased fish. As it turned out, it was a very large area for his wild otters to feed. Just imagine the expense he went through to rent equipment to dig the lake and stock it, just to feed otters. A very strange man. His warped mind created stories to read. After a few drinks, there was no limit to what might be realized. It could be that living in such isolation had taken its toll. Could be he was just weird. Either way, he's still out there. Keep the children away.

I personally know he responds to hundred-dollar bills left at the gate. Placed in a jar and set to the side. One day, the jar is just missing. Maybe a small rock left in trade. This guy needs medical help. The residents of Pinewood need not worry. He's too old, too slow, and too fat to pose any harm. Just a novelty to discuss at Thursday's coffee. Hope this put a smile on you.

Story 59
"Her First Love"

There were two neighbors who became best friends. One had a son, the other a daughter.

Because of the friendship of the parents the children were always together. So, they grew up almost as brother and sister. Maybe because girls mature sooner, and boys don't, something changed. One day she stopped playing and just looked at Tim. For some reason, she noticed a change about him. She had never been in love before so she couldn't interpret her feelings. She found herself thinking of him more, wanting to be near him more often. Their friendship was going through a change.

Suddenly Tim became ill. Seriously ill. Everyone panicked and doctors did all they could. But they lost Tim. At the viewing she stood at the coffin and cried silently. "I've never even kissed him. Was never able to show him my love." With that she bent over and kissed his lips. Then turned and left. She could see no more.

She withdrew. Solitude is her best friend now. She had to work her way through this. She was both young and inexperienced. She hid her feelings from everyone.

Then one day, she sat on the steps at school when someone spoke. "I know of your feelings for Tim. You two never connected. I've given it a lot of thought. I don't want the same to happen to me. I want you to know I've admired you for some time now. I could see your love for Tim. I kept my distance. It was all out of respect for the both of you. I'll leave now, but I'd like to speak with you again. Maybe a shoulder to lean on. I'll help you with this. Push me away if you wish. But I can help you, I want to." And he walked away.

The next time he approached her she asked him to sit with her. She did need that shoulder. She needed to express her feelings to someone. She loved her mother, but it was an uncomfortable subject for her. You know sixteen-year-old girls. Their logic is somewhat a little different.

The rest of the story, well we know. Their first son was named Tim. It was his idea. He loved her so much and knew Tim was her first love. She needed that small attachment. To remember her childhood. To turn lose. She had a man whose love had no bounds. And because of that she showed her love to him and her family every day in return.

Is that not the way it should be?

Story 60
"He Saw His Mother's Love"

He was twelve when he lost his leg. His whole world changed.

Suddenly everything was a challenge. His mother was always there for him, but very little help. He had pains, he had limitations, he felt all of this was thrown in his lap. None of it was his fault. Why couldn't he vent his grief with life. It was justified.

The mother tried to help. We all have our pains. It's not for others to have to sit and listen. Keep it private. Do all you can to have a better life no matter what. "Easy for you to say, you have both your legs." But the mother never stopped trying to have him see he had powers over life. She cared for him the rest of her life.

Upon her passing he began to find out things he never knew. A rare bone cancer took her life. She had dealt with heavy pain for years. Never once did she complain. Her eyesight had been failing for years. He never knew. Problems with her feet, yet she stood and cooked his meals every day. She showed love and strength he didn't even know existed. He felt shame. His life changed.

If my mother, as frail as she was can be that strong, then I can be even stronger. He got out more. Had a leg fitted for him. When he walked no one even knew. Happiness filled his heart once again. He even met someone to share his new found love with. Yes, his life had changed.

We don't control the cards dealt to us in life. But we do control how we play the hand. A positive attitude can lift you in the darkest times. Understanding you weren't singled out for your pain. It was just the card dealt. So, draw your inner strength and have the best life possible. You deserve that.

Story 61
"Timing"

How many believe life is all about timing? Events happen to each of us were, a few moments before or after, the outcome would be wildly different. You can say with a hushed smile, "The timing was perfect." This can be very dark also. "Such horrible timing." It's sometimes just a roll of the dice.

You meeting the love of your life. Was timing involved in that? Both of you in the right place at the right time. Was it chance, fate, an accident, or maybe just perfect timing? Who really knows? There were those times when timing meant everything. Your life was affected. You met a new friend for life, only because of the timing of you both in the place where you met or were introduced. So many chains of events had to happen. A variance of any kind, and a different outcome. Something to ponder. Time is one of the big wonders of the universe. Its impact on all of us is mostly taken for granted. People say every moment counts. Timing is everything. I was so lucky. I want to find that pot of gold too. Everything has to happen just right. And I think, *The timing will have to be perfect*.

Story 62

"The Value of Love"

What if I could never love again? Would I be mournful or bitter? Maybe a mix of both. But for sure I wouldn't be who I am today. Love covers such a vast area. The touch of the back of your hand on the cheek of your lover. What about an exceptional sunset? A favorite song? Your pet that you are its world. How would you be affected?

The lack of love in your life must be devastating. Do you feel you could be unaffected by the laughter of a baby? Not really care? Look back on a picture of your parents, long gone and feel no love at all? The desire to hold hands any longer? Where does it end? We love so much more than we hate. We just need to remember that.

A heart filled with love is good for the person. Sure, we deal with the opposite of love all the time in today's world. It's sometimes shoved down our throats. Know when it's time to tune it out. To take control of the happiness in your heart. The agendas of those who want to move your feelings down a darker road must not be allowed to happen.

So, fight for the ability to love. Love the people around you. Separate yourself from the haters. This is a beautiful world. Full of beautiful flowers of nature. Birds of unimaginable beauty. And people who will give their life for a stranger. When you give your love, give them plenty. The inability to love would be so wrong. Cherish your ability and never lose it!

Story 63
"A Woman So Special"

Her personality was such that you couldn't help but love her.

Not a complainer really, we all so some. But she never takes it too far. She is more of the gentle conversations and holding hands if you're special enough. Not a lazy bone in her body. Always busy. Doing the work required. Knocking it out so she might have free time of her own.

Going to town is a production in its self. She would never consider just walking out of the house "as is". No, details are taken. Hair, makeup, outfits. She always wants to look her best when out. And understand it's not an ego thing. Not at all. She's a very modest lady. It's more on the line of taking pride in her appearance. She takes pride when her man is told "she always looks great".

A stay-at-home wife. She enjoys her role. House cleaning, cooking, all the little things that shows she cares. Ladies, if you live long enough, all of you will experience it. She knows your favorite meal. The dessert of choice. All the things that make you smile. Be sure to reciprocate in that one.

I've met many women that take pride in being the best they can be. Not a single thing wrong with that. They deserve a partner equal to the love shown. To the care given. Go to the mirror and ask if your grade would be passing. If even close to a "no", start that repair today.

Story 64
"Letter to Santa"

A young boy wrote a letter to Santa. And these were his words:

I know the tooth fairy is just Mom and Dad. And a wishing well is not really a thing. But you are special. The bigger boys make fun of me and push me around. But I believe in you. I've written many letters letting you know what I want each year. Mom has said you pick the thing I want most from the list. And that has been true. So, I believe. This year is different.

My dad lost his job. People are getting sick or something. Now I see him worry. He leaves every day, trying to do work to make money. I hear them talk. I saw my mom crying after they talked one day. She said he could get sick himself and bring it home to us. He just kept saying, "What can I do? We have to eat."

So, this year, will you bring food? Enough so my father can stay home. I don't want him to get sick. I don't want to lose him. My mother is scared; give her strength. Let her know it will be all right. She needs that right now. Do this for me, and I'll never ask for anything again. I believe in you. You can do so much. I just ask for a little. I'm going to get you help. I'm going to mail this. Then I'm going to pray. I'm going to ask Jesus for help also. We never miss church. I say my prayers every night. I don't know if it's wrong to ask for a favor. But it's important. So, I'll ask.

So many must be asking for help right now. Do what you can please. I need to start my prayer. I'll put this in the box. And I'll wait. I know you'll do something.

Love,

Billy

Story 65

"First Kiss"

A boy. A young man wanting to be strong. The most beautiful girl he has ever seen stands in front of him. He wants his first kiss. But his confidence is low. Her smile takes his heart. They're close enough he can smell her hair. He knows he just needs to lean forward just a little. She tries to help. She looks up into his eyes. Moves a little closer herself. It's up to him to kiss her. Will he? Confusion fills the air. He takes a breath and pulls her in. Their lips touch. His heart soars. She smiles and lowers her head. Her first kiss also.

The magic of the night. Two children growing up. Never to return to the age of inexperience. The seed of love planted. What now?

This is how it starts for so many. Their introduction to love. Not aggressive. Soft. Tender. Holding hands. Wanting more words between them. The bond grows daily. Not a bad thing. Very natural. Without a full understanding of love, they work out the bumps. Time is on their side.

Introduction to each other's parents. Now a couple. Thinking it will last forever. We wish for the best. We wish them success. So, few of us love only once. We stumble, we fall. But we get back up. We continued the quest. Never allow your heart to wither. Never stop looking. It's out there for all of us. Look how it grows. Family, friends, nature, taste, smells. Once set free, love spreads everywhere. Allow nothing to stop it.

Story 66
"None of us Die Alone"

I heard the words "you die alone" in a song.

At my age I've seen death many times. Friends, family, and strangers. I've held hands, closed eyes, and shed tears. But I don't think anyone dies alone. Generations before surround that person. The spirit family will always be there. They stand and wait for you to see them. To take the journey to another place. There awaits even more of the ones who are a part of your life. Even lost pets.

So then what? Be sure confusion is at the forefront of your feelings. But also peace. An understanding you never possessed till then. It will be "your" heaven. Your start on another life. Yes life, but very different. No pain, no sickness, no turmoil of any kind. But a life none the less.

So know none of us die alone. If your life was good, good awaits you. It's that simple. And if you had no belief in a life after your physical death, well I'm not sure what happens? But why test it? Leave a back door open just in case.

Story 67

"What a Mother Sees"

A mother was watching her daughter trying to smell a flower.

They start so innocent and so clean. Then, when exposed to the outside, they are introduced to real nature. Dirt on the new dress. A fall and a skinned knee. Tears rolling down a cheek. Laughter and beautiful colors. What is a mother to do?

She'll protect as best she can. She'll teach as the child grows. Those will be some of her fondest memories. But each day, she grows a little. Almost undetectable, but shoes become too tight, clothes too short. She crawls, then walks, talks, then before you know it, she's going to school. Still, you teach her about life. You become friends but always still a mother.

The day finally comes that a boy enters your world. How you accept this is critical. She's becoming a young lady. Dad takes it the hardest. And your teachings continue. A wedding day comes, and you have to give her away. How you would like to go back at least for a day and watch her try to smell a flower.

She'll always come to you for advice. Your mother-daughter bond will never be broken. One day, you have a grandchild to spoil. And spoil you do. The cycle starts over. Your teachings never end until you fade away.

Yes, you can see the future. But today she'll smell that flower and look at you with a big smile. You'll pick her up and hold her a little tighter. She is your world today. A memory that will never be forgotten.

Story 68
"Blessings"

The day was like no other. Never before and never after.

He removed the covering of the last number. Haven't even looked yet. He studied and looked up and went over the numbers very slowly. He was a winner. Millions of dollars. Only one winner, and it was him. Now what?

Let's go back in time. He worked just like so many others. The provider for his family. A very hard worker. His wife was dealing with medical issues and couldn't work outside the home. He had to sometimes work two jobs to properly provide for the ones he loved. Each and every night he prayed: "LORD, give me strength tomorrow, I'll need it. My family needs me. Keep them safe. Everything happens for a reason. I trust in you. Amen."

This morning on his way to work he stopped for gas. As he pays, he sees the scratch off tickets. Five dollars was a lot. But something drove him to buy one. He knew he really couldn't afford it right now. And he really wasn't a buyer of tickets. Somehow today was different. His light was green as he moved through the intersection.

He regained consciousness in a hospital. Under insured and with a merger job, he saw his world fall around him. How could he provide now? He finds out he'll heal. But that will take months. He'll be able to work again. But what about till then. So, he prays: "JESUS You know I have a merger life insurance policy, take me so I can help once more. Please do this for me. I know everything happens for a reason. How do I recover from this? I need your help. Please!"

A doctor enters the room. Pulls up a chair and speaks. "Things may look pretty dark right now. You are strong, always have been. All of your possessions are in an envelope in this room. Ask for them," and with that he leaves. The man is confused, he has nothing there to help him. His depression deepens. He falls to sleep and dreams. The doctor returns in his dream. "You will be stronger tomorrow than you are today. You trust in your faith. You have said that to me many times. Remember your trust. Ask for the envelope."

The rest you know. We are tested each and every day. Depend on your strength. Trust your faith. Know and believe there are bigger things out there watching over you.

Things happen for a reason!

Story 69
"Dreams"

I woke up on a bed of soft grass. I had no idea where I was but I seemed very happy.

All was so strange. So much at peace. Where was I? I walked. All was so green and lush. The colors of the flowers so deep. Birds moved about and sang their songs. I was in a paradise. A really nice one!!!

But how did I get here? I found a soft place and took a short nap. Best sleep I've had in years. I continued on my way. Eventually I came upon a high point. I could see mountains in the distance. A valley with a river moving slowly along its length. Such a beautiful sight. Nature showing its best side just for me. Slowly it began to make sense.

I was dreaming. I was awake and alert but sound asleep. You have those dream sometimes. You don't want to wake up. More time in your fantasy is all you're asking. You open your eyes and sure enough, you're in your bed. You want to sleep again. Return to your paradise. Recapture those moments. But that's not to be. You're awake now. A smile is there. A foggy memory of a wonderful night.

Today is going to be great one. Your mood is perfect. You're so totally rested, it's just going to be a great day.

We all have those nights every now and then. Our subconscious works out the stress that has built. A reset sort of thing. Your glass has been emptied for you to be able to handle more. You want to remember all the details but you can't.

But a revisit? Well, that may just be waiting for you. You sleep every night. And you always remember the good things.

Story 70
"A Daughter Returned"

She was at the hospital giving birth to her first child.

The nurse laid the child across her chest. And so her role as a mother began. The little girl wanted for nothing. Always dressed up like a play doll. The center of attention for sure. Time moved slowly forward.

Now her teenage years were beginning. The close relationship was beginning to strain. The girl argued with her mother daily. The father had died years earlier in a car crash. So the mother was raising her daughter alone. She had spoiled her so badly that the girl demanded her way. She was disrespectful. The rules of the house didn't apply to her.

At seventeen, she ran off with her boyfriend. She wasn't seen for years. Then the worst happened. The mother had a stroke. It was a bad one. Ann heard about it from a friend. So she went home. At the hospital, she saw her mother in the bed with tubes everywhere. She looked so small. So fragile. All at once, all was forgiven. She didn't have the anger any longer. All she wanted was to care for her mother. She entered the room and held her hand. But the mother slept. The daughter made all the arrangements for her mother to be taken to her home for care. Now it was Ann's turn to be the caregiver. Her mother was there for her as an infant. Protected her from harm. Feeding and cleaning her. Caring for all her needs. For the first time, she realized how disrespectful she had been. Her mother could no longer speak. She could move her head just a little. And she could squeeze only one hand. The stroke had done its damage. And after a few months, she died.

Now Ann sits with her husband. She recalls holding her mother's hand. How she would tilt her head and look at her. She was talking with her eyes. The tears would flow. She wanted to speak so badly. So much needed to be said. All she could do was try to express it with her eyes. So the daughter would talk. She spoke about how unfair she had been to her. How ungrateful she had been. She asked to be forgiven. She got a weak hand squeeze. She talked of good times they had together. The memories held the dearest. She was by her side till she passed.

And what did she carry away from this? To love better. To care more. And time can be too short when the unexpected happens. She looks up to her husband. She says she is ready to have a child of her own now. All the anger is gone. She wants to be a mother.

Story 71

"Friendships Sometimes Changes the Odds"

Her cat sat at the back door and continued to call. What's up with that cat? So, she goes to open the door. There is her cat standing over a baby bird. First, she was shocked to see the bird alive. Second, it didn't have a mark on it. It had been very carefully picked up and brought to her. So unusual for her cat. It killed everything. Nothing came into their yard.

She begins feeding the bird. It was slow but it grew. She named it Peter. Didn't know which sex it was. But that seemed like a good name. So, Peter and her James bonded. Anytime James was in the house he would find Peter and play. So gentle yet so playful. They would spend hours together. And the bird grew. She knew she would have to release it soon. And the day came.

Her bird went to a nearby branch and looked back. It had no interest in leaving its friend. Finally, she had to place seed out. A week or so passed. Then she hears something hitting her window. As she goes to investigate, she sees it's the bird hitting the glass. When she opens the door, the bird flies a few feet and returns. And does this over and over.

So, she walks towards it. Now the bird moves farther away and waits. She continues to follow. She's led to James.

He had been hit by a car. Not dead but hurt. She gently picks him up and rushes to the vet. Repairs were made. And he could return home. In the coming days Peter sat on the branch and waited. So, she sets up a bed in the yard and takes James outside. Peter flies to him immediately. Spends the day with his friend. Knowing he was safe, he flew and was never seen again. The favor repaid.

We can be different. We don't have to look the same. We just have to accept the other. Friendship crosses all borders. Acceptance is the key. Old enemies can find peace. A lesson learned!

Story 72
"A Fathers Love"

A teenage boy and his father were always arguing. The boy was both disrespectful and rude. He treated this mother the same. Things were just bad at home.

The kid comes home one Friday to find out he was going to New York with his dad on a business trip. "Why do I have to go? This is so lame". But his bags were packed. The dad said they were going to find common ground and do a lot of talking. Things had to change between them.

Once checked in the father said "let's go for a walk". So, they went on the streets. They came up on four thugs looking for trouble. "Hey old man, this just isn't your day". "You can have all I have, I'm not looking for trouble". "There's just one thing I want 'your life', maybe both of you", he says with a smirk.

The father turns to his son. Looks into his eyes one last time. "Take care of your mother, now run". With that he turns and attacks the gang. He yells "RUN" once more. So run he did. After about three blocks he sees a police car. "They're killing my father, help"!!! He points down the street. Lights come on and tires squeal. He runs back.

There he finds bodies and blood everywhere. His father and three of the thugs lay dead. He stares at his father. He hears one of the policeman say there was a fourth one dead in the alley. He kneels next to his dad's lifeless body. The cop tells him his father fought a brave battle for his life. There was just too many of them.

The boy places his hand flat against the side of his father's face. He looked at him through different eyes. "He didn't fight to save his life", he says. "Look at how many times he was stabbed. He knew he would die. He fought to make sure my mother would not be alone. My dad died for our family".

A former Marine, he knew honor. You give your life for GOD, for Country, for family. Without people of honor to protect this great Nation of ours, all would be destroyed. That boy became a man that night.

From that moment on he wanted to walk in the footsteps of his father. To be like him. To honor his sacrifice, he was so willing to make to an ungrateful son. For his family.

Children will always argue with parents. Only a few will get to witness how much they are really loved or how far a parent will go to protect their family.

Story 73

"You're Fishing for a Dinner Date"

An old-timer went to the same spot to fish all the time.

He enjoyed his fishing. It was across the street from a neighborhood. So, people could watch him fish, and he could watch them work in their yards. He did this on a frequent basis all summer.

One day, a lady who watched him fishing for months crossed the street to talk to him. She said, "Are you really that bad at fishing? I have never seen you catch anything. I think I would have given up by now."

He smiled. "I don't even use a hook or bait. I'm not here to catch a fish. I drive by here all the time. I've seen you working your yard and plants. I've wanted to meet you but wasn't sure how. So now I carry a pole in my trunk. When I see you in the yard, I drive around and pretend to fish. I watch you care for your flowers. So gentle and so loving. I can tell you live alone. And you are much too pretty for that. So I stop every chance I get, hoping to catch your eye".

"My name is David. I'm alone also. I would like to be your friend. Companionship is healthy. No one needs to be alone in their senior years. I have a dog; his name is George. You would like him. I know you have a cat. He enjoys cats. May I ask you to a dinner soon? I want to know all about you. I'll just call and talk till you're comfortable with me." He stares into her eyes, waiting for an answer.

She smiles. "My name is Mary. Can I offer you a cup of coffee?"

Story 74
"We All Can Change"

An old woman sat on her porch. She kept to herself. Didn't really want contact with others. People irritated her. There was a young couple who had moved next door. She made sure they didn't want to talk to her. They had a daughter of about four and an infant son.

The little girl would always say hi to her when in the yard. She would just turn her back to her and ignore the child. One day she felt a tug on her dress. Looking down she sees the girl. She wants to present her with a flower. A flower she picked from the lady's flower bed. She glares at the girl and tells her to never pick her flowers. The small girl bows her head and says, "if you don't give them to someone while they're pretty, they just die. Don't even you see that?" The lady just storms off.

Inside the house she thinks about what the girl said. She took pride in her flowers, yet she just let them wilt and die. The girls words touched her. The next morning, she asked the little girl to help her pick some flowers to cut and place in a vase. The girl became her only friend. With time she noticed her looking less well. Then one day she didn't even come out. Her parents went to their car each morning showing their stress and were gone all day.

She finally approached the mother and asked "where's little Karen?" The mother broke down into tears. "At the hospital, she's very ill. Our insurance isn't that great. I'm worried. We may lose her. That would kill me also." She goes inside crying.

The lady goes in, gets on the phone, and finds out which hospital she's at. She smiles then drives there. She meets with the director of the hospital. My family founded this hospital. You will take personal charge of this case. You will spare nothing. And if this hospital lacks the expertise, move her to one that does. And no one will know I was involved. Not even her or her parents. Come up with your story why this happened. And with that she walks out.

A couple of weeks pass and she sees her parents bring her home. She's frail but getting better. Later the parents hear a knock on the door. There stands the lady with a vase of flowers. Place them by her bed. She always loved my flowers. I'll bring fresh ones every day.

Story 75

"The Beauty Your Eyes See"

We see people every day. But some stand out.

Some stay above the bar you set. You may never meet, but that's not the point. You can appreciate a flower that stops you in your tracks. You stand and stare. Such a thing of beauty. So impressive. You don't pick it, you brag about it in the days to come.

Beauty is very personal. Just as taste. It's beautiful to you because it struck the perfect nerve. Maybe not as much to someone else. You look and smile. You feel good about what you found. It hits its mark with you. Look around every day. Find the seeds of beauty in nature. Then give it water.

No one will ever be as beautiful as the woman you marry. Keep the love alive and the beauty will never leave. Not at any age. Respect and loyalty is the water of marriage. You can never run dry if you're true to your heart. True to your partner.

So seek them out. Do something special. And that could be holding hands and having a glass of tea under a shade tree. It's unlimited what you can do.

Story 76
"Be the Example for Good"

How you live your life!

We are all products of the lives we live. The ones who burn and loot with no remorse have a very dark stain on their souls. They will answer one day. They are the end result of no morals and *the world owes me* lifestyle.

But there is better out there. The ones who watch out for their neighbors. The ones who stop and help a person in need. People who have God in their hearts. They know their roles. They know when to step up and volunteer their help. And why? It's the life they choose to follow. They are the counterbalance to the evil in this universe. You help with no repayment expected. It's a gift.

Some will take advantage of your generosity. They are out there. But you don't care. It's a gift you gave them. Your life and feelings will continue to flourish. And don't think going to church each Sunday and sitting in the front row buys you anything. Someone else is there who knows you better than you know yourself. So what is your role to others? Be kind. Offer help when you see it. Feed the hungry. Give people some of your time. You have plenty. Help when you can.

You won't change this world. But you can change the world of a person really in need. We lose focus. We get so wrapped up in our day-to-day lives we forget the ones in need. And yes, there are imposters out there. But do what your heart tells you. We make mistakes all the time. A mistake helping someone who doesn't deserve that help is still a good thing. Your heart showed love. Never hold on to that too closely. It's meant to be shared.

Today, do something positive for a stranger. It can be as simple as holding a door open for another. Smile. Be understanding. You will be admired for being who you are.

Story 77
"The Pressure of Not Disappointing Your Parents"

They were just kids. They went to school together. They enjoyed each other's company.

But one day the boy's father came to pick him up and saw them together. Once in the car he made it clear he was never to speak to her ever again. He said their kind don't mix.

But she was his friend and he saw no reason not to keep her friendship. This began a secret that lasted for many years. They were just drawn to each other. And as they grew older, they fell in love. But they made sure they were never seen together. One day she asked, "is this our life? Always in the shadows?" He took her hand and said "you know how it is. We would never be accepted by our families. We have no choice."

Then one day the worst happened. She fell ill. Very ill. She was in a hospital never to recover. He came to her side every day and held her hand. The father saw one of his friends just by chance one day and said, "I think you work with my son."

"Used to, he quit about two weeks ago."

Now the father was confused. His son lived on his property and left for work every day. So instead of asking, he followed him. He drove straight to the hospital.

The father saw which room he entered. He went to the door and watched. He held her hand and began to speak. "I should have married you. I didn't want to disappoint my father; I love him also. But how I handled this was wrong. I love you so much. I'm a lesser man. I can see that. I should have stood by your side. Now I'm losing you. It's too late to fix anything." His tears dropped to their hands. He heard her soft words. "You are a fine man. Your heart is big. And yes, I too wished we had married. But I know your father is proud of you, he would have no choice."

The father's head bowed in shame. He turned and walked away. The next day he came back.

With him was his Priest. "Son, you know father John. He is going to bless your friend. And then if you both want to, he will marry you. I've set aside two side by side plots at the family cemetery. They are yours. Dan will be able to still see you every day." He now takes the girls hand, "forgive an old foolish man. I didn't change with time. I will regret this forever." And he kisses her forehead.

The son hugs his father. They cry together. "Dad, will you be my best man? Because yes, we do want to marry." She didn't last very much longer after that day. And the son did bring her flowers regularly.

We can't explain why things are the way they are. But we're all capable of change. We just need to take our first step.

Story 78
"Trust"

There was a boy who loved his father very much. And his father showed him so much love in return. The mother was very proud of their relationship. And why shouldn't she?

The years flew passed. And the day came when the father lay in his bed propped up with pillows. His son by his side. His father was passing. With very little strength he told his son a confession. The last time he spoke.

The son was now in his thirties. He walked from the room and held his mother. "He's no longer with us", he spoke. "I'm sorry mom". After he was laid to rest, the son approached his mother. "Dad told me he was my stepfather. Why was that held from me"?

The mother takes his hand and a deep breath. "I had an affair. It was very wrong of me but I did. I left your father to be with this other man. We had you. He cared for nothing really. Especially you. Eventually he left me. I had nowhere to turn. So, I came back to your father and asked to be forgiven. We spend almost a year talking. But I moved back in. He never allowed me to marry him again. I use his name. But the condition was you were to never know about that part of my past. He was protecting us both".

"He never blamed you for any of this. I'm sure you realize that. He loved you dearly. It was full acceptance with you. He was a perfect father. And a good husband to me. I broke his trust and I paid a big price. I honored his request. I'm sorry I kept all of this from you. But I just couldn't break my trust your father had in me now. He always said it would be him to tell you. I guess he did. He also didn't want me to deceive you any longer. Now I'm asking for your forgiveness also".

Marriage isn't the perfect arrangement with no bumps. As humans we sometimes sin. It's the forgiving part that separates us from lesser species. Our ability to see pass a betrayal. To know the problem can and will fix itself if both parties want that.

You may feel pain at times, Love will allow it to pass. Take strength in that!!!

Story 79
"Time Never Rest"

A little girl just out of diapers walks with her mom.

They move along the sidewalk side by side. The mother full of pride, and the child full of wonders. Days never forgotten.

As time goes by and the child grows older, she sees her mother differently. She is her best friend, her first love. Sure, Dad gets his share, but her mother is the center of her universe. A thousand questions, watching every move, listening to all her words. Her mother is her hero, while the mother looks at her with pride, knowing the teen years are ahead.

Then one day, there they are. Arguments are frequent, raised voices are common, but the love and respect still hold things together. It's a rough time for the mother. She knows so much now. And the girl, well, she thinks she knows just as much. They push their way through.

One day, the mother becomes the grandmother. All the years of calm and understanding are paying off. The daughter knows now that her mother was her best friend, even though she lost sight of it for a while. Their bonds are stronger now than ever.

Holidays come and go. Special meals are prepared, and the daughter sees the age of her mother for the first time. She will not be here one day. And she is facing becoming a grandmother herself. Where did all the time go? What can she do now for her mother? She feels so helpless.

So one evening, her grandchildren say, "Tell us about your mother!" She smiles and says, "Gather around me and get comfortable. I have a beautiful story to tell!"

Story 80
"ABCs to Relationships"

You want a forever partner, what does it take? Romance, consideration, dedication, soft music, slow dancing in the living room, honestly, acceptance, soft touch, and words, understanding, willingness to give your all for the other, a balanced partnership, the end is not in sight. Giving your all is just that. Sharing everything. A loving team to keep love alive. Will every day be perfect, hell no. Understanding, acceptance, love will get you through the difficult times. You rely on the strength of the other when needed.

Remembering the dates that are important to the other. Making the other feel special and appreciated. A two-way road. If you can keep the fire of that love burning bright, you'll go through life holding hands and will be studied by others. The secrets to a long love hides in plain sight. Be the "role model" others need. Be the beacon of hope and success. Love is not complicated. It just needs to be clearly defined in your heart. Will you always walk the perfect road? There's not one. But can you weather any storm? Most definitely. The strength of two is always greater than the strength of one. A piece of advice I would have given myself. Experience is a rough teacher at times. Love is like the sun, if you see it or not is not what's important. It's the blind trust that you know it's there. You've seen it so many times before. Bask in the warmth of a strong love. It's the life all married couples strive for.

Story 81
"Depression"

This writing is a little darker but words that need to be said out loud.

Depression affects many. My understanding is there are good days and bad. The good days don't last nearly long enough and with time you move back to the dark corners. Why you can't just move into the light and remain there is not understood yet. The battle is fought every day. Yes, there are meds, but that's only a false solution. It's so much deeper than a simple pill.

Robin Williams seemed so happy. Such a funny person. Always smiling and making others smile with him. But internally he fought a dangerous battle. A battle he lost with time. There are so many who make up our world. All unique, and still so common. Just looking for internal peace. Is that so much to ask for?

Be a friend to many. If you have strength in that area, share your strength. It's needed. We all depend on each other. Together we're invincible. A power strong enough to change a dark fate. Know your capabilities. Don't worry about embarrassing yourself. Understanding is there for you to feel. Opening up to others you trust is a benefit, a privilege. Don't try to mask your feelings. Discuss it with the ones you feel most comfortable with. And don't forget the professionals.

Help could be just a few conversations away. Help that could put you on a more positive outlook that you can beat this.

Story 82
"When Paths Cross"

It was a chance meeting. But it brought their worlds to a temporary halt.

Their eyes met from across the room. Memories raced through their heads. A second covered ten years. One heart rose, while the other sank. Over the evening, the awkwardness of what to do, what to say, grew. There was a meeting that had to happen, and it was up to him to see it done.

"Hello, Green Eyes. Nice to see you again. A total surprise, to say the least."

"Well, David, it was a shock. How have you been? I didn't know you knew Bill."

"We've been friends for years. I just got back in town. He asked me over. You look very nice. What's it been—thirty years? If not longer."

She looked at him and smiled. "Thirty-five as a matter of fact. Did you ever marry?"

"Well, maybe a couple of times. But who counts? And you?"

"My husband will be here later. Is there a wife here with you?"

"No, I think destiny has me down as a single. It's not bad. Before your husband arrives, I have something to say. I'm not making a move, just unspoken words that need out. I miss you. I think of us still. Time has been your friend. Your husband is a very lucky man. Lives touch and drift apart. Fate is fate. You will always have a place in my heart. I'll never forget your smile. Ever. I just wanted you to know this. I'm not going to stay. I have business tomorrow and a flight out right after. I'm glad this meeting happened. A load has been lifted for me. I've been wanting to tell you this for years. Just had no idea where you were. I need no response. I think I should go now."

He pushed his hand out for a handshake. She moved closer and gave him a hug. "Take good care of yourself. I'm glad you spoke. Now we know Bill knows us both. It was nice seeing you again. Fate is fate. I agree. But you never know when it will speak. Good night, David. Maybe our paths will cross again someday. Maybe!"

Story 83
"The Loss of a Dear Friend"

She was such a pretty puppy. You couldn't help but fall in love with her.

Full of affection, she was always near. Playful and seeking approval, she showed her love constantly. A natural protector always alert. At an early age she ran by your side. On guard for any danger. Ready to sacrifice herself for your safety. There's really nothing that compares to the love a dog has for its owner. People could learn so much.

She enjoyed her treats. Liked you to bring them to her. That made her feel special, as if she wasn't. She would look at you with those dark eyes. You knew her love for you was to her core. At night she slept by your side. One ear always up. Always on alert. Protecting her family was her job.

Without any fear she ran into the dark. Leave this place or suffer her rage. She was such a special animal.

With age she began to change. Such a powerful dog. Small changes at first. But you knew a change was taking place. She became more aggressive. Her love had less trust in it now. Something you loved so dearly was becoming a threat. How does this happen? You want to discount the reality. It's not really so. But others see it also. Such a powerful dog. A dog you can no longer trust, the dog you love so much.

Now she's a memory. You said your goodbye. She's still in your heart. You reach out but her space is empty now. No more treats to deliver. She is greatly missed. This dog you loved so much.

He stands by a grave remembering. She'll be missed. Though he stands, a part of him died also. Things are no longer the same. He can smile with the knowledge of years passed. But a smile won't stop the tears. They come and go.

As the winds of time blow pass, it does get easier. Acceptance settles in. But you still think of your friend. Joy shared. A wish for more time together. Knowing that will never be. She lives in your heart now. You do get to visit when your eyes close. Kind words are spoken to your friends. She used to do this. Remember when she would do that. Stories that bleed from the heart.

Losing a close friend is never easy. It takes time to heal. Do you replace? Should you look for the same? She was special. To me at least. Yes, it gets easier. She wasn't the only pet I have. The others want their stroking and special attention. They're your friends also. Company when you need some. They all make you smile. Joy returns. I miss my friend. It should be this way. All part of the cycle of life. Now I give a better quality of attention. Spend a little more time. Hug a little tighter. Pets are a source of comfort. They depend on you. A responsibility that's welcomed. Can you get too attached?

Well, they do sleep with me!

I really miss her. I put away her favorite toy. A place of honor. She was my protector. Out here danger is only steps away. That snake could have gotten me. But she got it first. She did her job. She will always have a permanent position in my heart. I said my goodbye. I'll say no more.

Story 84
"Life"

When life first entered her being. She had a heartbeat.

Things were so different developing. Changes every day. One day came when she could move her fingers. So very different. Everything about her mother flowed through her. She understood without any way to express her understanding. She felt what the mother felt. Joy, pain, depression, hunger, happiness was the best. Because of her mother she knew birth. One day she would use her developing lungs. This would allow her to cry for her mother's attention. Excitement filled her.

Her mother, out of love did all things correctly. Ate proper meals. No drinking. Didn't smoke. She loved this child so much. She would sacrifice anything for her. One day she understood her name would be "Pudden Legs". She couldn't understand that one. But she trusted in her mother.

Things started to change very quickly. Space became too small. She fought to get out. Then one cool morning she was at her mother's side. All was different. Touch, feelings she never had, breathing.

That was the start of her new life. The other would fade with time. A loving bond developed that would never end. One day she would care for the mother. That would be many years in the future. A mother and her daughter's love bond never ends. Today she just snuggled close and loved her new life.

Story 85
"Just Separated"

What does it mean to be alone? Some people are alone in a house full of people. Others are never alone no matter what. Is it a state of mind? When you carry peace on your shoulder, you have a friend. You can be your best friend. You can keep you fulfilled. But not everyone can. Some people need companionship. Some more than others. If you need those friends or family for additional support, there is nothing wrong with that. It's who you are. I'm not a hermit. Nor do I reject society. I enjoy my alone time out here. I see it as a privilege. A privilege others want. I don't go months without seeing friends. I don't call and visit on the phone. I get in trouble for that. I stay busy. I have my pets and my projects. So I never feel alone. I enjoy my company, but in the same breath, I enjoy getting my place back, just me and the pets.

I watch the show *Life below Zero*. They live alone. Too far removed for me. I'm not that kind of isolationist. I enjoy going to get an ice cream if that's what I want. So, I'm not alone. Just separated.

Story 86
"Being Together"

I lie by her side and watch her sleep.

This flower of life. How my heart lights up when I'm near her. I feel so content. She needs her sleep, so I watch. Maybe steal a kiss. She sleeps, so it goes unnoticed.

I think of our day together. Holding hands, enjoying each other's company. It doesn't really matter what we do as long as we do it together. I stayed up late watching shows I really had no interest in. But she likes them. And I try to give her what she likes. We stretch out on the bed, facing each other. Getting in a little more time with her is what I like. We talk, laugh, discuss tomorrow. She'll lay her head on my chest and tell me of her love. She is so precious to me.

But soon I hear her breathing steadily and deep. She's drifted off. I'm not ready for that yet. I need a few more minutes feeling her touch. Tomorrow, I'll give her coffee in bed. She really likes that. And I must say, so do I.

Valentine's Day is just around the corner. I think a pretty necklace would bring out her smile. We'll sit home and have wine. I do my best to look my best. I do it for her. She's the champagne, and I'm the glass of beer. She loves me for who I am.

We'll grow old together. We have so much love to look back on. There is no one I would rather be with. I'm a very lucky man.

Story 87
"The Heart Knows Best"

Titled by Carolyn Nolan Millhouse

We all fall in love. Everyone does. For some it's great. Others get hurt somehow. The way life works.

A man saw the same girl many times. Always at a distance. So, one day he asked her out. She replied she would have to find a sitter for that night. It caught him a little off guard. He hadn't considered she might have a child. Ok, one date isn't a proposal. He wasn't sure about dating a girl with a family.

The date went well. Actually, very well. He enjoyed the dinner and even paid for the sitter. Now what? He sat and thought about his situation. Was he wasting her time? If this relationship moved forward, the little girl would be his responsibility also. He had never thought about falling for someone with a child. He looked deep within. A light slowly grew brighter.

The commitment required didn't scare him. She was beautiful. He could tell they were compatible. He took a breath and called asking to see her more. They ended up a very happy family. A great ending to a nice story.

There are a lot of circumstances out there. Some you will accept, some you won't. Love and happiness can always be found when the right combination finds you. Sometimes you don't pick the one you love. Your heart does.

Story 88
"Potential"

The morning was early. Most of the city still asleep.

He drank his coffee as he drove, a routine very familiar to him. But today was going to be different. Today he was going to ask his love to marry him. Lack of confidence overwhelmed him. Why would she commit to him? He could barely afford to date her. He had dropped out of school. Way too smart to waste his time there. Never did go back.

He worked small odd jobs to stay above water. And he wasn't very good at holding a job very long either. Then he met Mary. So kind, so pleasing to his eyes. He got the nerve up to ask her out. They date but her father didn't approve. His daughter deserves better. Somehow, they stayed together. She had such a warm heart, why did she stay with him? Because of his low self-esteem he only saw his faults. She deserved better than him. Or so he thought.

After work he showered, put on his best cloths, and even purchased a new cologne. He had asked her father for her hand. With reluctance, he had no choice but to agree. He knew his daughter loved him.

He arrived, took her hand, and led her to the bench on the porch. Then he asked her this. "Why do you tolerate me?" "I love you with all my heart, but I'm no catch." She smiles.

"I not only love you but I love the man you're going to be. You are so caring. So protective of my well-being. You will marry me one day. No woman could ask for a better husband. A father to our children. A provider. Better jobs will come to you, to us. Our love will be our strength till then. I have full faith in you. Together we will handle anything that comes our way."

"Now, my father wouldn't allow me to go out tonight. Said you were coming over. Very strange for him. Do you by chance, have something you want to ask?" She smiles, leans back and looks into his eyes.

That was day one of a new start in both of their lives.

We at times see only our faults, while others see our potential. Believe in yourself!!!

Story 89
"Final Words"

There was a father if only by title only. He never gave his family much of his time. He had better things to do.

Then he went in for a regular checkup and blood work. The results were bad. He wouldn't be on this earth much longer. To his surprise, the family was very complacent. His years of placing them in second place had come home to roost. Now a caretaker gave him the care needed. And at a cost to him. He was waking up to the life he led. Why should they care really? He never made time for them.

It's sad, but in reality, he wronged them. In the short time he had left, how could he repair his damage to the family? He took up paper and pen. He had a wife and three children. He wrote each one a letter. He knew nothing else that might work.

To his wife, he wrote, "You lost your love for me years ago. I understand. I was a horrible husband. I gave my money and not my time. There is no good reason for you to forgive me. But I'll ask for your kindness toward me anyhow. I'm very sorry I was the failure to you that you married. I ask for your forgiveness and your compassion while I lie on my deathbed. I don't want to die alone."

To his son, he wrote, "Jason, you've grown to be a fine man in spite of me and my example. It was you who was the pillar for the family. You don't have to come and be by my side. I was never there for you. Take care of your mother and sisters. They will need your strength. Goodbye, son."

To his first daughter, Gwen, he wrote, "You were such a beautiful little girl. You enjoyed sitting in my lap and having me read to you. I don't know why I stopped. But I did. I'm ashamed of that. You've grown into a beautiful young lady. Your mother did well. Don't let the man I was scare you from love. You deserve a true romance. Let your brother give you away in my place. Wish I could be there."

And to his small flower, he wrote, "Because of your age, you are probably the closest to me. I wronged you. Your time was so much more important to me than I realized. I am so sorry I was a poor excuse of a father to you. Visit me every now and then. I love you."

He asked the nurse to mail the letters after he was gone. But instead, she hands delivered each and every one.

He was slipping away more each day. He no longer opened his eyes. He no longer ate or talked. He could hear the equipment connect to him. He heard the door open. He could feel the hands on his face and hands. One by one, they said their piece. They all forgave him. He was assured he would pass as a loving father to them. It was their promise.

He left the world a loved father.

Story 90
"The Wonder of Ageing"

The morning is early. The air is cold. He doesn't wear a light sweater in the house yet but close. He's observed the senior's age. They move a lot slower.

No, their balance is not near as steady now. And doing the small things are a little more challenging now, but life is good. The pains are there. You see your doctor as much as any family member, no big deal. So, what is your value now?

You can't lift heavy loads. In many cases you shouldn't be driving. A fall may just be your end. All of your friends are slowly leaving. People you really valued their friendship. And have for years. So, what is your value now?

You are the storyteller. You have hundreds that will captivate the youth. You've seen and done so much. You were raised with technology long gone. The youth of today are amazed with your life. The hacks and shortcuts you know leaves them speechless. And your stories, well they brag on you all the time. And what do you do now? You think about your past. The friends you've had. The family lost, the new people you will meet. Maybe a love you share or will share. You're not dead yet. Life is still an adventure.

Don't spend too much time in a chair. Spend more time outdoors. Weather is your friend. Never fear it. Wear that sweater if that's what you require to be comfortable. Adjust to the life of being alone more. Heck, if nothing else try writing a book or two. Live your life to the end. Happiness can be in the pen you hold or the story you tell. We all enjoy walking a road where you're surrounded by make believe. It's a nice distraction. You will have only so much time here. Live it to its fullest. Live it in spite of your pains. We all should have taken better care of our bodies when younger.

If you can slide out of bed and put your feet flat on the floor each morning, feel thankful. You have more time to tell another story or share a memory. It will be their memory of you.

Story 91
"Hours Left"

What if at 8am one morning you found that at 5pm the next day, you would die? What would you do?

Get things in order. Understood. Then what? Anyone you should maybe call? Any fences to mend? A song to hear for the last time? A last favorite meal? Could be a simple bucket list thing you kept putting off? The ideas can go on for hours.

We are all different. Our priorities vary. But you have only so much time then it's over. Would you speak of a hidden love? Bear your feelings? What regrets would you have? You only have hours, you must choose wisely. A last visit to a grave? A family member? So many choices and so little time. A last confession, a wrong corrected? A dark secret reviled? Your mind would open up. Ideas tucked away forever rise to the surface. Take a few of your precious minutes to place words on paper? A recording? All of this will be you after your gone?

It's not impossible all you want is to quietly leave. To do nothing? We are all so different. So now bring your thoughts back to the present. Are there things on your list that should happen? Things important enough to make that list? Should they happen now?

No, you're not looking at such a short group of hours, but you do have that list. Now, would you do anything special today? Now is the time to fix things. Later may be too late.

Story 92
"Dark Clouds"

There was a young man who really didn't express himself well. But he fell in love anyhow.

That next level in his life was wonderful. He was so happy. He knew she would be his wife one day. Time went by. He turned eighteen. He felt it was his duty to serve his country. So he joined.

His world changed entirely. He really wasn't ready for such changes. He would write her, and she would write him. He just wasn't good at expressing himself. His letters slowly began to drop off. She would write, but letters would go unanswered. Then he got his Dear John. It wasn't a shock. He also knew it was his fault. He was just lost. He still loved her, but he had no idea how to fix it.

He came home on a leave and found out she had married an old friend. His heart sank a little, but once again, he knew it was his fault. So, what does a man do now? He dated here and there, even married a couple of times. They didn't last. They weren't meant to. He just wasn't able to speak his heart. He figured his destiny wasn't going to be the regular path. And because of this, he loved less.

After quite a number of years, he met a special girl. He was very slow with his affection. Like rungs on a ladder, he slowly moved up. Years of dating went by, and he fell into his old ways. And with time, he lost her as well. He always knew it was never their fault. He had only himself to blame. He would see the couples in love and think, *Why not me?* He was happy but not complete. He felt his life was set and there was nothing he could do. But in spite of everything, he loved once more.

This time would be different; he would not allow himself to mess this one up. He wasn't the glue. Never would be. She, on the other hand, could read his heart. She knew what to do and say. This time, it worked. They married. His love for her flourished. He had learned from his failures. They went through their lives holding hands. Soft words and frequent kisses were their glue. Respect and desire to spend their time together filled many more years in their cup of life.

They died just days apart. One didn't want to leave, and the other didn't want to stay. No matter how dark a cloud is that seems to follow you around, the sun does comes out. Never think otherwise.

Story 93
"We All Need What We Don't Ask For Sometimes"

She was a little girl of six. Her mom said to her "let's go for a ride." That day they drove to the local animal shelter. She was told they would rescue a puppy. As excited as she was, it wasn't a puppy she wanted. She had her sights on a kitten.

She went into a room where cats were held. And sure, enough she saw the perfect kitten. It was blonde. So small, so cute. Such a sweetie. She named him Sandy. They took to each other immediately.

Sandy acted almost like a dog. Always seeking her out. Always near. They truly loved each other. The years passed. Fifteen to be exact. Sandy's age was showing. Her friend of so many years was fading away. She would stroke his fur and tears would come. She did all she could to keep him happy, make him comfortable. Then one day he didn't wake up. That was a very dark day for her. Her heart was broken.

Cats are so different than dogs. They have this regal attitude about themselves. They show their love so differently. But they give their love just as strong. She missed her Sandy terribly. But the thought of replacing wasn't right yet. She buried him under a tree close to a brook. A place worthy of her most precious memories.

She couldn't bring herself to replace her Sandy. No other cat could equal his spirit. Why even try. Then one day her doorbell rang. She opened the door to find a box. She looked around to see no one. The box had a bow wrapped around it. She heard a sound from within. Inside was a new kitten and a note. My name is Jake. I'll give you my love if you'll keep me. You can even change my name. I think you need me right now.

No one ever owned up to leaving the kitten at her door. Jake turned out to be a wonderful cat. Playful and full of understanding. He could read her moods. Cat people are special in their own way. The love shared is uniquely different. And as for the cat, their independence is their personality. No, she never found out who left this special friend.

We all have Guardian Angles who come to us when we need them most. A piece of life not accepted or understood yet. But a reality, nonetheless.

Story 94

"What you Teach, They Learn"

A more beautiful child would not be easy to find. Her parents were so proud.

Spoiled, I'm sure. Be so loved. Loved to a point that at an early age she began to understand its meaning. Love came from deep in the heart. Not on the surface.

Soon she was in her teens. Her body was changing. The boys looked at her in a way as never before. Her understanding was reawakened. She was being asked out by boys who wanted her as a statement of conquest. That they had her and nothing more. A bragging point. This was totally unacceptable for her. She was not a trophy. She was a loving caring person. Her parents raised her better.

This somehow made the boys want her even more. She withdrew into a shell of sorts. Her studies gave her the recognition she desired. A beautiful young lady at the top of her class. Then she met James.

James was five years older. An academic as well. At early ages five years is a big spread. She too young and he too old. She fell in love with him none the less. Now what? Time was spent to be closer to him. A girl always chased by the boys was now trying to chase a young man. And she did it through her studies. Got shared classes. Sat near him. Showed the class, and him, just how smart she was.

Finally, the day came he asked her a question about a problem. She was only too glad to answer. She moved in even closer. Their friendship grew.

Children share common ages. Common experiences. But they are as different as night and day. Boys and girls. Tall and short. Heavy and thin. Children of good manners and character and ones with less. Work with them. Give them your time. Share your experiences. They want to learn. They ask for your time with their eyes.

It is you who'll build their future, they need you and others no matter how they act. Some are getting a late start.

Story 95
"I can't explain it"

Titled by Richard Speed

I met her in her twenties. The way she filled her jeans, well let me say "wow"!!! They were a great set of years. Such a wonderful girl. We developed a love for each other but never married.

Then came the thirties. We both grew. The little girl in her matured. She enjoyed all the fun things. Was comfortable in any setting. From cut offs and a T-shirt with holes to a formal banquet. Excelled in her career. People respected her talents. She moved up the ranks.

In her forties I saw her first gray hair. I noticed mine a couple of years ago. We are still best of friends. We're considered a "couple". We only see each other. This special lady I would die for. Time is being kind to her. Her personality matches her beauty. She's so special, I'm a lucky man.

Her fifties were somewhat of a challenge. Our bodies were changing. The curves weren't quite the same. We sag in areas now. But still a good-looking couple. Our talks are a little more serious. Planning a future together. As a couple we were outside the standard mold. I think that's something we both took pride in. But age is creeping up, for both of us. She's still so gorgeous.

We hit our sixties now. Looking retirement in the face. Plans are set. A date is locked in. The honeymoon is all planned out. Waiting this long to marry the woman of your dreams isn't a bad thing. We've spent a full life together as best friends. Now we'll change the title. Husband and wife. Sounds nice.

Both in our seventies now. We travel a lot. Still enjoy each other's company. Still best friends. It has been a wonderful adventure. We're in good health, so we'll try to slow down in our eighties.

But don't count on it!!!

Story 96
"The Romance of Holding Hands"

How often do you hold the hand of the one you love?

We hold hands as an expression of love. You help them step down. Or maybe you're just driving to a location. Holding hands while driving seems to disappear after marriage. But it could be a safety issue.

It's a clear message for others to know you're together. That you're in love with the other. I can say my hands are dirty, and she may come back with, I don't care. She enjoys the feelings she receives. It's worth it.

We hold hands starting early in life. The meanings are obvious. You care for each other. You share love. When sick someone holds your hand. When scared it gives comfort. When nervous we sometimes hold our own hands together. So why? Why do we do this? Do we really require an answer? Maybe it's just good enough to feel the comfort. Isn't that something we enjoy in our lives? Comfort?

Hold hands more. Enjoy the person you share this with. It is truly an expression of love.

Story 97
"Love"

She left him alone. How was he to live?

His love of over fifty years. His purpose in life. To show his love, to make her smile. Taking care of all her needs. A task of love. So much love returned. A perfect couple so everyone said. But now he sits alone. Holding tight to the memories. His heart still breaking. The tears still flow, he's still not in control yet. It will come but not yet.

He looks at her chair. He can kind of see her there, busy fiddling with something. Looking up to smile at him. Asking if he needs anything? Just one more touch, just one is all he asks. But that won't be. He knows it. He spins the ring on his finger. Wears one on a chain around his neck now. He'll be buried with it.

Life does go on for the one left. So many calls now. Everyone checking in. Making time to stop by. Loneliness comes only at night. The house so empty. It also seems bigger, but he knows it's not. Her dog comes to him now. Not sure when she'll return. Stroking the dog softly relaxes him. A tear will still sometimes roll down his cheek. He's adjusting.

Five years later now she's been gone. He still goes to visit her resting place. He'll lay by her side one day. And he's sure the dog will also. He's full family now. Fresh flowers. A peaceful talk. When he walks away now, he's smiling. Feeling good they've talked. Adjusting wasn't really that easy. But with time, things are possible.

Long term love is a precious gift. Be one of the ones lucky enough to experience it. You'll be a better person because of it.

Story 98
"Giving is the Reward"

Titled by Mary Evans Speed

How you live your life!

We are all products of the lives we live. The ones who burn and loot with no remorse have a very dark stain on their souls. They will answer one day. They are the end result of no morals and *the world owes me* lifestyle.

But there is better out there. The ones who watch out for their neighbors. The ones who stop and help a person in need. People who have God in their hearts. They know their roles. They know when to step up and volunteer their help. And why? It's the life they choose to follow. They are the counterbalance to the evil in this universe. You help with no repayment expected. It's a gift.

Some will take advantage of your generosity. They are out there. But you don't care. It's a gift you gave them. Your life and feelings will continue to flourish. And don't think going to church each Sunday and sitting in the front row buys you anything. Someone else is there who knows you better than you know yourself. So what is your role to others? Be kind. Offer help when you see it. Feed the hungry. Give people some of your time. You have plenty. Help when you can.

You won't change this world. But you can change the world of a person really in need. We lose focus. We get so wrapped up in our day-to-day lives we forget the ones in need. And yes, there are imposters out there. But do what your heart tells you. We make mistakes all the time. A mistake helping someone who doesn't deserve that help is still a good thing. Your heart showed love. Never hold on to that too closely. It's meant to be shared.

Today, do something positive for a stranger. It can be as simple as holding a door open for another. Smile. Be understanding. You will be admired for being who you are.

Story 99
"True Love"

The girl I love doesn't really need makeup, but when she does, she's hot.

Her beauty is very natural. My eyes only see the best in her. When near, her eyes tell me to move closer. We hold hands when together. Very little phone time then. Our focus is each other. Her voice enchants me. I could listen to her soft words all day. I love her very much.

We dress for each other. We make a cute couple. She does such a better job at that. Myself, well I ask for approval before we go out. I think it shows my desire to look good for her. Randomly I stop at a jewelry store and have her pick out something nice. That brings out a big smile. It's not expected and that's part of the shared love. She's the center of my universe, and she knows it. Other women I have no interest in. Mine has ageless beauty. And I'm proud of that.

The road to this place in time was a little bumpy. I did reach it though. Now I'm a very happy man. Very much in love. And willing to place my life on the line for her. When she reads this, she'll be a little embarrassed. She'll blush. But I'll get a call telling me she loved it and loves me.

Yes, my universe makes me always want more time with her. To feel her touch more often. Time apart also keeps the flame bright. Just wanted to say a few words about my girl.

Story 100
"David and Mary"

He was out for his evening walk, just the same as so many before. There was a pedestrian lane by the road. So organized, so safe. But this day, all was different. Two cars collided, and one was going to roll over him. He would die that day. Time stopped. He got to remember. All was in order for his wife. She would want for nothing. Everything was together in an envelope.

He thought of her. His beautiful Mary. It would be thirty-five years next month. He had made plans in secret. That trip to the islands she always wanted. His eyes teared up. He was looking forward to seeing her surprised smile.

Mary was such a loving wife. Never complained about anything. Was always there for him. Always looking out for his needs. Life had been a little hard on him. Too many doctor appointments. These afternoon walks were good for his health. And this day, it will remove him from his love and best friend. Then in a flash, it was over.

So strange this feeling. I'm no longer here, yet I am. I always was a believer. My faith was strong. Something was happening. A feeling of calm wrapped me like a blanket. Then a finger touched my forehead. I woke up. I was in a park. Things seemed familiar, yet all was different. My old life was fading away, and a new me was taking over.

He needed to sit. He saw a park bench with one person sitting there, tossing bread to the ducks. His looks were different, his health better. He sat. All was complete. The bread hitting the water caught his eyes. There sat a lady very pleasing to the eyes. She was at one end, he was at the other. He said, "Do you come here often?"

Her eyes were so soft, her smile so appealing. He was just naturally drawn to her. "I come here now to pass time. I lost my husband two years ago."

"I'm sorry. My name is David. May I join you?"

She looked closely at him and smiled. "Sure. My name is Mary."

They spent the next few hours visiting. It was so peaceful there. But Mary had to leave. She thanked him for the day of conversation; she really enjoyed it. As she walked away, he called her name. "Will I ever see you again?"

She looked hard into his eyes. She broke into a smile. "Sure. I come here almost every Tuesday. I love the tranquility. It recharges my batteries."

He turned to walk away, joy bursting from his heart. *I can't wait till Tuesday*, he thinks.

So what is heaven? This space somewhere occupied by the good? Or maybe the feeling of happiness. We don't really know. He chose to allow these two to continue their love. To be examples of what a respectful marriage should be. Neither knew. But they would live out the rest of their lives together and see the heaven for them. Such wisdom.

David and Mary's story is not that unique. People everywhere share such strong bonds. Love was created to be shared. Treat your Mary with all the love and respect you can muster. He would want it that way.

Story 101
"The Road of Life"

I had no idea it would be this hard!

I just wanted to grow up. But getting there I broke my arm. I broke my heart, and I lost my father. I never asked for any of that, and they were hard on me. But I made it.

I wanted a proper education. I worked two jobs and because of my studies got little sleep. My dad taught me not to borrow money I couldn't pay back. And what I did borrow, I paid back. Things weren't easy. But somehow, I managed to survive. I wanted to give my heart to someone who was willing to trade theirs in exchange. That road was very rocky. My personality, I guess. After a long search she found me. We've been married ten years now, the brightest star that shines in my life. But wow, marriage requires work. I always thought it was smooth sailing after the "I Do's." We're both stronger because of it.

Now children, I expected a little challenge. But the love returned took me by surprise. How could anyone take a life for convenience? Their action is hard on me. Children's hearts are full of love. They haven't been stained with hate yet.

Old age. Very hard on the ego. So many things you can no longer do. You work to provide for your family only to sometimes now not being able to provide for yourself. Yes, I never dreamed it would be so hard. But it was the path I took.

What would I change? Nothing! Every experience I faced built the person I am today. Pain is sometimes required to reach your goals. Our path is not perfect. Potholes are here and there. Do your best not to trip in one. But you will never avoid them all. You have strength, resilience, and the ability to solve problems. Always trust in yourself and be open-minded to ideas not your own.

Story 102
"In my Fathers Image"

He was the pillar in my life. My mom called him the perfect man. I just called him "dad".

Always there for mom and me. Always trying to set the example for me to live by. We had so many talks. His advice was free and plentiful. He kept a watchful eye out on me. He knew the kind of man I should grow up to be. And he understood his part in that. Over the years we would clash. Even I knew he was right. I just was at the age I just wanted to push my will.

My studies were very important to him. More so than myself. Just another area to bump heads. But I understood the "why" that he cared so much. He loved me. Always someone I could turn to. Always made the time to talk. As I grew older he asked me to look into the military. Said it would build even a stronger character. He wanted the Marines, but I went Air Force. I qualified to be a pilot. It made him very proud. He said so many times.

Then one day I got that call. He was in the hospital and would probably not leave. My mom passed earlier that year. I think he was dying of a broken heart. Now I came for him. To be there for his final hours. I held his hand and spoke soft words. My heart was breaking also.

I buried him next to mom. They rest together once more. Never to be separated again. So I stand at the foot of his grave looking at his tombstone. These are the words I had placed on it.

A better "step dad" no man could ask for. He was an honorable man. I was raised in his image. If I ever have a son, he will carry his name.

This world takes many twist and turns. But some are so grand, the right words to describe such things are not that easy. Love and care for your parents. They deserve it in almost all cases. And if you feel short, do it anyhow!!!

Story 103

"Morning Coffee"

What is it about drinking coffee by a campfire that's so relaxing?

The warmth on your legs, hands, and face as the fire dances before your eyes. Or maybe just the fact that you've moved outside for coffee that morning. Well, summer coffee and winter coffee have their own personalities.

Summer coffee, I watch the sunrise. I watch the land wake up. Birds become so active. The early-morning air is so fresh. I have a fan on standby in case the humidity creeps in. Everything is so green. Life is everywhere. Really great memories.

Winter coffee is so different. Was thirty-eight degrees this morning? I set up the outside fireplace the night before. A single match, and I go back in and start the coffee. I crawl back under the covers and let it perk. With time, the smell calls my name. I know it's ready. So it's sweatpants, a warm shirt, heavy socks, and a warm coat. Now I'm ready to take on the world.

My first cup warmed by an open flame. All the animals gather close. They like the fire just as much. I know it's the same coffee, the same pot, but it tastes so much better by the fire. I'm lucky for such a privilege.

Story 104
"Letters of Love"

There was a father if only by title only. He never gave his family much of his time. He had better things to do.

Then he went in for a regular checkup and blood work. The results were bad. He wouldn't be on this earth much longer. To his surprise the family was very complacent. His years of placing them in second place had come home to roost. Now a caretaker gave him the care needed. And at a cost to him. He was waking up to the life he led. Why should they care really? He never made time for them.

It's sad but in reality, he wronged them. In the short time he had left, how could he repair his damage to the family? So, he took up paper and pen. He had a wife and three children. He wrote each one a letter. He knew nothing else that might work.

To his wife, he wrote: You lost your love for me years ago. I understand. I was a horrible husband. I gave my money and not my time. There is no good reason for you to forgive me. But I'll ask for your kindness toward me anyhow. I'm very sorry I was the failure to you that you married. I ask for your forgiveness, and your compassion while I lay on my death bed. I don't want to die alone.

To his son he wrote. Jason, you've grown to be a fine man in spite of me and my example. It was you who was the pillar for the family. You don't have to come and be by my side. I was never there for you. Take care of your mother and sisters. They will need your strength. Good bye son.

To his first daughter, Gwen, he wrote: You were such a beautiful little girl. You enjoyed sitting in my lap and having me read to you. I don't know why I stopped. But I did. I'm ashamed of that. You've grown into a beautiful young lady. Your mother did well. Don't let the man I was scare you from love. You deserve true romance. Let your brother give you away in my place. Wish I could be there.

And to his small flower he wrote: Because of your age you are probably the closest to me. I wronged you. Your time was so much more important to me. That I've realized. I am so sorry I was a poor excuse of a father to you. Visit me every now and then. I love you.

He asked the nurse to mail the letters after he was gone. But instead, she hands delivered each and every one. He was slipping away more each day. He no longer opened his eyes. He no longer ate or talked. He could hear the equipment connected to him. He heard the door open. He could feel the hands on his face and hands. One by one they said their peace. They all forgave him. He was assured he would pass as a loving father to them. It was their promise.

He left the world a loved father.

Story 105

"Marriage"

Marriage, how do you rate?

You find the one you love. You want to be with them forever. Is that really what you want? Lust and desire is a foundation made of sand. It can't weather the storms. It weakens. To really love is one thing, to desire another. Blinded by love, ever heard that? Love is a powerful emotional experience. You are not really in control. Emotion have taken the wheel. You're the passenger now. That road can be hurtful if not careful. What do you do?

First is to slow down. Forever is much longer than a few months. If the desire for sex is pushing you forward, your foundation is weak. "I have no problem that she has children". That's now, what about ten years from today? Will you call them yours or hers? How is your "will" set up? How did you balance things? Interesting question

She stayed home and you brought in the checks. Do you control the dollars or both? Answer this one wisely and with honesty. You can say you're fair, but you're judge and jury when you say such things. Move slowly and stay neutral.

Will the desire to please be as strong years in the future? Do you still date? And if you do, how often? Do you put financial pressure on your account to do something special for the other? You did when you started going together. So many areas to look at. Updates might just be needed? Everything needs maintenance to work properly.

But it's worth every minute.

Story 106
"A Letter to GOD"

A small boy asked his mother, if he wanted to send a letter to Jesus, where would he mail it? The mother looked down with loving eyes and told him they would mail it at church on Sunday. So the next day, he was sent to visit his grandmother for the day. The mother remembered his question. She went to his room to look around. And sure enough, she found the letter. She sat to read it.

Jesus, my parents argue a lot right now. I hear them from my bedroom. It's always over money. I guess we don't have enough. Can you do something for them? It's probably wrong to ask you for money, but we do go to church every Sunday. We never miss. I heard my dad say how expensive I am. How mom spends too much when it comes to me. I must cost them a lot. If you could take me early, I could help them. I don't want to be a problem for my parents. I love them. So think about this. I want to help.

The mother broke down sobbing. How could they have been so blind? She called her husband home to read his words. They cried together. They talked things out. Then they drove to pick up their son.

The father said, "Son, God works in strange ways. You talked to his son, and he used you to talk to us. We were too wrapped up in our lives we stopped thinking of yours. You are the most precious thing we have. We're sorry for the way we reacted to our problems. None of that is any fault of yours. So please forgive us." From that day forward, they showed how a family should be. They still had money issues, but their son never heard another cross word. All things worked out for the best. That day changed all the lives in that house. Never forget your faith!

Story 107
"Life in between"

Titled by Rebecca Dixon

An old man was slowly walking along and came upon a small boy playing in the mud. "You are covered in mud! Won't your mother be upset?"

"Sure," he said, "I slipped and fell. And since I landed in mud, well, I thought I could go ahead and play. Have you ever played in mud?"

The old man looked down and smiled. "No, I haven't. But when I was younger, maybe I should have."

"Get in we'll play together. It's fun!"

"Tell you what I'll do. I'll join you but I'll need help to stand again. Can I count on you?"

"Sure!" was the reply.

So, he removed his shoes and sat. He laughed so many times. Found out his new friend was named Jimmy. Jimmy was five. He was having real fun with the child. The mother showed up and was not happy with the picture. "Jimmy Taylor Baker! What are you doing? And who are you?"

The old man looked at her and said "don't be angry with him. A hose will clean him up. His clothes will come clean. His shoes are plastic, no harm done there. He's just being a child trying to have some fun. You should be very proud of him."

She calms down some. "Jimmy, go to the back yard and let me hose you down. We've got to clean you up." She turns to the old man and asks if he needs help standing.

That night he laid in bed when a glow of light entered. A small ball of light. "Tonight, you will leave with me. Your days here are done. I tried to give you a very pleasant final day. I saw you smile often. More than in many years. I think playing in the mud was good for the two of you. Jimmy will lead a very good life. Be happy for him. You were a positive influence on him. So now come with me."

We don't know what happens after we pass. It doesn't need to be something to fear. It's just part of the cycle of life. We are born and one day we pass. How you live your life between those two points is what's important. Be a good person. Play in the mud at least once in your life. Laugh often. Give some of your time to children. It's good for them. Contrary to what some believe, it doesn't just end. And how do I know this to be true? A small ball of light told me.

Story 108
"He wouldn't give up"

A boy was born. So small. So helpless. But a healthy baby boy.

He was raised without a father. His mother was the "rock" he depended on. He grew tall and strong. Did quite well in school. Then the news came! His mother was sick. A sickness that with a short time would take her life. He knew he must help somehow.

So, the field of medicine consumed his life. Failure after failure, new approaches, experimental drugs, all he could think might work. His mother grew weaker. Very late one night a coworker asked "how he could not give up on this?" That's my mother. My flesh and blood, I owe her life". His work continued.

His mother did pass away one early morning. But his work did pay off with time. So many others were saved. But he always knew if he had started sooner, he might have saved his mother. A regret he never lost.

Chapter 2

Story 1

"Remembered Stories"

A man goes into church to pray.

"Dear Lord, I offer my life to you. I'm not half the good person as my wife. But I'm strong. I don't want her to leave. I'm scared. They sent her home to die. Die! Is there nothing I can do or say to change this? I have to be so strong in front of her. But inside, all I do is cry. My world is falling apart. I quit my job. They said I had no more time to be gone. So I quit".

"She sleeps now. She won't take her medicine because she wants every second remaining for us to be together. I have to break them up into powder and feed it to her on ice cream. I feel I'm being deceitful, and she eats less every day. I love her so. This is my request. I beg of you to take me instead. Amen."

He returns to her side and waits for her to wake. His tears drip onto her hand. Her eyes open. She draws on all her strength and speaks. "No more tears for me. I'm leaving you, I know. But I'm going to a place of beauty. You will miss me, but be happy for me. I'm going to sit by the side of Jesus. I find strength in that. We don't have much time left. I need to see your smile again. Talk to me and let me listen. Talk about our fun days. I want to smile with you."

With time, she passed. But he was so grateful for her words. He talked for days. He laughed as he told their stories. They said she could hear him. So, he kept talking. She was truly his strength.

Now things are so different. The house so empty. But he feels her presence. He sees her smile still. They'll see each other again one day. Until then, he goes about his life. Mother's Day is today. The kids are coming over. Joy and laughter will fill the house. She stills brings him joy, even now.

This may seem a little dark for today. But mothers are center of the home. They will never leave. They will always be by your side. But hug them now. Show them how special they really are. Make them smile today. Do for them. It's their day, but they will fuss over you.

Story 2
"We Should Never Lose on Love"

Somethings seem to just fall in place. And others are like trying to put the square peg into the round hole. It just won't happen.

Deep in the past they shared love. Why it didn't work out is not the issue. It just didn't. Not all people in love spend the rest of their lives together. Their paths split. But their love for each other doesn't just end. It's carefully placed in a special place in the heart. Pulled up often and tenderly held. Thoughts of what could have been, surrounded by the reality of what is.

By accident she finds out her lost love is in the hospital. Not doing well, not even conscious. Her instinct is to go to him. Give comfort. Say goodbye. How would she explain this to her husband. Ask for his blessing to be by the side of a former lover. Her heart is breaking over this.

She holds his hand. Whispers words of the past. He's slipping away. Tears flow. Yes, she still carries a love for him. Holding his hand now is the most beautiful thing she can do for their past. He leaves this world. Kissing him on the forehead was her last act of love to him. She returns to her husband crying.

She looks up and asks why he allowed this time with him. He looks down and smiles. "We've been in love for many years. I never have, nor ever will doubt your love for me. My love for you is just as strong. Why take a part of your past and destroy it? You would have thought less of me. You would say your goodbye and return to me; return to our life together. I will always respect your feelings. Honor your requests. As you would mine." And he kisses her gently. "Let me order in dinner tonight. I think a quiet evening would be nice."

The boundaries of love are wide. The tenderness of the heart is never dying. The ability to show love is important in this world today more than ever. Hate and anger need to fade into the mist. And a love separated doesn't have to die. Just tucked away in a special place.

Story 3
"Guarding Angles"

She awoke from the dark. Confused but not afraid. Moments later she's greeted by an adult. Take my hand, your training starts now.

She was taught the ways of people. Their strengths, but mainly their weaknesses. Why their decisions can be so harmful. So hurtful. So thoughtless. With so many, their hearts are good. Their intention are for the best. But failure wants to follow them. They need a helping hand. Someone to watch over them.

This is the reason GOD created Guardian Angles. He gave HIS people a free will. This was good. But very powerful. Sometimes the free will controls the person, not the other way around. So a helping hand is given to everyone. You may say you had a brush with death but got very lucky. Maybe, just maybe your Guardian Angel helped. Your time to leave wasn't today. There are bigger plans for you. You're thankful for your luck not knowing the true story.

Maybe in another life you will receive the training. It will be you always near. Ever watchful. Caring for someone assigned to you. Doing the bidding of the ALMIGHTY.

Can you think of a better way to spend eternity?

Story 4
"People of the streets"

You see them in the streets. Begging for food. Who do you trust?

We as a people have turned into the haves and have-nots. I really have all I need to be comfortable in my life. I have shelter, food, warmth. Hot and cold running water, a warm bed. Cool air in the summer and friends I can trust. But what if I lost it all overnight?

Would my family or friends come to my aid? I see the ones standing on the corners with their signs. I know nothing about them. How do you trust them? Who do you trust? Should you even trust? It's so easy to look the other way. Pretend they're not seen. But you see everything around you. When I see someone healthy, more than capable of work, I give them nothing. I want to drive them off the corner. I want them to allow the space for a worthy individual.

I watched Missy for two years. Never gave her a dime. I observed. And with time, I determined she was legit. So, I stepped in. I was able to influence her life for the better. She deserved compassion. And I was glad to assist. There is another couple who plays music in the Kroger parking lot. They just want to pay their rent and feed their children. I love their music. I always give them something. They work to provide a concert for your enjoyment. Nothing smaller than a ten. They work for your donation. They never beg. Their sign explains why they're there. I believe them.

So, my point is that we who have money tend to waste a lot of it. It's our money and our privilege to do with it as we please. Living off-grid on solar energy means you never waste energy. And in life, I never want to waste money. But I will share if I think someone is in real need and needs a helping hand.

Isn't it the way things should be?

Story 5

"A New Dad"

This small child lost his father in the war. They never had the chance to meet.

As he grew, he could tell he was different because he had no father. His uncle Jim did his best to fill in for the part, but he could only go so far. He had his own family and children. His love for little Jeffrey was without bounds, but he was not the dad he wanted. One day Jeffrey came to his mother and asked, "will I ever have a dad?"

His mother placed him in her lap and held him close.

"I still love your father. I can't seem to find love anywhere else. And I won't marry unless it's equal to the love I had for your dad. Your uncle Jim tries hard to fill those shoes for me. I just need more time. But I am looking."

One day Jeffrey goes to the front yard and notices a man in a rocker on the neighbor's porch. "What's your name?" he asked.

"Bill. You can call me Mister Bill. And you?"

"I'm Jeffrey. I live here," and points to his house. "Where did you come from?"

"I've come to live with my daughter. This is my home now also."

So, Jeffrey sat in a second chair and talked with Mr. Bill every time he was out. They became good friends.

Finally, out of the blue he asked Mr. Bill if he would like to be his father. Bill looked down at him and said he was better suited for the job of a grandfather and smiled.

"I have a grandpa. I need a dad."

Bill could see the care in his eyes. "I'll tell you what, I'll be your dad till a better one comes along." A big smile broke across little Jeffrey's face.

Bill played the part with real earnest. Some days he would drive him to school. He told the mother about their deal, and she was fine with it. She just wanted her son to be happy. As the boy grew up Bill attended all his games. He gave him pointers on improvement. And Jeffrey would introduce him as his dad to others and dad became his name to Jeffrey. The years went by. Little Jeff grew tall. Not so little any longer. His mother never remarried. Bill filled the need for her son. All was working out just fine.

Then the day came when his mother came to the school and picked him up. "Jeff, Bill is in the hospital. It's bad. He's had a heart attack. He's asking for you."

Tears swelled up. This couldn't be real. He had just talked with him this morning. He seemed fine. He enters his room. He looked so frail. So weak. The reality sank in. He was going to lose his father. The only dad he had ever known. He takes his hand and leans in close.

"Dad, I'm here. I'm scared. I don't want you to leave. We can get through this."

Very weakly Bill squeezed his hand. "I don't want to leave either. But some things you can't control. I'm a proud father. You've grown into a good man. You'll be fine. You can carry on. Take good care of your mother. She needs your love. You're the man of the house now. I'm very proud of you. As far as I'm concerned, I'm your second father. An honor for me."

Bill's been gone for over a year now. Jeff still comes to the graveside to talk now and then.

Friendships come in many forms. They can be different and outside the traditional box. They're just as real as any. A friendship is a sacred bond. Never betray a friend! And be a friend to all.

Story 6
"Young couples in love"

An old timer was walking along a path. He sees a young couple on a blanket on the grass. So he stops and watches for a few minutes. They hold hands. She'll laugh and lay her head on his shoulder. So much in love. Their eyes tell the whole story.

He thinks "I once loved like that". It wasn't so many years ago. Sure age has taken its toll. But he remembers. Soft kisses. Words of love. Feelings that wrap you up and keep you warm. Those memories aren't gone. Maybe allowed to settle from the top. Replaced with a peck on the cheek, a helping hand around the house. Conversations when time permits. A show of love for sure, make no mistake about that. Maybe the flame has been allowed to simmer with time. Almost unnoticed. It sometimes takes seeing the young in love to force those memories back to the top.

The phone now, the television, they want so much time. Yes, back to basics is in order. He'll stop for flowers. Order dinner in. Tonight, he'll shower her with attention. Make up for the lack of swooning he's guilty of.

Sometimes seeing the young can remind you of your duties in a marriage.

Story 7

"Coffee in bed"

We met at a party. It was the classic "I saw her from across the room."

Beautiful eyes, a really nice smile, and the right age. I kept an eye on her to see who she was with. I wanted it to be a girlfriend and not the other. It was a large party in a big house. I would lose track of her. Finally, I heard someone speak my name. I turned, and it was her. I was quite surprised and asked if we knew each other. Her answer embarrassed me. "You kept looking at me, so I asked who you were." We talked the rest of the party.

We exchanged numbers. I told her I would call from Beaumont. It wasn't long before I talked her into coming to visit. Everyone wants to see off-grid living. She stayed two nights. She slept in PJs and told me not to assume I had privileges. To this day, I smile over that.

I served her coffee in bed—a thing I do still today. I keep her cup in my room. I prop up her and myself with pillows, and we talk over coffee.

It wasn't long at all before I found out I had cancer. So, no out-of-town trips for me. She still worked and cared for a family member. There were long gaps in seeing each other. Then the pandemic hit. We had no face contact at all. That's why I splurged for Valentine's Day. Our first time together in months. Now we're both vaccinated, but this is where living off-grid comes in. I can only be gone one night at a time. I can't ask anyone to come way out here to feed my animals. And she can only get away mainly on weekends. And I have so much company now because my family wants to escape to the woods and leave their houses.

We're working it out. A little challenging to say the least. But we're working it out.

Hope this was a good read for you. I should have learned how to cook. And I still hate washing dishes.

Story 8
Growing Up is Not a Cake Walk"

The knowledge of age and time. Where does it take you?

As you grow older you learn things. Never touch fire. Never trust a politician, things like that. Experience is a great teacher. We all don't learn at the same pace. You have the ones who will touch the hot metal after the fire is removed. It doesn't look hot! We older ones know.

You carry all the debt of youth. You must have it now. You never are paying things off before you add more. We know better. They carry stress and pressure because of bad calls. Were we any different at such a young age? But that is not who we are today. We've picked up knowledge along the way. Knowledge that the youth don't want to acquire. They're smart now. They know what's best for them. They just need a dose of age still. And when their world crashes, where do they turn. Who do they want to fix things for them? Would it be that old couple who wanted to give guidance? The ones who had valuable advice for you, but you didn't want to listen? The ones with age and experience. Funny how that works out.

This new role, teacher, and student. They want to share knowledge and skills to help you grow. Yet they want to help develop your ability to just step back and ask yourself "is it necessary right now? Can I afford it now? Did I save for it or just wake up and plowed head long into another debt?" At this junction you and they are partners. A team to assist both parties.

Don't hesitate to ask for an opinion. You don't give up the right to decide. You just want more data. And age and experience have a lot to offer.

Story 9
"Love that doesn't die"

It took years but his love for her finally could not be denied.

They dated for years in their youth. But the strong connection just wouldn't connect. So, they went their separate ways. Only thing, she never left him. Years, a lot of years went by. She was the measure all others had to measure against. And of course, she was the only one who was her. He was never really happy.

Then one night the words slapped him in the face. You never got over her, you'll never be happy with love until that changes. So, what to do? Both had new lives. That clock could never be turned back. The bigger problem is that he did still love her. He didn't want to "get over" her. So, what now?

That was many years ago he realized this. He made contact as an old friend. Just checking up. Not wanting to cause a problem. Doesn't get to talk often. Just keeping the friendship open. If lucky a lunch visit. On one such visit music was playing in the background. Then a song is played. She says she wants it played at her funeral.

That exact song was on his phone. He never listened to it the same. He had to remove it. The thought of her passing. Laying there. It was more than he could handle. The piece of music he loved so much now brought tears.

Made him think about losing her again. This time would be the last. So, he deliberately placed space between them. He had to leave once more. She didn't realize the change. It was so infrequent they talked anyhow.

He never married and one day she did pass. Such a dark day in his life. He visits her grave and talks to her still. Can't leave flowers. Still never wants to cause a problem. Doesn't want anyone to ever think ill of her. The tears still roll down his cheeks on his visits.

We have what we want but are sometimes too arrogant to see that. We stop the special treatment and begin to drift apart. Respect what's in your care. You can lose it forever!

Story 10
"The road to Manhood"

A set of loving parents gave birth to a son. Time flew by, and soon he was five. For his birthday, they gave him a dog, a small puppy that would not stay so small. "It's your friend. You give him a name," said his parents. So the boy and a dog named Sam grew up together. Sam really did become his best friend. He was as gentle as could be—unless you wanted to bring any harm to young David. They were always together. When he started school, it was very confusing to Sam. David would never leave his side. But with time, he adjusted.

David was very shy. He poured all of his feelings into his dog. But as he grew, there was a girl he so badly wanted to talk to. Years went by, but he could never build the courage to speak to her. Finally, he graduated. His choice was to go into the military. He was sent overseas. Then one day, he got the horrible news. Sam was no longer. He took leave to return home. His Sam was a jar of ashes. But he wanted to lay him to rest himself. So the family went to the family plot, and there Sam was laid to rest.

David, dressed in full uniform, knelt and shed tears. He felt a hand rest on his shoulder. He looked up to see the girl he had loved from a distance. She said she asked his mother if she could join him on this day. She told him that she always wanted him to talk to her, but he left. She promised herself that she would wait for him to return, and she would speak first.

With time, they married. They spent a beautiful life together. Then a day came where David lay in a hospital bed without much hope of leaving. His wife held his hand and spoke in a soft, loving voice to him. "David, I fell in love with you because of the way you loved Sam. My father always told me any man who can love a dog at a young age would be a great husband. 'You learn to care past yourself. He will be a good provider. You will be under his care and will want for very little. He'll know compassion. He'll know you.' And that is why I waited for your return. So don't leave me yet. I should have told you this sooner. I regret that."

A couple of days passed. Then the doctor came to her. Miracles do happen. He told her, "Your husband will leave this place. Not for a few days, but make his bed ready. He's a true fighter." She sat down and sobbed tears of joys.

Never think they can't hear you. Always continue talking to them. You could be planting a seed of a miracle.

Story 11
"My Destiny"

A small boy of four came to his mother. "Mom, what is destiny?"

The mother looks down and says, "it means you are going to do something that is probably needed. Why would you ask that?"

"In my sleep a voice told me that. I didn't even know what it meant."

The mother looks at him deeply, then goes about her business.

The coming years brought change. He somehow understood things. Words, pictures, and expressions missed by most. He could explain things without effort. He for sure had a special gift. The day came when he came upon a serious police event. A man had a young girl at gunpoint. He stated if anyone came close, he would kill the girl. Totally unnoticed he walked past the police linc. All hell broke loose. He ran to the gunman. He stopped and they made eye contact.

"You don't want to kill anyone. What has you so upset? I'm coming to you and you will release her and take me. We can talk. I care about your problem." Eye contact was never broken. The man felt an unexplained ease. "Come to me" he barks. "You need to fear me. I'm dangerous."

"No, you're not. Just scared and confused. You're actually asking for help. I feel it."

The man later dropped his gun and gave up. His problem was a dying child. He needed help for her. He thought he had nowhere to turn. But this small boy promised to help. And help he did. What he did drew so much attention that everyone wanted to know him. He went to the family in need. His mother, who understood his special gift took him there.

He then talked. "There is a girl behind those doors who will die soon if she doesn't get help. The father was willing to die for her to save her.

He's safe now but in a lot of trouble. Will we as a people allow this child to perish? She needs help!"

She was saved and the father released on probation. A good ending?

This boy proved his ability to solve even the most complicated problems. His mission in life was to help people in real need. His destiny. And what did he ask in return. NOTHING!!!

This may be an exaggerated example. But there is good all around us. People willing to help. People who care. They're not after a huge salary, an obscene bonus. They want what's best for mankind. All this craziness today is not their concern. It will find its balance. It is for others to solve. They want people to have a peaceful life. Is that too much to ask! Is that not the perfect destiny?

Story12

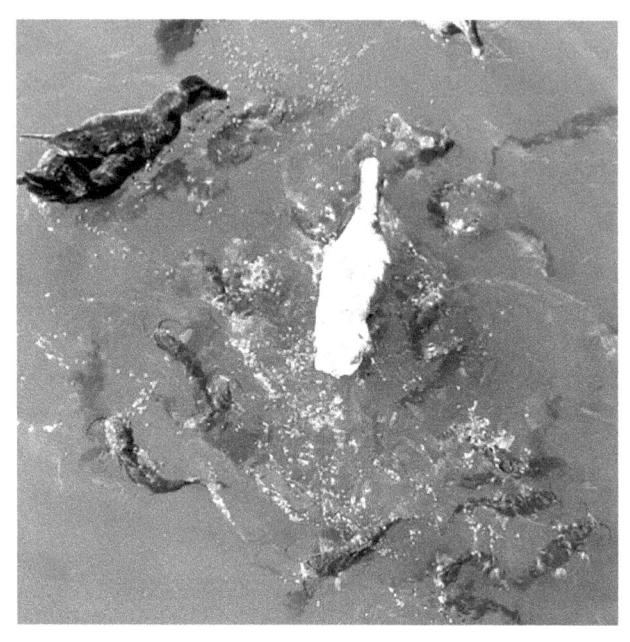

"The influence of a bird"

A woman far along in years sat on her back porch one morning as she has done for many years.

She lives alone now, her husband past three years ago. This morning turned out to be different. A song bird landed close to her. They made eye contact. The bird saw no danger so it stayed. It selected a small branch and perched itself. And it began to sing.

The woman was totally impressed. Never had she just sat and listened to a bird sing its song. Note after note came. The pitch rose and fell. Such beautiful sounds from a creature so small. She smiled. With time the bird flew away.

She decided to set up a feeder. Whatever she could do to draw it back. The next morning, she got a repeat performance. She couldn't fully explain it but her spirits were lifting. Energy was returning to those old arms and legs. She was excited each day for the coming morning.

This went on for more than a year. Other birds visiting. She even bought a book to identify the different birds. Then one day she noticed her original song bird was missing. Age takes everything with time. Mother Nature is no exception. The gift this bird, a small little bird with a beautiful song, gave her was priceless. It changed her life. A change for the better.

We are influenced by our experiences. Our needs must always be addressed. And sometimes, just sometimes, the smallest influence can be just what you needed.

Story 13
"Why I Love your Mother"

A small girl seeks her father's lap. A place she enjoys very much.

"Daddy, tell me why you love Mommy."

Very surprised, he says, "OK. See her in the kitchen? She says that's her room. I'm only allowed to go to the refrigerator. Other than that, it's her area. She takes a lot of pride in that."

"But, Dad, you didn't know that when you met. Why did you fall in love with her?"

"Her smile. I fell in love with that first. We met by accident. I think I fell for her within minutes. I knew I needed to speak to her. I had to bring her into my life. A decision I've never regretted. I quickly learned she was quick on her feet with a cute line. I still love that about her. And talents. I feel uneducated sometimes around her. But she is so modest. And very forgiving. I'm a bull in the China closet. But she accepted that in me. And I really love her for that. She can be firm yet so tender. You'll learn to respect and love her for those qualities too".

"Over the years, I've seen how blessed I really am. Does all of this explain my love for her to you? I can go on. I can go on for another hour."

"No," she says, and she snuggles close.

"Now I want you to do something for me. Go tell your mother what I told you. Then go out to play. We may want to lie down and rest for a while."

Story 14
"Enduring Love"

Titled by Audrey Geissler

He was at the hospital and the doctor had a long talk with him.

His wife of fifty-three years was leaving him and there was nothing he could do. Arrangements were being made to send her home to finish her time there. Hospice staff would assist him. The news was so dark. At home she just lay there, eyes closed, breathing so shallow. His heart was breaking.

He had to get out and breathe fresh air. Have some time for his thoughts. He got a friend to watch her, and he walked to the lake. There he sat alone and cried; he had things he needed to say. Feelings he wanted her to hear. It just wasn't fair. Then for the first time in many years he said a prayer. He prayed for strength for himself. No hand would come from the heavens and make her well again. He understood that. He just asked she wake up one more time so they could talk once more.

He returned home and sat by her bed. He held her hand and spoke soft words. His head lowered and a tear fell and hit her hand. He feels a squeeze. Then the words, "don't be sad dear, I'm going to a good place." His eyes open and she's looking at him. It was the answer to his prayer. It was his time to say what his heart was feeling.

And so, talk he did. Everything was on the table. She couldn't laugh but her smile was there. He expressed all his feelings of love to her. Things that should have been said but for whatever reason wasn't. She gave him comfort. Gave him words of deep felt love herself. They talked till the wee hours of morning. Then she said she needed rest. He knew what would happen next. They kissed for the last time.

He found his religion again. Started going to church. He prayed for the strength of others. The gift extended to him was forever appreciated and held in honor in his heart. He spoke to her daily even if just a few words. They would see each other again in time. He truly believed that now.

Story 15

"Aging"

Sure, he's aged a lot. The fun things aren't so easy anymore.

He gets up early but leaves the house for coffee. The wife likes to sleep in and he makes way too much noise. Besides he has friends there. The visiting is nice. A bunch of old men sharing stories and enjoying their coffee. Events are planned out. Fishing, hunting, or a project they are willing to help with. A good time for men of their age...

As much as he enjoys this time, he knows his wife will be getting up soon. She likes being pampered with her coffee in bed. He knows what all she does for him. A small repayment in the big picture. So he goes home to prepare for her getting up. Maybe a little more noise now to make sure she starts waking up. Maybe a little avocado toast on the side this morning. She likes that.

Grandkids are coming over for a short visit. He'll try to get them to leave the kids for a while. He gets fresh baked cookies if that works out.

Aging isn't so difficult. A few aches and pains here and there. Bruising of the skin and you don't even know why sometimes. Other time you say "that will leave a mark" sometimes a little ugly to look at, but you're fine.

Days are full of time together. A privilege you didn't have when working. But your love has grown much deeper. Maybe no longer physical but a higher level that you will one day envy. Holding hands, a peck on the cheek, a special smile that speaks volumes.

Aging isn't such a big deal really. Just a different journey in your lives to make you smile.

Story 16
"The Final Walk"

A father saw his son for the first time. He was late because of traffic. But there he was. Tears rolled down his face. His emotions were in a scrambled state. Where was his wife? Then he heard his name spoken. "Please follow me, Mr. Davis. We're going to a more private place."

He started demanding answers. "Where is my wife? What's going on?"

He sat in a chair with his face in his hands. He had just received the worst of news. He sobbed quietly. "My beautiful Jess. She's gone now. How will I ever be able to do this?" His hands trembled.

Then a door opened. A nurse walked in with a small baby. "Your son," she said as she handed the baby to the father. "I'll let you two be alone for a while. He hasn't been named yet."

Such a small little life. He saw the baby's mother in the eyes. He pulled him close. He whispered in his ear, "Your name will be Jesse, and as you grow, I'll teach you about your mother."

And grow he did. His dad didn't read children's books to him. He told long stories about Jesse's mother and about her plans for them. The years passed.

He went to college locally. He didn't want to leave his father alone. His father had friendships with women, but he never allowed them in close. And sure, Jesse tried to introduce him to the right one, but he had love for only one. He knew he would be with her later. Time continued on.

He was much older now. He made it to ninety-three. But his health wasn't good. His son was always there for him. He deserved a better life. He should have married. His love for his father and the sacrifices he made for him were his focus. Then one early morning, the father woke up to Jess sitting on the bed. Her smile was so beautiful. She looked so young.

He then noticed he had gotten younger himself. She reached out a hand to him. "We need to go."

"What about our son? He'll be alone now." Her touch was so soft.

She leaned forward. "He will meet his wife today. She'll bring paperwork for him to sign. I've taken care of everything. Now, let's walk. I have so much to show you."

Story 17
"Always Keep Them Close"

You lose someone you truly love. But when are they gone?

If the memories of a lost parent, spouse, child, or pet are a part of your everyday life, are they gone? If they still live in your heart, do they still carry life? True it's not a physical one but a life just the same. You might hold a conversation in times of need. In your subconscious they listen. They care about your problem. They want to help. You can clearly see their willingness to help.

A lost loved pet that looked into your eyes so many times before. You notice the transparency beginning. Slowly they fade. Then at some point their name is mentioned to express a point. Something changed. They are finally laid to rest. Acceptance of their loss acknowledged. Not an" uncaring". You have moved on.

With people the rules change. Your pet at best was part of your life for 12+ years. But with people it may be your entire life. 60, 70 years. According to plan they leave first. With all the important dates, they spend time in your heart. They're not really gone yet. You still hold on. Not wanting to lose that grip. This acknowledgement give a ghostly life." Here" but not. Talking only in your dreams. And yes, you will dream. You bring them back into your life if only for a brief night. Love is shared.

The clock runs out. You wake up. Feeling blessed for the visit. Knowing they're still around. The memory alone may bring a tear. But at the same time a smile. You snap back from a daydream. You don't really control the meetings. Not at first. Never allow their name to be spoken just to make a point. They deserve more. If you speak their name, take the time to speak of your love for them you still carry.

There is an order in life. Not iron clad but an order. Your seniors will probably leave first.

Accidents happen. Sometimes the child leaves before the parent. The rules for remembering still apply.

Accept this now. The adjustment will be slightly different. It will never be easy. As long as you love, no one ever truly will leave you.

You will meet again.

Story 18

"Who We Are"

There are those who marry but really shouldn't have.

Their version of love has not yet fully matured. So they're together for a few years then it starts to unravel. I was one of those. But others have it more together. They move at a pace different from the one I took.

I brag at lasting eight years with one former wife. They say with a smile and a raised chest, they are celebrating fifty years together and they were their first love. I can find nothing but respect in that.

I take pride in living to 73 and knowing I have many years ahead of me. My health is good, and my finances are in order. I led a good life. I guess that's my marriage of 50 years. We all walk our own paths. Mine is different form yours. But I'm no less happy. And just like you, we can say, so many didn't make it that far.

Many of you have accomplished both. That makes you exceptionally special.

We have but one life on this earth. Make the most of it. Never lose your honor. Help others in true need. Have understanding. Never regret the past. Those day are gone. Learn, then move on. It's your future and how it's handled, that counts now. Fine the humor around you not the anger.

Do all of this and my hope is that our paths cross one day. I think I would be a better person because of that.

Story 19
"Growing Up"

A boy was sitting with his father and said, "Dad, I'll be thirteen in two days. It won't be long after that I'll be an adult. What's the difference between an adult and a responsible man?"

The dad looked at him with surprise. "You are growing fast, and you will be a man one day. What makes a man is not that big of a secret. Your morals and your character are the foundation. You must always ask yourself questions. 'Do I want to work and contribute to society? Or do I want the government to send me checks while I sit at home with other losers and do drugs?' Now that doesn't include all of them, just the ones who are capable of working but have the workers of this nation give them their money. They lack character. Instead of working for something, would you steal it? Would you steal something just because the opportunity is there? It's not yours. Someone else worked hard and paid for it. And would you just take it? Those people lack morals. Would you ever strike a woman in anger? You're bigger, stronger, and can inflict great pain on her. Those people are cowards. They are adults who never grew up. They have no self-esteem. Can you love a wife and only her? Can you be faithful? Many can't. But are you man enough to say yes to this one? Can you place your family's needs over yours? Being a man requires sacrifice. Not daily, but you will be called upon. By being a man, you gain respect. You are admired by others. You are the example for younger men to follow. Just being an adult doesn't get you this. So how you live and the decisions you make determine your manhood. Others are your judge, not you. I've watched you grow up. You've made me proud to be your father. Don't stray from your path, and you will make a fine young man. You are off to a great start. I will always be here to answer your questions. Include me when you need me. Other than that, enjoy life. Find a girl and treat her with the upmost respect. She may be your wife one day."

Story 20

"Living Alone"

Living alone isn't so bad as long as you're busy.

It's quite time. Planning time. Pets love it. They can fill your need to talk. Might be a form of one-way communication, but after time you do understand their questions.

You want out? Ready to eat? Need water? Hear something? And I could go on and on. They have moods just like us. Treats make them smile. Having to stay home doesn't. All of this makes for a good day. Without pets I'm sure things would be different.

So, I share my time. I share my food. I'm sure I would place myself in harm's way to protect them. They would die to protect me. Would never allow me to face danger alone. People that's friends! Yes, there are dangers out here. But I feel very comfortable being here. Nature allows me my place. We have a sort of agreement. We both leave the other alone. Just in case, the dogs roam the yard. Insurance in a way. A gun is never far.

I'm sure I'll be remembered by living off the grid. A lifestyle I chose and have no regrets for. My day-to-day life is an interest to almost everyone I meet. I'm asked a thousand questions. I try to take the time to answer most. "Don't you get lonely"? One of the more frequently asked questions. And believe it or not "do you have TV" is a close second.

So, I'm propped up having coffee. Figuring out what I'll do today. Waiting for daylight. Enjoying music. Wouldn't trade this for anything. Planning for the changes of season. Hurricanes.

Maintaining the solar. All busy work. All necessary. The volume of oak I cut and split, to cook with, would surprise many. But I enjoy grilling over an oak flame. My needs are unique too out here. Been out here eight years now. And I love it!

Story 21

"Family"

They were raised together. The connection was very close.

As soon as they could move freely they played. The energy of the youth has no match. Chewing on everything, what came off the ground went straight to the mouth. And let me add there were no restrictions

The first born a little more pushy. I think dominant is the word. Always wanting is/her way in this case. A bit controlling. But separation was not an option. They were always together. If you wanted to bully one you had to take on both. As I said the bond was very tight.

Not always that good at sharing. But occasionally. As life goes everyone grows up. The mother forces independence. Some hang around a little too long. Some leave too early. But know the contact isn't broken. The chain that kept them together may now be a very long thin thread. Long thin, but strong.

      This is the way of families. Of generations. The family tree has so many branches. Not easy to know every leaf. But once established as a family member all doors open. Hands of welcome extended. Food is shared. Conversation and laughter for hours. The offer of a bed for all.

      Keep your family strong.

Story 22
"Letters of Love"

There was a boy who was raised without much love. He knew that when his chance came to be a father, he would be a great one.

He grew tall and strong. Then one day, he married. His life was going as planned. His wife soon gave birth to an infant girl. He held her in his arms and cried tears of love. He couldn't get enough of her company. His wife could clearly see his love for tiny Ann. She was so proud.

A few years passed, and he noticed a lump under his skin growing. He ignored it at first. Figuring it would just go away. But it didn't. The x-rays told the dark story. He had less than six months to live. His whole world crumbled before him. His wife and child would no longer have him in their lives. So he began to write.

He had so much to say and such little time to say it. He and his wife spent hours talking and taking care of arrangements. All he could do for Ann was to write his feelings.

> Ann, I'm sorry I left you while you were so young. Your father loves you so very much. I had such big plans for the two of us. I wanted to take you to see the ocean and let you play in the sand. I've asked your mother to do this for me. I wish I could, but I'm so tired now. I can tell I don't have much time left. I wanted to walk you to your first day of school. You're such a beautiful girl. I knew a boy would show up at our door one day. I knew how I was going to handle it. Poor kid!

> I wanted to walk you down the aisle. All dressed in white, a huge smile on your face. I would have been glowing with pride. By then, your mother may have experienced love again. He would have my blessing to stand in for me. Your mother would only accept a man of good character. I know you would have given us grandchildren. To bounce that first child on my knee. It excites me even now.

But I won't be there in person. My spirit will be by your side each and every day. Take care of your mother. She'll need your love. I think I need to rest. I'll talk more tomorrow. Think of me often with fondness. These words are all you'll be able to know me with.

Know I would have been a great father. I knew the choices needed to grow our love. I miss you already.

Story 23
"The wonders of Aging"

Titled by Cindy Walker

I look into the mirror and see time has left its mark. My youth has been replaced with age. An older version of me. So how do I accept this?

It's not really that bad. Aches and pains are more common. But I've learned so much. Completing the task is somewhat easier. Tools and leverage do the work now. Family and friends. I use them all. At this age you need less. And that's because over the years you acquired what you must have. And believe me your neighbors know this.

Sure, I move slower. Maybe a little less brisk. Not bed ridden by any means. I'm careful on how things get done. I'll reward myself much easier. Half days of work are my norms. I have no problem with that. Let the young ones work all day. Besides I get sore muscles now. I look at the job and decide to farm it out or take a few days to get it done. I'm happy with either.

So, I stare at my reflection. I can still smile at myself. I've run a long race. Still running. But I know my pace is slower. At my age the women don't care about your "dad body". Are you healthy? Are you a provider? Is your heart tender? The small things. And heck, if you can catch fish, clean it, and cook it for them, well you might get lucky!!!

So, the mark of time upon me is just part of the cycle of life. Still in the race. For me retirement is just fine. Every day a blessing. But remember, I'll tell a yarn to a kid without hesitation. Screen everything, I say. That's my fun. And to stay young, stay fun!!!

Story 24
"She Met Sam"

Her parents noticed the changes around age five. She just seemed to have a better understanding about things. Things far beyond her years.

Her quest for knowledge couldn't be satisfied. All she wanted was to learn. Her school soon learned they were being left behind. What to do? So they started placing her in advanced studies. Even they weren't challenging enough. This girl was gifted.

What was the price paid? A little socially awkward, but not that bad. No, her price paid was in relationships. She only could relate to men much older. More experienced. So love never really ever crossed her path. And this was her life for years. And one day all of that changed. She worked in a lab, a very advanced lab. And one morning she met Sam.

She and Sam shared the same childhood. Both very smart. Neither had ever met an intellectual match. Not till that day. The competition began ever so slowly. Then grew rapidly. Each trying to outdo the other.

Feelings began to emerge. Neither had ever been in love. So as smart as they were, they both missed the signals. It was her whose eyes opened first. She began to see the cute side of him. Choose to work a little closer. Things started to change. And him? Well, being a guy he was clueless. The smartest guy in the room but still standing in the dark.

Good feeling lead you to good places. Yes they did fall in love with each other. No matter the life you have experienced, good feeling seek you out. Be receptive. Want that happiness. It found you. Your leap of faith could be the best thing that can ever happen to you. Be known for being a happy and uplifting person. People out there need friends like that!

Story 25

"What is your Happiness"

What do I require to be happy? We all must ask ourselves that every now and then. Do an update, if you will. We all want happiness in our lives, so what do we require to have it?

Our life is ever changing. Absolutely nothing remains the same. Is your requirement stability? Sorry. You will grow. Your children will develop and one day move out. Your health or the health of someone near you may change. But stability is a loose word. Working for the same company for twenty years. Being a good provider is the job of both people. You both go into retirement and look back and smile. Another couple may not share your comfort.

Maybe just having people around is the answer. Your requirement for happiness is less demanding. To some, happiness is easier. Others may have to work a little harder to get there. But we all want it. There are even those who have separated themselves from society and have animals as friends. Whatever works.

Happiness is not an elusive dream. What makes you smile? When was the last time you laughed out loud? If the answer is "Too long," then figure out a solution. Ask for help. Get a pet. But make a change. Right now, there is a surplus of hate. Happiness can and will change that.

Story 26
"You're The One Who Chooses"

Today is supposed to be a blah day. No sun. Rain. I guess some might say a nasty day.

So, what do I do? Well, I'm a very lucky man. I pick how I'm going to feel. I choose my attitude out here. Today will be fabulous! I have Mother Nature all around me. I party with her. She needed water. And the water came. So why shouldn't I be happy for her? I'm the only human for miles in any direction. Aren't her needs just as important as mine? She deals with her version of equity and inclusion. Enter my land and you will not be turned away. I'll include you, just respect my home. Don't throw trash, damage the land, or kill trees or animals for fun. Once you go back to the houses piled high, then act a fool, if you wish.

It's hard to be upset out here. There are things that won't get done today. But you know what, I don't care. Today is her day. It's her that provides me with wood for a warm fire. She shares. Who can't respect that? My days are filled with wonderful experiences. No loud noisy vehicles. No racing to the next thing to do. I'm more laid back than that. No stress to speak of. I like that.

So, I start each day with the best coffee this side of the Mississippi River. My music is all handpicked for my enjoyment. And my surroundings were sculptured by GOD himself. How could I find any problems in that?

Story 27
"Remembered How"

What do we want to be remembered for after we're gone?

Myself, I want family and friends to see me in their minds eye as a god person. Not perfect, good is plenty good. Someone who would share. Someone who would help someone in need. Who always cared about this world we live in. Cares about its people. We all have our personalities. Our quirks. But do we want to find fault in people only because they have succeeded better than any one of us? Does being different offend?

The more we can accept in others, the better we get along. Honor and integrity should be the foundation we stand on. The rule to live by. Will that make you perfect? Not at all. Who really wants to be "perfect"? Who wants to live forever? Our goal is to a good example for others to see. To inspire others for all the great things in our lives. And yes, great is a personal interpretation. To lift the ones who could use a hand right now in their life.

None of us will live forever, how do you want to be remembered?

Story 28
"The Journal"

The long-awaited day was here, but something was wrong. The doctors were trying to deliver her child and save her life. Twice they almost lost the mother, but they did their job and saved them both. The mother's life was forever changed. She never fully returned to her former self.

As time went by, she realized her life would be shorter than she hoped. She knew she would be leaving her husband and daughter. So she began to write. She bought a journal. She recorded all her daughter's special moments. All her words reflected her love for her little Sharon. Time passed. She never allowed her daughter or husband to know about or see her writings. They would be her final gift to her family. Then one day, she passed. As her belongings were gathered, they found a box. A pretty ribbon and bow wrapped the box. And in the corner was written, "To my lovely Sharon."

She was twelve now, old enough for feelings and strong emotions. She took it to her room to open it. Inside was the journal. She took it out and opened the book. The first lines told her that her mother would never leave her really. "And in days of loneliness, read a story. I've written many for you. See how you grew up." There were stories of birthdays. Stories of school. Her first interest in a boy. Her love for her parents. To her surprise, stories just about shopping for clothes. So many stories about her growing up.

Tucked in between were words from her mother to her. Advice to her when she would no longer be there. Tears ran down her cheeks. She never realized just how wonderful her life really was. That book was her prized possession. So she went out and purchased a journal of her own. She began to write her own entries. One day, both books will be passed down to her girl. She'll finish her last page just as her mother did for her. Words of such profound love and wisdom for her daughter to live by. A path of understanding and guidance. And the final entry, "I will always love you."

Story 29
"The Power of Caring"

He never married. Never had children. Business was his life at an early age.

In his senior years he was kind of lost. He had plenty of money, but no one to share it with. Didn't trust the women who showed interest in him. He felt they had motivates to secure a retirement with his dollars. So, what to do?

Then he sees a fundraiser for a local hospital wanting to provide health care for the most underprivileged at no cost. He went in to investigate to see how the money was spent. What he saw was children. Many children. All with serious issues. The doctors and staff did not live a life of luxury. They gave their all out of care for the kids. They were doing what they could.

He walks into a room. There was a child with many hookups to all types of life saving equipment. The boy looks in his direction. His eyes told him he had given up. Just lying there waiting to die. Not on his watch! He calls the nurse, and they go into the hall. He learned the drugs needed were not covered by any insurance. The hospital itself couldn't afford them either. So, it was down to just comforting him.

"If he gets the meds, can you save him?"

"It's close but, yes, I'm sure."

He returns a few days later and finds a woman crying in the waiting room. He places his hand on her shoulder and asks what's wrong?

"My son is going to live! A stranger, a white man has saved him!"

"When you give up all hope, a miracle can still happen. I'm glad you got such good news. I'm happy for you!" And he walks away.

He tells the director he wants no one to know about his support. He will continue to pay for the lifesaving drugs.

"Help all you can. I'll be a silent donor. And if a family is in need personally, let me know that also." And so, he gave. The money he had placed such a high value on, he was now giving away. Giving it all to people in need.

He died alone. The only way of life he had ever known. As each child recovered, he was given a picture of them leaving. And a box containing over a hundred pictures was buried with him. So, was he ever really alone?

Story 30

"The Love of a Son"

He's working hard to save a life. Being a doctor has a lot of stress.

A nurse catches the sweat on his forehead with a cloth. His mind remembers days past. Being a small boy afraid of the dark. This strong man telling him not to fear the monsters, he was by his side. He would keep the monsters away.

His real father died in the military. He wasn't even born yet. And this big man entered his life. He took care of his mother and sister. He grew to love this brave man. He knew he loved his mom. Would bring her flowers. Make her smile. But at night I could call his name and he would enter my room. He would sit on the edge of the bed. He was a protector. Always telling me I was safe. Placing a strong arm around me till I went to sleep.

No he wasn't my real father, but he was the only father I ever knew. He had us call him by his first name. Told me he was just doing the work for my real dad. They were friends, it seems they knew each other at one time. My mom loved him very much. We lost mom with time. And taking care of dad was a work of love. And yes I did say dad.

He returned to the brightly lit room. He's working to save a life. A life so important to him. His hands steady. His mind so focused. He'll save this life. Nothing can stop that. It's now his turn to keep the monsters away. To save the life of this man who has shown so much love for his family.

A step parent is not an easy balance. Caught between two very strong emotions. The love of a new relationship, and the love of the children. But you do your best. Not always successful. But just continue to keep the monsters away. And all will work out as it should.

Story 31
"Strength"

There are days you rule the world, and there are days you are just part of the tide. What makes them so different?

Some days, you're invincible, and some days you are so weak you don't want to get up. How's your day today? The pendulum is not just the extremes; there are many points between. Your focus and your attitude control your life more than you think. It's easy to give in, but to stand in defiance takes strength. Takes a winning attitude. Takes your inner desire to be in control. It's not those easy many times.

Look at the actor who recently died of cancer. He made movies till the end and didn't discuss his problem. What determination! He knew he was dying. He just wanted to leave his mark. A positive mark. Do you think there were days he didn't want to get up, much less go to work? He has my respect.

So, do your best. Be in control of your day if possible. Appreciate your friends and don't hesitate to ask for help. They are your friends.

Story 32
"Getting Through"

A small girl was the quite one in class. A total outsider. Why was this?

The teacher would just look and wonder why? She had no marks on her. No signs of pain. Why? She was plenty smart, with no problems with lessons. But always at a distance. One day the teacher approached her and asked if she would be her helper. She needed someone to dust the erasers. She had always shown kindness towards her. She just looked ahead and said nothing. Then one day she set the erasers on her desk and asked if she could have them ready before the next class and left the room. When she returned the girl was gone. To her surprise all the erasers were cleaned and neatly stacked on her desk. This brought a tear to the teacher. She had broken through to her. Now what?

Not wanting to scare her off, she had to think of her next move. She set a stack of papers on her desk with a note asking her to look over them for mistakes. Once again, she comes in to find the papers neatly placed on her desk. All corrections marked in red. Zero mistakes.

Finally, one day she is asked to go to the principal's office. There sat a couple. They're very nervous.

"Miss Anderson, this is John and Mary Davis. Ann's parents. They asked to speak to me about you. I thought you should be here."

She looks at them a little confused. "Yes?"

Mrs. Davis begins to speak.

"You have changed our daughter. A change for the good. The very good. She's not the girl we raised any longer. She looks at us now. She helps around the house. Her room has always been kept tidy, but on her caulk board one day we found your name. There was a heart next to it. That was the first sign of love we have ever seen her express. You have a gift. You've penetrated the layers of her isolation. You've accomplished what we could never do."

The mother's eyes tear up. Mrs. Anderson walks to her and gives her a hug.

"Your daughter is very special. And I fell in love with her months ago. There is more work ahead of us. But I feel Ann has started her journey to leave her shell. And know I'm honored to be a part of that."

And Ann did just that. Her teen years were very normal compared to others her age. Miss Anderson passed with time. She was buried in the family plot. And Ann, every year on her birthday, she and her family would bring fresh flowers. This lady did a miracle with her. And she wants her children to know it.

Story 33

"What is Life"

What does it mean to be alive?

Sitting in a recliner and watching TV all day and saying you've earned that privilege. Well, not me. Moving around all day staying busy is more to my liking. My reward is awesome and pain form the work prior is common. Not a bad life really. Feelings of satisfaction. Looking out and seeing the accomplishments. Knowing you're somewhat healthier because of your lifestyle.

It helps to keep a bunch of the pounds off. Not all for sure. Age slows you down. But if you stay active it doesn't put you down. I have the advantage of property. That in itself means work. A lifestyle I chose. I've worked as far back as I can remember. And I guess I'll be busy till the end. But what do you want? Friends help me frequently to do the jobs. The two or more people jobs get their turn when they show their face. I just have to show patience. In the end it all gets done.

So, what does it mean to be alive? That definition is personal. I've just told you mine. No regrets at all. Best move I've made in my adult life. As you grow older, live your best at your age. Your time of "rest" will come. Don't rush it.

Story 34
"Friendships"

There was a very quiet boy at a school for boys with a main bully.

He was picked on every day. The bully would push him around daily and laugh about it. Then one day, that changed. The bully was messing with the quiet one when he heard someone say, "Leave him alone." He looked over to see the new kid.

"Shut up, punk, or I'll knock your block off."

The new boy charged the bully and knocked him down. The fight was on. The new kid took a bad beating. His nose was broken, one eye swollen shut. The fight was stopped. The quiet one came to help him up. He looked him in the eye and asked, "Why? Why would you help me, take such a beating, and you don't even know me?"

He smiled through a busted lip and said, "We all need to help the underdog from the ones who want to push them around." They became friends. Over the next few grades, he fought the bully three more times, with never a win. With time, all went their separate ways.

New kid (James) married and had children. He was a hard worker. He just never really got that big break. He took his family and moved to the city. A fresh start might be the answer. He put in an application, was interviewed, and got the job. The best pay he had ever received. He was quickly taken under the wing of management. He was trained for more responsibilities. His career was always moving up.

One day, he was in the cafeteria having lunch when a stranger asked if he could join him. "Sure," he said.

"How do you like the company?" he was asked.

"A really great company. I've been treated like family. I've received great training. I'm providing for my family better than I ever have. I hope to go far here."

"Well, I've been asked to deliver a note to you. Our CEO has watched you move up here. He's a very secret person. Many have never met him. He likes your work and attitude. Keep up the good work, and your future will be very bright." He slipped him a paper and left.

A little confused, he unfolded the paper and read. "We all need to help the underdogs. Especially if their heart is good. Good to see you again. Continue your training, and I'll have you running one of the companies one day. It's the least I can do for a boy willing to get beaten up to protect me."

Story 35
"When It's Important, Don't Accept a No"

I spend more time thinking of what might be. I want to be the most of a man I'm capable of. I'm in love and I want her to be impressed by me. Is that so wrong?

When she reflects on our time, I want to know she smiles. Now a warm glow covers her skin. The way it is with me. Falling in love with her, I was powerless to stop. I want the same of her. The good in her is my standard now. My goal. If I can be the man that she is a woman, that would be my greatest accomplishment.

So, we hold hands when together. Speak soft words. Show our feelings. I'll marry her one day. With her I'm complete. My value is not measured with money. With her it's my character. My word. Not so much to ask!

Tonight, we're having dinner in a nice restaurant. I'll break the ice on the subject of marriage. Watch her eyes. Read her face. My heart will be put out there for her to break. But I feel good. We're in love. It's the next logical step. I'll ask if I can buy a ring. A token to show we're committed to each other. To show we're a couple. As if no one knows!

Yes, I'm in love with her. Only her. I'm wanting us to spend the rest of our days on this world together. To date her till I'm no longer able to walk. Have other couples to look at us with envy. Such a beautiful image.

Must get ready. A special date tonight. My whole future rides on it. And if she says no! Every batter gets three strikes. I'll do even better when I ask next.

Story 36

"You Touch Lives"

There was a boy who was always told by his mother that he was very special and he would do a great deed for mankind. He came to believing this himself.

He decided medicine would be the way to achieve his calling. So, he studied. He put in long hours to understand everything. He was sure this was his mission in life. The years passed slowly. He improved cures for deadly diseases. Extended life where there was no hope. At his level he was recognized for his accomplishments. But this wasn't his answer. He expected something better. He dug deeper.

At the age of 93 he lay in a hospital bed. His time here was ending. He was disappointed in himself. He never reached his goal. Or so he thought. A woman appeared at the foot of his bed and spoke. "Mr. Davis, look at you, so sad. You have done more in life than ten men could do. You never gave yourself the credit you deserved. So many owe their life to you. You saved lives where death was at the door. And one life in particular will finish your work. That was your mission. Never giving up! You inspired so many. You achieved what no one before you could do." She smiles and tells him his work isn't complete. And he will leave this bed.

And sure enough he did. Now he walks into a room where a chair awaits him. He looks at all the eyes watching his every move. He's at an orphanage. He's come to speak about his life. To help them believe in themselves.

He sits and with a big smile he says "let me tell you about my mother".

We are all here to do something special. You just may not see the big picture. You touch lives. Make sure it's a positive influence.

Story 37
"My Beautiful Flower"

What is it about flowers that is so obsessive to humans? Could it be something as simple as colors? Our choices are driven by color. Even if your house was gray without, it's the color you picked. Our clothes, cars, how we decorate our yards are centered on color. Why? Maybe it's their unique shapes? Like snowflakes, no two are alike. Very close but worlds apart. You pick a flower, hold it to the light, and feel a pleasurable experience. You selected that one flower out of many. It touches you.

Could it be the combination of color and the uniqueness of that flower? Everyone wants that green thumb. The great thing is only a gifted few have the talent. Those get the praises of the onlookers. They take a true pride in their ability. But the rest will hire people with the green thumbs to decorate their houses and yards. Nothing wrong with that. I can't draw, but I will purchase a drawing that appeals to me.

Animals, birds, insects, other flowers, they all depend on the interactions between themselves. So why the attraction? I have no idea. But just looking at a beautiful flower makes me feel good. And the girl I love, I affectionately call her my beautiful flower.

Story 38
"Believe In Angels"

"Mother, how many Angels are there?"

She looks down with a smile. "I guess it depends if you believe in Angels to start with."

She wipes her hands and sits by her daughter. "I'm a believer. So, I feel there's millions of them." "They don't fly around with a harp?"

"No, I think they walk among us every day. They observe to see how and who they can help. They may be the one who died in a fire saving someone's life. A hero to the survivor. Someone who comes to the need of a person whose life has been turned upside down. They are the answer to hope for many. It's even said we all have a Guardian Angel. An Angel who is with us at all times. I have one and you have yours. We get a girl Angel. She keeps us from harm. Or does her best. So how many of them are there? How many people need their help? That's the number. And I think even those who don't believe still have one to watch over them too. I think your brother has two. If not, he needs two. I worry about him constantly. How about we bake some cookies for dad. We'll kind of be his Angels today. Think you might like that? Let's get started."

Story 39
"The danger of speed"

He's in bed looking out the window. Today will be like yesterday and the day before that. Tomorrow will be like today.

They say I'm lucky to be alive. But who is really the judge in this? They will walk to their car today and return home. I'll still be here. Alone with my thoughts. Along!

It was my fault. Speed and immaturity. That curve came up so fast. I just couldn't control the car. My family warned me constantly. I didn't listen. I was into me. So many times, over the last three years I've relived that day. Just a little more responsibility on my part and it would be me going home. But that's not to be. I must pay the price for the judgements made. And understand, I know that now.

No one but another paralyzed person understands the feelings. Awake at night. Dark thoughts. Wanting to end this nightmare. I don't have a drunk driver to blame this on. It's 100 percent on me. It was me who ruined my life. You just don't know the feelings I experience daily.

But today did turn out different. A machine was rolled into the room. A way for me to express my feelings. Not in anger. But in earnest to help another not to do what I did. I'll be able to type my words. And believe me I have a lot to share. No one wants this.

Maybe I can inspire another to let off that gas a little. I'm not sure but I must try. And you know what, I feel I have value again. I smiled for the first time in a long time. Wish me Luck!!!

Story 40
"Life and Stories of Love"

He was standing in line at the grocery store.

He looked over a few lines and saw a beautiful woman. Her clothes were perfect, showing her figure nicely. She was just a gorgeous woman in his view. Her hair was long, straight, and blonde, just what he liked. Now the question—was she married? He quickly looked at his place in line and hers. He would be checked out first. Perfect!

He pushed his cart to the side and watched her hands. No ring. He knew he had a small chance at least. Finally, she pushed her cart passed his, and he followed. Once outside, he called out to her. "Excuse me, I don't mean to be forward or make you uncomfortable. But I think you're beautiful. I see you don't wear a wedding ring. I would like to introduce myself to you. My name is David. May I ask you for yours?"

She looked him over, smiled, and said, "I don't know you. It's not appropriate." Then she continued to her car.

A little discouraged and a little heartbroken, he turned and left. As he loaded his car, she drove past, looked at him, and smiled. That made him feel much better. After a few weeks and about fifty trips back to that store, he saw her again. He pushed his cart close to hers and said, "Hi. Do you remember me? I don't want to bother you."

She looked back with a smile and answered, "Yes."

"Then you kind of know me now. David. Remember?"

She looked him over a little closer and said, "Ann. My name is Ann. I want you to know I'm not interested in a boyfriend."

"The second half is fine with me. Everyone needs to have plenty of friends. I'll leave you alone now. Don't want to ruin a good thing. But the next time we bump into each other, I'll ask you for your number. I would like to call you one day. Have a good day." And he walked on. She did the same, smiling.

This time, he waited for her to drive by, to check out her car. He just wanted to increase the chances of a meeting. And again, weeks went by. Until the day came and he saw her car. He grabbed a cart and started walking the aisles. As he turned a corner, he came face-to-face with Ann. She had a man by her side.

He didn't expect this. "Hi, Ann," he said and went to move past her.

"Hello, David. Meet my brother, who is also David. I have something for you." She picked up her purse and pulled out a sheet of paper, folded ever so nicely. "Try to convince me to go to dinner with you. I'm interested in what you have to say." She smiled and walked on.

When you want something badly enough, just be persistent and show manners. Life has its love stories. Find yours.

Story 41
"Churches"

Where is the church really? That building tucked back with all that colored glass? Let's look at this.

The buildings can be quite grand. A lot of respect is given once you enter the doors. So many rituals are performed here. I think it is an important part of life. Morals were taught. Understanding of good and bad. Pretty much every city has multiple places of worship. Each one is a little different. They all have their purpose. A good thing really. Is that the required location to speak to GOD?

Even those who claim to be a non-believer will question themselves under the right conditions. I kind of understand their position. I mean there are religions out there that will kill you if you don't accept their way. It's a tough world. Just look at the number of choices to worship. Kind of staggering. We just try to do our best at it.

Isn't the church within? That voice that can speak in which only you and GOD can hear? On Sundays all the true believers come together. Common beliefs. An acceptance of your place in life. They sit and listen. Sing, pray, and admire their surroundings. Fellowship abounds. Can you be alone in nature? A beautiful place to talk to the ALMIGHTY? At that moment can that be a church? All the colored glass is nice but not required. We do need a place for all to come together. That is one day a week. Your church travels with you. Its bricks are your beliefs. Its glass are your morals.

So, look within, see the size of your building. It travels with you everywhere.

Story 42

"Reunions with Purpose"

They come out in small groups, these hunter friends of mine.

They arrive heavy with smiles. Loaded down with hope of the coming days. They're going back in time. A more prime evil period in the fast moving world. Having fun with stories of the past. The liquor flows freely. Mixers always in demand. Jokes move around the camp. A camp to them but my home to me.

Their dogs are included in the adventure. Every creature gets to experience a time passed. Dog treats make their way out all day. Even a dog can smile you know! The cats aren't nearly as excited. But there's harmony mostly. No fences, no collars for some. Freedom at its finest.

Around mid-morning they start returning. The biggest smiles belong to the ones with spent shells. Everyone pitches in to process the animal. Get it on ice quickly. Then the story of events begin. When it was first seen. The shot. In the back are the ones who missed their opportunity. Knowing they must endure the jabs of being the butt of the jokes. (And I must say some have more experience than others).

So the end of every year brings old friends back together once more. Time has claimed some. But their spirit returns. And that's good enough. Hunting is not a lost art by any means. If you're a hunter you understand. And if not the curiosity will still reach out and hold your hand. And I look forward each year to see the smiles. Hear the stories. You can't beat good friends. I'm proud to call these hunters mine.

Story 43
"I Love You Dad"

One day, I was alone, or so I thought. I had been in a lonely mood for days. I looked up and asked for help. I sat down and closed my eyes. Suddenly my eyes were filled with a bright light. Then a voice told me I could spend a day with anyone I had ever met. Daylight till sunset. Anyone. I chose my father. There he was standing before me. I knew his smile, wearing that old hat he enjoyed so much. I hugged him. I couldn't hold back the tears. I asked, "Dad, will you go fishing with me?" We walked and talked. The feelings were overwhelming. I picked up the poles, and we walked to the water. I picked a shady spot where we could visit in comfort.

He caught the first fish. He was always a better fisherman than I, and I was pretty good. We laughed, told stories, and really enjoyed our time together. I noticed my watch. It was already three. Where had all the time gone? A small panic came over me. My father said, "When you receive a blessing, never find fault. Our time together was a gift from heaven. Let's just make the most of it." So the remaining time was the best. We talked old times. Laughing frequently. We had caught four fish, two each. Then I noticed he was leaving.

Becoming more transparent. He said, "I love you, son. Thank you for the time together. I'll see you again another day." *He was gone*.

I opened my eyes. And I was back where it started. Was this real? Did this all happen? Was this nothing more than a wonderful dream? Then I looked by my side. There were four fish in a bucket. Dad had given me his. He always did that when I was younger. I love you, Dad!

Story 44

"The Power of Love"

As a small child, he was drawn to her. They were life-long friends.

Finally, the day came for him to go off to college. But he just couldn't get up the courage to speak his true feelings. So, he left without words to her. A leaving he regretted for years. He poured himself into his studies. He was top in his medical class. But he thought of her daily. Finally, he got up the nerve to call. His disappointment was huge. The family had moved, and he had no idea where. He could find nothing. She was lost to him.

He was a trauma specialist. The one everyone turned to as the last chance for life. One day he walks into the waiting room to give good news to a frightened couple. He notices a woman. He stares for a moment. When he finishes, he walks to her. "Mrs. Davis?" She sees him and begins to sob. Her daughter was dying, she was in a horrible accident. The mother was the first to arrive. Her husband and the husband of Stacy were on their way. His whole world shattered. "Sit tight and let me investigate this. I'll come back."

He found the case. It was assigned to him. He began to study the broken body immediately. It just didn't look good. He went to work immediately. Saving her was the only acceptable thing. He worked for hours. Nineteen straight hours to be exact. Finally, he was finished. Now it was in GOD'S hands. He could do no more than pray.

She did recover. Her life was totally changed. She needed a wheelchair to get around. But with time she might be able to stand again. Behind the scenes he monitored her every improvement. And with time she and her family were able to take her home.

We experience love. We learn skills. The ability to express feelings is something everyone should improve at. How this story may have changed no one can guess. Maybe it was meant to be as it happened. His connection to her saved her life. His leaving and acquiring the skills to save her could be part of a bigger vision. Something we don't see clearly. Sometimes our Guardian Angel is a best friend. And the power of love can make miracles happen.

Story 45
"Years of Friendship"

I love just holding her hand.

This dear friend. We're not teenagers any longer. More matured than that. Our comfort together tells another story. Grey hair and many years piled high, we read each other's needs. Quick with wanting to help if it's called upon. But I always hold her hand when I can.

Her fingers close around mine. I see her smile. Maybe not a lot said. Small talk at best. We just enjoy the time to visit. Catching up is always fun. I think maybe a little "spoiling" is always in order. Back to that maturing attitude, you just understand better. Communication is so much easier. Not all the words are required to be spoken out loud.

It's just that holding hands speak also. A feeling of contentment flows between you. Such contact makes you one. Calms the inner self. We can all use that "calm" now and then.

So I look and smile myself. Friendships of many years are the best. Keep in contact with the ones who always make you feel better. The ones who make you smile. Compliments should flow like wine. And smiles are free for the asking.

Story 46
"The Changes of Life"

The old man takes his daily trip to the park.

His cane in hand, he shuffles along. With humor, he calls it his daily run. He gets to his bench and sits. It only takes minutes for the squirrels to arrive. They run up his leg and go to his pocket. They know what's there. He smiles. He talks to them softly, then reaches in for their treat. They all have names given to them over time. He gives them each a peanut, one by one, and they settle down to their snack.

Soon a mother and her child walk up. He is greeted with smiles and a hug. He pulls a candy from his other pocket for the girl. He visits with the mother, gives the girl a second candy, and they move along. His small friends ask for more peanuts. He happily complies.

This is his life now. Not a bad one. On the bad days, he sits on his porch and looks out into the neighborhood. His neighbors wave when they see him. Overall, he's a very happy man. He misses his wife still. It's been three years now. He knows he'll see her again. But not too soon he hopes. He wants to live to be a hundred.

So now he looks forward to sunny days, his trips to the park, and visits from family and old friends. His life is good. Old friends are growing fewer. He understands that very well. He is no longer depressed over that. They go to a better life. He just has his last goal of becoming a centennial.

I hope he reaches his goal. He's ninety-seven.

Story 47
"When Love Matures"

Life for each of us follows its own path. What's an acceptable way for one may not be the acceptable way for another. It's part of the beauty of life.

This man is deeply in love yet lives alone. Not a lonely person. But found a very compatible lover. Both enjoy their independence. They are both loyal to each other. And their time together is devoted to pleasing the focus of their love. Is this so strange? It's not sexual any longer. Based so much stronger on respect for the other. Let me say there can be happiness in a relationship like this. More than you might imagine.

Sure, I'm always hungry for more of her time. I'm up in years and so is she. So, the question is how different is love in the 70's than in your 20's. Well, the quality is very different. Your eyes don't wander. Your appreciation for her is your light. Something the younger men could learn.

Holding hands, dancing to our favorite song, staying off the phone and just talking to her is the pleasure. Smiles and laughs out loud a regular occurrence. I do tell her if she could run a chainsaw our relationship could move to the next level. I never think she takes me seriously.

So, this is my beautiful flower. I don't have enough time to explain her any better. Just take my word, I love her that much. Love in your senior years is so much more fulfilling. You young guys will just have to be patient and learn.

Story 48
"Ever Changing"

We all have our "likes and dislikes", but they constantly change.

I think it's just a human trait. What we're impressed with today may not be as welcomed tomorrow. Why? Are we ever changing? Not really. People marry and live the rest of their lives together. Friendship are kept for a lifetime. So once again, why?

Well, I think we are looking for that well of satisfied feelings. We're always willing to see what we've found. And sometimes it's just not treasure. But others! We feel good about our discoveries. We "trust" our instinct to explore this opportunity with your life. In spite of what you see nightly, the good is out there. Believe me when I say that. Explore this great world. Meet its people. Happiness surrounds you. Spend more time smiling. You won't regret it!!!

Story 49
"Do you enjoy being in Love"

Do you enjoy being in love? As with any beautiful flower, it requires loving care.

If your heart is attracted to the other half, then that relationship can never be neglected. Do you tell your love how important they are to you? Each and every day? If not, bring your focus in closer. The one you love never should become every day to you. Go on dates. As I've said before, they can be simple. But you must inject something grandiose every now and then.

When you know your spouse makes you the center of their universe, and shows that to others, your smile is larger. Your days are happier. The stress, much weaker. You know, together, your combined love will defeat your problems. Communicate. Never shield the other from your issue. You are a team. A strong one.

Both parties must realize their value to the other. Their children must see the love and respect. Time will run out one day. Don't be the one to look back and know you should have done more. Your floor is cluttered with opportunities missed. Be the example for others to be inspired to follow.

And know a love note tucked away in a spot where it is easily found makes the heart glow. Both parties benefit.

Do you enjoy being in love?

Story 50
"Memories – They Remain Raw Longer Than Wounds"

Titled by Kathy Morris

We are all raised differently. Each parent picks the values they choose to pass down.

Once I was old enough to work, I was put to work. 100% of all monies earned went to the family. I did mostly outside work, so my days off were rainy days. It was the rules laid down. The rules I had to follow without question. As I grew older my place was on the shrimp boat. My dad's help at no pay. I could keep fish. They had to be cleaned and the meat cut away with no bones. The prime cuts were kept for the family, and I was allowed to sell the rest and keep the money as my pay.

My grades had to be at an acceptable level. Church every Sunday. I was even volunteered to be an Alter boy, which meant walking to church for the 5am mass. But you know what? I had no issues with any of it. It was the way I was raised. So, because of my upbringing I always worked hard. The pride taken from a full days work is very gratifying. I'm exposed to young men today with "terms and conditions," they never get my work. And I pay a descent pay for the work accomplished. But I'm the one in charge. Not them.

So, at my age I do the work. It keeps me active. My friends who visit are more than happy to help. Maybe this arrangement will buy me an extra few year on this earth. I don't even know how to spell the word laze.

Story 51
"Time and its affects"

They watched him age. Slow but happening.

It finally came down to one parent. Against the odds it was the father. Sure, he's slowed down quite a bit. Overall, he's still in pretty good health. Aches and pains rule now. Bad elbow, trick knee, can't see quite as good. And we won't even discuss hair loss.

One day your flesh seems to just hang. No real tone to speak of. Age is taking its "old" shape. But how is your attitude? Are you still "you"? Your shape is different for sure. But are you still "you"? How do you feel? Age 75 or age 50. It's a privilege to last through so many years. Especially if your health isn't in that rough a shape.

So time marches on. More and more that favorite chair calls your name. Watching not necessarily doing is the new norm. But still time marches on.

Story 52
"If I died tonight"

If I passed this night, this is what I would humbly ask of the Lord.

Take care of my wife. Her love was unconditional. More than what I deserved. That was my job, but, well, you know.

Help her with my passing. It will be hard on her. We were so much in love.

Give her your shoulder. She needs one on occasion. She's very strong, you see. But every now and then, she needs my shoulder.

Make her smile. Her happiness is very important to me. Make her laugh out loud. Help her to always see the positive.

And most important, make her love again. She has so much love; it can't be wasted.

If you would please do this for me, I will go back to earth and save a million souls for you.

I promise you.

Story 53

"The Loving of Pets"

He got his pup when it could fit in his hand.

For whatever reason he felt he needed a dog companion. So, their life together began. The joy delivered to him was unexpected. His dog had the perfect personality. A rescue dog picked up from the local shelter. Nothing really special, but that statement ended there. He was a most loving dog. He wanted to be by his side every moment. They named him Duke, and Duke slept at his feet every night. He developed a genuine love for his dog.

When sick, Duke was by his side and never left. He would move in even closer and lay his head on his chest. Their bond was strong. And so, the years passed. His wife would dress him in outfits, Duke didn't mind, it was all just attention to him. Age was catching up on Duke, and it was then that he really became aware he would outlive his close friend. Time was moving so fast now. They went for long walks. An effort to keep Duke healthier. The walks became shorter as the months passed faster. Now his friend no longer wanted to leave the house. His face all white, his gate so stiff. As with all the ones you love, they age before your eyes. You know your days together are numbered. So, you try to do more.

Then one day Duke wouldn't get up. When you tried to move him, he showed pain. It was a Thursday. They went to the vet. On a Thursday he got the bad news. Duke would not live through the weekend. His life was ending. He cried all the way home. He gave the news to his wife. They cried together while petting their good friend. "Get our things together, we're going to Dukes favorite camping spot. He always loved to go there. That's where we'll bury him."

Duke died with his head on his owner's leg. He stroked his forehead till dawn. They left without their best friend.

The ones that matter most to you will not be around forever. Make time while they're still in your life. Those same tears will someday be yours.

Story 54
"Memories make experience"

There will come a time I won't remember many things. Age takes such a toll.

But what I will remember is a lot of my life. Many of my friends who passed with time. My family. My first love. My love today. I'll remember friends I went to school with. Ones who I served with. People I've helped and who helped me. I'll remember my time in the woods with Mother Nature more than my time in the city. So many food memories. It makes me smile even now.

I'll remember fishing trips. Hunting elk. Pretty girls. Rain storms and big winds. I've experienced so much in over seventy years. Shrimping will never leave my memories. Neither will my hard work. My first time to ever fly in a plane. That was special.

But what do I not want to remember? Different bouts with pain. Heartbreaks. Bad deeds by me. None of us are perfect. Fights both physical and emotional. Hatred. Why remember any of that? You know a list exists here also.

But maybe I'll be lucky and remember it all. It's all of such things that makes us who we are. Experiences. I should be so lucky.

Story 55
"Neutrality"

A small boy of about eight years is walking down a country road. He sees movement. He squints his eyes and finds a baby rabbit. He goes to it to see it's been hurt. Not really bad but hurt. He picks it up and brings it home. Over the next few days, he cares for the animal. The rabbit rebounds to good health, and the boy releases it back into the wild. What does this tell you, if anything?

Rabbits have been food for humans for centuries. Yet this small boy tends to the health and then releases it. A good deed. Is it that when you are still in your youth, you have more compassion? He didn't look at the hurt animal as a meal. He only wanted to help.

The small get along with everyone. They only want to be friends. To enjoy one another's company. There is no prejudice in their innocent lives yet. Their parents haven't started their training. The parent says, "I don't eat meat, and neither will you," or maybe, "I don't like certain people, and neither will you."

The fault lies with the older generations, not the younger. We as a culture need to look at how we raise our children. We don't impose our lifestyles on innocent children. What is good for our children and what is not? Such a slippery slope. As a male, if you want to dress and act as a woman, it's your choice. But do not impose your feelings on your child. It is their job to decide, when they feel they are ready, if ever. You must remain gender neutral. That is your responsibility as their parent and mentor. Allow that child to grow up and make their own decisions. Is that really such an impossible task?

Story 56

"Love Your Pet Equal to Their Love for You"

I hear all the time about the love and loyalty of a dog.

They'll lay on the grave of their best friend and grieve. They'll never hesitate to place their life in danger to save yours. Stories abound out there. No opponent too great. A small dog will attack a bear and die if necessary to give you the time to escape. They know no other way. You are the center of their world.

A parent will die for their child if called upon. Will not hesitate. That is the type of love your pet has for you. You are their family even if in some homes they're not allowed on the couch. They try to understand, but they obey.

Love your pets. You accepted the responsibility to raise them. To bring them into your home. Make them family. They deserve such a small act. A full commitment in return. They will die for you! How many others outside your family will do that? When they pass, we bury them. They're given a place of honor. When replaced, the new addition is always compared to the first loved pet. But in time your heart will be captured.

Pets come in so many different creatures. The one you pick is the one you have a love for. But a dog is by far the most loyal in my opinion. They are a big part of my everyday life. I'm surrounded by them even as I write. Do they ever just piss me off? Show me how such a bad judgment call on their part impacts my life? Sure. But like a child, they're forgiven. They are dogs you know.

Keep treats at hand. Make them more valuable than your phone. Give them their time. When they come to you for attention, give it to them. My dogs are a part of my family. They will sit and wait for tid-bits given to them from me at the table. They pretty much eat what I eat. But as snacks only. They have their food.

Once they placed themselves between me and a real threat. Our lives were in danger from a wild boar I walked up on. He was set to attack. But my dogs moved in. They were protecting me. I was able to escape. On that day they placed their lives on the line for me.

What do I owe them for that? My total loyalty in return. They have my love.

Story 57

"Children in the park"

This is my type of favorite story.

    The old man sat on his front porch. Leaning forward on his walking cain for a little extra support. A daily event for him. Soaking up life knowing his days are running out.

    He watches the people walk their dogs. They always wave and give him a smile. An occasional visit would make him smile even bigger. People just don't seem to do that any longer. The younger ones bicycling by. All dressed up in clothes that fit tight. I guess that helps the rider. Wouldn't really know. The bikes are so fancy now. Nothing like what he had in his youth.

    But his favorite is the mothers walking the very youngest. A flower in hand. A smile brighter than the sun itself. Not all that steady on their feet. Just loving the outdoors. Developers want to buy his home.

Build something new. But he won't sell. They don't know he left it to the city to place a children's park here. What they don't know they can't prepare for.

So each day he comes to his chair. Enjoying his day. Never been an indoor person. Recliners show him no interest. That old wooden chair is his friend. His porch, his living room. He has a heater for cold days. Only wind on a rainy day can force him inside. He has a large front window for those times.

He'll be missed one day. Not for a while of course. But he will have left a gift for the mothers and the young. His large trees will stay for the shade. Each will have a bench. A nice place to watch the children play. He smiles in his heart. Money is set aside for the play things. All for the very small. He's thought it all out. Took care of all the paperwork. And he firmly believes he will look down to watch the children play after he's gone. A continuation of his life. That would be good.

Billy is coming down the street. He always stops to say hi.

The park will be called "Billy's fun park". He may tell him one day. But today he'll just talk to his small friend. Talk and laugh. And sincere smiles.

Story 58
"After Life"

He finds himself walking, not knowing where he is.

A dog runs up. "Jake, is that you?" It can't be, but he knows it's his Jake.

Then he looks up and sees his uncle walking toward him. "Uncle James, I must be going crazy. You died six years ago."

His uncle says, "I've been selected to walk you in. You are with us now. There are so many wanting to see you again. You were loved by all."

He stops to allow all of this to sink in. "Am I dead too? Is this heaven?"

The uncle smiles. "Call it what you choose. But it is your afterlife."

"Mom?"

"Yes, she's waiting for you. Your sister you never met also. It's just easier to walk and talk a little first. Life after death doesn't stop. It changes. You were able to go to this wonderful place. Everyone here has a good soul. You will like it here."

"But what about my past life? Is it over?"

"Kind of. You can never go back; they will come to you. Not all. The ones with good souls you will see again."

"We're almost there. Do you understand things better now? Are you ready to meet everyone and be a part of this new life? Everything and everyone that ever mattered to you is here. Jake will be by your side forever now. Time doesn't exist here. When you walk through those gates, you are a part of this new life. So many are excited to see you. Let's not keep them waiting."

He's still a little unsure but very intrigued. "Let's go," he says. "I'm ready."

Story 59
"I See Beauty Everywhere"

It's said you must see ugly to find beauty. Probably so.

But beauty comes in many forms. Beauty to one may be ugly to another. So, is personal taste a factor also? Beauty may float around till it's pulled and an interpretation that you like is applied to it. Some things look so nice it's universal. A couple may find themselves in love yet look so different. Others may not see what you've found. Love, happiness, a special caring for this beautiful partner. The one you want to spend the rest of your years with.

Yes, our eyes speak to us. Approve this or disapprove of that. But our world continues. We see the beauty in nature. Flowers, birds, everyday life. A kind heart will always see the best in anything. Know that. Your eyes will open wider. The unseen becomes visible. A peace will flow within. You become a better person.

So, what is beauty? You tell me. It is mostly personal. The wonderful things you see are pulling you in. Asking for your approval. Today is a good day to totally give in. See the beauty in everything. You'll smile often.

Story 60

"Let's go fishing today"

It's her that admires him in his sleep. This man of honor.

He's so respectful of her. Opens doors. Pays compliments seemingly all day long. Loves to give flowers. And doesn't hesitate to help her so they have more free time together. He makes her feel special, and don't think she isn't. He knows how I like my coffee and likes to serve it in bed. He sleeps so peaceful.

He enlisted to defend our Nation when so many wouldn't. Willing to give his life so that others he never met could sleep in peace. He's special in his own right. It's sad so many no longer take pride the way it used to be. Things change for some I guess.

Today I'll make sure his day is a better day than yesterday. It's the least I can do for him. He works so hard. Always giving his best. Making sure my happiness is protected. We complement each other. Maybe I'll suggest we go fishing today. I know he'll like that. A casual day of tender words and ample smiles. Sounds good to me.

So, this morning I'll serve the coffee. Sit up close to his side. And I'll tell him about my thoughts on today. Yes, he'll like that. And we'll have another wonderful day together.

Story 61
"The neighbor's boy"

She had been at the hospital for days when suddenly doctors, nurses, people she had never seen burst into the room. She was pushed to the edge, losing his hand, and in a sudden state of panic, she saw him die.

She could not come to grips with the fact that in his last few minutes of life, she was asleep in that chair. She lost her son and blamed herself that she was not awake. Her life was changed forever. She became bitter. She only wore black now. She never smiled any longer. She wanted no one's company.

Time passed. Then one day she sat in a chair on her back porch, drinking coffee, and she heard a Hi. It was a small boy. She had seen the moving van from the window, but she just didn't care. How dare he speak to her; she went inside and slammed the door.

Days later, she was back with a glass of hot tea and heard the Hi again. With hate in her eyes, she looked to the fence to see no one. She scanned the yard to see him behind a tree. And again, she left in a huff. How dare him. She just wanted to be left alone. Now something was different though. She was not sure what. The next day, she looked through the screen of the door and saw no one. She moved to her porch. About time she could enjoy a cup of coffee in peace. After just minutes, she heard the Hi. She looked with anger but saw no one. Out of the corner of her eye, she caught a movement in a bush. It was him. She said with a firm voice, "I want to be left alone. Say nothing to me." But the boy had made a game of this.

The next time out, she looked closely at every section of the yard. She was by herself. She drank her coffee. As she got up to go back inside, she heard "Bye." She did not even look back. But she did something she hadn't done in years. A slight smile came to her lips. So a game had begun.

The next time, she went outside and adjusted her chair for a better view of the neighbor's yard. It was pretty much the same time every day she had her coffee. So she was sure he was there. She studied the yard. She turned to go back in, but just before she entered the house, she said, "The camo cloths don't help."

As she walked in, she heard "Bye!"

Then one day, she looked to see where he was before going outside. He was just standing at the fence. She turned and walked away. The next day was no different. Finally, she stepped on to the porch. She sat down and sipped her coffee. He stepped from behind the tree. "Hi. My name is Jimmy. What's yours?"

A tear comes. "My name is Doris. You're a very good hider. I had a son who was good also." A friendship that lasted the rest of her life began that day.

Story 62
"The Unexplained"

A nurse was standing looking at the newborn babies. Her heart was filled with love and sadness as she looked. Then she felt a hand take hers. She looks down at a small little girl. "Who are you?" she asked. Without hesitation she answers, "I'm your daughter." She smiles but her sadness deepens.

"I don't have a daughter. I've always wanted one. I can't have children."

"Well, I was sent to you to make sure you don't lose hope. You will be my mother one day."

The nurse looks at the babies once more. "Well, today we need to find your people." But when she looks down the child is gone. She can see down the hallway in both directions. There is no child.

"Did I just imagine this?" she thinks. "I'm tired. It was a long shift. I need rest." But she was glad about the message.

I do need to keep the hope alive. I was having a weak moment.

But with time and advances in medicine she became pregnant and gave birth to a beautiful little girl. Her life was complete for her and her husband.

Her child walked early. Spoke words sooner than most. Her first word being "mommy." At age four she asked her mother, "do you remember you and me talking? I was a little older but we talked." The mother dropped her glass and it shattered on the floor. "What did you just say?"

"We talked. I don't remember what we said, but I remember holding your hand."

In total shock she relives that morning.

There are people who care for our souls. When we need them the most, they come to us. We may never fully understand or grasp the moment. Guardian Angles exist. They know what to say and when it will mean the most. Both listen and believe. Don't question too much. Accept things that sometimes you can't explain. Believe there is more to this life than we realize.

Story 63

"What are you thankful for?"

He was young, but not so young.

He sat by himself in the school yard. A teacher noticed and walked to him. "Why do you sit alone, do you have a problem"? "No" responded the boy. "Thanksgiving will be here soon so I'm thinking of all the things I should be thankful for." Quite surprised the teacher asked "may I hear a few"? He looked up and began speaking.

"I'm thankful for me. I exist in a not so perfect world, but I exist. Life is precious. So I'm precious also. I live in a house and eat every day. So many do not. I have friends. Some my age and some much older. I'm very thankful for all of that. My health is good. I thank GOD for that. I've seen kids my age who can't walk. They will probably never walk without help. But you know what? They're precious also. I tell them that."

"I have good parents. Brothers and sisters. I love them all. I even have a dog named Sargent. He's a best friend. I'm very thankful for him. So my list is small right now. But it will grow. And you, what are you thankful for"?

"I'm thankful I met you this morning. My eyes are opened a little wider thanks to you. You belong on a stage to tell your story to everyone. You could change so much. Is there anything you want to change?"

"Yes, I think Thanksgiving should be everyday by everyone. We forget sometimes." "Yes unfortunately we do. I would like to meet your parents one day. I think they're very thankful for you."

Count your blessing every day. The world would be a better place for that!!!

Story 64
"Maturing"

There was a man. This man fell in love too easily. He was never satisfied. So, what was the cost of such a lifestyle?

Well first of all, his life was never stable. Always looking for the new and fresh. Any pretty girl who looked too long caught his eye. Because he could always find fault, he never stopped looking. The thrill seemed to always diminish. So, girls got hurt. Their confidence got shaken a little. But he moved on, and he never looked back.

As time went by, he grew. Slowly, very slowly, he began to understand himself. He convinced himself he wasn't out to conquer women just for the bragging rights—a lie he lived with for years. But he grew. Now how do you make the repairs? How do you change your life for the benefit of others? You may be envied by some men but dejected by most women. So, what do you do?

Friendships are a good start: being a good listener; making the time to help a woman in need; knowing where the line is and no longer crossing it; knowing that everyone has issues they may feel alone with. Listen and read between the lines. You can do for them and not steal the limelight. Go mostly unnoticed.

There is so much a man can do for a woman that doesn't require an invoice. Open a door. Help with a heavy load. Pay a compliment. It's an expression of respect. Her day was made nicer.

This is not a confession for myself. I think about things to write about. How can I put words out there that can make a positive impact? Words to make people think. Our world is very much in turmoil. We need to step outside the box. What can we do at any level to help society get along better? All of us can be victims. But is that your choice? Just be the best citizen you can be and know there are people out there who will come to your aid. Really know that!

Story 65

"Daddy's Love"
Titled by Debbie Champagne

Things I remember about my dad.

He worked hard all his life. Getting to go to town with him was a special privilege. He always had a few pennies for some candy. No seat belts back then. You could stick your head out the window and feel the wind in your face. As soon as you could handle the work, you were put to work.

He took us to church every Sunday. He was a provider. We had a big Sunday dinner. Company was usually there. Mostly family. Dominoes after dessert. A table set up in the living room.

Television was mostly a night thing. He maximized his time with family because he would leave on the shrimp boat and be gone for weeks. His next trip was always just around the corner. As a family we would go to the docks and wave him goodbye.

When he returned, we always went camping. Cat fishing on a river of choice. After all that time with water as far as you can see and a 65 ft. boat was all the room you had, the woods were very inviting. Our grades were very important, he only went to the eighth grade. Missing school wasn't an option. If you said sick, you'd better be sick.

In the later years having a cigarette and a beer in his chair was the reward for a life of hard work. He laughed a lot, I miss him. There are so many stories about making ice cream in the back yard. So many stories. The cigarettes finally took their toll. But his memories live on. So, every now and then I feel it necessary to tell you a few stories. So, you can meet my father. He was a good man.

Story 66
"My magic window"

I have this magic window, but maybe not what you think.

First I must say I'm in love with a precious lady. If she was a stone she would be made from a blend of gold, diamonds, rubies, and all other gems of value. While I, on the other hand, am a rock in a field. Run over a hundred times by the tractor and hit by the plow a thousand times. Beat up, scared but I hang in.

Then one day I was noticed. Not for my tattered appearance, but for me. This special lady wanted to slow dance outside on the grass. And this is my magic window. Our lives are so different. Yet in each other's arms, swaying to the soft sounds. Holding each other, her head on my chest. My arm around her waist. This is my window of time.

Our lives are so different. Out time together so limited. But this is our love for each other. Our short windows together. So I work at being noticed by her. Dancing in the grass when possible. Swaying to the music. Whispering words meant for just for the two of us.

With time the window closes. Separated once more. Waiting in anticipation for the next dance. I think this is a great way to love. Always looking forwards to the next dance. Looking forward to the feel of a head on your shoulder.

Marriage can be just as romantic. It starts out that way. Never stop dancing, holding hands. Whispering the soft words. Feeling the warmth.

Story 67
"The Thief"

I once married a thief. I probably should have known better!

It started out many years ago when she stole my heart. I had no way to stop it. It wasn't my choice. She controlled my heart from that day forward. What can you do? She then began removing my time. She wanted all of it. Such a demanding woman. We were always seen together. She held my hand as if it were a leash. I never tried to escape.

She demanded a home, children, the nicer things for living. I complied. She took my money, and she was so clever about it. Dinner, movies, weekend trips just the two of us. Called them dates! But the money left just the same. I had to buy makeup, nice clothes, pretty shoes; she always said it was for me. So clever. Why she even had sleepwear that almost wasn't there. We had five kids.

Then one day, she stole my happiness. She left this world for another place. I would give anything to have that clever thief back. I miss her. I still cry sometimes. Don't smile nearly as much. If I could just have her back for one day! So much needs to be said. I do talk to her. I look at the pictures. It's not the same.

Now I keep an eye open. I know someone else wants to take advantage of me. Somehow, I feel my love wants that. My happiness will show up after I've given up hope of ever seeing it again. But this time, I think it will be me who is the thief.

I once married a thief. I probably should have known better!

It started out many years ago when she stole my heart. I had no way to stop it. It wasn't my choice. She controlled my heart from that day forward. What can you do? She then began removing my time. She wanted all of it. Such a demanding woman. We were always seen together. She held my hand as if it were a leash. I never tried to escape.

She demanded a home, children, and the nicer things for living. I complied. She took my money, and she was so clever about it. Dinner, movies, weekend trips just the two of us. Called them dates! But the money left just the same. I had to buy makeup, nice clothes, pretty shoes; she always said it was for me. So clever. Why she even had sleepwear that almost wasn't there. We had five kids.

Then one day, she stole my happiness. She left this world for another place. I would give anything to have that clever thief back. I miss her. I still cry sometimes. Don't smile nearly as much. If I could just have her back for one day! So much needs to be said. I do talk to her. I look at the pictures. It's not the same.

Now I keep an eye open. I know someone else wants to take advantage of me. Somehow, I feel my love wants that. My happiness will show up after I've given up hope of ever seeing it again. But this time, I think it will be me who is the thief.

Story 68
"One More Time"

Titled by Corrie Cabral

If I could hold you in my lap just one more time. Our children are our joy as new parents. We show them off as the prize won at the carnival. There are bad nights and days. At our wit's end, they just won't stop crying. Nothing you can do. Those are the bad days. The rewards are when they snuggle close and sleep. You can kiss a forehead. Listen to the rhythmic breathing. Your world is so complete in those times. The peace of a loving family.

But they all grow up. Won't even fit in your lap any longer. Your time together gets less and less. They have their own small children to hold now. They'll visit and give you a turn at holding. You reflect on the past. Smile a little. You look at them and see them in diapers running across the floor. That was so long ago. Yet only yesterday. Now the hugs of a grandchild fills the need of closeness. Not wrong. But you look at your child and think "if only I could hold you in my lap just one more time."

Story 69
"The Classics"

The little boy, barely three years old, came to his dad with an earnest look on his face and asked him if he could teach him how to soar through the skies.

The father looked down and smiled. "Is this something you truly want? Because I can give you your wish. But it will take some time on your part. Each night we'll practice. Deal?"

So on the first night the father took the boy's hand and led him to his room. He gently tucked him in and sat in a chair beside his bed. He opened a book. "This book is called Moby Dick. Close your eyes and see what I read." And he read. Over four nights he read. The small child would dream about the story. His mind soured.

Next came Huckleberry Finn. Then Captain Hook. The boy looked forward to his stories every night. With eyes closed he lived each and every story. He and his father grew even closer. But the clock of time never stops. And with time the boy became a man. He was with his father when he passed. Visits his grave regularly. He loved him so much.

Of course, he married the one he loved. Together they had a beautiful daughter. The days slowly passed. But he finally hit her three's. That's when the father asked her if she wanted to meet some wonderful people?

So all tucked in and warm he pulls up his chair. Tonight, you'll meet a girl named Cinderella. After that a girl named Snow White and her very different friends. So close your eyes and let me introduce you two.

Read to your children while they're young. Their imagination is at its best. They'll love you so much for what you're doing. Those will be their best memories after you are gone.

Story 70
"You are always cared for"

A man stood in front of the large doors, wondering what to do next.

"Do you need help?" the voice asked. He turned to see a boy around age seven or eight standing behind him.

"The doors are locked, I think I should go."

"This is my Father's church. I have the key to the doors."

"Let's go in." He unlocked the doors and opened one for the man. With a smile, he said, "Come in."

"What do you need?"

Reluctantly, the man moved forward.

The boy said, "I'm my Father's helper. What do you want?"

The man entered and sat on a bench.

"I got some really bad news yesterday. It turns out I don't have long to live. I thought I should come here and say a prayer, but it's been so long I'm not sure I'm welcome anymore."

The boy looked at him a minute then took his hand. "I don't think the heavenly Father cares about such things. You are here now. Tell him what you want to say."

"I'm not sure where to start or what to say."

So, the boy said, "I'll help you with this."

They spent about two hours together. The man poured his heart out. A lot was said, and finally, he was ready to leave. He thanked the young boy for his help, got up, and moved to the door. Just as he reached it, it opened. He could easily tell it was the preacher. The preacher asked him, "Why are you here, and how did you get in?"

"Your son opened the doors and allowed me in. He is a fine and caring child. Thank you for having such a son."

The preacher looked at him, confused. "I have no son," he said. "I'm not even married."

The man turned to see that he was alone. His eyes teared. "Thank you for use of the church. I should go now."

He was not able to explain what had happened that day other than he was helped by an angel or the son of God himself. But for sure he no longer feared his fate.

Do you believe such stories?

Story 71

"He Wants Her for His Wife"

The morning was early. Coffee hot. Big plans today.

He's going to ask for her hand today. With so many years behind him, he's still nervous. The day has to be perfect. No details left unchecked. He's loved her for years, just couldn't find the door open for him. Now he knows he's caught her eye. She wants time with him. Her smile tells a story of love. His heart now soars when thinking of her. Yes, this day has to be perfect.

He has tickets to a romantic island. Two weeks of holding hands and words of love.

She once said she would love to spend a honeymoon there. He never forgot. Being in love holds on to your youth. Your desire to please her is bursting from your heart. You've waited for this day for years. Your smile is deeper. There's a bounce in your step, even at this age. Your future will be hers also. You love that.

Dinner reservations, flowers delivered to the table, champagne, a ring in his pocket. It will be perfect. She deserves nothing less.

We find our happiness in many forms. But happiness in love is the envy of all. May this evening be your best.

Story 72
"We Choose"

We choose the one we love. We're not forced into that decision. Convenience isn't a justification. We Choose!!!

So then what? Why that choice? Looks, stability, maturity. That list is endless. But we picked something. Your life is changed. Colors seem brighter. Our ability to sit quietly and smile comes more often. Our happiness is much closer. We can touch it.

If the one you picked is just as happy about your choice, you have entered a new life. You are no longer "one". You've entered into a partnership. Everything evolves around your feelings for the other. The bond just grows stronger. Now do you move it to the next level?

A lifelong promise. To be together under one roof. Each day spent together. Will all that much change? Not if the true love was planted and flourishing. It can only get better. You each watch out for the comfort of the other. That is what true love is all about.

So stay committed. Grow old in a deep love. Hold hands often. Kind words. Coffee in bed together. That's your best friend you're looking at. And sure the dog won't agree. He'll get over it.

Have a great day. And if you're alone, know your mate won't knock on your door probably. Get out and let the world know you're available. You are a jewel, never stop believing that!!!

Story 73
"Under Orders"

A small boy found a dog. He wanted to bring it home. His parents said no.

He later returned with a box and picked up the puppy. It was a male, and he named him Jake. It wasn't long before his parents noticed him leaving the house with food. So they confronted him. He had no choice but to confess. While upset with him, they allowed him to keep the dog. Their bond was already strong. They couldn't be separated. The boy truly loved the dog, and the dog loved him.

Jake had to adjust to his leaving for school. That wasn't easy. Then one day, he left for the military. He would be gone for a while. The boy got down on one knee and told Jake to protect his family till his return. Jake looked at the parents, then back to Bill. He understood. He was much older, but so were the parents. Then very early one morning, an intruder entered the house. It was a teenager from down the street. He had a knife. He had been drinking and wanted money. The old couple was his best choice. But he didn't plan on Jake.

They could hear the breaking of glass. And it was moving closer. Neither had their cell phones. They locked the door, and Jake never made a sound. The boy yelled, "Open the door, or I'll kick it down!" They just yelled for him to leave. With one strong kick, the door flew open. Jake's attack was instantaneous. He attacked with maximum aggression. The yells of the boy only lasted for a minute. Jake killed him.

So now the police were involved. Jake was removed from the house. And because he killed, he had to be put down. Bill was out of the country. Things didn't look promising for Jake. He was to be put down the next day, when out of the blue, a government lawyer showed up. He gave papers stopping the execution. And with time, Jake was in fact returned. He was left to protect the parents. He had been under orders. This placed him in a separate position.

Our dogs are so loyal they will die for their owners. They will kill if necessary. They will protect! Cherish your pet. They are your best friends.

Story 74
"Keep The Fire Burning"

They were drifting apart, and he hadn't noticed yet. The comfort you seek in a relationship can be both a good or bad thing. Relationships must stay interesting to both parties. The balance must satisfy both. To say you don't dance and not take her dancing could be a fatal crack in the glue of the relationship. You may have met her at a dance. Taken her dancing while dating. But with time you stop. And no matter how much she enjoyed it, it happens no longer. And when you tell her no, the disappointment in that answer is directed to the crack.

So how or what do you do to compensate to keep the balance? An occasional weekend romantic trip to another city. How do you show her value to you? A roof over her head isn't the answer. She already had that. What do you add to her life and her to yours? To now say we're saving for our senior years is not a legitimate reason. You can do both. Children added to the equation, still no. Never stop dating. Keep the fire alive. Keep it warm and glowing. The image you strive to project should be for one another. The others don't matter.

Don't separate roles. She cooks and you mow the yard. Do things together. Give her the lightest work but do the work together. Show her the value you are to her. And she will do the same. Love isn't so complicated. Real good communication is. Just telling the other you're having a bad day and don't really know why doesn't have to be an emotional lashing out. A soft request to be held for a while will suffice. Love is really a simple thing. Keep it to the forefront and don't drift.

Story 75

"A Stranger today, a Mother forever"

She grew up in an orphanage. A life not always the best.

At 18 she did her exit. Never looking back. She wanted a new life, anything but what she had. This is her story.

She went to a church for help. Not totally giving up on the good in people. Was given a place to sleep till other arrangements could be made. She met couples who wanted to help her. But the one she noticed never asked if she could help. So, she approached. "Why don't you want to help me"? The lady looked down at her and spoke.

"I'm well advanced in years. I don't think you would be happy staying with me." This time it was the girl who looked. "No one knows me better than myself. And just looking at you I could see you could use my companionship. And I could use yours. Together we will overcome the odds. Give me a try." And so it began.

Years passed. Plenty bumps in the road for both in adjusting. But a love for each other grew. Respect. Something the girl was not familiar with. She learned. The day finally came where she was at the bedside holding her hand. This lady's time on this world was drawing to a close. The girls began to speak.

"You are my mother. The only mother I have ever known. I tried to be a good daughter to you. I hope I did well. You showed me I could love again. You took time to teach. Lessons I needed. You shared your wisdom. Wisdom that will stay after you are no longer here to share more. When I go I'll be by your side once more." She smiles.

So on this day she stands next to a grave. Fresh flowers in hand. Tears flowing. "I miss you mom". "I want to follow in your footsteps. I have an appointment at the orphanage today. They have someone they want me to meet. I'll seek out the child in need. Wish me luck."

Not everyone gets the family environment they need. They're gathered up and placed in the care of the state. This care should be the best care there is if a family isn't there. The children left out there alone. The children without parents need our care. Make sure the money is there for them.

Story 76
"Separation"

There were two lovers not allowed to see each other. The quarantine didn't allow physical touch. Each day, they would talk. Speak of the small details of the day. This went on for a year. One day, the girl received a card. The boy tried to speak his heart. He started out, "You must know my love for you. I also know how much you enjoy our talks. I do my best to keep them positive and upbeat. I worry this separation will take a toll on our love. Over the months, I've memorized your every feature. I close my eyes and see your smile. The shine of your green eyes. I hear your soft voice. You are my everything. This will be over one day, and I'll be at your door. That I promise you."

She smiled. She could hear him speak those words of love. She pulled a sheet of paper and began to write. "My love for you is limitless. It has no boundaries. You are the other half of my soul. Time has no meaning when it comes to our love. We speak soft words every day. You make me smile. You rejuvenate our love daily. Yes, this will end. And when you come over, I want to marry you. We won't be separated from each other ever again. You will be the father of my children. My husband. We will look back on this and see it made us stronger. So, feel strong about our love. And call me every day until we kiss again. I love you!"

Story 77
"When We Move On"

He lies in a bed. Nurses move around. He fully knows his time has run out. This is his last hour of breath. He remembers as a small boy he would climb the neighbor's tree for apples. So fresh, so sweet. He enjoyed his visits with him. They were friends. Going to school. Remembering his first day. He was brave yet scared. He liked school. Met a girl. Only had other boys as friends. She was different. His first love he's pretty sure. Took his first job as a teenager. Sacked groceries. Wasn't hard and he even got tips. Finally got his license to drive. How that changed his life! So many doors opened. Things were moving fast. Finished school and joined the military. Fought in a war. Realized the horrors of death. Never talked about it. Got to travel a little but ended up back home.

His eyes were closed but his ears open. Heard the nurse say he doesn't have much time left. His breathing is so shallow. He can feel himself drifting away. But he wants to remember his life. Not yet! He never married, maybe that's why he will die alone with strangers. Wishing someone would hold his hand one last time. One last touch. Is that asking so much?

He retired after 30 years of work. Then he was alone. Fed the birds at the park. He did miss the company of his coworkers. Slowly his body began to die. Small things at first. Soon he couldn't make it to the park any longer. He really didn't have a life now. He just sat each day while the caretakers handled his needs. Not much of a life at all.

Now here he lies. Waiting for the end to come. That's when he feels the touch. Someone has taken his hand. There stands his dad. "Come on son. Your work is done here." His dad helps him sit up. He could see all the nurses moving so quickly. But that didn't seem to matter now. He was with his dad.

They left together. To a place so different. So peaceful. He saw others standing and calling his name. He smiles and joins them.

Death will visit us all. It's just a matter of time. Not something to fear. Just the next stage of our lives. Something new to understand. The body may be laid to rest, but our essence will continue. There's more to us that just this short time on earth. Take comfort in that.

Story 78

"We just love dogs, you can't help it"

A man and wife were together many years and very much in love. But she passed first.

His heart was broken. His house no longer the same loving place. Sadness consumed him. Then one day his daughter came into the house with a puppy. A light brown lab. Said to him he needed a friend.

Dad wasn't all that thrilled. This dog could never replace his Linda. But the daughter left without it. So what to do? He had all his shots. She left food and his own bowl. He looked down at the pup. His tail wagging, wanting to be picked up. He shook his head and tried to walk away. The pup wouldn't have none of that. He was right on his heels.

Dad sat in his recliner and watched the dog struggle to join him. He had no choice and picked him up. "Sam. I'll call you Sam." A friendship began that day that took him by surprise. They never owned a dog before. It was just him and the wife. His world had changed. Now he had a friend to share his grief with. The most loyal friend he ever knew, other than his Linda.

They did everything together. Trips to town. Walks in the cool evenings. They were now never separated. And this went on for years. But age was taking its toll on both.

"Sam, I think I'll leave this world before you." A tear swells. He holds him tight. He tries to speak but can't. He kisses his forehead and allows him to lick his face. He looks at the dog and tells him he will be taken care of. He'll live with his daughter. My ashes will be there with you. And after you pass, our ashes will be buried with my Linda. You'll like her.

The attachment we all make with our pets is very personal and extremely deep. Our responsibility is their care. And theirs is total devotion to you. Care for them with love. You are their reason for being on this earth.

Story 79
"Repairing a loss"

There was a small family. Husband, wife, and twelve-year-old boy.

The mother got sick first. She didn't last long. This virus was a killer. So the son asked his father, "Dad, if you get sick, what happens to me?"

The father looked down at him and said, "Don't worry. I won't get sick."

"I have no aunts or uncles. What will happen to me?"

In less than a month, he was gone. Now the boy was alone. He had lost both of his parents and now lived as a ward of the state. His life had been turned upside down. He withdrew. He became an unwanted child of the orphanage.

Then one day, a couple walked in. They had read the bios on the children. They searched him out. They spoke his name, but he didn't acknowledge their presence. The mother pulled up a chair and sat behind him. She began to talk. She talked of the son she had lost. She shared the gaping hole in her heart. The number of times she cried herself to sleep. Finally, she said she had to leave but would return tomorrow. And they would talk more. Or at least she would.

And so it went. For many days, I might add. One day, he turned his chair around and faced her. He spoke for the first time. Inside, it broke her heart. But she knew she had to be strong for him. So they talked. This time, the father sat with them. They were there for more than an hour, with the conversation going back and forth. But the time came to leave.

"Will I see you tomorrow?"

Her eyes filled with tears. "When you're ready, you will leave with us and never return."

"You'll take me to visit my parents' grave? I never got to tell them goodbye really."

"I'll take you every day if that is what you want. You will never replace our son, and we will never replace your parents. My promise to you is we will love each other."

He looked down at his feet. And in a very soft voice, he said, "I think I'm ready. And I want to call you Mom and Dad. Is that OK?"

He grew up to be a fine man. And with time, he laid them to rest. They taught him love. He learned compassion. He married with time. Then one day, he and his wife stood at a door. They held hands. Looked into each other's eyes and took a deep breath. And armed with only a sheet of paper, they entered the orphanage.

Story 80
"A Prayer to His Father"

He was raised by a single father. It didn't seem all that different. He never knew his mom.

His father worked in both roles. His son was his life. The only connection to the one person he thought he would grow old with. But that wasn't to be. There was a woman who wanted to be close to him, be a mother to his son. He kept his distance. Somewhat withdrawn. Opening his life and sharing his love with another was a betrayal to his wife. He just couldn't come to terms with that. So, he lived the role of being both parents. It seemed right.

His son graduated and chose the life of a soldier. So proud his father was. Within only a few years he found himself on the battlefield fighting for his life. A battle he lost. His face pressed to the dirt, he prayed.

"Take me into your protective care. Dad, I really need you right now. I need your strong arms around me. Protecting me as you have done all my life. I'll never walk away from this. I'm sorry. But now I'll watch over you. To lose both your wife and son could make you bitter with life. I'll be your strength. Always! I'll miss you."

The day of the funeral his father stood at the grave. His heart was broken. Everyone had left but him. He feels a hand take his. He looks to see the one who has always loved him. Always trying to get close to him. Maybe now was the time. His heart was bleeding. It was he who needed to be held. She pulls at his arm. Let's go home. I don't want you alone tonight. Allow me to cook you a meal. You don't have to talk if you choose not to. I'm there for you.

As they walk away, the son watches and smiles. His dad will be fine. Love will come back into his heart. He walks slowly behind them. "Like I said, it's my turn to watch over you. Both of you."

Story 81

"Paths cross and cross again"

The paths of people cross. Small introductions, a smile or a slight bow of the head. Usually, eye contact is made and that is the beginning of a much larger story for a gifted few.

Those crossings can no longer uncross. A connection unbreakable. So you see each other again. Soon you are a couple. Best friends. Lovers. But marriage doesn't seem to happen. And for whatever reason you part ways. The bond stays unchanged. That path will never uncross.

With time a phone call may happen. A chance meeting in a store. Your hearts reach out. Memories race to return. Smiles are shared. Maybe even a longing for days past. Why? The love never died. Tempers cooled down. The reality that you still love each other shows in the eyes. Now what goes through both heads? A smile and a "nice to see you". Or a rekindled hug maybe a little too long?

So many years have passed. Extra pounds, wrinkles. But the younger self never left. The spark can still shine bright. Holding hands and a walk barefoot in the sand is still very romantic to both.

Some loves require more time than others to accept the true path. To know they were meant for each other. Something that nothing can change. Maturity was the missing ingredient found now. And this second chance at love, well you each know the other so well now. Why wouldn't it be the final chapter?

Story 82
"You make your life"

Are you living or dying? Once you hit your peak of life, it's the beginning of a downhill ride. You don't know you've entered that phase. Each day is pretty much as the day before. But time will awaken you. At age ten, you have no idea you will die in a fatal accident at age twenty. You were on the downhill ride and oblivious to that. Only if you could have known. So many out there can accept their fate, but a heads-up could have changed so much.

Your life would change. You would either become the person you were inspired to be, a much more focused person, or you might go into a deep depression. Or a blend of both. But your life would change.

But age will awaken you. I'm seventy years old. I hear every day of the people who don't make it this far. Do I have seventy more years? Of course not. Reality is a comfort. I don't want to live forever. I just want to live my life and leave a positive footprint when I go.

I can be thankful for my life or criticize it. The choice is mine. I can help ones less fortunate or, with my bitterness, turn my back on them. You make your life. You are the driver. You are not driven. Know that. No matter how heavy the load, you can get it done. In the race of life, many can finish first. Look at your footprints. Are you proud of them, or is an adjustment needed? Believe in yourself. Others do. When you're drowning in the swamp, it's not the alligators you're worried about. Just survival. Clear that. Then see where you're at.

We all have much to be thankful about. Look deeper into that. Smile more. Laugh more. Look around and smell the flowers. They are everywhere.

Story 83

"Morning Coffee"

The morning coffee taste a little better this morning. Sun hasn't come up yet. The air is crisp. He takes a sip. He wants his coffee as hot as he can take it. So, the sips are small.

Rain has started to fall. Won't be all that wet today. That's good. The chores never end. The wood heater feels great. I worked all my adult years just to live in the past. A little strange in my book. When you live way off the grid your life is different. Electricity is a precious commodity. You don't waste that. Everything you do you check what the power requirements are. Recycling a must. Maximum use of everything required. Using objects in ways not intended an everyday occurrence. Trips out at a minimum.

Just me and my dogs to entertain each other. And believe me dogs can be funny. Yesterday I drove up on a baby pig. He somehow got separated from the group. He'll be fine. They'll come for him after I'm gone. But a nice encounter just the same. Every day brings in their surprises. No two are alike. One of the values of not living in a neighborhood. No people, roads, or sidewalks. Kids don't ride their bikes past. The night sky full of stars. Wouldn't trade this for anything.

Looks like it's time for a second cup. Yes, the coffee tastes a little better this morning. The rain still falling. Peace and harmony rule out here. The morning light will show soon. Another great day ahead!

Story 84
"You make your life"

As a people we are all unique. Different taste, different likes. So how do you judge people you see?

I have no tattoos. Yet I see all the time both men and women covered from head to toe with them. Do I judge that as excessive? Do I pre-judge their character? I've never spoken one word to them yet I'm forming an opinion. Over the years I've learned there is no honor in that. They are who they are. If I must judge, then I must introduce myself to them. Spend a little time talking. And the goal is to judge myself. Can I just be friendly to a stranger so different from me? And really it might just be in the exterior appearance. We could be much more alike than I realize.

So with all the unrest today I think I need to acquire a better sense of understanding. A better tolerance of people not like me. I'm nothing really special. But some of the others I might try to judge could be.

Yesterday I helped a young man in need. I did a little extra. Instead of smiling and walking away, he told me his name and shook my hand. Said what I did would buy gas to get him and his wife to Houston or very close.

You never know when a little help will do the most good. Will help someone in real need. And believe me, the tattoos don't matter. It's the individual.

Story 85

"Call me Teacher"

When you look into the mirror, what do you see? I see age. Experience. I see the wrinkles earned in life. The skin thin now, the body tattered. I see a teacher. A teacher for the young. I see my children, my brothers and sisters. I see my father. I know so much yet so little. The eyes of the very young trust me. They feel secure. My hands are still strong, but a baby will sleep on my soft shoulders. I tell them stories of my youth. They hang on every word. I watch them grow. One day, the firstborn finds love and starts a family of their own. They show their love, their respect. My place in their hearts is without question. Time marches on.

    Soon, I don't move around as much. They proudly show me their children. I get the credit for starting it all. I do my best to share as much as possible. I'm still a teacher. I relish my role. I nap way too easily. I dress a little warmer. I don't talk as much. I eat smaller portions. I look so different. I won't own a dog any longer. It's too hard on me when I outlive them. And then one day, it's my turn to begin to pass myself.

I'm propped up with soft pillows. A child holds my hand. My grip is so fragile now. I know I must go, my stay is over. I fall asleep for my last time. Tears are shed. My son steps up and tells the small ones not to worry. He will fill my shoes. He says, "Call me teacher."

Story 86
"Never Refuse to Help Someone in Need"

She wasn't your typical woman. She had money. A lot of money.

Her first husband died of a heart attack. He was somewhat over insured, so her check was big. With time she married again. After a couple of years, it was found out he had contracted cancer from his job. So, when he died her settlement was huge. But she was a woman single with a large bank account. She worked with an investor who had her money making more money.

All she was ever after, was a loving husband. To hold hands with and speak words of love. Was that so much to want? Now because of her wealth she didn't trust the men who wanted to be close to her. Did they want her love or her money? Then she met Dan. Her car had a tire go flat on a busy road. She pulled over and called for a tow. It would be a while. Dan pulled up behind her.

"You don't need to be stranded here, let me change your tire." She saw the heavy traffic and reluctantly agreed. But she took a phone shot of his driver's license for safety. He worked and changed out the tire. She wanted to pay him, but he refused. "A man will always help a lady in need. Have a good day and get that tire fixed as soon as possible." He left.

She pulls up his pic on her phone. All his information was there. Over the next couple of days, she kept thinking of him. She hires an investigator to gather information about him. He was her age, single, nice looking, no criminal record at all, and led a modest life. So, what now? Does she do something? She made contact. She explained he impressed her, and she wanted to get to know him better if he had an interest also.

Fate will always intervene in our lives. Sometimes an answer, sometimes an issue. But with or without our consent, it touches our lives. Once she knew he was in love with her, she told her story. She found love. And him, well he was in shock. His love for her was his core attraction.

Fate is more a friend than a mistake. Keep an eye open for the meeting.

Story 87
"The feelings of Love"

I get up in the night for a bathroom break. I'm quite so not to wake her.

When I return, I look down to watch you sleeping. So peaceful, getting your rest for a busy day tomorrow. You asked me to grill you up a ribeye. I picked out two nice ones. I'll grill to perfection. Bake potatoes to go along.

We'll spend the day talking. Maybe sip on a drink. I really enjoy our time together. She constantly makes me smile. I picked up fresh spring flowers for her. Lots of color, plenty of fragrance. She lights up every time she walks into the kitchen.

But for now she rest. Coffee is all set up for in the morning. I think she enjoys her coffee as much as I. A slow start to the day. Not really caring what gets done. It's the time together that adds the value to the day. She'll insist on a dance or two today. I enjoy that myself.

Yes we're up in years. The romance is as strong as in our youth. She is my better half. So back to sleep I go. A great day planned tomorrow. I want to impress her with those steaks. She hasn't seen them yet. I think wine with the meal. A good choice.

I'll move a little closer. I get to sleep faster that way.

Story 88
"The Song of a Bird"

A man was sitting on his balcony feeling very down.

He was the kid bullied in school. Although he was very smart, that is what kept him from other people. He just couldn't mix in. He went on to college, and not much changed. He wasn't being pushed around but was totally ignored.

He graduated with honors and got a good job. Yet still, he couldn't make friends. He did not like his life. Day after day, he came home and sat on his balcony, upset with his life. He lived on the ninth floor. He knew he could end his misery if he just jumped. But he lacked the courage for that. So day after day, he looked down and wished he were a stronger man.

Then one day a bird landed on the rail. It was a beautiful bird. It would sing. He was totally captivated by this strange event. The dark areas of his mind were being given light. He came to understand that the bird was allowed outside for him to experience freedom. This went on for days. Very slowly, he began to smile more.

He did his work with a new vigor. He was quickly noticed. A bounce came to his step. Each day, he looked forward to hearing the bird sing. It was the most beautiful sound he had ever heard. Then one day at the water cooler, he was approached by a fellow coworker. She was a loner too. She said she noticed the change in him. She liked it. Then she asked if he wanted to hear a bird sing. He was taken back. What was this? "A bird?" he asked.

"Yes, it showed up around a month ago. My spirits were not good. Then it sang. My world changed. And I want to share it with you, if you agree."

Of course, the bird never returned. They enjoyed tea and conversation. Never had a girl wanted to visit with him—never. They became good friends and talked about their birds on many occasions, never really understanding what happened. And in time, they married. And they lived very happy lives together.

Our guardian angels watch over us. They fix our problems. They care for our happiness.

Story 89
"A Father and His Daughter"

She was a daddy's girl from birth. For whatever reason, she wanted her dad.

She would sit in his lap, have him read to her. Slept many hours on his chest. The relationship was beautiful. As she grew older, she still demanded his time. Frequent calls and visits. Happily married but her dad was still her number 1. Calls in the early morning. Coffee when it could be. Always checking in. Wanting to know his movements. Not smothering, caring.

They lived not far from each other with her always offering her mother and father any help needed. By every measure a really great daughter.

What's your relationship with your living father? How often do you talk? How often do you go to see him? He's always there when needed. Someone you have depended on all your life. Too many parents aren't missed till it's too late. When you can no longer sit and visit. You want that time so bad, yet while you had it you were busy. Or so you thought.

Look at the time spent with them this past year. Do a better job this coming year. You are both aging. But time is on your side. One day a memory is all you will be able to hug. And a memory doesn't hug back.

Story 90

"The Picture Box"

I was a four-year-old once. A very long time ago.

    I don't remember much. Almost nothing. But every now and then I see the pictures. My father and his. My mother and hers. So long ago. In many of them I'm still in diapers. Cloth ones. So different from today. All those pictures. All of my ages growing up.

    I have many of my first days of school. Sometimes just me smiling. Sometimes holding a sign. Pictures of the first of many things. Me missing a tooth. A first haircut. Sometimes all dressed up. Others I'm covered in mud. We have pictures of family members. Aunts, cousins, uncles, brothers and sisters when everyone was young.

    The pets with me, and long-gone ones. I guess we've always had pets. Us on trips. Everyone smiling. I love going through the picture box. Now it's so different. All of them on a chip. It requires a screen of some kind to be looked at. I guess that's alright. But still enjoy the old way better. Soon no one will even know about rolls of film to be developed. It's almost there now.

Sit down with your children and look at the past together. Set time aside for that every now and then. It's the only way for them to know family passed. A quick second of time captured for the future. Take lots of pictures for your children. They'll want to show them after your gone.

Story 91
"I wanted you to know"

It's early in the morning, and they sit holding hands outside, watching the sun rise. Drinking coffee.

The wife says, "It will be sixty-two years tomorrow we've been married. Sixty-two wonderful years. You have been a very caring husband. You have shown me love greater than I deserved."

"Why are you saying these things with such deep eyes?" asks the husband.

"Last night, I dreamed it will be me who leaves first. You are in such better health than me."

"Well, I wouldn't last long without you; of that, I'm sure."

"Only God himself knows that."

"You'll be around for a while." He gives her hand a squeeze, leans over, and gives her a kiss. "Let's stop this talk. It makes me sad."

"Sure, I just wanted to be certain you know how much I love you. How good a husband you've been. Let's watch this beautiful sunrise and let me rest my head on your shoulder."

She fades away. She said what she had to say to him and left. That was two years ago. Nothing has been the same except the sunrises. He sits alone now. The children come by more often, and that helps. He remembers the memories as tears roll down his cheeks. He finds the strength to be brave for her. He wouldn't want to disappoint.

Story 92

"Make Time for Your Child"

His son was hit by a car in front of the house. He was lost that day. They waited days before boxing up his room. A day that broke his heart.

The things are placed in boxes with loving care. The father comes across his backpack for school. He pulls the papers. And one stands out. It's titled, "what makes you happiest at home?" He sits and reads.

"I like it when dad talks to me and not the phone. When he doesn't tell me to leave the room. I really like that. Also, when dad holds me and not the dog. He really loves that dog. I wish I was the dog. I wish he had more days off from work. I get to see him more. I sit closer and watch him. He's a great dad! Maybe one day he'll take me to catch a fish. Billy's dad takes him. He says it's really fun. I don't want him to bring his phone.

Just a couple of hours of just us would be fun. I know it's not home but that would really make me the happiest."

All the father could do was cry.

Now he stands at the foot of a grave. He visits often. Trying to give his son all the personal time he needed in life. The pain is still very deep. If only he could have just one more chance.

That chance is gone. Never to be held again. Our priorities need to be examined constantly. They get out of balance and adjustments are necessary. A phone should never compete for time with your family. And this includes both parents. Nothing in your house deserves more quality time than your children. Place them in your lap more than the dog. A strange request, but a reality.

Story 93
"Habits of Dogs"

It takes a dog lover to enjoy this story.

A person gets a dog and in the process, they pick up a very close friend. The dedication of a dog is by far greater than a humans. But there are a few "flaws" you have to deal with.

One of my big ones is this. I have hundreds of friends. I don't talk to all of them on any regular basis, but not even one of them, except my dog, will take a leak on the bathroom floor within steps of the toilet. For some reason they can't seem to make the connection.

I have a set of shoes I wear daily. One of them the top has been badly chewed up. I can still wear them around the house here, but they look pretty bad. I hadn't owned them two weeks before the dog found them and I wasn't looking. I'm trying to get some of my hundred dollars back. Name even one of your human friends who will chew up one of your shoes!!!

Drinking water. What a mess they can make. No matter what you do they can figure out how to get water on your floor. I bought a watering dish that was supposed to prevent that. They dumped it over. People you invite over have never made such a mess.

You open a door to walk out and a dog wet and covered in mud runs in. And I can go on and on. But I want you to know I love those dogs. I would place myself in great danger for them. They would die for me. And that's pretty impressive.

Yes they will be forgiven. I will overlook many of their shortcomings. And they do learn some boundaries. Never will be perfect. But could I ever say that about me? I do know this, they will always be best friends to me. And I will care for their needs.

That's what best friends do!!!

Story 94
"You Never Die"

I see my eyes in the child of my child. It's said we never really die. Is that so? Maybe I have a better understanding of those words now. I see a part of me in my grandchild. It's there, no doubt. Most of us can't go back even four generations, much less five to six. But which distant family member walks with me? Someone I never met is a piece of me. Or am I a part of them?

Family members will say, "Don't you see Grandma in little Susan?" And the answer is I've always said that. So you live on in the eyes and hearts of the offspring. Your presence never leaves. Your children should embrace that. If you were loved and respected, they continue to see you. They feel you watching over them. A parent can never stop caring for their family. Your protection by the past should be listened to. It's described as a feeling. Your good judgment says, "Don't do this." But it could be a past loved one touching you, protecting you from harm.

You may live forever. There are things in this universe not fully understood. You pass in one reality only to take your place in another. I would like to think that's so. I would have the chance to watch my family flourish.

Story 95

"Compassion Can Come from Anywhere"

He was a kid on the streets. About eleven, he wasn't sure. His mother was heavy into drugs. Did tricks for the money and for more. He seldom went home. The air was just too bad there. Sometimes he would pass her on the street and wasn't even recognized. He did small jobs for change for food. His life wasn't easy.

One day a lady approached him and asked about his parents. His answer was his dad worked overseas and his mother was a teacher. She looked on with suspicion.

"Well, I need help here at my shop, are you interested in a job? Only a few hours a day and it includes lunch. What do you say?"

He couldn't believe his luck. "When can I start?"

"First, we need to clean you up. You'll be near my customers. And maybe a few fresh clothes wouldn't hurt."

So, he took his first step on his new path of a normal life. A life that made him a man. "There's a room in the back if you ever need to stay over. You can fix it up to your liking, I don't use it." She unofficially adopted him. He never saw his real mother again. His life had done a 180. His education was next.

He worked a half day and was homeschooled the other half. He was bright. Eager to impress the one who changed his life. His love was the love of a son. A son who adored his mother. She taught him all about the business. And when she had business elsewhere, he ran the store. This went on for a few years. He even met a girl he liked and started dating her.

Then one day his "mother" called him in. "Today we close early, and I need to have a conversation with you. Let's walk."

She let him know she had a cancer. And this one was going to take her. She had only a few months. He was devastated. "No, you can't leave me, I need you. I've always needed you. Please don't leave me!" He cried himself to sleep numerous times after that.

"I'm sorry, but I will be leaving. That I can't stop. I've left the shop to you. All I own is yours now. I've paid for a plot to be buried in. I purchased a second one for you by my side if you want it. We never know what the future brings. I love you, son. You have brought so many hours of pride into my life. That dirty little boy from the streets. Thank you for all the good you've done for me."

And she passed. He looks back on different moments of his life with her. Memories he will never lose. He sees the love she shared to a stranger. Yes, she was his mother. He will love her forever I might add, that was a black owned business. He wasn't black. Her loving care was not defined by race. And his love for her wasn't either.

Something we all can learn.

Story 96
"I'm 27,375 Sunsets Old"

The word "old". One of those tricky ones.

Is age the qualifier for you to be called old? And if so, when is that exact moment? At what point is that transition completed? I can say there are people younger than me who are much older. And I'm not speaking of maturity or wisdom. People can look at me and say "time has been your friend". While the young can say "you look old to me".

I look around and see so much. Mostly I can smile. My sense of humor is still strong. I see ones older than I going full speed ahead. Others moving so slow, you're not sure they're moving. The active and the inactive. Do you know way too many doctors now? Is your pill box the large size? As you age you seem to need a pill for all of your activities. A pill to sleep. A pill to wake up. A pill to get lovey-dovey. Are the number of pills the indicator of "old"? Or is it attitude?

If you feel young, are you? And just as easily said, if you feel old, are you? Yes a tricky word for sure. Science and medicine have joined forces in the battle of the aging. And doing pretty good I think. Some people have that little dimple on their chin. But know that in some cases it's their navel. Their skin has been pulled so tight. But if they're happy, well I'm happy for them. We try to keep a firm grasp on our age. Not allow it to move too fast. It can't be stopped. We don't need to allow it to define us either.

So I listen to my music from days gone past. Tell stories of life before the internet. Have no tattoos or piercings. Dress like I have no money. I smile a lot. Children seem drawn to me. I have that "grandpa" look now. The doctor says I can still chase women, I'm just not allowed to catch one!

OLD, three small letters that can mean such different things. I'm old and have no problem saying that. I'm more active than so many others my age. We are all given an allotment of time here. Be sure not to pick up your "old" label too early. Smile a lot. Never really grow up. Go to your grave like a teenager sliding into home plate. Keep life fun!!!

Story 97
"I Hold His Hand"

I sit in a chair by his bed, holding his hand. He's sleeping. Resting for his last time. His sun will set early today. I see him and remember.

I wasn't very big then. He wanted to teach me to swim. His strong arms held me safe in the water. I did learn. Another time, he took us camping. He could carry so much firewood. Those times make me smile even now. I see him sleeping. I should have made more time for him. I kept telling myself I was so busy. Soon he will no longer be with us. Foolish is what I was. Thought he would be here forever. No one is.

I could turn to him for anything. He was always there for me. Here I sit holding his hand. I want to say so many things. But those chances are gone. There will be so much sadness in the days to come. Just one more day of talking. Is that so much to ask?

We used to make ice cream in the backyard. I would get him his beer. He helped me catch my first fish. He was so proud. He helped me learn to drive. I came to him one day and told him I was in love. He said, "Treat her nice and with respect." Mom said he was a good husband. I lost her two years ago. I should have come by more often. I know that now.

So here I sit. Looking down on a man I love so much. I have a son with his name. They're best of friends. He'll take it hard. I'll be there for him. I'll be his strength now. I see so much clearer. A tear drops to his hand. He slowly slips away. I'm alone now. I cry.

Story 98

"Into The Wild"

Titled by Cynthia Reed Gillette

My yard is so different than most.

 The visitors are so varied. I have no roads, no sidewalks. They walk on dirt or grass. In some cases, they fly or swim. Or even soar. I might find a deer watching me. Wild pigs moving past. An otter is not a rare event. I had a loon in the pond the other day. They are fish eaters at the highest level. Fox, raccoons, possums, hawks, owls, coyotes, animals, and birds I can't even identify want my chickens. All types of snakes want the eggs. Even my guest attacks the eggs.

 My fish are always looking for a free meal. I watch them leap up to two feet in the air to eat dragonflies. The pond is a water source for birds of all kinds. Wild ducks, bats, Martin's, migration birds. Sometimes quite a sight. Alligators, bobcats, Wild dogs, stray cats, and maybe a glimpse of something you have no idea what you saw. But you did see something.

All the crows. Songbirds of every breed. Hummingbirds, you name it. Every now and then a noise of a bird or animal that makes you wonder. Am I scared of any of this? Cautious at the very least. My dogs will protect. So sure, my yard is different. I hope change doesn't move too fast.

Story 99
"What We Love"

How many kinds of love are there?

A wife may love her husband. So deep. Filled with emotions. Can it even be matched?

The same woman has three children. She loves them. Just as deep and emotion filled, but it's different. She would willingly give her life to protect them. But that love is truly different than that for her husband.

She owns a dog. Never goes anywhere without him. He's nine years old and she has had him all his life. She tells everyone how much she loves that dog. Gives him hugs and kisses. She does love that animal. So what is the difference? Let me say it like this, would you die for your dog? Place yourself in great danger for him, sure. But would you die? A gun is placed at your head and one at the dogs. A trigger will be pulled. You have to pick. Which is more important, that you be there for your family or the dog? Hard question!!! As I've said, she would die for her children.

She says she loves a certain plant. It's her favorite. She has had it for years. She boasts to her friends how much she loves that plant. Now someone wants to buy it. She needs the money for her family. What would be the price to part with it? It's the only one she has ever seen. It wouldn't be able to be replaced. But she loves that plant, what would you do?

Her favorite song plays. She stops everything she's doing to listen. She loves that song. Is love the right word in the situation? Can you love a song, a picture, a memory? It can go on and on. One day you may look back and say you love your life. You love yourself. We use this word so frequently we never want to devalue it.

Can it be overused? I hope not. With all the anger out there today. We need to speak of love all we can. Our world would be a much better place.

Don't you agree?

Story 100
"I needed to remember"

She was so upset with him. All she asked was for him to bring bread home for dinner. That was all. And he showed up without it.

Things had been rocky for a while now. *Is this marriage still worth it? He just doesn't seem to care about us anymore.* She poured a glass of wine and sat. *He can fix his own plate.*

Then for some odd reason, she began to remember. They met in college. He was both handsome and shy. She had to initiate their first kiss. They dated for a couple years, then married. She didn't know it, but he had been saving up for their honeymoon. He knew they would marry before she knew.

Her pregnancy was very hard. She couldn't work. So he took on a second job. It seemed he was always gone. But he never complained. He would bring flowers to make her feel better.

She went for a second glass.

He could always make her laugh. For a grown man, he could be so silly.

Time flew by, and we both grew older. He would still work to cheer me up, but the stress took its toll on me. Never enough money, the kids cost so much, and they demanded all my time. Then suddenly I realized the problem. It wasn't my husband; it was mostly me.

I have a wonderful husband. A beautiful family. I somehow forgot all that. I allowed the value of my life to cheapen.

She got up and told everyone to get ready for dinner. They would all sit together and eat tonight. No exceptions. It was fantastic. They talked and laughed, and she bonded with them again. A weight was lifted.

She discovered that happiness starts from within. That the burdens of life aren't really that heavy. A good attitude makes for a good family. She takes the time to look better now. Everyone noticed. *I came close to losing the most valued thing I owned.*

A glass of good wine can do wonders in the right situations!

Story 101
"We All Live for A Reason"

Two teenagers saw a man sitting on a bench. So, they decided to have some fun with him.

"Hey old timer, why aren't you dead yet?" They look at each other and laugh. The old man looks up and speaks.

"It's not because others didn't try. As a teenager I was in a gang. Almost died twice. Shot once and stabbed twice. That knife almost won. The courts placed me in the military. Went to Vietnam. Our post was overrun. All but three of us died. I should have went that day. Luck was on my side, I guess. Got out and went to work at a chemical plant. I was in a block when the explosion happened. I'll never forget the burns of the hot gas. That's how I lost this leg."

"So, you boys ask me why I still live. I live because I'm a survivor. Because my presence is still needed on this earth. Maybe just so we could have this conversation today. I really don't know." Those two boys grew up a little that day. Their outlook on people changed. Neither one ever made fun of others ever again. And the strangest thing? The old man passed away only weeks later.

We go through this life trying to survive. To find our happiness. To leave our mark. With age comes knowledge, experience. The tools we need to share with the ones who ask for help even if they don't realize they're asking.

This is a good world. Sure, there are rough edges. Just do your part to smooth them out. Everyone will benefit!

Story 102
"Valentine's Day"

He was lost in the woods, this young boy of sixteen.

Night was approaching fast and the winter cold was dangerous. He kept looking to find his way, when he came upon a hollow tree. He crawled inside for warmth not finding much. He knew his fate. All he could do was wait for what he couldn't stop. And then it happened.

A small glow of light appeared. It must be the cold he figured. But it began to take form. Before his eyes stood a fairy princess. Many many years ago another with a heart full of love entered here. Her name was Ann. A maiden of such beauty. When you slip away from this life, you will meet. Slowly the cold took over him.

This is when the tradition of Valentine's Day began. In his sleep he saw a beautiful flower. A flower of such rare beauty never seen. He could sense someone smiling at him. But all he could see was the flower. The princess spoke again. She died in this same tree hundreds of years ago. She turned to dust after such a long time, as will you. She touched his forehead with her finger and he began to change. His spirit changed into a magnificent sunflower stalk. At that moment he could see the maiden. A beautiful girl of sixteen herself. And magic filled them both. Fireflies lit the room. He took her hand. The cold was gone. The rose gave all of its pedals to give them a soft place to rest on. They fell in love.

The rose and the sunflower took root at the opening of the tree. Nothing was ever allowed in again. This became a place of magic. One night a year they came together to share their love for each other. This fourteenth day of February. This special day. Twenty-four hours of tender words. Smiles. Looks expressing love for each other. The princess had cast a spell of love. A spell that would never be broken. A spell that persist even today for people in love.

Be with the one you love today. Show your feelings. Make this day as special as it was intended. It's the one day a year for lovers. Show you love.

Allow the magic to flourish.

Story 103
"I Want To Remember"

"Why do you come to the park and just sit?"

He looks up and smiles. "I come here with my wife to visit."

"But you're alone!"

"Not at all. She is by my side always. You see, we used to come here all the time. You might say it was our favorite place to visit. Almost a year ago, she passed on. And I'm not willing to let her go yet. So, I come here still to visit with her. You're young. After fifty years of marriage, you sort of become one. You might see this one day. So, I'm not ready to accept I don't have my Ann anymore. She's in my heart, so she's still by my side."

"We talk about happier times. Holidays. And times we spent together. So many good memories. She was a hell of a cook. We traveled all over the world. A little sad we never had children. But it was the life we chose. You would have liked her. Enough of this talk. I don't want to be rude, but I want this time for her. I'm holding on as tight as I can. But she is slowly slipping away. One day, my heart will be broken. I'll know she's really not by my side. I don't want that to be today, not tomorrow, not next week. I'm pushing back as hard as I'm able."

"I want to remember our time in France. I want to hear her laughter again. I want to relive every day. Every day we were together till we can be there once more. I want to remember!"

Story 104
"You Can Always Help"

He worked hard all his life. His work was his life.

Dedicated as he was, he had no time for a personal life. And so, the years went by. But finally, the day came to retire. To walk away from it all. It was then that his being alone really hit him. He had no family. No friends to speak of. His life became day after day of nothing to do. What was he to do?

He walked his neighborhood. Saw the children in the streets playing their games. He could also see the danger. An accident waiting to happen. He found a cause. How could he change this?

He talked to the children. What did they need? What would help the most? He spoke to parents, to the city, to the parks department. A park! Get them off the streets and onto the grass. How? He needed space. Around six connecting lots. Could it happen?

Once a need is identified, and a solution found, then the funds and action are next. He made it happen. He got those kids off the streets and in a safe area. A first-class park in a poor neighborhood. All because he cared and was willing to go the extra mile for strangers. Retirement isn't the last sentence of a long book. Just the beginning of its latest chapter.

Who knows, maybe your choice might be to help others get clean water in a foreign land.

Retirement is never the last sentence.

Story 105
"She Needed Help"

He was raised very poor. But he worked hard each and every day. With time he built a very successful business.

One day his H.R. person came to his office with a paper. "Per company policy I plan to terminate this individual, here is the required document you asked of me. I would like to wrap this up this week. I have a replacement I've been talking to." And left the room.

He picked up the paper and read. Absenteeism, falling asleep at her desk. Mistakes in her work. All serious infractions. He thinks for a minute and picks up the phone. He gives the person on the other end the information and tells him to get back within three days.

He receives his report. Miss Jane Wilson. Widower. Mother of three small children. Holds down two other jobs. Barely makes it pay day to pay day. No social life to speak of. Goes to church every Sunday with her children. Probably her work performance is because of exhaustion and stress. Termination seems justified. But the termination will put her underwater.

He thinks about the situation, paces his office, and then calls in his H.R. man. "John, you've been with me for four years now. I'm very pleased with your work. But I'm going to ask a favor of you. You won't like it. I want it done anyway. There will be no rebuttal on this." John looked at him with concern.

"You are going to create a manager's position and promote Jane. She will get a hefty pay increase and her own office. Make this happen." "But why" asked John? "She doesn't deserve this. Why?"

"There are times when people need a hand extended. They are in real need of some help. They are doing all they can but are on the verge of drowning. Their children will suffer the most. We as a company will extend that hand. We will step in and be the help she needs. So go and make this happen and leave my name out of it. Tell her if she is willing to make this position a success, she will receive another review in six months. Her salary will increase again if all is on tract. If you were in her shoes, I would do the same for you. Please go and do as I ask and tell no one."

Large companies wield a lot of power. The large bonuses need to filter down to the rank and file also. The very top could get a little less and the employees could get a little more. Do this and there would be no needs for unions. Everyone would work as a team for the success of each other. Everyone would take home more in the long run. Life is really not so complicated.

Story 106

"Smiles"

A mother sees her child for the first time. Ever so gently, she takes the child into her arms. She smiles and cries. So small, so fragile. But the most beautiful girl she has ever seen. She speaks with soft words and kisses her cheek. She's a mother now.

She tells her about her future. How she'll be the center of her world. How much she'll be loved. They'll spend time together in the kitchen. Holding hands for hours on end. She'll brush her hair. Tell her how to pick her clothes for the day. So much for her to learn. Who will teach whom?

With time, she'll ask about how she knew she was in love with Dad. "What it's like to love?" The mother sees a twinkle in her eyes.

"You probably need to learn about makeup. Well start light. A little color on the cheeks." She hugs her daughter, knowing she will leave one day. It was always there, but this hug was different. Once they find love outside the home, they grow up so fast.

Now she bounces her grandchild on her knee. It's a boy. She looks at her daughter, knowing her turn is now here. All the love, all the sacrifice, all the growing. Her world is changing daily. Now the daughter looks at her mother and smiles. They both know they're good mothers. They'll always be best friends. They smile once more.

Story 107

"The Love of A Pet"

The mother kept carrying her daughter to the doctor. Nothing seemed to work. Then she finds out "cancer."

Her bright shining star was not going to live. And there was nothing anyone could do.

Her tears flowed every day. Her heart was broken. She had lost her husband, and now her daughter would be gone. She would be alone.

One day her daughter spoke. "Mom don't cry for me. I'm going to a good place. Daddy will meet me. I've asked for a puppy. I've always wanted one. He'll do that for me."

"What kind of puppy do you want?"

"A brown one that won't get too big. I want it to sit in my lap so I can love on it."

"A girl or a boy?"

"A boy I guess, so I can say I have a boyfriend."

The mother had cried so many tears she had none left. "And his name?"

"Blake."

"I like that name. Can we go and pick out a Blake for you tomorrow? The animal shelter might have one. And after you're gone, I can care for him to meet you later."

And so, it was. The mother and beautiful little dog were alone in the big house. Every day she hugged Blake and loved him dearly. He was her connection to her lost family.

When we lose loved ones, we require a connection of some sort. A picture and memories are a good thing. Although a little hollow sometimes. But a loving pet will strengthen your heart. Give you a way to touch them still. Their love will come the closest to the love you lost.

Story 108
"Enjoy Each other"

We had a chance to talk. I could hear the excitement in her voice. It made me smile with pride.

When it comes to the one you love, shouldn't it be that way? After five, ten, twenty years, that excitement should never lessen. But how do you hold on to such feelings? After years have passed do you still act as if you're still dating? If she wants a new dress, would you not set a limit, just ask she be reasonable and wink and tell her to splurge a little. You both eat a meal, do you both clean the kitchen together? Clown around and make it fun. Laugh together. No TV, no phones, just each other that evening. At least a couple of times a month.

It takes work not to become complacent. Understandings at a higher level. A deeper love. Stoking the embers of the flame of youth. Do you remember the smiles of the past? The eyes talking to each other? Such fond memories tend to be locked up in the heart. Viewed at times of endearment. Those feelings need to be worn on the chest like badges. A constant reminder. A reminder of a passionate youth.

Feed the love. Cut corners to enjoy a date again. Show your level of love. Holding hands comes free. But is says so much. Saying I love you and showing it cost nothing really. The value of expressions that keep the embers glowing warm! That value is large, larger than you think. So large, you smile with pride.

Chapter 3

Story 1

"Responsibility to your family is utmost"

There was a man, not unlike so many others.

His life was blissfully rewarding. But things slowly began to change. Changes so small they were hardly noticed. But changes nonetheless. With time, the weight of change caused the balance of his perfect world to wobble. His job was threatened, his marriage was on the rocks, and then one day he yelled, "God, why did you choose to punish me?" He now slept alone. He silently harbored his hatred for believing in God at all. He finally drifted into sleep.

He dreamed. There he stood at the foot of God himself. God spoke. "Why do you no longer believe in me?"

With the question asked, he unloaded. When his rant was over, God spoke again.

"Was it I who told you to go drinking with friends? To leave your wife and family alone for your pleasure?"

"Was it I who told you to make the bad deals for you to make money and others to lose?"

"Why did you stop going to church with your family? Do I need to continue?"

"I gave you a free will. You were taught responsibility. But you turned your back on me because of your own selfish ego. The road you're on is a dead end. There is only one more exit. Then it's over for you. You have a free will. What is more important to you? Me, your family, your soul, your life after death, or your false success? You must decide—and decide tonight."

He suddenly woke up. *I will not throw away this chance.* He got up and went to his wife. "Darling, I need your help. I'm weak. I need your strength. Help me be the man you married again."

She looked long and hard.

"Let's all get ready for church. We'll go as a family again."

Story 2
"Finding Love in a Crowd"

He sees her for the first time at a dance. She was with her friends, smiling real big and enjoying herself. He lacked the confidence to ask her to dance that night, but he knew he would one day. She held such beauty in his eyes, he had to meet her somehow. Down the road he sees her again. But this time she is with another boy. His heart sinks a little.

Instinct told him he had better do something quick or his opportunity will pass. So, the next day at school he works his way close to her. Finally, they make eye contact. "Hi I'm David. I've seen you at the dance a few times. Do you mind if I ask you to dance also?"

"Sure, I love to dance. I'm going this Friday, see you there."

He remembers this as if it was just yesterday. She's about to deliver their first child. It'll be a girl. He wants so much for her to be like her mother. He carries enough love for them both. Her pregnancy wasn't an easy one. So many failures. So many disappointments. But at last, the day was here. He was assured all will be fine. He just needed to be patient. Not that easy in a time like that.

Finally, the nurse comes out and asked him would he like to meet his daughter?

And now look at her. In a wedding dress, so much in love. Wanting to share that love with the man of her dreams. Time seems to move so fast. Her mother tending to all the details for her that day. Love was in abundance like so many others.

Now here I sit waiting for that nurse to announce we're grandparents. The anticipation has made time stop. The great news was finally delivered. We had a grandson. A real day of joy. So boy, that's pretty much the story of your granny and me and your mom. And you're getting way too big to sit on my lap now. My leg goes to sleep.

He lays the flowers by the stone. His favorite story told so many times. "If only grandpa could tell it just once more." He takes the hand of his daughter. "You know, I think I can tell you a wonderful story about your grandma. Let's go and have some ice cream."

Story 3
"It's hard for love to leave sometimes"

Once upon a time I held her in my arms. That was long ago.

Now I look forward to that chance encounter. A few moments we exchange kind words. I soak up every second of it. She's married now. So I can't give away my real feelings. I just smile while my heart breaks a little more. Her smile, her fragrance, her person. All the things I think about after we go our separate ways. Some things just are not meant to be. I accept that. It doesn't hurt less. But I accept it.

I turn a corner and there he is. The past love of mine. I don't go out of my way to encounter him. In a small town it just happens. We make eye contact and I know he still cares. I love another now. Our chemistry just wasn't strong enough to keep us together. The price of young love I guess. I'm with a great man now. He loves me and I love him. Life is just a little complicated. I have no regrets. It was the path that led me here. So I smile. Take a few minutes to talk. Exchange a few pleasantries. Then we both go on our way. It's the way it should be.

In our lives we may love many times. Sometimes only once. Falling in love is for sure necessary to complete you. Love is an emotion that drives you. The family you love. Your country. Yourself. All necessary.

Never hesitate to love. You may feel pain sometimes. But the bliss is even greater.

Story 4

"The Bond of Friendship"

There was a typical boy with a typical pet dog. They went everywhere together.

As they grew, their bond thickened. Angie was her name. She was very protective of her owner. Nothing was allowed to harm him. One day, he took her to the park. They ran, played, and were having a great time. And in an instant, all that changed.

A large male dog came out of nowhere. He was angry and had the boy in his sights. He charged. He almost reached him when Angie attacked. The male was too large. Angie was being killed. That's when Dale jumped in. He attacked. He began beating the dog with a big stick. He had no fear. He wanted to save his friend. The male grabbed his arm.

Blood was going everywhere. He was losing. Angie attacked again. Nothing was going to stop her this time. She bit down hard on the dog's back leg. He let loose of the boy and turned on her again. This time it was brutal. He was going to kill her. And once again the boy jumped in. He got in a lucky blow. The dog staggered. He gave one last swing, this time finishing the male off. Bleeding badly, he picked up Angie. Holding her tightly, he blacked out.

When he woke up, he was in a hospital. His arm had been stitched up. Blood was being pumped back into his body. He remembered what he last saw. He had been holding his Angie. She gave her life to save his. He began to sob. He had lost his dear friend. At such a young age, it was very dramatic.

He felt a warm hand on his side. He didn't care. Then he heard a whimpering. It was his Angie by his side. They had both been saved. He didn't remember, but he kept saying he wanted his dog—over and over. So the hospital decided it was in his best interest to do so.

Friendships don't have boundaries. They are what they are. But the friendship of a dog is unique. More loyal than a person. Willing to protect at any cost. Any!

Angie now rests in a small box on the mantel. They will be buried together one day. He will never leave his friend. Never!

Story 5
"Chance meeting"

He backs up in a store and bumps into a lady. "My goodness, watch where you're going!"

"Excuse me, it was an accident."

"I don't care if it was, watch what you're doing." And she storms away.

He stares and thinks she seems stressed out. But as life would have it, he sees her again in a Lowe's. She goes to move an object and a full display comes down. He walks over to help her. "Thank you so much, it was an accident." She then looks at his face. She smiles and says "I feel so stupid now."

"Well accidents do happen," he says and smiles back. He looks and sees no ring. "Maybe a small break would help us both? Next door is a coffee shop. Can I interest you in a cup?"

"You know, maybe that would be a good idea."

That was thirty-eight years ago. She thinks about that day all the time. How in love they are. He's a perfect husband. So kind, so courteous. He makes her feel very special, very loved. They're walking in the mall holding hands, she gives him a squeeze.

"Why do you always come with me shopping, I know you don't enjoy this."

He leans over and kisses her cheek. "Someone has to make sure you don't tear down a display case." And has a chuckle. More time passes.

Now age sets in. Stiffness and pain are normal. But so are their smiles. They're having coffee on the back porch. He reaches into his pocket and pulls out a small box. "For you darling."

She opens it and finds a pretty necklace. "You'll have to wait for one of the children to visit, I don't think I can work the clasp."

He smiles big.

With time they were put to rest. They lay side by side for eternity. Their children always spoke of their love for each other. The respect they showed. There are many such couples out there.

It's not that rare. Love still abounds even in today's problems. Maybe a trip to the mall holding hands would be a nice break. Maybe someone needs to see your love. It gives hope.

Story 6

"Love is a choice"

I didn't choose to fall in love, it was forced upon me.

Is that the way it seems sometimes? The responsibility of loving is so great. All of your weaknesses and shortcomings laid out to be seen by another. But with time all is exposed. If you spend the time together, you learn the person not projected. Our "show" side, the side we want others to think they know of us, well it's not always the complete truth. This artificial side protects you.

Then one day you find interest in a stranger. You think "can they be trusted"? Should I speak? Well probably your eyes already did. Will your heart be broken again? I know nothing about this person. Will I regret speaking? So rejection prevailed. And I quickly move away. Fate is the driver, not me. I find myself thinking of him. Kind of looking forward to another chance encounter. And that happens. Time and time again it happens. Then at some point you're talking.

You probe. Find out all you can. You enjoy the talking. You are moving closer weather you want to or not. Love is being forced upon you. But in this case it's a two way street. Holding hands for the first time. That first kiss. It all adds up. You're in love again. Happiness flows through your body again. It's a good feeling. You remember it well. So now it's the future that scares you.

Love is such a strong emotion, we're helpless fighting it sometimes. Never lose the ability to love. The dog or cat is not the same. It's great the love they give. And the love you return. It's the love of family, friends, and yourself that moves your heart. It's the passion that moves the world.

There's too much prejudice out there today. Accept more. Forgive more. And know there are sins of the past that can never be changed. How do you want to shape your future? With love or prejudice?

Story 7
"While he forgets"

Titled by Cathi Sue Beatty

A wife came into a room to find her husband sitting alone. "Is anything wrong?"

He looked up with a tear in his eye.

She moved in close and took his hand. "Tell me what's wrong!"

"I'm forgetting you. It's just the beginning, but its happening. I will sometimes look around and not know where I am. It just lasts for a second, but it happens. What I fear the most is seeing you and not knowing who you are. It happens to people all the time. I think it's happening with me."

"I'll set an appointment with the doctor, but we'll do this together. I will never leave your side no matter what. For better or for worse, remember?"

With the passing of time, he did forget. She would take his hand and walk him to a park bench. There she would talk about their past. The love they shared. The wonderful things they did together.

Finally, the time came when she went to the bench alone. Her life had gone through so much change. Only memories of a love once so cherished. Longing for the touch of a man never to return. Sadness filled her heart. One day, a cat came and sat next to her. She looked around and saw no one. She looked down and smiled. She reached and scratched his head. He rolled to his back, and his little motor started. He loved the attention.

As she returned, the cat always ran to her. One day, a collar was added. A small metal heart had an inscription: "Enjoy my cat, but let it come home every night." She never met the owner, but the cat for sure became her friend.

This small cat was able to lift her burden of grief. Bring her smile back. She one day realized she would be fine. She goes to the park less now. Her cat friend still runs to her when she does visit. She met a nice man. A real gentleman. And he wants more of her time. And you know what? She feels the same.

Story 8

"Your Weakness Can Sometimes Be Your Strength"

There was a child not raised by parents.

She was without parents within months of her birth. The sole surviving family member of a horrible accident. With no one to take her in, she was placed in a home for children who have nowhere to live. It provided a roof and food, but not much of anything else. As she grew older, she was even more withdrawn. She was considered mentally handicapped. With time she turned eighteen. So, the process to put her into society and out of the home started.

Then she met a lady named Mary. Mary was kind and full of understanding. She took this girl under her wing. Since she didn't mix well with people, Mary introduced her to the internet. Computer training was next. And in a very short time she excelled. She started a data research online business. She filled a niche needed by many. So, Mary hired a young man to assist her.

Our girl was not comfortable with the change. Such close contact with a stranger. And a man at that. She was assured he was a good addition and she trusted Mary. With time she not only became more comfortable but was attracted to him. What Mary had done was to expand her exposure to society. Her exposure to a male. None of it was by accident.

They eventually married. Their first child was a little girl. They named her Mary. Over the years, as a family, they did a monthly visit to the grave. They spread a blanket on the ground and ate lunch. But our girl, (Sharon) had a small box built into the grave stone. Every year she wrote a letter to her mother. The only mother she had ever known and pushed it into the box. Just a short note expressing her thankfulness to her mother.

She was buried next to her. Her gravestone also had a box. And over the years many notes filled her box also.

Story 9
"I was granted my wish"

A good man led a good life. Long and fruitful. The days passed.

The day came he rested in a hospital, his days at an end. His daughter ready to give birth to his first grandson. You only have hours left. I'm very sorry. He comforts him and has to leave for another patient.

So the man is by himself. He looks up and speaks. "One more day. Just one more day. Allow me to meet my grandson. To say goodbye to my daughter. Am I asking for so much? I've prayed so many times for you. Raised her in the church. Shared your teachings. Would you grant me just one more day?" His eyes closed for the last time on this earth.

He finds himself in his daughter's room. She is sleeping. He's confused. A hand touches his shoulder. He sees no one but knows he's not alone. "You have been given your wish. Your grandson will be here soon. Your daughter will sleep again. You then will be allowed to hold your grandson. Say goodbye to your daughter. You'll have the day to observe them for the remainder of your wish."

"You'll hear her name the child after you. She'll tell him about your kindness. The wonderful father you were. You were dearly loved by her. I'll return later to lead you to another place. Enjoy your time. Touch your daughter. A feeling of acceptance for all that's happened will help her grieve. I'll return later."

We have no real understanding of what happens when we pass. You lead a good life. Your afterlife will be a blessed one.

Story 10

"The Journey"

A mother looked down at her new son and didn't know how she'd raise the child. But she would. Just the two of them will give the other their strength. It will all work out.

She was holding down two jobs but always made time for Jason. He grew up to be a fine young man. But now she was in the hospital, very weak, her life slipping away. Jason was there holding her hand. His wife, Mary, held the other. She said, "The baby can lie next to you if you wish." Her grandchild. Such a lovely baby. But she was so weak.

"Jason, I tried to do my best giving you a happy life. Your father left us before you were only inches long. He got so sick. He was a good man, and that's why you carry his name."

"I know, Mom. You did good."

"But, Jason, the accident almost destroyed me. It broke me."

"That's why we're here with you, Mom. We won't leave your side."

The doctor came in. "How are her signs?"

The nurse replied, "Very weak. She has no one left. We'll turn off the support before her organs begin to fail. She doesn't have much time left."

Her son squeezed her hand. She looked up. "You know you haven't aged a day since the accident. Losing all of you in one day was more than I could bear. It was the church that saved me. But the years became so lonely."

"You're here now, and that's all that matters. You should have remarried. You shouldn't have been alone all that time."

The equipment was turned off. Jason said, "Take my hand. We can leave." They all walked together. She held the baby. "You know, Mom, I have a surprise for you."

"What is it?"

"You're going to be really shocked."

"What? Tell me."

"Dad is in the lobby. He's waiting for you. We're all together now, all of us. We have a journey to make. Wait till you see where we're going!"

Story 11
"Sometimes Your Life is Chosen"

An Angel bends over for a closer look. "Well little child, I was sent here to alter your life. This world needs your wisdom. I will always be close to you." With that said, she touches his forehead.

As the years passed, he learned. Not in the top of his classes, his learning was different. He observed everything around him. Unknowingly he took a particular interest in the way people reacted to change. This drove the direction of his future. He would become the youngest Mayor of a large city. Change was the main ingredient of positive impact.

He spent time talking to the groups in most need. The ones with most influence. And the most corrupt. Everyone had to change. Everything was self-interest. Crime in every form helped the criminal. Greed helped the greedy. The love of mankind needed to be redefined. So, he had to change things and being a political leader was his answer.

He started with a city. Then a state. And finally, a Nation. We became a Nation of pride. Money was no longer in control. What could we as individuals do to change our surroundings? Who would help to accomplish the goal? Respect was a big player. Respect at all levels. Teamwork came back. Solutions the priority. He did change our Nation. Other Countries followed. Life became better for all.

Then one day while working at his desk, in walked a stranger. "Can I help you?" he asked.

"It's time for you to leave with me. Your work is done here. You're needed elsewhere."

His eyes squint a little, then he remembers. A touch on the forehead. A touch to give him the skills to end the widespread hate consuming our people around the world; a remembering of the way things were. The pride knowing his role in change.

"What needs to be done now? How can I do better?"

"That is for me to show you." And the Angel opened the door and his spirit left with this heavenly spirit.

The next changes start today. A very small child lies in a hospital bed in the nursery. He enters the room and says "I'm here to alter your life. The world needs your wisdom." With that said, he touches the forehead of a beautiful little girl. The "good" given to us all will never die. It's always reborn!

Story 12
"A Bible on the bed"

"Mama, who is Jesus"? Quite surprised she asks "why would you ask that"?

"I heard some people talking in the hall. They said it would take Jesus to save their daughter. They were crying." "Son, we're not people of religion. We live a good life. We care for others. We raised you with the same beliefs." "Can you save her?" "No, maybe no one can." "I was told we used to pray in school. Would a prayer help?" The mother was almost at a loss for words. "Prayers will not save her. They are only letters on the page." "I heard them say a prayer. Those were kind words."

"I'm going to talk to someone about the privacy here. You shouldn't be subjected to such nonsense." "Why do you choose not to believe in prayer?" The mother looks down at him again. "You almost had a sister. I caught a bad fever and lost her. I prayed plenty, but I lost her anyway. I've never prayed since." "So did Jesus kill her or the fever?" "You are far too young to ask such things." "But I want to know. Did Jesus kill my sister?"

The mother sat expressionless. The question was too big. Her buried feelings were rising to the surface again. Her anger was softened. She hugged her son. She could see she was wrong in the way she handled it all. Now she doubted she was right. She told her son to rest. And left the room. With some anger she asked to speak to a supervisor.

Upset, she questioned their privacy policies. "Children should never be subjected to hearing the heartbreak from another room. That was wrong!" The supervisor rang for the floor nurse to come to her office. Once there she was asked how this could have happened in the first place. The floor nurse looking quite confused asked "the floor where her son has a room"? "Well of course. I'm not sure what happened. He's the only patient on that floor. There is no girl there. No other people." Confused even more, the mother returns to the room. "Are you sure you heard those people?" "Yes. They came back out and I saw them. They even looked at me and said things were going to change for me now." The mother got up and stormed across the hall. She opened the door to find out for herself. The room was empty. A Bible was in the center of a made bed. Nothing or no one else.

In a religious world, people sometimes lose their way. They are affected by things they can't stop and look up to assign the blame. Everything happens for a reason. I think Jesus will accept blame to ease your pain. But with time you will heal. It's then when he calls you back.

Never lose your faith.

Story 13

"Pictures in a box"

The day came when the house needed to be addressed. So many memories. Kathy's grandmother had passed away. They had been very close. Losing her was hard, but it is the way of life. So it had been decided to sell the house, and it had to be emptied.

She and her husband worked for hours. They wanted to keep some things and sell the rest. Kathy did her grandmother's room last. She did that room by herself. So many reminders of the love shared. The pillow where she laid her head. Her favorite nightgown. She sat on the bed and ran her hand across the covers. She closed her eyes and remembered lying by her side. She loved her so much.

But a job needed to be done. She began her work. As she cleared out the closet, she noticed a box. Tucked in the back and tied with a ribbon. She picked it up and sat on the bed. A pull, and the ribbon fell. She removed the lid, and the tears flowed. Pictures. Hundreds of them. Wrapped in small groups with rubber bands to keep them in order. Pictures of her as a baby. You could tell they had been handled many times. Each bundle was a year of their life together. That little girl with that loving smile. Holding hands. Her in her grandmother's lap. In the highchair with birthday cake. Every year of her life was there. Being pulled in a wagon around the neighborhood. A day at the beach. Getting off a school bus. She never noticed so many pictures taken. *The tears flowed.*

One bundle stood out. Thicker than the rest. Pictures of hugs and kisses shared. From a baby to just weeks ago. She could do no more today. This precious box needed to be held. A connection to her where she still was alive. Her husband took over the work. That box now had a place of honor. Every year, it was taken down, and Karen handled the pictures. But it was no longer about her. It was now all about her grandmother. She wasn't in the ground. She held a deeply loved space in the hearts of everyone. This lovely woman with a camera. Turned out she was more than just her grandmother. She was her friend, her best friend.

Story 14
"It's You Who Makes Your Future, Not Your Surroundings"

His life was so hard to be so young. Not every child comes from the perfect home.

He had no father he knew of, and his mother was always in and out of jail. He enjoyed school just because it got him out of the house. His good grades gave him the attention every child needs. His life was so different it was hard to fit in comfortably. School was his home really. And all his studies paid off. He was awarded scholarships for college. He finished at the top of his field. Not too bad for a boy of his background.

He was asked what he would change if he could. He thought about his answer. Then spoke. "Probably not much. I was loved by my mother. Sure, she stayed in trouble, but I don't think she could help it. She is who she was. Never met my dad. See no reason to meet him now. Mom said she told him he had a son. He never tried to meet me. That's ok. My past belongs to me. I own it. I still did alright. Now, what I can affect is the better question! I have skills and talents. I can share what I know. I can help other children in tough situations. I can not only relate to them, but I speak their language. I can do good. So no, I wouldn't change much about my past. I'm going to focus on the future of others. Others that need my help. That's my real calling. So, I need to go. I have a family to meet. The father thinks this is a waste of time. The mother will probably not even be there. But those two kids. Well, I'll win them over quickly. I'm going to give them a shot at reaching their potential. Watch me!"

Story 15
"Show your Love"

I've loved her for so long. All I ever wanted was to be near her. To feel her touch.

It's not always easy. I went to work each day. She stayed home. Our worlds were so different. She always showed her love for me when I entered the door. I made sure to hold her in my arms. Tell her I missed her. She seemed to love that. My touch on her back. Running my fingers through her hair. The little things.

I change and sit in my soft chair to relax. She's always by my side. Those dark eyes. Looking for any attention I may show. To be so loved, why is it so obvious? Am I really that deserving? I'm a good provider. I know that. But to receive so much love! More than I really feel is mine. It makes me smile.

So we'll go for a walk later. Something we do almost every evening. The walks good for me. They help me unwind. I do all the talking. She just looks up and smiles. And for her, it gets her out of the house. Special time we can share. The walks aren't that long. But they are special.

Your pet can bring all kinds of joy into your day. Make the time for them. They show a love few can match. They are your family also.

Story 16

"Family"

A man was walking one day. It was a beautiful day. He came upon a child crying.

"What's wrong?" he asked.

The child looked up and said, "I'm hungry."

So the man looked more closely. The child's clothes were tattered, but the child was clean. "Where do you live?" he asked.

"Over there." She pointed.

"Let me walk you home."

He went to the door to find a very defensive mother. She grabbed the child and pulled her close. "What do you want?" she demanded. He could see past her into her house. Old furniture, very old, but a clean house.

He said he was just walking by because it was such a nice day. A couple more blocks, and he would be at his car. "Your daughter was crying. I thought she might be hurt. I just wanted to help."

The mother relaxed a bit. "I'll take care of her now. Thank you." She turned to leave.

He said, "Wait! I have no family to do things for. Would you allow me to send some things here for your family?"

He could now see another pair of eyes looking from around the corner. "Why would you do that?"

His eyes lowered. "I am sick. I don't have a lot of time left. You would make me happy if I could do this, not just for you but also for me."

She softened. "Sure, if you want to."

So later that day, a delivery was made—food, plenty of food, and a note. It read that he set up an account at the local store. Any groceries needed were now covered. She didn't even know his name. A few days later, a lawyer came to her door. He explained the house was now hers. And new furniture would be arriving soon. All had been taken care of, and he left his card and told her to call if she and her family needed anything. He left, and she sat down. Tears swelled. A total stranger had changed her life. The lawyer would not give up his name.

The small girl asked, "Is that our daddy?"

The mother looked down and said, "If you want him to be. That is what fathers do for their loved ones."

So, the mother decided to try to find out who he was. She went to the different places but didn't talk to management. She was sure they would give no answers. She went to the helpers. She created her story, and after many tries, she got a name—and from that an address. She went to the home. There she found a note on the door. Mr. Edwards was in the hospital; for any assistance, contact this person. There was a name and number. She called all the hospitals and tracked him down.

She and her two children went to the floor where he was. They were told only family could enter. The mother told them they were family. The small girl said, "He's my daddy." The doctor was sure she meant granddad. So they were allowed to enter. Now it was her turn to be the giver. She held his hand. She told her story to the sleeping man. She introduced the children to him. She gave thanks for all he had done. They were with him when he passed.

No one is ever really alone in this world. If you are a good person, you have thousands of family members.

Story 17
"Courage"

Titled by Corrie Cabral

They lived in the country. Far removed from the rest.

Each day the mother would go for a walk down a trail in the woods. With her walked her three-year-old daughter. The day started out as most but quickly changed. They were always accompanied by the family dog. Her name was Grace. A medium size animal. Full of spirit and love for her family. The only family she knew.

On this walk the mother kept hearing something following them. The dog was on edge about something. And then it happened. A cougar stepped into the trail. A big one, and it wanted the child. The mother was without any defense at all. Never needed anything till then. She snatched her daughter up knowing she might die that day. That's when Grace moved to the front. All her hair was bristled up. She would defend her family in a battle she couldn't win.

Grace was the one to attack first. As fierce as any warrior she lunged at the cougar. The fight was on. Fur and blood went everywhere. The mother was horrified by what she saw. But she kept moving backwards. Finally, she ran. The safety of her child was the most important thing.

She came back with her husband and a gun. They found Grace. Alive yet not to survive. So badly injured. So gently they picked her up and brought her back. Tended her wounds and made her last hours as comfortable as possible. She was buried under a large oak in the yard. A small fence around the grave. She gave her life for the only family she had. There is so much honor in that.

We need to see everyone as an extended family. Separation is not needed right now. I hope change is in the wind. I hope we can come closer together as a Nation. We can always hope. Let's make change one small step at a time.

Story 18

"Umba"

He was a doctor. Very skilled at his work. But he had a dream.

He wanted to live in a village where he could do the best for everyone. A village in the deep Congo. He wanted a tribe to provide for him while he cared for them. He has a daughter. And she has no mother. Could he put her in such a life? His belief said all will work out for the best. He left his civilized environment.

With time he found his village. He was given a hut and his food was provided. He set up a network to replenish his supplies. His daughter became his nurse. This went on for years. Soon the sick and weak from other parts of the land came to be helped by him.

Then one day the daughter wakes to hear her father arguing with a young warrior. Not just any warrior, he was the son of the Chief. A warrior Prince. Her father kept answering back "it's not our way". The Chief to be storms off. When asked, he said he wanted to buy her. Make her his own. A very worried look came across her face. "You have no worries. This village places honor above everything. He'll accept my decision." And so the days passed.

Then while walking one of the paths to the village, he appears in front of her. He places a hand on her shoulder and speaks in a language she has never heard. He places an ancient belt around her waist that held a knife she could see was very old. Then he says for her to never leave her hut without it. It will give her protection. And he walked away.

When the villagers saw her wearing the knife, her life changed. Nothing was the same. She was given a respect she didn't possess prior. One day the Chief came to her door and asked to speak with her. My son picked you to wear this, pointing to the knife. It's a sign of respect above any other. Cherish it. Never lose it. You are one of us now. Even more than your father. With that he leaves.

The young Chief to be never approached her. His promise to her father was honored. Till one day. While walking back to the village a large male Lion stepped in front of her. Fear filled her body. She pulls the knife. Her fear was so great she trembled. She is shaking so that she drops her knife. The Lion starts his charge. Her life was going to end. Out of nowhere the warrior Prince was between her and the Lion. He grabs the knife and yells to her "run". He yells it once more as the Lion attacks. She runs to the village for help. His life was in danger from a Lion. A group of men ran to his aid.

After what seemed like a lifetime they returned. On their shield lay a dead Prince. On another the Lion. The knife still lodged in his neck. They placed him on the ground. She felt someone take her hand. The Chief led her to the body. Honor him. He gave his life for you. He fought such a large killer so you would live. Honor him. The Lion had been stabbed eight times. He fought bravely.

The sum of the events overwhelmed her. She fell to her knees and cried. She couldn't hold back the tears. She took his hand and held it to her chest and cried even more. One by one the villagers filed by and touched her shoulder. Some would say "Umba". But every single one paid their respects. The villagers then prepared for the burial.

The warrior Prince and the Lion were buried together. Facing one another. She stood by the side of the Chief. Held his hand. When it was over, he placed the knife back onto the belt. "No other man will ever approach you. My son lives in you now. It's our way. Your name is now Umba. There is no greater honor than to have a king give his life for one he loves. And to fight a Lion with a sacred knife, a fight he could never win, puts you in a special place. When I die I will be buried with him. And will you. You are Umba now. You will learn your place."

She looked deep in his eyes. "What is the name Umba?" "You must understand, Umba is not a name. Your people have no words for this. It is best understood as a title or rank. Umba answers to her people and everyone answer to her. We have not called anyone that in over 10,000 moons. Your story is traveling in the winds across the lands as we speak. The ancients have passed down the story since early time. Even I went to the next village and spoke to their elders. Every village knows the story."

A young woman not from our land will come to our villages. She will be a helper of the sick and injured. Her heart will be pure. All she wants is for all the people of our lands to flourish. She ask nothing in return. A great king will love her. He will fight a Lion saving her. But he and the Lion will both perish. A king and a Chief are the two sides of the same leaf. You are the story. You are Umba.

And so, it was. Her life had changed. Leaders from all the lands near and far came to meet her. All promised their alliance to her. She spent her time learning the languages of the tribes, and working with her father. He passed with time. The old Chief called for her one day. He had her sit near him. He told her his moon would set for the last time. It will be she who will rule the tribe. No new chiefs will there be for any tribes. All will answer to her. She was Umba. People had waited a thousand years for her. He would be placed by his son. And when her time came, she would be wrapped in white and placed next to the Prince. And peace will sweep over the lands.

A group of maidens tended to her needs. World leaders met with her. All she ever asked for was doctors and hospitals. To place them all around the land. Seed for crops. Wells for water. Never money. Her life was simple. Like her people.

One day a small boy asked to speak to her. He told of a war brewing. Two tribe's wanting the others land. Many would die. "How far is this?" "A three days journey" he said. "We leave at first light." Her maidens and six warriors for protection from the wild will make the journey. They moved with haste. As they neared the battlefield, they could her the drums beating loudly to reduce the fear. She didn't have much time.

Finally, she stepped into the center. On both sides all instruments of war began to fall to the ground. All warriors bent to one knee. This swept like a wave on water. No one was allowed to have a weapon in her presence. Not even a chief.

She looked over the field. Then asked for the chief from each tribe to join her. Both moved quickly to face her. To one she asked for water for her and her people. The other was asked for food. The sun was hot. She asked that the five best from both sides prepare shade and a table to eat on. Everyone moved quickly to please her. Once her people were seated with food and drink, she asked the chiefs to walk with her.

"Why a war? What are your needs? There aren't many chiefs left. And you two want war? I ask again, what are your needs?" One side needed more room. The other more food. "And for that you would kill? Break the peace we all enjoy. You both have children of age. You a daughter, and you a son. They will marry. Your tribes will become one. You will share all you have. I will return in one year. I will be an invited guest of this new family. Solve any issues. Peace will prevailed." Her word was law. But it was fair.

We don't pick our futures. No matter how well planned, the unexpected can happen. She ruled for over fifty years. And never once organized an army. There is always a peaceful solution in the wings. Remove the greed and serve your people. Learn to be true to the good in this world. Once she died all went back to each land having a Chief. She was buried in the Royal tomb by her Prince. As it should be. Wars were no longer an option. Everyone understood there was always a peaceful solution. Maybe this world needs an Umba? Maybe right now!!!

Story 19

"Early Mornings"

I wake to darkness, a little foggy but ready for coffee. I hear my wife still asleep, her steady breathing, and I think, *I love her so much. She is my world, and I like that. She always wants to look her best and forgives me for mine. I'm actually impressed by the ways she shows her love. Her smile, that special look, her soft words. I know I'm a very lucky man. I try to please her. Make her feel secure. It's not that hard when you're loved so much. I don't get sick often, but when I do, I'm in better hands than at a hospital. She always checks up on me, and I might drag it out a little longer, but I can see the love in her eyes. We do a date night at least once a month. She is truly a beautiful woman. We have dinner, then go to a quiet place and slow dance. Don't get me wrong; we have fun and fast-dance dates too. The slow ones are always the best. I don't have her cook all the meals. I enjoy cooking for her too. But I use a pit, not a stove. I mix her a drink and attend to her needs. Treat her like the queen she is to me.*

She stirs a little. My heart just melts watching her sleep. I'll wake her soon with a cup of coffee. A smaller cup with an ice cube floating. She doesn't like it too hot. I'll prop her up with pillows and turn on the lamp by her side. Morning coffee is my job. But some mornings, she'll whisper to me not to get up. She'll do the coffee this morning. She is so special. And I'm so lucky.

Story 20

"Senses"

Titled By Patti Dyer

A boy in his early teens saw a blind man sitting on a bench in the park.

He walks to him and asks what it's like to be blind. "I don't want to offend you, but I would like to know more." The man lifts his head and told the boy to sit beside him.

"I have never seen so much since I lost the use of my eyes. A new and fabulous world opened up to me. Your name is James. You come here often with your friend Kenneth. Ya'll throw a frisbee almost always. I bet it's with you now."

The boy is taken back by what he said.

"Your other senses step up. I think you see better with hearing than with sight. I can remember the colors of this park, but I didn't realize all the smells. The grass, the flowers. Next to you is a rose bush. Had you ever even looked at it? Probably not. I can smell the food vendor's selection. And taste the ingredients. I bet you didn't think I can cook. Every day!"

"I was very discouraged after my accident. But ever so slowly I began to realize I didn't have a handicap. In fact, I became stronger. By the way you had eggs and bacon this morning for breakfast. Smelled that right off."

"So, what is it like to lose your vision? You never do. How does your life change, well that depends on you. In my case it really was for the better. I'm so much more alive now. Can I stumble and fall, sure. But you know what? So can you. We aren't so different."

"Go enjoy your day. And be careful. And know not to pity me or others like me. I'm thankful I wasn't killed. And my life is full of mystery. I enjoy that. And I no longer judge anyone by their looks. That's a great thing!"

Story 21
"Nothing remains the same"

She takes a moment to reflect. Nothing ever remains the same.

Her marriage to her husband was the answer to a dream. So much in love. Two children followed. A boy and a girl in that order. But nothing stays the same. He started going out to have a couple of drinks with coworkers. One night a week moved to three. Coming back late, drunk and in a bad mood. That marriage fell apart. He was very angry about the entire situation. Not that he was losing his family, but who would cook for him. Wash his cloths. His change was an embarrassment. How so bad so fast? A question never really answered.

Today a single mother. Single for three years now. And sure it's very difficult. She has no choice but to get through each day. She didn't want another man in her life. They can't be trusted. The lesson she learned was "nothing remains the same". As much as she hated to admit it, it was a truth she couldn't deny.

So today she sits with her daughter watching her son play ball. She never misses a game. She noticed a man whose son also played on the team. He never missed a game either. She would catch him looking at her. A quick glance but a look none the less. One day, her son said he asked him her name. Change was in motion.

We all experience both positive and negative emotions. Sometimes they will leave a mark. If you believe things can always change for the better, your world will follow your beliefs.

Nothing ever remains the same. That I promise you.

Story 22
"The strong and the weak"

There was a boy around eight years old.

He was a quiet kid who just wanted to be a good student. But as life would have it, he was bullied. Older boys see they are so much stronger than the younger kids that they push their weight around. And in his case, being withdrawn and smart, he drew extra attention.

One day, he was being bullied extra hard. The bus driver did nothing because one of the boys was his. A poor parent at best. When they came to the smaller boy's stop, the bigger one decided they weren't done with him. They got off too. The biggest and really the meanest of the bullies started to hit the smaller one with his fist. He laughed while he made the other cry. Then everything changed. Out of nowhere, a dog tackled him. He had him by the arm and was doing damage. The dog let the boy go and stood between the smaller one and him, growling. They all ran. Then the dog turned his attention to the boy. The boy could see he was in no danger. He knew every dog in the neighborhood, and he had never seen this animal. Once the boy was on his feet, the dog left.

Now the father showed up, demanding the dog be turned over to be destroyed. No one knew where this dog was, much less who owned it. His son had sixty stitches and rabies shots at the father's cost. The smaller boy smiled at the hardship the bully had to endure.

The smaller one was never picked on again. He would just say his dog was watching. "If you don't believe me, push me down." None of the older boys were brave enough to try. That dog was never seen again. But because of that, the boy never lived another day without a guardian dog as a pet. He learned the weak can pair up with the strong. And the bullies of the world are really scared of equal strength. Pretty smart for a young kid. Don't you think?

Story 23

"Happiness is always just around the corner"

She always felt alone. Even in a crowded room.

    She was considered gorgeous by almost any standard, but that was the cause of her always staying distant. Men only wanted one thing, and women were jealous of her looks. She just wanted acceptance. But that seemed to be out of reach for her.

    Then one day while reading outside she hears a voice speak. A man asked if she would allow him to share her shade. With heavy sarcasm she said this wasn't the only tree. Move along!!! Well, this one is easy for me. She slammed the book shut and looks up for the first time. Embarrassment floods her face. There sits a man around her age in a wheelchair. "I'm so sorry, please join me." "Understand if I'm intruding, I'll move on." "No, please stay."

They talked. Talked for hours. She told her story of rejection. Her lack of trust in men. Somehow there was comfort in talking with this man. He could relate to her feelings. 'Well, I think you're a beautiful person inside and out" he said. "It's their loss. I need to leave. Believe your match is out there, be who you are". And he started to leave. She scribbled her name and number on a piece of paper and handed it to him. A bold move for her. "Call me anytime. I would like that."

And as fate would have it they married one day. She fully accepted him as he was. She had so much love to share. Unconditional love. His legs didn't work but that was all. They had children together. You never know where your happiness will find you.

We all carry problems. More than not it's in our insecurities. In the head. Storms move on. The sun will shine again. Trillions of people came before you. Your problem has already come and gone on this great earth many times. You're not the first to feel this way. Find strength in that!!!

Story 24
"Respect this life"

She lay so restful, her time ending. Her husband by her side.

She looks up and speaks. "I've loved you since the day I first saw you standing in the park. I knew then we would be together." He gives her hand a squeeze. "I've had a wonderful life with you. I've loved you every day. When I'm gone I will look down and still love you. I still think you need me in your life. But that call has been made." This time it's her that gives his hand a squeeze.

"Do this for me. Don't grieve for me too long. That's not good for either of us. I know your love for me." She looks into his eyes and smiles. "I'm so proud to have the life you provided for us. That is mine forever."

"I'm going to sleep now. I'm so tired. Stay by my side till the end. Hold my hand. Give me one last kiss. I want to meet GOD with that on my lips." The tears rolled down his cheeks. They fell on their hands. She slowly passed.

We will all pass one day. Love dearly. Smile plenty. Respect this life. It will someday come to an end. Leave your mark. And make it a positive one.

Story 25
"Revenge"

There was a boy in his late teens. His parents gave him everything. He cared about nothing but himself.

He drove a jacked-up truck with a huge bumper. You've seen the type. Many nights, he took a shortcut, returning home going through a dense forest. There was always something crossing the road, which he took out with his truck. To him, it was just fun.

Then one night, he spotted two deer by the edge of the road. He swerved to hit them both. It was a mother and her young fawn. The mother quickly jumped to the side, protecting her child. Of course, he swerved again to hit her. Her body flew through the air and landed hard. He got back on the road, smiling about what he had just done. Evil was in his heart.

This was no normal forest. Spirits lived there. The deer looked down at the lifeless body and begged the spirits for help. Suddenly, a heavy fog rolled in. It covered the mother, and her body vanished. Revenge for the fawn was going to be his.

The next time the boy drove down that road, he looked to his side to see a deer watching him. Such dark eyes. And so it began. More and more creatures of the forest lined the edge of the woods. All watching him drive by. He thought this was a little creepy but didn't really care.

Then one night, a night of a full moon, he was drinking. He took his shortcut. And there stood the deer. His life was his. He swerved. But when he would have hit the deer, it turned to mist. His truck hit a tree. He was pissed. He saw the deer again. He grabbed his whiskey, took another drink, and got out. He had a pistol in the glove box. It was in his hand now. The deer walked into the woods, and he followed.

The moon gave all the light he needed. But the deer stayed just ahead, and he couldn't get his shot. The air was getting cooler. Birds began to move in the trees above. Animals of the forest moved all around.

So many eyes watched his every move. The temperature continued to fall. He stumbled and fell into a small, wet area. Now soaked and drunk, he wanted to go back. He realized he'd dropped his pistol. He wanted nothing more of the wet ground. He just wanted to get back to his truck. A truck he'd never see again. He was lost. Now animals were everywhere. A deer walked just behind him. He wanted to run, but it was so cold. The whiskey had him confused and off balance. He fell to the ground. All the birds and all life gathered close. It was they who would watch him die. The earth claimed his body.

Searchers never recovered him. Only a mostly empty whiskey bottle and a handgun. A deer watched him lay dead as he had seen his mother. His revenge was complete. The soul of this boy went to hell where it belonged. The spirits made sure of that. The world became a little better place that mystical night. A full moon has her powers.

Story 26
"Greatness"

A small boy around the age of four came to his mother. He asked, "Who is God?"

Why would he ask such a thing? "He sat with me in my room and told me he will call me to his side but not before I do great things." The mother was speechless. Her eyes teared up. She held him close. From that day forward, she tried to balance her time with him. Nothing was so important any longer. She prayed for him to not be taken anytime soon.

Then one day, he came to her side again. "God said I accomplished one of the great things he wanted."

She looked into his eyes, her hand trembling. "What was that?"

He said, "I brought you back to him. He said you drifted away. But now you talk to him every single day. Is that true, Mom?"

"Yes, son. Every day."

Time went by. As he got older, he could see the pain of the homeless. He could see their need for help, love, and understanding. He stepped up. He organized businesses, motivated people, and got organizations to provide shelter. Food was donated, and everyone gave thanks. But one day he could not get up. He was sick. The mother had passed away years earlier. There was nothing anyone could do. He had been called at last.

Finally, as he lay there, his mother appeared. "Take my hand. Let's walk. Look at all of the lives you touched. You did well. The people will keep this going for years to come. You did a great thing."

Story 27

"He can find your smile"

The doctor enters his room. Smiles and introduces himself to Jayson.

He sits on the side of the bed and ask if they can talk. "Sure, about what?" "About you" he says. "I want to know why you're always happy. Your life has been very hard. Seventeen surgeries over three years. You were abandoned and left to die. When you were brought here, you were very near dead. Your operations were very complicated and recovery was extremely painful. Yet you are the happiest child in this hospital. I want to learn why?"

He looks at the doctor and begins to speak. "I'm eleven years old. And that was the number given to me. My mind blocked out all of my life prior to being here. It must have been bad. Yes, I remember the pain. Wishing I would die. But very slowly I was being healed. I remember when I was asked to walk the halls to get my body to strengthen. That is what changed me. You're the doctor but walk with me on my rounds." So they leave the room together.

He stops in the hall and points to the door. "This is Billy's room. He's my best friend. He has no legs. Lost them both in an accident along with his parents. I think of his pain and feel lucky." They continue walking. "This is Sharon's room. She's not going to live much longer. I see her every day. All her parents do is cry. They can't help it. But she needs smiles too. I give them to her. David here is better also. He doesn't like me to visit, or so he says. He has no one. He's mad all the time. He was pretty sick also. So I stop every day. He always yells at me to get out. So I do but I leave a note each time. He reads them I know. Let me drop off this one now." "May I see what you wrote?" "No, it's private between me and David. I think you'll understand."

"This is a children's ward. Every room has a different kid. I know them all. I say goodbye to the lucky ones who get to leave. And I meet the new ones who replace them. That takes time sometimes. But I meet them all. We all need smiles in our lives. I've made it my duty to be the one who freely gives them out. Does that make sense?" The doctor looks down at him in a kind of a shock. "You know you are healing quite well now. One day it will be your turn to leave. What then?"

"That day will take care of itself. Today I'm a badly needed friend to them. I relate. Almost all of them know that. I think this is what I was meant for. Or at least that's what I think."

So fast forward five years. There is this young councilor walking the ward. He goes in and out all the rooms. It's his job to help heal the minds. Always smiling. Always happy. And you know what?

That's very contagious!!!

Story 28
"Unending Love"

He fell in love with her in his early teens. Little did he know she would be his only love. So many say, "Forever," but it's not so easy as you grow from a teenager. Years went by. Many of them. All this time, he never introduced her as his wife; it was always his lover and best friend. Sure, she would get embarrassed and a little upset sometimes, but in her heart, she loved it. Their children thought it was romantic. They got their house back with time. Their days were always filled with smiles and great conversations. They did everything together.

The grandchildren were their most fun. But even they grew up. It's just the way it works. Loneliness wasn't in their home. They always had each other. One day, he came in and found tears streaming down her cheeks. He quickly responded to her. "What is wrong, my flower? Why the tears?"

"I fell asleep and dreamed I would pass before you. It was so real. I don't want to ever leave you alone."

He gave her a very loving hug and said, "Our lives have been full, and except for a tragedy, one of us will go first. That will be a very dark day. We have family to support us then. And we both know we will be together on the other side. You're my lover and best friend. It can be no other way."

He gave her a passionate kiss. "We will savor this moment. We will never lose the taste of the other's kiss. We will feel our touch, the warmth of our bodies showing love for the other. Never forget this moment, and we will never be separated. That I promise. Now show me that pretty smile. Let's go out for a breakfast. A new place has opened. Let's check it out."

Story 29
"No Matter What, You Can Always Do Something"

There was a doctor who was exceptionally talented at his work. The hospital considered him their best physician. His skills saved many.

Then one day while working on his land he had a horrible accident. His hands were crushed. He woke up in a hospital only to realize both his hands had been amputated. The shock was devastating. His reason for life, his hands, were gone. He went downhill from there.

Then one morning he hears a knock at his door. He didn't want to answer but the knocking kept up. His security camera shows a woman standing there.

"You need to leave, I'm not interested in seeing anyone," he says.

"Well, you will see me or call the police."

He had a way to open the door. "What's this about?"

"It's about my dying son. Now let me in."

She hears the door unlocked.

He greets her with anger. "What is this all about?"

"My son is dying, and the hospital says you're the only one with the skills to save him. He needs you right now! And we don't have time to waste!"

"Look!" He holds up his arms. "I can't even open the door by myself!"

She looks around. "I see no one. So, you did let me in. I need you to look at my son! I need that now!"

She goes into a rant. "You are so full of self-pity, do you think you are alone in this world with problems. You would allow my son to die because you feel sorry about yourself? Get your ass up and get dressed. My son will die if you don't."

He yells at her to get out. She comes back with "you lost your hands, not your knowledge. Not your ability to heal. Get ready and see my son." Her words struck a chord. He left with the woman. "What if I can do nothing?"

"Then I'll accept that, and you will have tried."

Long story short, the boy was saved.

After devastating accidents depression will consume you. Your value in life may be shaken. But others can still see the value you possess. The person you still have inside. You are the only one just changed. At some point you must rejoin life. It may seem impossible. But with the help from strangers and friends, you can take a hand and make the walk back. Not everyone will understand the new you. The changed you. Don't let that stop you from making the journey.

Story 30
"Inseparable"

They were inseparable from the day they met. Can love touch and leave its mark at such an early age?

He would search her out. Look till she was found. Both from different families. But they formed a quick bond. She would always be by his side. Always involved in his affairs. They grew quickly. They only grew closer. Friendship really, but interwoven with love. They may not realize that, but that is what it is none the less. Others can see they love each other. Just looking makes you smile.

They're still young, but it will endure. He'll one day protect her with his life. Not saying he wouldn't do this now. His caring and strong friendship with her is in his eyes. Sometimes he just watches her. Turns his head a little. I would love to know what's going on inside that head. He'll just watch her. Is that when his appreciation is the strongest. Today she's a best friend. His favorite companion. Tomorrow will bring more surprises.

His name is Thunder. Her name is Daisy. Even now he's laying close to her while she sleeps. Best friends for life. Such different backgrounds. But that doesn't matter to them. Just a little rest then their fun starts all over. Yes, inseparable. The only word describes them. I think it's cute.

Story 31
"The Friendship of two boys"

There was a very rich child and a very poor one.

Of course, they went to different schools, and their lives were very different. But against all odds, they met. Being so young, they accepted each other as friends. Their differences didn't matter to them. They were friends. The wealthy parents didn't approve of the friendship. They quietly discouraged their seeing each other. Time went by.

The one boy had met all of his friend's family, and they accepted him as their own. The richer child gave his friend shoes, shirts, and pants as was needed. His parents never even noticed them being gone. Time went by.

One day, it was discovered the poor boy was sick. His health was failing. His family was poor, and they relied on charity for the hospital cost. He was going to need a kidney. So the rich boy went to his parents to help. To his surprise, they didn't want to get involved. "He's my best friend. You have to help him." The answer stayed at no. He pleaded, "We have so much, and he has so little. Don't you care?" In retaliation, the parents forbade him from seeing him again.

So, the boy would climb out a second-story window to see his friend. Things were not looking good for him. The day came that he fell from the second floor. The fall killed him. He wasn't found till the next morning. His parents were totally devastated. In his pocket was a note and some money. "My parents won't help, but I will. I'm selling things I don't need. It's not much, but I'll do what I can." This added to the tears already flowing.

At the funeral, his friend and his family stood in the back. Mark was in a wheelchair. Security came to the mother and asked if they should be asked to leave. She looked back to see the family and Dan's friend. She said, "No. Escort them to sit with us." And so, they did. She knelt in front of Mark and gave him a hug. "My Dan told me you were best friends; your future will be different."

She kept her word. Mark soon was walking again. He had gotten Dan's kidney. The mother had the organs of Dan harvested to save other young boys in need. She made sure Dan and Mark would always be together.

Wealth can sometimes blind. Makes you think you're above others. And that is what killed her son. It took him losing his life trying to help his friend to teach her that. The two families were never separated again. And a part of Dan never left his mother and friend.

Story 32
"Asking For Help"

There was a doctor who handled the most critical cases. He was the "last hope" for the medical care to save a life that was lost by all standards. When he could find a few moments of rest he would go to the gardens on the ground and reflect. On one such occasion a mother burst through the door screaming at him. "My daughter is dying in there and you're just enjoying your day! You are both insensitive and incompetent of your responsibilities! This is not where you should be! My daughter needs you!"

He slides over and says, "I'm praying for her right now, join me." She was totally taken back by his response. She stood there looking at him, speechless. He reached for her hand and pulled her to the bench.

"I'm just a man. I work every day to save the sick. I don't always win. I lose both my confidence and my faith almost every day. I can't do this by myself. So, I come here to ask for help. Yes, your daughter is dying. She needs a miracle which only one person can give. And that person is not me. So, I ask for help. I have seventeen people under my care right now. I cannot save them all. I will lose some, maybe all. I'm their last hope. Your daughter is Jennie. She's seven years old. She was flown in from California to be under my care. I'm doing all I can but she's slipping away. I'm here asking for help. I don't want to lose her. I need inspiration. And I'm talking to the only one who has the capability to help."

"Do you believe in GOD? Do you believe in HIS ability of miracles? Do you believe HE listens to your prayers? I do and sometimes HE is my only hope. The only hope for the one under my care. I will fight the evil attacking Jennie. I'll leave no stone unturned. Go be with your family. They need your strength. I now have a good feeling about this. Maybe you were sent to me? My faith is restored. I feel stronger. I'm ready for battle again. Thank you."

Story 33

"Good in everyone"

There was a small boy always consumed with anger. He wasn't well liked.

He bullied both boys and girls. Showed little respect to adult, mostly none. His parents were helpless as to what to do. They tried to get him into programs to help. He only saw this as an effort to get rid of him.

Then early one morning a little girl fell over on her tricycle and couldn't get up. He stood looking at her crying. An old woman stood at her kitchen window and watched this unfold. He carefully looks in all directions, then bend over. The lady expecting him to harm her in some way turns to come to her aid. But she was shocked.

The boy helps the girl and consoles her. Never had she ever seen this side of him. There was a good side after all. So the work began. She said hi to him every chance she had. Would say what a nice day it was. He would only look down and quickly walk away. She talked to the parents about him. Not showing her hand. She just wanted to know him better.

Then the break came. As he walked pass she said "Happy Birthday William" I made a cupcake for you. He stops and looks at her. They make eye contact. Then he quickly moves along. At that moment a change happened. No he didn't just warm up to her, but something changed. Now as he walked pass he would secretly glance over to see if she was out. He had never had a friend before.

On a hot day, as he passes he sees her on the porch. He hers her words, "come out of the heat and share some Lemonade with me, it's cold". The ice was broken. He sat and they talked.

We see all sorts of people. We all have our problems. Caring for others is strong medicine. Medicine needed by some. "Care" about the welfare of others. Try to be a positive influence. You can't help them all. But you maybe the help needed in a life at that time. There is good in everyone. Dig a little deeper.

Story 34
"A Prayer answered"

It was a time of war. Hundreds of brave men and women died every day because of their honor and belief. On this day, a battle between two great forces shook the ground. The smell of death, the cries of pain were everywhere. This needed to end. But how?

A small, unimpressive man looked at the carnage and knew it would be him to end this. He would save thousands by the sacrifice of himself. So, he prayed. "Give me strength. I'm weak. Give me courage because I'm overwhelmed with fear. Bless my family. I will never see them again. I give my life because to save thousands is just. You gave your life to save millions. I follow your teachings. No one will know my name. No one will know my sacrifice. Just you and I. But I do this for humankind. I do this for my unborn child. I do this for you. So, how? Force a retreat on both sides. Destroy the ability to give commands by either power. Without direction, without structure, wars can't continue. So, how? I kneel to you. I ask for your wisdom." At that moment, a bomb exploded. He was thrown back. He was unconscious. Now the rumbling of the ground became intense. The earth began to separate. An earthquake rose to the surface.

Implements of war were swallowed up. Men on both sides ran for their lives. There was no more war. Both armies were in retreat. The man woke up in a hospital. In his unconscious state, he heard a voice. "Your prayer was answered. You will meet your unborn child. I needed to know such sacrifice still lived in the heart of man. The war ended that day. The power of prayer is infinite. The love of man for his fellow men will be their salvation. I have spoken."

Story 35
"Strange Events"

A small boy walked up to his teacher and told him he had the same mark on his shoulder.

"Really, this is a birth mark. It's kind of unique."

"Look at mine, they're the same."

So, the teacher turned him around and saw his mark. A shock ran through his body. The boy looks back at him and says "I think you're my dad."

He looks at him not sure what to say next. "What's your mother's name?"

"Clair," he says. Again, he's taken back. "I knew a Clair once. She moved off years back."

"Well, we moved here about a month ago. This is where she used to live."

"Is she here today?"

"No, I came with a friend."

He sits in a chair, his mind racing. "You never had a dad?" he asked.

"No, mom won't talk about it. She says when I'm older."

He looks at the boy and studies him for a moment. "Are you and your mother happy?"

"Sure, that's a funny question."

"Excuse me for asking such questions. I just want to know you better."

"Are you my dad?" he asked again.

"Well, I can't answer that either. We may just have a similar birthmark. Will your mother bring you tomorrow?"

"Well maybe. I don't know."

"Ask her to. Tell her a teacher would like to speak with her and say nothing about the birthmarks. Will you do that for me?"

The next morning the small boy and his mother entered the room. He looks up and their eyes meet. He had never seen her before. His feelings were scrambled. He's not sure just how he feels. For a moment he thought he and Clair would meet again. No longer. He smiles and asks her to sit.

"Why am I here?"

"Well, I don't want you upset with me for this, but it was important for me to speak with you. It's all cleared up now. Do you have time for a coffee, I have a story to tell. I think it will surprise you too."

Story 36

"The strength of my love for you"

What would happen if I lost you?

Devastation would take over my life. My feeling of loss would consume me. For the first time I would feel the emotion of loneliness. Tears would flow. It would be hard on me. Very hard!!!

How would I adjust? I really have no idea. You are my universe. My beautiful flower. Life without your smile will break my heart.

I would have no choice but to accept the present. You would be memory now. I'll speak to you in my dreams. See your smile. But at some point I'll wake. I'll start another day without you. Longing for night and sleep again. Holding hands. Slow dancing. Even mixing a drink for you. All will be lost.

So for now you are under my protection. Allowing nothing to harm you without my intervention. Trust in my strength. I'll give my life for you. On that you can be sure. Until that day, walk by my side. Share your moments. Hold my hand. Kiss my lips. As we grow old together, you can move to the cheek. Not now. I love you. Know that!!!

Story 37

"The value of a child"

What is the value of a child? Well, to some, not much. But to others, a value can't be reached. To hold that newborn for the first time and know you helped create that life. You swell with pride and love. Is there work involved in raising that child? Sure. But the work is work of love. One day, your name will leave their lips. Might be *mama* or *dada* first, but both will come.

The crawling, then walking and unfortunately running. But you smile. You dress them up for special company or events. They are truly the center of your life right now. The breaks are cherished, though for not too long. Then the big day comes. They tell you they love you. That's a special day. It will be said many times in your life. But the first time is always cherished. Now we all know some days you want to tie a rock to their leg, toss them, and deny you ever had a child. After a little recovery and a glass of wine, the full love returns. You do so much to protect and nourish them. It's tiring. Once again, I can say it's work woven with a lot of love.

You'll do your best. They will give you grandchildren to pretend being a parent again. By then, time is moving so fast. You know it, but they don't. You'll see less of them as they grow to adulthood. It's just the way it is. You'll always be placed on a pedestal, but everything is so busy now.

Then the day comes when you're passing away. You were there when they came into this world; they will be there when you leave. They will regret more time wasn't made. Nothing can change that now. You become a cherished picture, stories of love from the days lost forever. In spite of such a sad ending, the love still lives. It is still felt. Out of nowhere, you'll have a dream of them. A nice one. Know you were kissed on the forehead. They sit by your side and talk to you. Relive their time with you. What is the value of a child? Priceless!

Story 38
"How Commitment is Defined"

You hear the words "they, he, she lacks commitment." But what is the base line for that judgement?

We are all so different. Many may follow a similar path in life. But never the exact footprints. So, who has the right to make that call? If I choose not to get engaged and just want to date, does that make me a person who lacks commitment? For the other person, what is their commitment to the relationship? You need to commit or go your own way. I don't have forever! Between the two who was more committed?

I think that example opens the door to what really is a happy and solid relationship? My gage to measure is not the same as yours. You might be influenced by others. They push their opinions on you. Then one day this happy relationship isn't as happy any longer. The definition of love comes into question. Everything can change so quickly.

Isn't that what dating is all about? Finding the common ground. Identifying shared interest? Communication at its finest. Or it should be? Most people will date many in life. You can't marry them all. You weren't meant to. Can you separate as friends? Speak well of each other? The ability to make that call soon enough is important for both parties. Waiting too long causes the relationship to sour. Tears may be shed, but it's for the best. That ending is that day or days down the road.

If it was repairable, then it would be repaired. Both must want it. It's not a lack of commitment but choices and common ground. The clock will take care of itself. Never allow your emotions to rule your life. Like butter on a slice of bread, don't add it too thick. The right amount helps with the balance. Adds to the flavor. Stay in charge. Fall in love. But do all you can to keep the friendship if the love doesn't take you where you want it to. I've been in love many times. I'm in love even today. And I've tried to remain friends with every love that didn't pan out. I have a greater capacity to remain a friend than an enemy. I would never want to hate someone I once loved. Never!

Story 39
"A bottle of pills"

She sat on the bench a bottle of pills in hand. She had finally given up on life. Why live?

Raised in an orphanage, her brother adopted early, and she was left with no one. An innocent trip to the store changed her life forever. She thinks she remembered a last look from her before the other car hit them. Her mother died there. She was told she had no father or other family. She had lived a very "unloved" life. So why continue?

It was then a man sat next to her. " Cassy, I don't mean to alarm you, but I have something you want to hear". "Who are you, she says"? "My name is John. Look at this." He lifted a picture to show her. There stood a small boy and a little girl. Their last picture together.

"Johnny, can that really be you"? She looks deep into his eyes. She can see her lost brother. "How can this be"? They hug as her tears flow. "Cassy, I've been looking for you for a long time. A couple of times I almost gave up. But I knew I had a little sister that needed me. So I never gave up. I've been following you thinking of how to introduce myself. I could tell you were not happy. All of that will change now. So come with me, we have a lot of catching up to do." As they walk past the trash bin, she tossed in a bottle of pills.

Now, it could be argued that a divine hand had been placed on her shoulder just when she needed it most. Maybe her Guardian Angel made the decision to change her life. Decided she had suffered long enough. That she needed the weight of such pains lifted. She needed reasons to smile and feel happy again. Just maybe!

It could also be argued that it was just her good luck. Non believers like that explanation. I want you to stand in front of me. Look deep into my eyes and tell me to the bottom of your heart you really believe all of this was just luck? That there was no chance it could have been a divine action. He couldn't answer.

When we are at the bottom of our darkest pit, that's when our words are the loudest. Prayer has power. Hope can become strong again if just the smallest spark is kept alive. No matter how dark your life is right now, prayer can change the direction. Trust me, Trust in GOD!

Story 40

"Change isn't a bad thing"

For so many, this will be a wonderful day. It could be your birthday. A new member of the family will arrive. You will spend the day with someone you love. And that could easily be your dog that's been lost. Joy and satisfaction are not that long of a reach. It may seem so, but in the big picture, it's not. The sun and cool temperatures are not here every day. Our planet and we need the changes of the seasons. If it gets too hot or too cold, we have technology on our side. Fix the situation. Understanding that storms will enter our lives but will not stay should bring comfort. All bad will pass with time. In business, it would become necessary to terminate someone. They were seldom pleased with that. I'm 5'5". Basketball is not in my future. But I did try. Sales is not for everyone. But not being good at one sport doesn't mean give up on all sports.

I've had former employees thumb their nose and say, "Look at my success." They were salesmen. Just not in my field. I was very proud they found their goal. My termination was the best thing that could happen to them that day. I know many who found their niche. It was never in my field. So, see through the dark clouds. Know that times to celebrate are always just around the corner. You may be restricted to your homes. But soon you'll be able to spread your wings and soar again. Keep your smiles.

Story 41
"A Beautiful Dream"

I hurry about the house. It's four in the morning. Very important day ahead. I've set up a fishing trip for me, dad, David, and Maggie. Of course, dad shows up early. The coffee is hot and an ashtray is on the table. David, on the other hand, will always run a little late. Dad settles in and I introduce him to Maggie. They're friends instantly. Maggie even lays at his feet. Sure enough David enters with that "I'm sorry I'm late" smile. But forgiving him was easy.

We jump into dad's small white truck, all piled in on each other and head for Surfside to his favorite spot. We're after redfish today and maybe a flounder or two. I fill the 5-gallon bucket with water and dad throws the cast net. We have bait in minutes. To my surprise Uncle Bert shows up. Fishing pole in hand.

We all bait and cast. We spend all morning there. I gave dad his hat. I got his boots from Beth. He looked as he always had. Maggie stayed at his side. Looking over every now and then for approval. She somehow knew she was his dog now. That trip was the best. We all talked and laughed. Never caught a fish but who cares. I sat next to David. I wanted to get in the most visit I could.

Slowly they became a memory again. It was never meant to last. A gift from GOD I guess. So here I lie. Wanting so badly to go back to sleep. To pick up where I left off. But it wasn't to be.

We never completely lose our loved ones. They now reside in our hearts, our memories. They visit at moments when we least expect. Just a brief stay. Just to let you know they're thinking of us. One of the blessings given out in the night.

So, until the next time I wait. Longing for a quick return. It will come. I see his hat hanging on the wall. A small reminder he's never far. Time for coffee, I guess. Smiling, I go to the kitchen.

Story 42
"The Power of Hope"

It all started at about age fifteen. A small boy was dying in the hospital. He really had no hope. This is where she came in.

Finding out he had no family, no one to be with him in his last hours, she stepped up. She actually slid into his life. She held him close, whispered soft words into his ear. For two days she never left his side. And to the astonishment of everyone he got better.

This young mother came to her and asked if she would comfort her child. She gave a small smile and agreed. That child got better also. Coincidence, probably. But it was seen as something greater. And so it began. Over the years she held hundreds of ill people. Many died anyway. But their death was wrapped in dignity. Many got better. She was called a "healer". She never corrected people when this was said. She would just smile softly and walk away.

Being a "healer" became her life now. She married and had a daughter with time. And at an early age her daughter told her mother she would carry on her work when she no longer could. And that day finally did come. The mother wasn't sick. She had just aged. Her time here was over. The daughter asked how she could take her gift and use it for the same good.

The mother took her hand and began to speak. There is no gift. Just an understanding of life. People need hope. As long as hope lives, miracles can happen. All of us begin life listening to the heartbeat of our mothers. That alone benefits life. The sick need to be held tight and close. They need to hear that heartbeat and feel warmth. Their minds go back in time. Their mother's care is reconnected. Age doesn't matter. It's the security. That is my secret. Never talk of this to anyone. Everyone must believe you have a gift. A gift to save a life. And in a way you do. Their hope will begin to repair as soon as you enter the room. It's them who help themselves. They do the work. Speak softly, hold them tight, and allow them to fight the battle of life. As long as they believe in your power, their power does all the work. Never, ever, tell anyone the secret. You will kill their hope. Take the credit you don't really deserve. That's not a bad thing. They get their life back.

Story 43
"The Power of a Prayer"

A man was walking on a trail and looked up to see a bear in full charge, coming at him.

He knew there was no way to save himself. So he took a knee, and this is what he said in his last words.

"Lord, please accept me as I am. Allow me to enter your kingdom. I'm not without sin. And I don't ask for more time. Just accept me as I am. I've tried to live an honest and fair life. I've shared with those who had less. I know I didn't enter your house, but you know I've talked to you. I've spoken to you in times of hardship. When the hardship was both mine and when it belonged to others. I asked for your healing.

"So don't judge me too harshly please. I do have a good heart. I'm ready to meet you if that's your wish."

He could feel the ground move. He could hear the heavy breathing of the animal. His time was up. A peaceful feeling fell over him. He knew his words reached their destination. He felt the fur brush him as the animal ran past and disappeared behind him.

He opened his eyes. The danger was gone. He knew there was only one explanation why he still lived. When you take a knee, it's not to protest; it should be to pray. And when you pray, have the words come from the bottom of your heart. They are heard.

Story 44
"Happiness is Sometimes Hidden"

There was a small girl. Her life didn't follow the regular patterns. She just couldn't find happiness. This is her life story.

Her name is Liz and she was sad and not smiling most of the time. Her parents did all they could. Doctors gave meds, but never really fixed the problem. It was classic depression. Why her? She was so young. Not much changed over the years.

In her early teens she sat alone on the bleachers at school. That's when she noticed a boy separated himself. They made eye contact. A cry to the other for interaction and understanding. A few days later she was at the gym again. She looks around for him. When she finds him, he's a little closer, but not looking at her. And so, this "game" began. Ever so close they sat. Then one day she looks for him, he's not around. She hears her name spoken. He had moved in behind her. She looks forward, not moving.

He says his name is David. Talking to her back, he speaks of himself. The loneliness of separation. How others just don't understand their life. Their advice didn't apply. Their worlds are too different. He tells her he knew she would. He stands to leave. She in turn tells him maybe another day they could visit again. It's the smallest actions that open the largest doors.

And visit they did. Conversations of their feelings in life. Why they felt so distant. Why their meetings were opening doors to their common inner insecurities. They fell in love with time. Their world was changing. With the help of each other, they emerged from their shells.

Real understanding can cure many problems. The correct approach hits the mark. Sometimes the answer is love. Unconditional devotion for the welfare of the one you love. A building of confidence from the ground up. A path traveled together. An abundance of patience. When love is involved, it's not really that hard.

A happy ending for two. How many more are out there needing their hero. Their partner of understanding. I have faith in this land. Good is everywhere.

Story 45

"Time is only so long"

She sat on the couch wrapped in a blanket. Eating a snack and enjoying her favorite show.

A typical Friday night for her. Not in the dating scene, and really not wanting to be. Her life was simple but all of that was about to change. She hears a knock on the door. Who could that be she thinks? She opens the door to find her mother standing there in tears. Their eyes meet and the mother says "I'm dying. I need you, I'm scared."

The daughter quickly brings her in and gives comfort. "What? What is this? Talk to me." And so the mother explains. "I got the news just this afternoon. My doctor says I have a fatal blood disorder. They can't help me. I have approximately three months. It's going to move quickly. " At a loss for words the daughter hugs her tight and asks what can she do to help?

"Take care of me like I cared for your father when he got ill. Be my nurse, my best friend, my loving daughter. I'm sorry to put this all on you but you're all I have left. And I'm so scared. So much to take in. So much to do. I need you now more than ever." And kisses her forehead. "Mom, I want you to rest. Sleep in my bed tonight. Try not to think about things. We'll solve it all tomorrow. I just want you to rest now. Are you hungry?" "No, I think rest is the best idea." She put her mother to bed. Gave her a sleeping pill to insure the sleep. Then went to work. What all needed to happen? In which order. How could she give the best care and still be her mother's daughter?

She took a leave from work. It took about two weeks of steady work to accomplish all the details. But she did it. Now she turned to her mother. "We're going on a trip together. Where have you always wanted to go to see? Name anyplace." "We don't have the money for such a thing." "Mom, it will be our last big trip together. Let me do this." She takes her hand and looks into her eyes. "I'm asking for a mother/daughter trip. Allow me this small pleasure here at the end. I should have been there more for you. This is my chance to make it up a little. Tell me someplace you always wanted to see?"

The mother looks at her with tears falling. "I want to see Rome. I've always wanted to walk the streets. Maye a little shopping. Your father was always going to take me. We just ran out of time. I'm not sure I'm strong enough for the walking?" "Leave that all to me. Thank you mom and kisses her cheek. Thank you so much."

The funeral was small. The daughter carried a hidden smile. She had memories of her for life. Her smiles. Her looking with amazement at the sights. Hearing her mother tell stories of her childhood. Of their family when she was too young to remember. She wheeled her all over the city. She was always smiling at her mom while her heart was breaking on the inside.

We all don't get the chance to have such a special time with a dying parent. It seems they're gone in a flash. A way of life I guess. Pay attention to your time. Pay attention to how you use it. Your time with them is worth much more than money. Seeing them smile is priceless.

Story 46
"Mother Nature"

The wind howls, the trees shake, and Mother Nature steps to the forefront.

Every so often, Mother Nature demands the attention of all humankind. It is she who is all powerful on earth. Water is her weapon. Combined with the powers of wind, she holds your life in her grasp. Nothing made by humans can stop her. She is truly in charge.

But her anger doesn't last. Given a little time, she calms down. She opens the skies and allows the sun to shine down again. Her point has been made. Those who ran from her anger can now return. She leaves no doubt about her displeasure. The landscape bears scars.

She will move across the land. Millions will lose their power, and some will lose their lives. Yes, when she wants your full attention, she gets it. We still don't fully understand Mother Nature. We are getting better at predicting patterns. But control—it will always be hers.

Story 47
"Introductions"

Who is she?

This smile across the room? Such a nice smile. Some people are just lucky that way. Not me of course. You can tell she takes pride in her looks. Her hair, each and every one in place. The look she wants. She holds a glass of wine. I've yet to see her take a sip. But it fits well with the picture she projects.

I've moved a little closer, I can hear her speak. I think her voice is sexy. Maybe I'm just wishing she was talking to me. Her skin looks soft. Age has been nice to her. Her scattered grey fits her well. She's not wearing a ring. I wonder why? A story I would like to hear. Her eyes are green. Not that common. I like that.

She just looked at me. We held eye contact for a moment. She smiled and gave a slight nod. That has to be good. I'm nervous. I'm not sure why. I want to introduce myself to her. Steal some of her attention. I want to talk with her. Learn more about her. Let her know me better. Why am I so nervous over this? At my age? No matter what happens I will speak to her. I have to. She still hasn't tasted her wine. Maybe that's my opening question? I'm not sure.

I look up and she's walking in my direction. Just a few steps.

"Hello, my name is Cory. I love this house, what's your thoughts?" The hell with the wine question!

Story 48

"Brave Parents"

She sat on the edge of the bed bolding his hand. His father sat quietly in the chair knowing his son would not make it much longer. For such a big man his heart was breaking. He very quietly cried.

The mother stroked his forehead. Without moving, her son asked if she could hold him once more. The nurses were called to fill his last request. Different tubes and patches were removed. She slid into the bed beside him. Cradling him in her arms. Very weakly he says, "I know I'm going to a good place. I will miss ya'll greatly". "You will be met by family passed. We'll join you later. Know this." With a shallow breath she says, "take care of Willie, he likes to be scratched under his chin. Tell him bye for me. I love you both, I'm sorry I'm leaving. I'm scared. Hold me tighter please." With tears streaming, she heard his last breath leave. They all hugged for the last time.

In the book of life the parents are to leave before the children. It doesn't always follow the script. I don't think anything is harder than seeing a child pass before your eyes. It's not supposed to be that way.

Willie's name was changed to the name of their son. A final small thread to hold on to. They found comfort in that, in their own way.

Story 49
"Kindness"

There was once a homeless man. He had lived on the streets for about two years.

The company he had worked for let him go. Not because he was a bad employee; they just eliminated his position. At his age, he couldn't find another job. His money didn't last, and he lost his home. Basically, he lost all he had. His hope, his pride, his world fell to the ground. So now he slept on the streets.

One cold, lonely night, he heard a whimpering. It was really cold that night. He got up to check it out, and in a dark corner, he found a young dog. It was shivering and freezing to death. So he took him in. He placed him in the blanket with him. And that was the beginning of a miracle friendship.

He shared everything with his Joey. They became best friends. A couple more years passed. Then one day, he noticed Joey was getting sick. It got worse every day. His dog was dying. So he scratched out a sign.

"Please help me save my dog. I love him and don't want him to die. He needs a vet, and I have nothing." People began to stop. They asked questions and gave money. A vet even stopped and examined the animal. He told the man it was serious. And he would have to take the dog.

"Take all I have. Tell me what you need. But please, please save him … He is the only thing of value I have. He is my friend." Almost immediately, donations began to pour in. The old man was given a room with meals. Everyone wanted to help. He was even offered a job. But without his friend, all of that meant nothing. The gods favored him. As I said, it was a miracle friendship.

Because of a freezing dog and his kindness, he got his life back. That chance meeting got him off the streets. His friendship with a dog, his love for that animal—there was a lesson to learn. Kindness itself can plant the seed of change. Love will make it grow. And with that, nothing will remain the same.

Story 50
"Different Lives; Common Happiness"

They're different from most children. But a wonder of a beautiful life just the same.

The body is bent. Born that way. Not every tree grows tall and sways in the wind. It's one of the things about life that makes us all stop and look. Marvel at the workings of the ALMIGHTY. HIS reasons aren't easy to understand sometimes. Is it to build my strength? To pull my stored love and bring it to the surface? I've been tested in so many ways. I just don't know. But there is a reason for sure. I keep searching, asking myself questions. I trust in HIM.

This life is so innocent. Holding my hand. Showing their love. Depending on my care. Sometimes I just look and stare. Sure, some days are a real challenge. We all have our tough times in life. For some the weight we carry is a little heavier. But we were picked for this work. Chosen by GOD himself. What an honor.

A mother's love is without bounds. Not clearly understood by men. But they try. We all go about our day. The wheels of life turn. A fresh start every twenty-four hours. I'm strong. I have help. I have friends and family I can depend on. That's good. I guess I need a small break every now and then. Who doesn't? A recharge of the batteries. Then I'm ready for another day, a week, or a year. Whatever is asked of me.

So don't judge my life. Help me celebrate it. Everything's for a reason. My smile is just as beautiful as my heart. And my heart is just as beautiful as my child.

Story 51

"I'm my father's son"

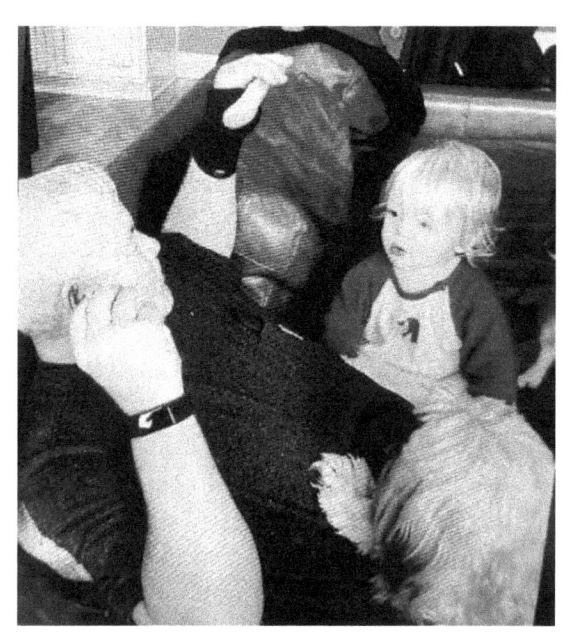

I'm my father's son. I see that so clearly now.

My father was so much older than me. We did things together, as all children get to do. Boys time is different than girls. I think the softer side showed more. He was a good father. Did his part in raising us. He was just so much older. As I grew, so did he. I could never catch up. This strong man I craved to be around.

The outdoors was his church really. On Sundays he went with the family. But in nature is where his soul fit best. So many trips over time. Always a helper. That was my job. Help the family is what we were taught. We did our part as best we could. The children grow up one day. They start their own lives. They leave the home to be on their own. Not always a pleasant separation. With time all is forgiven.

You see your father very differently as an adult. This much older guy. Not as strong now but still very active. Age has taken its toll. He's still so much older. He's slowed down a lot. Has friends over more. Dominoes still spark his interest. One day he passes. His age stops. All memories and all pictures show him as he was. Time for him no longer moves forward. That's just the way life works!

Your aging continues. Sometimes at just the right angle I see him in me. I still try to make him proud. I still hear his laugh. I've already lived more years than he did. Longevity is in our genes. How much more will I go? No clue. But I'm my father's son. And for that alone, I'll do my best.

Story 52
"That inner voice"

A small girl was in the yard playing. She saw a flower, a very colorful flower. She picked it and looked closely. And for no reason, she decided to eat it. As she moved her hand to her mouth, a hand stopped her. A voice said, "Don't eat this flower; study it." She looked up and around, but she was by herself. But being such a small child, she shrugged it off.

The advice stayed with her. As the years passed, her study of flowers flourished. She extracted color. These colors were used by artists to make beautiful paintings. She was able to enhance the quality of the flower to bring joy to everyone. Lifesaving medicines were created from the flowers. All of this happened because she didn't eat a pretty flower that would have killed her.

We have angels who watch over us. They interact with the very young. They are your inner voice as you age. As adults, your free will can cut off your feelings. Block your inner judgment of what's right. Refocus occasionally. Reset your outlook on life. We move from the center because our life drives us like a rut we can't seem to escape. So you slow down and make the adjustment. We will see the evil around us. We'll question, "Why?" The answer isn't clear. But remember, you have a guardian angel. You have protection. Listen to your heart. Be the example.

Story 53
"Sometimes the One You Love Will Fade"

What happens when we lose someone we love so dearly?

When two people separate, it's not always a bad negative event. Sometimes our love is taken from us. A car crash, a terrible accident, so many more ways. But they are gone and it's something your heart will have to accept.

There are times when the separation is slow. The mind is slowly fading. It takes years. You hold hands more. Speak soft words to each other. Always knowing you will lose them one day. Their body may still be there. But you'll be forgotten. You become the caretaker for this person you still love to be the center of your soul.

Then one day you stand at a grave with fresh flowers. The memories overwhelm you. You drop to your knees and cry. You do a lot of that now. You know you will have to "move on" but not right now. The heart mends slowly. And sure, you will most likely find love again, this love will never be replaced. No one wanted it to end. That love was taken from you.

So, listen to this song and remember those fond memories. Never forget them.

Goodbye by Kenny Rogers.

Story 54

"Don't grow old alone"

He was old yet happy with his years. He'd lived a long life. Not really ready to go yet. But understood the process of life.

He remembered his life as a small child. A one room classroom. Three grades in his. All separated into groups. Wasn't that bad. Very strict. Was too scared to cause a problem. Sees kids now and shakes his head. They have no idea.

Joined the Army at seventeen. World War II. Got shot and thought he died on the battlefield. Woke up days later in the hospital. It still hurts on very cold days. But he lived, and is thankful for that. Later he worked at a factory. Long days and hard work. He scraped by. Never did marry. Thinks that big scar on the side of his face was the reason. Not much to look at. But he did live!!!

Retired and moved into a small apartment near a park. His days are much slower now. Just gets by. His only fun is the park. Fresh air, people, children, and the squirrels. He'd feed them both. He's not really lonely, been an outsider all his life. Adjusted years ago. Just thinks a companion would be nice. That's not to be. So a slow walk home ends the day. A bowl of soup and a little TV then a good night's sleep. Nothing ever changes.

      The elderly needs more stimulation in their lives. At least some do. Don't allow them to age with a mundane existence. Do more for them. Share your time. Figure out a way to bring smiles to their experienced faces. Something as simple as a conversation will work. A little time given freely, it would go a long way.

Story 55
"The sacrifice of love"

A small boy kneeled at his bed and folded his hands. This is what he said: "Jesus, we have spoken many times. I say my bedtime prayers every night. Tonight, I need your help. My sister is very sick. I heard the doctor tell my mother that sis is so small to be as sick as she is. She may not be strong enough. She's only four. I'm almost six. I'm much stronger. I'm asking you to give me half of her sickness. The bigger half. I don't want to lose my sister. I can help. I've always been her helper. I'm asking for your help tonight. Amen."

The next day, he entered the hospital very sick. He was put in the room with his sister. Their eyes met. Very weakly, he said, "Don't worry anymore. I'm helping you." They fought so bravely. Their mother cried so much she had no more tears. Then things started to change. The sickness began to fade. In his sleep, he saw his mother. She looked different but was smiling. She said all would be better. She was helping them both. They lost their mother that night.

As he grew older, he never forgot those hours … His sister fell in love and married. He understood the sacrifice his mother had made out of love. He understood it well.

Story 56
"The Honor Protected"

There was a quarterback and a virgin, their paths crossed.

The football player had his way with the girls at school. He really showed little respect. Then one day he noticed a pretty young girl who wasn't interested in him. So, he told his friends he would "bed" her in less than two weeks. And so, his pursuit began. What he didn't expect was her confidence and morals. She cut him off at every approach.

Finally, she had him listen to her. "I'm saving myself for the man I marry. I will pick him more than he will pick me. I have standards, standards you have long lost. I'm after a marriage that will last till death. Not some weak fun in the backseat of your dad's car. So go on your way and let me be."

But his pursuit of her didn't go unnoticed.

Another girl became very jealous. She wanted to destroy her. She placed drugs in her locker and turned her in. And sure, enough the drugs were found. It was looking bad.

She sat in a chair across from the principal with police on each side of her. She was about to be taken in when the door opened. There stood the quarterback. He entered the room. "What is this about?" Asked the principal.

"I'm here to confess what was said. I placed the drugs in her locker because I knew she would never be suspected. I didn't want them found on me. I set her up."

She looked up to his eyes. She could see he was lying. A quick-thinking policeman asked him what they found. His story quickly fell apart.

"Why would you try to help this girl?" He sat down and began to speak. "I had a chance to talk with her once. In that short time, I saw my weakness and her strength. She has more character than all of us combined. She is innocent. On that I'll stake my life. I don't know who did this to her, but I will stand my ground, it was me."

"Your life would be ruined!"

"What about hers?" he asked. "What's happening is not justice. I'll stand for her innocence. And I will not back down!" In the end she was released.

Out of the blue he got a call. It was her. "You once asked me out. Is that still there? Just for a coke and ice cream. But we could talk."

"Yes, it's still there. And I'll treat you with all the respect you deserve. Trust me."

Years later they had children together. And to this day their love for each other grows stronger.

Story 57
"We're here for a reason"

Do you believe we were all placed on this earth, given life, to do a job for the good?

What if as a much younger person you picked up a sharp object and gave it to an adult. What if just days later a diabetic walked passed and wasn't harmed. A puncture to the feet is dangerous. Your action may have saved that life. What if? Maybe your quick reflex prevented an accident. The life of a person you don't even know was saved. The world we live in is very complex.

The dark may take your heart later in life. But you saved a life and really didn't know it. You were place here for that job. The other one may have been needed at a later time. And it was you who provided it. Maybe we're all connected in some way? The bigger picture most people don't see.

Instead of people protesting for the right to end the life of the unborn. Maybe more than one life was taken? It's not the children or the young who chooses to end the life of the unborn. Sadly it's adults. But that is a whole other discussion.

As in bowling, the ball strikes one pin and the chain reaction begins. It doesn't last long, but a lot happens. That's the way life works. Your life can affect so many others. The influence can be a positive one. In other cases not so much. Some don't care about the big picture. They live for today. If greed didn't exist, how would that change our live? How would that change the world?

There are those who take and those who earn. Very different people. Not on the outside but internal.

Who are you?

Story 58

"Our Pets"

Yes, I love my dogs. My cats are pretty special too. Having a dog or dogs is a big thing. Are they perfect? Not at all. They want attention when you're busy up to your eyeballs. You just don't have the time. But you make it for them. They show such love. They only want to please you. To be your best friend. And when you stop your busy day to touch their heart, give them your love, the love they ask for, what can I say?

They do smile. They move in as close to you as possible. To give you dog kisses on your face is their reward. No matter how big they get, they still want your lap. They are best friends. Dogs come in all shapes and sizes. Each one has their own unique personality. They would give their life for you without question. And for what? A small amount of special attention just for them. Dog treats? Or just to be allowed to be treated like people and be on the couch or sleep by your side.

Yes, without question, their loyalty is second to none. Being a dog lover speaks well of you. You have enough love that you can share with animals. Some can't accomplish that with people. So I see them lying around me on my bed, trusting I will care for them as I would any family member. They don't live nearly long enough. And their passing will cause me great grief. I'll cherish my time with them now. That future will come to me at its own pace. I'll deal with it then. But today, I'll show extra love. When this writing ends, cookies will be given to each one. And they do love their cookies.

As for my cats, they are so different. And different in a good way. Where the dogs will knock me over when called, the cats require I negotiate terms. They'll stand back and just look at me. They ask, "What is he doing for me? Why should I walk to him? No! I'm not doing it." They just walk away. Cats! But I wouldn't give them up.

Story 59
"We Can All Look the Same, Yet Be Very Different"

An old timer was raking the leaves in his yard. A small boy walks up to him.

"Mister, I'll rake your leaves for a quarter. I'll do a good job. Can I?"

He looks down at the child. He can see his cloths are well worn. He notices two areas sewn on his pants. "You from around here?"

"Kind of. Can I have the work?"

The man studies him for a minute then hands him the rake. Soon he hears a knock on his door. There stands the boy asking for bags to pick up the leaves. The old man steps out to see his work. All the leaves are in a single pile. All the leaves. He was impressed to say the least. Soon all the leaves were bagged and set by the curb. The boy returns to the door and asks if he could be paid now.

The old man compliments him on his work and pays him five dollars. This brings tears to the boy, and he runs off. The next morning, he hears a knock again. There stands the boy. He steps on the porch.

"My mother says I owe you more work for the pay you gave me. What else can I do?"

"She said that, did she? Where do you live?"

He hangs his head a little and just says "a couple of blocks over. What do you need done?"

"The rest was a tip. If you do more work, you will be paid again."

"I need to speak with my mother first." And he turns to leave. Curious, he follows him in his car. The boy enters an old run-down building. The man returned home.

Sure enough the boy returns. "Mom says ok. What do you need done?"

"I saw where you live. Tell me your story. We're friends now. Maybe I can help?"

They sit on his bench and the boy talks. He came from South America. They were immigrants. They have nothing really. Afraid they may be returned. So, he does work for the few dollars he can earn. His mother depends on him. Now he understood. Where he came from an American quarter was valuable. He knew he needed to help. These were good people worthy of help.

"Do me a favor. Would you introduce me to your mother? I can help your situation."

That was years ago. Both are doing well. His church sponsored the family. Juan is in school now and making good grades. The mother works at the church. She doesn't receive any government money by choice. She was raised very proud. She's not afraid of work and lives within her means. A lesson many need to learn. We have some who just want an easy life. We also have many who need that "fresh start." Never judge all harshly. The good fruit and the bad are always mixed. They just need to be recognized and separated. A lesson for our government!

Story 60
"We are all unique"

Such a beautiful child. But all babies are. This one was no different. Or was he?

As time passed it was understood he was indeed different. Very quiet, not speaking at all. Withdrawn. This was his life. Anxiety his norm. Didn't like noise, being touched, or strangers. Eye contact not his thing. Yet he wanted to just be himself.

He would withdraw to the back of his mind. Looking out through eyes only he understood. If it was noticed he was watching, he quickly looked away. He never wanted to draw attention. He saw others. Others his age. They were so different. All of them. Somewhere in his mind he knew. It was him that didn't fit in. A part of him wanted to, yet another part didn't care.

Time moved on. His best friends were his family. They all loved him dearly. Didn't want him lonely. Lonely in a house full of love. He aged like everyone. One of the few things he shared with other people. This boy grew to be a man. His body had the appearance of an adult. His mind stayed withdrawn.

Did he ever adjust to his surroundings? I guess it would better be described his surroundings accepted him. We're not all the same. No matter what we share, we're still very unique. Acceptance needs a few adjustments. Acceptance isn't that easy for everyone. Especially the immature. Find peace in your world. Accept the different things you're exposed to. Know the picture is bigger that you.

Compassion is not something to shun. We all have understanding, the parents need to teach their children in their early years. The whole world will benefit!!!

Story 61
"Together Always"

When you look at the one you love, what do you see? A best friend maybe. A stabilizer for your life that sometimes gets out of control. You share everything. And your time apart is always felt. Your day is so much brighter when you're together visiting or just sitting in silence and holding hands. She feels your love. You look at her and see a caring heart. A woman who understands you. No one knows you like her. Her smiles makes your heart soar. You melt with her words of affection. She's always interested in what you do. What you say. You feel blessed because you know you're really not that exciting, but she gives her heart to you. She makes you feel special. She is the love of your life. All she asks for is your unconditional love and your respect.

I never want to lose her. Never!

Story 62
"The Orphan"

There was a small family. Husband, wife, and a twelve-year-old boy.

The mother got sick first. She didn't last long. This virus was a killer. So, the son asked his father, "Dad, if you get sick what happens to me?" So, the father looked down at him and said "don't worry. I won't get sick."

"I have no aunts or uncles, what will happen to me?"

In less than a month he was gone. Now the boy was alone. He lost both of his parents and now lived as a ward of the state. His life was turned upside down. He withdrew. He became an unwanted child of the orphanage.

Then one day a couple walked in. They had read the bios on the children. They searched him out. They spoke his name, but he didn't acknowledge their presence. The mother pulled up a chair and sat behind him. She began to talk. She talked of the son she had lost. She shared the gaping hole in her heart. The number of times she cried herself to sleep. Finally, she said she had to leave, but would return tomorrow. And they would talk more. Or at least she would.

And so, it went. For many days I might add. When one day he turned his chair around and faced her. He spoke for the first time. Inside, it broke her heart. But she knew she had to be strong for him. So, they talked. This time the father sat with them. They were there for more than an hour with the conversation going back and forth. But the time came to leave.

"Will I see you tomorrow?" Her eyes filled with tears, "when you're ready, you will leave with us and never return."

"You'll take me to visit my parent's grave? I never got to tell them goodbye really."

"I'll take you every day if that is what you want. You will never replace our son, and we will never replace your parents. My promise to you is that we will love each other."

He looks down at his feet. And in a very soft voice he said, "I think I'm ready. And I want to call you mom and dad. Is that OK?"

He grew up to be a fine man. And with time he laid them to rest. They taught him love. He learned compassion. He married with time. Then one day he and his wife stood at a door. They held hands. Looked into each other's eyes and took a deep breath. And armed with only a sheet of paper, they entered the orphanage.

Story 63

"How old are you"

What is old?

A teenager would call someone in their thirties old. Someone in their thirties may call someone in their late fifties old. The fifties call an eighty-year-old "old". But someone ninety-seven might call that eighty-year-old a "kid". And so, it travels in reverse. The teenager now calls the ten-year-old a kid. Is that all so undefined?

The years lived count. It's called "experience" plenty of times. Those who exceed a hundred years impress everyone. Are they old or experienced? Both maybe. How did they live differently? Was it in their genes? Lifestyle plays a part. A glass of wine a day. No fatty meats. Staying active. Don't drink excessively. The list goes on.

In your youth you, don't want to age. To get old. Isn't it a badge of honor really? The hard part is to outlive so many. Family, love ones, friends, and even people you never met. They go younger than you. Older than you. Same age as you. When you get up there you have a better understanding of age. An appreciation of your accomplishment.

So, what is that magic number that defines you as old? Is it even a number? Does your attitude pull years back? A more active lifestyle keeps you younger. I've been told by many senior to me "they're not old". And I'm sure they're not. We can't deny age, but how old you are is in your hands. Not in the opinion of others.

Story 64
"What the young believe"

"Really, Mom, I think I'm a little too old for the Santa and Easter rabbit and tooth fairy game any longer."

The mother said, "Let's get some chocolate and visit. As a small boy, you believed. You would get so excited. Some of the milk was gone, a bite taken from the cookie. The gifts under the tree that came from the North Pole. Money under your pillow, colored eggs in the yard. You were a believer for sure then. We as parents helped with your imagination of such important times. We were able to sit back and see the excitement all over your face. Back then, it was all very real."

"Everyone knows their children will grow up one day. One day the picture is a little clearer. But what did we accomplish? What are you going to do with your children? Tell them none of it is real? I think not. All the special days will live through you one day. Even Peter Pan might join them. Little Sue next door, she still believes. Do you want to go to her and say it's not true?"

"Keep the spirit in your heart. Keep the flame of believing burning bright. Include the teachings of the church. It builds character. So I ask you to continue believing for the younger ones. Allow them to have dreams that they just might meet Santa one cold night."

"I'm glad you're growing up. You'll be a fine father one day. And I think you will place your children on your lap and tell them the story of Christmas. You'll carry them to bed and tuck them in. Your last words will be 'Now go to sleep. Santa comes tonight. He doesn't come till you're asleep.'"

"You'll walk away smiling."

Story 65
"She Just Wanted to be a Nun"

A small girl was at church on Sunday. Her mother was talking to a Nun before church. The little girl was mesmerized by the woman dressed in black and white. Her mother took her hand to leave and as they walked away the Nun waived at her and smiled.

"Mother, who was that lady?"

"She's a Nun, she's a helper in the church who has given her life to GOD."

"Her life?"

"As you get a little older, you'll understand better. But they are very special people."

As she grew, she always took the time to speak to the Nuns. There were two of them at the church. She would ask many questions trying to understand their choice in life. She would ask her heart if she could possibly be a Nun herself. She wasn't sure if that was her "calling." Then a boy asked her out. She thought he was very handsome and polite. Her feelings were confused. She went to the church and asked to talk to the Nuns.

She told them of her feelings about possibly being a Nun from a small age. How much she enjoyed talking and praying with them. Now she didn't know what to do. The senior Nun looked at her and studied her face. Then she spoke.

"You should go out with the young boy. You are not sure what you want to do. I advise you to speak to GOD and ask for guidance. Your heart has to speak to you also. Being a Nun is a major lifetime commitment, or it should be. Take some time to figure this out, I'm here if you need me."

So, she sits on a bench resting. She's been at the hospital all day. A doctor walks up to her. "Sister, I'm sorry to bother you. I have a man on the third floor asking for a priest. We have none in the building. He isn't going to last much longer. Will you meet with him?"

"Of course, lead the way."

The next day was Easter Sunday. She would have a full day tomorrow also. She had a special class to teach. It was going to be all girls of different ages. And I said class to teach. It was really just going to be her telling her story as to why she became a Nun. How fulfilling her life is. How great a life GOD has given her. She enters the room. She pulls up a chair and holds his hand. "GOD is with you now through me. Put your mind and heart at peace. I will stay as long as needed. I'll say a prayer for you. GOD himself will bless you. What you need to say but can't, you can say when you sit by HIS side."

Story 66
"Together Forever"

They met in college, this young couple.

Fell in love so quickly. Everything was moving very fast for them. Just prior to graduation they married. Children soon followed. The early years were hard. Never enough money. Every dime was closely watched. Doctor, clothes, all the work of raising children. Pressures experienced by all with a growing family.

But their love held fast. Their time came late at night. An occasional dinner date. When mom and dad took the kids for a weekend. They did for each other. They shared the work. Kidding around with smiles showing. Kisses and hugs. Each sharing a shoulder to lean on. Years went by. Children grow up. Leave for school. Fall in love themselves. It all moves so fast now. Then one day you have each other alone in a big house.

The stress isn't nearly as hard. As a matter of fact, love is growing stronger. The birthdays and anniversaries pile up. You move a little slower now. Grandkids visit. Love still fills that home. A little traveling now. But not that much. Homebodies could describe them now. They still hold hands when walking. Somehow the kisses have evolved into a peck on the lips or cheek. Don't doubt them, very much in love they are.

They finished their years in that old house. They lay side by side now. Together forever. And when talked about. It's always said "they were inseparable" so much in love!

Story 67
"Another day together"

It was early, a little earlier than most mornings. He turned on the light. Shuffled into the kitchen and started coffee. He found his phone. *We don't read paper news now*. He got his coffee and went back to the bedroom. Pillows were propped up, and he settled in. He glanced at his wife sleeping and started to remember. It was first grade, and he saw this little girl. The first girl he thought was prettier than his mother. She would understand. He gave her his first Valentine's card. But he wasn't uncomfortable about it. He looked for her smile. Time marched on. It was the fifth grade. They sat side by side. They were best friends. And he didn't like it when other boys talked to her.

They were growing and changing. High school was very busy, but they always made time for each other. She wore his ring on a necklace every day. They were dating now. With time, he went to her father and asked for his blessing. He then went straight to her, got down on his knee, and asked her to marry him.

That was sixty years of marriage ago. He heard her soft breathing. Neither looked as they did in the younger years. But their love for each other had never faltered. Looks didn't matter as much now; it had been replaced with mutual respect. A stronger love for the other.

He smiled. So many years. Three children. The house had been theirs for years now. But no loneliness lived there. He knew another great day would be spent together. The weather was nice. Maybe a long walk by the lake, holding hands, would make the day. He'd discuss it with her. He looked down and smiled again. He touched her shoulder and softly whispered, "Darling, are you ready for coffee?"

She stirred. "Sure."

He helped her sit up and placed pillows behind her back. She took her first sip. "Darling, do you think you would like to walk around the lake today? It's going to be a beautiful weekend."

"Sure," she replied. She took his hand and moved closer. It would be a great weekend.

Story 68
"To Earth I Return"

The parents gave birth to a baby boy. A truly joyful day. All seemed very average. Maybe not?

In the yard the inhabitants of the ground and trees seemed drawn to him. It just couldn't be explained. Over the years he fed them from his hands daily. Other friendships didn't seem to matter. Nothing was ever aggressive towards him. They were his friends. He respected them and they respected him. To an outsider, something miraculous. The years moved on.

He married and shared his love. His wife loved him because of his caring nature. With him by her side she could approach the birds (her favorite) and other animals. But on her own they wouldn't come near. This went on for years with little change. As always age catches up to everyone. He couldn't sit for hours on end on his bench. With time he found it harder just to get out of bed. Things were changing.

In response the wife had the bed moved next to the window. The screen removed and a door installed. All birds and creatures of the forest still had access to him. It was not uncommon to find animals in the bed with him. Birds lined his bed post and sang to him.

The day came when she looked out the kitchen window and saw hundreds of everything wild in the yard. She dried her hands and quickly moved to the bedroom. To her shock flowers were everywhere. They covered the floor, the furniture, and the man himself. Thousands of flowers. All colors. Every variety, every variation. He looks at her and gives a weak smile. He was passing. She quickly goes to his side and takes his hand. Too weak to speak he looks deeply into her eyes. His look did the talking.

"Thank you for giving me a wonderful life. Thank you for your understanding. My friends will be yours now. Take care of them." She hears a lone wolf howl. She looks and sees him in the distance. Her husband had closed his eyes for the last time. There he laid, covered in flowers. His eternal rest. All sound had stopped. All knew he was no longer.

She sat crying in silence. A magnificent eagle lands at the window. In his beak he holds a flowering branch. He comes to her and places it in her lap along with a cup of seeds. He pulls at her dress to follow him. He takes her to the bench and all the wildlife gathers around her now. She was now honored by nature.

The old man was laid to rest under a large oak. And to this day fresh flowers cover his grave. Different animals are frequently seen lying on the ground next to him. No one can really explain why. One day his wife will lie by his side.

We live in a complex world. It's not required to understand everything. Just appreciate the good in life. Sometimes leaving reality for a kind story is good for the heart.

Story 69
"He saved her life"

He was nine when the accident happened. It changed his life forever.

His father told him many times not to touch his tools, he could get hurt. But today he didn't listen. It was the table saw. He just wanted to cut a board. He saw his father do it a thousand times. At nine years of age he had no skills yet. Soon he was in a hospital bed with a bandaged hand. He had cut off the last three fingers on his right hand. When healed it looked like a pointed stick with pitchers.

The boys at school made fun of him. It wouldn't stop. As he grew older, girls were uncomfortable around him. This went on for years. Feeling so depressed, he wanted to end it all. So here he stands, ready to jump. The fall would stop his pain. That's when he heard a voice.

"Please don't jump. I need you." Startled he looks to see a small girl looking at him. "What? Where did you come from?" "Please don't jump, you're the only one who can save me." He looks all around and sees no one else. "What are you saying?" She tells him if he jumps she will die also. He looks down at the water. "How can I possible help save you? I'm a freak!" He turns back to her and he's standing alone, again. Looking all around, he sees on one else.

He went back home. He wasn't sure why he didn't jump, his life didn't get any easier. Then it happened. He was on the subway on his way to work. He hears a frantic mother and people in a state of panic. A small girl was choking to death. A small toy was lodged in her throat. No one could get it out. No one but him. He quickly lifts the girl and opens her mouth. His dagger like hand could reach the toy. His pincher like fingers grabbed hold. And he extracts it from her throat. He saved a life that no-one else could.

He was a hero now. People said it was a miracle he was there at such a critical time. He was feeling very good about himself. The next day he visits the girl in the hospital. He takes her hand and asks if she's better? She looks up and gives his hand a squeeze. "Thank you for not jumping"!!!

    Is this story real? Would this ever be a reality? We all have a Guardian Angel watching over us. They work in mysterious ways. And the guy, from that day forward he saw his hand as a gift. He carried the memory of that event the rest of his life.

Story 70
"How fast things can change"

A mother wakes up in a hospital. She's very foggy. A doctor is standing nearby.

"What happened?"

"You slid on ice and hit a tree."

In fear, she asks, "Where is my son?"

The doctor replies, "Mrs. Edwards, we need to talk."

She instantly breaks down sobbing. "No! No! Where is my husband?"

"Your son is alive at the moment. Your husband will not be here in time. We can't save your Bobbie. But right now, he can speak. Let us take you to him. We'll leave you two in privacy; he doesn't have much time. Our equipment is the only thing keeping him alive. Let the nurses put you in the wheelchair, and let's leave."

They take her into a large room. There lies her son with wires and tubes connected all over him. The doctor tells her he's in no pain. He can't move because of his injuries. He can open his eyes and talk. "But he won't last long. Go to him."

"Bobbie," she says as tears stream down her face.

He opens his eyes and says, "Mom. What's happened? I can't move. Where's Dad?"

The mother chokes, then clears her throat. "We were in a terrible accident. Your dad has been called and is on his way. Are you in any pain?"

"No," answers the boy, "but I can't move."

"Don't worry about that," she says and takes his hand. "When you get out, we're moving to that larger house. The one you picked. You liked your bedroom because it was larger. We'll get you a brand-new bed."

"Can I put posters on the walls?"

"Bobbie, I'll let you do whatever you want."

He smiles. "Can you ask them to turn up the lights? It's getting harder to see you. Is Dad here yet?"

"He's on his way. I love you, Bobbie. Your dad is very proud of you. So am I." She gives his hand a squeeze.

"Mom, I'm very tired. Will you wake me when Dad gets here?"

She can barely say the words. "Yes, I will. I'll stay with you right here."

He closes his eyes, forever.

She sits in silence. The doctor returns. "I'm sorry we couldn't have done more. His injuries were just too extensive."

She looks up. "It's a miracle you gave me. I was able to tell my son goodbye. He was a wonderful boy. I'll miss him dearly. A part of my heart left with him. I'll bury him knowing every minute is precious now. You can lose everything dear to you in a blink of an eye. Thank you, Doctor. I need to go and be there for my husband. Bobbie senior. He is going to need me."

Story 71
"Sometimes There is No Map for the Road We Find Ourselves On"

Titled by Kathy Morris

Can you love, and I mean really love someone, you will probably never be with.

Life has so many wrinkles. You have no choice but to accept them in stride. Your feelings of love are moved to the back because of your love. You can't just come out and say what's in your heart because of the problems that would create. So, you love in the shadows. Unspoken. Never allowing it to shine in the light.

The other person, they know. Eye contact tells a story. But they also accept the fact of fate. So, two lives go about their days. They think of each other. A soft smile kept personal. A longing to one day hold hands. A private conversation shared. Yes, so many wrinkles.

Still, you love. You want no other. And time is not your friend. You begin to sag. Loose skin seems to be in charge. The memories try to fade. You hold on to those intense feelings you've had for such a long time.

Your role is to love as it is. To understand our world is not perfect. To know you just need to walk away. To solve the issue. But you can't. Your love is too strong.

Story 72
"I've loved her for so long"

I sit in the recliner, my favorite place now. I can hear her in the kitchen and the dishes being washed. I've loved her for so long now.

Our passion may have wained somewhat. At our age it's not our focus any longer. We're much heavier now. Both of us have a drawer full of pills. And to be honest, sex would probably give me a heart attack. But I love her so much. And she loves me. We've slowed down in our old age. Sex was replaced with laughter and sincere feelings. Our time together is very special to us. An appreciation only the aged can respect.

We kiss. We dance still. Visits from the grandchildren are our biggest highlights. We can talk for hours. We may work in a nap though. That's one thing we do more. To lie next to her still gives me a great satisfaction. In the old days she wouldn't have gotten near as much sleep. But that was then.

We don't argue much. Every now and then. We've learned not to stay mad very long. Nothing to gain. No one has to "win". It's silly to think that way now. I've loved her for so long. Her smile is my joy. Her comfort my reward. We may enjoy a bowl of ice cream together. And her pies are deadly. Our wants changed with time. We want to show our love for each other more now. Shouldn't we all?

I hear her walking back now. Her favorite show is starting soon. I always watch it with her. She thinks I like it just as much. It's the watching her smiles that I watch. We're going out to dinner tonight. The money doesn't stretch as far now. But it's our date night. We still do that. A carryover from younger days. I've loved her for so long now. I wouldn't have it any other way.

Story 73
"Friendships can weather storms"

There were two small children, a boy and a girl. Since preschool, they had been friends. They would sit close to each other and do their assignments together. Their friendship was strong. But as they grew, the girl changed ever so slightly. The boy, David, grew to love the girl, Nancy, but her love wasn't for him. Nancy was growing up, and the boys began to notice. Her popularity grew. She had less time for David now. So he got her alone and told her of his love. She broke his heart. "David, you'll never be any more than a friend to me. Look at me. I can have any boy I choose. Why would I choose you?" And with that said, she pretty much broke off their friendship. She ran with the cool guys, and David finished high school and went on to college.

A number of years passed. David was successful in his life. He never married. One Christmas, he returned home to visit with family. It was always good to see his loved ones. This day, his mother asked him to go to the store to pick up something she needed. As he rounded the aisle, he saw a crippled lady. She could barely get around. It was so crowded, and her cart took up space. He said, "Nancy?"

She looked up, and tears of guilt showed on her face. "Hi, David."

He asked, "What happened?"

"A fun night, a fast car—you know the rest. I was the only one hurt."

"Let's grab a coffee and visit for a minute."

With reluctance, she agreed.

"How long ago was this?"

"About two years now."

"Are you married?"

"No. I'm alone now. No one wants a cripple with them. All of my friends have moved on. David, I was so wrong to do to you what I did.

I've relived that day with shame so many times. My looks and popularity went to my head. I could be with anyone I chose. You were no longer important to me. And now I'm no longer important to them. They all left me, and now I'm having coffee with someone I hurt. I've had a lot of time alone to relive that day. You were truly a friend I could count on, and my ego destroyed it. I'm so sorry."

"Nancy, we do things in life we're not proud of. But if you recognize it, that is the first step in fixing the wrong. I carry no anger. And you are still my friend. Allow me to invite you to our family dinner. You will be welcomed with open arms. You will be with true friends. I think you need that right now. Come with me."

Story 74

"The Responsibility of Being the Oldest"

He was the oldest of four. Eighteen when his parents died in a crash. To keep them together he had to become the parents. A job he wasn't prepared for.

Life was hard for him. His sister refused to recognize his authority. There was nothing he could do to stop her bad judgements. She left home with a boy he never met. She was only seventeen. To this day he has never seen or heard from her again.

His younger brother was different. Always wanting to help. Willing to watch over the baby sister while his brother worked to provide for them. He had an understanding beyond his years. So that's how they all finished growing up together. They both loved and respected their older brother. He sacrificed every day for them. Working all day and helping with their studies in the evenings. He needed to give them the best chance for a normal life he could.

With time both of them left on their own. Their family bond was stronger than most. He missed his sister and thought of her often. He hoped to see her at least once more. But he spent holidays with the other two. He never married. Never really ever loved outside the family. His life was wrapped up by responsibility. The role of a parent never ends. He could look upon them and smile. He did good!

Over time they came to him when in need. He was always there. Always ready to help. Never wanting to judge. And if he did, he kept it silent. His age took its toll. Finally, he needed to go to a home for care. He just couldn't care for himself any longer. He was making the arrangements when out of nowhere a vaguely familiar face greeted him. His sister that left.

"I've always been too embarrassed to speak to you. I did wrong, I know it. I watched you sacrifice for the family. I need to sacrifice for you now. You'll come stay with me and my husband. You'll like him. Like you, he's a good man. I'll never be able to fill your shoes, but I'll try. You're an uncle. I want to introduce you to my daughters. We'll be a family once more. Forgive me and let me do this."

He lived out his remaining years happier than he ever felt. The bonds of family can be stretched thin, but never break. We all do what we're called upon to do. And for family there is really no limit.

Story 75
"Peace and Happiness"

He would be ninety-four in just another month. But his cancer would not allow him to see that age. And he was bitter. To have lived for so long only to have it cut short with a cancer.

The morning nurse came to his room. "Mr. Wilson, tomorrow I would like to take you on a tour of the hospital. Don't just lay there till you're moved to the hospice facility". "I don't want to just let me die" and turns a cold shoulder to her. "I'll be here at nine. It'll only take about an hour, and it will do you good." And she left.

The next morning, she came back with help to get him into the wheelchair. She began to push and listening to him complain. She took him to a window and he could see six babies. "I don't need to see the maternity ward. Is this your idea of a cruel joke" he scowls. "This is not the maternity ward. These babies are dying. Every one of them. Over your 91 years I'm sure you have some good memories. These children will die without even one. How do you feel about that?"

She takes him next to a special room where a woman was also dying. "She's the mother of five children. Yesterday her husband and all of her children were here crying. Would you give up ten years of your life to guarantee she lived? Eighty-one is still a ripe old age. She's thirty-five. That young and such a beautiful family. Maybe just five years? Would you give up five?" "Why are you doing this to me? Return me to my room right now!" "I will but we have one last stop."

"That young man has cancer also. We can't help him. He's donated his body to help others. He said "anything and everything we can use to help anyone". We will all leave this earth someday. The final days are your most precious. Why be bitter? You've outlived so many. Make peace with your fate. You were gifted with time. Such a precious commodity. You have great memories. Relive a few. Maybe a lot. None of us will live forever. Look back and smile. Look forward with peace. You still have strength."

She returned him to his room. He was quite. Her words and what he witnessed was what he needed. There was no reason to be bitter. He lived a good life. He would make peace with himself. And he did!!!

We all have anger over things we can't control. Things we didn't ask for. But peace and happiness is always there to comfort you. It can be your best friend in the end.

Story 76
"I Love"

I love, maybe more than others.

I love to take long walks with my friends. I love their company. I love watching the sun rise and set. I love sweets, though I wish I didn't so much. But I love. I really love watching children having fun. Hearing their laughter. Knowing the world is so big to them. I especially love family. The close bonds, time spent together. Other than your spouse, who do you know better or love more?

I love time spent outdoors. The rain spoils nothing. And as you've guessed, I love the rain. When was the last time you walked in the rain? It doesn't need to be watched from a dry area. I love to fish. A skill I've acquired and don't mind sharing. Eating fish is healthy.

In my case, I love a special woman. Her heart is tender. Her smile captivating. Her eyes beautiful. I feel very blessed to have her love. I have pets. And like everyone I know, I love them. They're way too big to sit in my lap, but they don't think so. They love me.

So, do I love more than others? As I write this, I think maybe not. I may have just taken a little more time to acknowledge the life I love. Holidays can be tougher than other times of the year. Look back on what you love. Take the time to really focus on the love in your life. It's there. Acknowledge it.

Story 77
"I See Great Things"

We get up every day, but what do we see?

Lucky me, getting up early is the best, it's my time. Coffee at my pace. Going over the jobs for today. Figuring out the order. So exactly what do I see?!!! I see I'm prepared. I see I've spent enough time planning that it all should go pretty smooth. My confidence is good.

What else? Well, I also see people. All doing their best. Each realizing they depend on their coworkers to keep the business flowing. All doing their jobs and making each other proud. What do I see? I saw a team. Not just any team, that's our team.

I see a boss that sets the example. Never late. Always planning the next move. Looking to hire. He wants the business to grow. What do I see? I see leadership by example. Someone who knows the names. (Or should) of all who work around the main office. A family man. A person of understanding.

People are driven to do great work. Sure, some more than others. Those are our next generation of leaders. Teach them. Test them always. They can handle it. I see so much more. We must always stop and look at the bigger picture. It's always there. Wanting to show the way.

See the positive in everything. You may not need to speak it out loud. But do see it. See that cup half full. See your strength. See all the good you are or can be. See me. See your efforts. I stand by you. I am a part of your success, and you are mine.

There is so much to see. Never stop.

Story 78
"Never get to comfortable"

Most single men treat women better than most husband's. Do you believe this?

I think most single men see the woman for her beauty. Her sex appeal. Single men stay hungry for a beautiful woman. While a husband will marry that beautiful woman and gets used to having her there every day. I've said so many times "don't stop dating your wife". If you become complacent, where does that leave her? If you don't quickly move to open her door, someone else might. She will smile out of appreciation. The husband might say thank you and walk in behind her. But what impresses her the most? The fact that this stranger opened her door or her husband told him thank you?

People that's how that strong bond of marriage begins to erode. Small tiny pieces at a time. But over time it eaves it's mark. Arguments may become more frequent. Time away from each other increases. The love begins to crumble. Is it the end!!! Not if that's not what you want. "We're together for the kids" what a horrible statement. What is your quality of marriage now? What is there to do? How can this be fixed? Do you still want to address this? For better or for worse. Not really practiced as it used to be. Divorces come more frequently now. And why?

Don't stop dating your wife. Never stop being that gentlemen and the gentlemen she fell in love with. Buy a cheaper vehicle and spend more money on you as a couple.

Its money well spent!!! You're spending the money either way. And ladies, always look your best for him. Be his eye candy on his arm.

Story 79
"The only child"

A father is fishing with his daughter.

She looks at him and says, "Dad, would you rather have had a son? I ask this because all we do is boy things. I am sorry I was born a girl. But there is nothing I could have done about it."

The father looks down and pulls her in close. "Darling, has your brother been complaining because he isn't here?"

"Dad, I don't have a brother."

"My mistake. It must have been your sister."

"What is wrong with you? I have no sister. You know that."

The father gives her a kiss on the forehead and says, "So, if I want to take my lovely child with me to spend the day, you are my only choice?"

The girl studies him for a moment and sees the trap she put herself in. "No, Dad. You know what I mean. All we do are boy things. You want me to play baseball. I want to take dance."

"Do you remember when we sat down and discussed this?"

"We've never discussed it. Why do you ask such questions?"

"Then why haven't you asked to speak to me about this? Why hold it inside? Does your mother know?"

"Well, no. I didn't want to disappoint you."

"Darling, I would never want to disappoint *you*. I love you. You and your mother are the most important people in my life."

"Your mother can never have any more children. Do you want a brother? We can adopt. Both of us want your time. You're growing up, and maybe we still hold on to your past. I'm sorry."

"Dad, I was afraid you wanted a boy. I was silly for not talking to you about it until now. I love you both so much. I want you to be proud of me. I now see you are."

"I'm going to talk to Mom about taking dance. And, Dad, I will always go fishing with you. When you and Mom grow old, I'll take care of you. And if you want a boy, you have to talk to mom."

Story 80
"Friends can be strangers"

A man was sitting on his balcony feeling very down.

He was the kid bullied in school. Although he was very smart, that is what kept him from other people. He just couldn't mix in. He went on to college, and not much changed. He wasn't being pushed around but was totally ignored.

He graduated with honors and got a good job. Yet still, he couldn't make friends. He did not like his life. Day after day, he came home and sat on his balcony, upset with his life. He lived on the ninth floor. He knew he could end his misery if he just jumped. But he lacked the courage for that. So day after day, he looked down and wished he were a stronger man.

Then one day a bird landed on the rail. It was a beautiful bird. It would sing. He was totally captivated by this strange event. The dark areas of his mind were being given light. He came to understand that the bird was allowed outside for him to experience freedom. This went on for days. Very slowly, he began to smile more.

He did his work with a new vigor. He was quickly noticed. A bounce came to his step. Each day, he looked forward to hearing the bird sing. It was the most beautiful sound he had ever heard. Then one day at the water cooler, he was approached by a fellow coworker. She was a loner too. She said she noticed the change in him. She liked it. Then she asked if he wanted to hear a bird sing. He was taken back. What was this? "A bird?" he asked.

"Yes, it showed up around a month ago. My spirits were not good. Then it sang. My world changed. And I want to share it with you, if you agree."

Of course, the bird never returned. They enjoyed tea and conversation. Never had a girl wanted to visit with him—never. They became good friends and talked about their birds on many occasions, never really understanding what happened. And in time, they married. And they lived very happy lives together.

Our guardian angels watch over us. They fix our problems. They care for our happiness.

Story 81
"Be the example"

A young boy was given community service for mischief he got into. He was to cut the yard of an elderly lady.

So he showed up and cut the yard. The lady came out and told him he should be ashamed of the job he did. Angry he went home and his father asked him what was wrong. So he told what the woman said. The father told him to get in the car and they went back to address the lady.

Once there he realized the lady was correct. He took the boy back home and loaded all of his yard implements and returned. The father gave a small lecture on pride in his work. And they both started working. At different times the father would stop and give instruction on how to do a better job with less work.

They worked all day together. And know that the son was enjoying the work. He and his father hadn't spent so much time together in months. He enjoyed learning from his father. And maybe that time apart was the reason he got into trouble in the first place. The lady watched from the window. She saw the care the father was giving. She made cold drinks and sat them on the porch for when they took a break.

Our children need, yes need time spent on them from their parents. They become better behaved. More confident. They know they're loved. Appreciated. They can see their value. Time is the most valuable gift you can give them. Don't be frugal with it. It's a great investment. Be the example for what you want them to be.

Story 82
"He crossed over to save his father"

His sixth sense told him something wasn't right.

But he kept walking. He looked down at his arm and saw bone. He was hurt and hurt badly. But he kept walking. He looked behind and saw a smoking car. He had had an accident. He heard traffic, but no one was stopping. He was getting dizzy. *If I don't make the road, I die where I fall.* He dropped to one knee.

Then he felt a hand on his shoulder. "Allow me to help." It was a small boy. "Put your hand on my shoulder and stand."

"I can't. I don't have the strength."

"Do this or you will die." So he mustered his strength and stood again. One step at a time. "Keep moving. We're going to make it."

They got to the road, and he sank to the ground. The last thing he heard is "You'll be safe now, Dad. Thank you for allowing me to help."

He woke up in the hospital. His wife by his side. He was still sedated but waking up. "Where is the boy?"

"Who?"

"The boy who saved me."

"There was no boy. You were by yourself. The sight has been swept—just your car and your footprints leaving."

He looked to his wife. "I think I was with Bobby. I'm sure I saw him."

"John, it's the medication. We lost Bobby three years ago. Just rest."

"I remember it so well. He was there."

"Just get more sleep."

A nurse walked in and gave him a sleep aid. He closed his eyes and slept again. The nurse handed her a package. "These are his personal belongings. They were removed when he was admitted."

As the nurse turned to leave, the wife poured the contents on a table. In astonishment, she quickly said, "Wait. You took these things from him?"

"Yes, I'm the one who collected them."

"This chain and cross, where did it come from?"

"He was wearing it." And she left.

She doesn't know what to think. What to believe. Their son had been buried with that chain and cross around his neck. How could her husband be in possession of it? She sat down and took his hand. She'd wait to hear what he had to say about what happened. How could that chain get around his neck? What did he experience? Whatever he has to say, she'll believe him.

Story 83
"Aged Friendships"

A man was at the beach. The sand on his bare feet felt so good.

He often comes here. Before his wife died, they bought a house in the area. But the memories were just too strong. And in his case not always that pleasant. Sadness would overtake him. He was not in control. So, he sold the home. Now he's a visitor like all the others. On this day he sat under his umbrella watching the waves. The air had the smell of salt. A cool breeze. Really a special day.

When off to his left a woman sets up her spot. She settles in and starts reading her book. He kept glancing up at her. Age changes your features, but you hold on to some. He knew her but couldn't remember from where. Later she stands and walks towards him to get something from her car. He remembers. "Mary! Mary Davis!" he says. She looks without recognition. Then her memory draws up the connection. "Well James, how have you been? It's been years, many years." She sits in the sand to visit. "You'll have to help me up when we're done." They both laugh a little.

She tells the story of her husband Bill passing a couple of years ago. Her life was different now but she's happy. "You know I always had a crush on you."

She looks at him and answers, "yes, my friends let me know. But Bill had my interest. Who did you end up marring?"

"Kathy Long. We had 42 years together. I miss her, as I'm sure you miss your Bill. Would it be improper or forward to offer a dinner invite?"

"I would really like that. So much time to cover. Maybe a yes?"

They had that dinner. And many more. Old friendships seem a little sweeter when a chance crossing of paths happen. Sure, we change, but the core personality remains. And I think a respect rises to the surface. An old one that was buried in the sand. Age and maturity are a gift. And a past love is always tucked in a very special place in the heart. It can be dusted off and continue growing where it left off. We mostly don't seek them out after so many years. But a chance meeting under the right conditions. Well fate just might be in your corner. Your love will never die. It can get into quite a disarray, but like a loved flower, it can bloom again.

Story 84
"A love story"

After so many years of love and marriage, it was winding down. Age and health were taking their toll. The husband takes her hand and speaks softly. "I've tried to show my love for you every way I could think of. And you to me. But I've decided I need to write you a love story. A love story about us. About the day we met. You have always been a beauty. My courting you, our honeymoon. The way you fixed up our first home. We had almost nothing and you did so much. You were my anchor. You drove me to be my best. When I was ever down you picked me up. You make me smile. The warmth of our love blankets me."

"I love you so much. I'm going to write this love story to you." She looks at him and says "write nothing". "You just told me the story I want. I'll remember every word. It was beautiful. Those words will live in my heart forever now. In my quiet times I'll revisit today and the moments here as you held my hand. Thank you darling for such a gift. I love you dearly. And will till my last breath."

Story 85
"Conversation with Dad"

"Dad, I want to grow up to be a man. How long will that take?"

"Well, son, that's a tricky question. You see, some boys never grow up. They just grow old."

"Dad, that doesn't make sense. All boys grow up unless they die. Even I know that."

"There are a great many things at your age that won't make sense for a while now. But one day, understanding will creep in, and that will open your eyes."

"Open my eyes? They're not closed."

"A man acts mature. He knows his role in life. He takes on responsibility. He will do what has to be done without anyone asking. He will be a good provider. He'll probably marry one day, and he'll be a good husband and father. Having fun is no longer his goal. It's quality of life for his family that rules him now. How can he better provide for them? He's willing to sacrifice so they won't have to. And something I hope you never see is that if the marriage doesn't work out, that won't stop him from being a great father anyhow."

"So, son, I'll do my best to be the example you need to learn by. You'll see me, and you'll see others. As I said, some grow up, and some just grow older. You'll fall in love one day. Keep her the center of your life. Don't stray. Make the time to show your love for your family. Give plenty of hugs and kisses. Do all of this, and you will grow up. You will be a man others wish they had. You're not the only one who will watch me. As a man, you're graded by many. Don't disappoint."

"Now go get ready. And anytime you wish to talk further about this, just come to me. And when you're ready, I'll tell you about women." And with a smile, he sends him away.

Story 86
"People Can Be Very Different"

A man in his 20's would take his dog to the park each day. He would spend a couple of hours with him. It was clearly apparent he loved his dog. But he was always observed by a girl who came there to read each day. She was always wondering how he had so much free time. He didn't appear to be a worker. "I would love to know his story," she always thought. Unknown to her he also noticed her. He carried similar thoughts.

This continued on for months. Then one day just by chance they meet face to face in the grocery store. Never before had they been so close. At a loss as what to do she says "where is your dog? I've never seen you without it."

He smiles and says "they won't allow him in here, I've tried."

A situation so awkward. Neither knew what to do next. So, she smiles and moves on.

Later that day she's at her spot in the park. She hears the request, "may I sit?" It was him. A little uncomfortable she tells him yes. His dog lies in front of them.

"I've seen you here many times and I've never seen you with anyone. I'm not into relationships but I do enjoy friendships. I'm very different. I'll| never call or ask for your time. If I see you here, I would like to know I could visit. I get all the companionship I need from Blake here, but he doesn't talk. I just ask that you accept me as I am and not judge."

"Well, that's different but I can agree to that." And a friendship took seed.

We live in a big world made up of a lot of different people. Your choice is to accept them or reject their way of thinking. The latter results in rejecting them. In the big picture does it matter how they wear their hair? Do you lose sleep over the number of tattoos someone else has? And right now, who they vote for or the color of their skin? You know mankind is bigger than that. A criminal deserves jail time. Innocent people don't deserve to be intimidated by thugs. And our political system is not a "get rich quick" system. So go about your day. Find happiness. Do what you can to fix the problems. We're all in this together.

Story 87
"A Grandmothers Love"

You all know her. She has that gift about cooking. Carries it to the next level. Who is she?

Never without that small towel to catch a spill or two. Can fix any dish on the planct. She'll always enhance the recipe to her own taste. She has learned a trick or two over the years. A turkey dinner starts days in advance. All the planning. Ingredients on hand. All the right dishes coming together. All the hungry smiles. That kitchen is hers. She calls all the shots. Won't share many secrets. All the ingredients are written down and stored lose in a drawer. She's done it so many times she doesn't even have to read them anymore.

Washes the dishes as she goes. Can't stand a cluttered counter top. Nor a sink full of dirty dishes. Always on top of things. She'll taste as she goes. The dishes have to be perfect. Her reputation is on the line. This cook of many talents won't allow a bad review. The way they fill Tupperware to take some home tells she hit the mark.

Now the young start asking to spend the night. A blanket and pillow is all they need. TV and popcorn. Just the right movie, seen a hundred times. Sure she's tired. But she has her place on the couch. The smallest ones snuggled up close. A beautiful ending to a full day. The kids look at her with love in their eyes.

She's called "grandma" or that pet name given to her by the first grandchildren. Grandpa's there but it's her that gets the most attention. And shouldn't that be the way it is? Who's up for making some fudge before it's too late? This goes on till they've all fallen asleep. She'll turn off the TV and lights. Slip into her bed by grandpa. Get some badly needed rest. They'll wake early. Pancakes and bacon will be the order. She picked up plenty of milk.

Yes, this superstar is "grandma". Cherish them while you can. They won't be here forever.

Story 88
"Not a bad life"

I retired at age sixty-five. Knew I would live out here. But there was so much I didn't know. Never saw the joy in living completely surrounded by a forest. All the different trees, all the wildlife.

I didn't build a place to live. I sculptured it. I spend almost every day outdoors. I really enjoy being here. With pets, you are never alone. Their days are best served being close to you. I look around me, and I'm surrounded by dogs and cats. Chickens walk around scratching for bugs. And the ducks are never too far.

So the arrangement of covered areas was built for comfort. I have so many choices. What is my mood? My music is all handpicked. Close to three hundred songs. Around eighteen hours of music I really enjoy. I get up each morning, Bluetooth, and mix. The arrangements change every day. And anytime I hear something I want to add, it's just a push of a button.

I seem to be always in a good mood. Doesn't take much to make me smile. I start out with the best cup of coffee this side of the Mississippi River. And it just goes up from there. No, I can't cook. Never could. But I grill. Do a damn good job with it. Thinking about living more off the land here. I've cooked and eaten more wild game than most. Raccoon, rabbit, squirrels, gar, and snake. All good eating if done right. I've just drifted away.

I'm seventy-two, so I don't have that many years left. When I go, I'll go with a smile. And I wouldn't change a thing (maybe have my lady here). Life is good. Lay the dark aside and celebrate the light. At one time, I knew more jokes than anyone I knew. Yep, not a bad life.

Story 89
"Always Have Something Nice to Say"

There was a man who just enjoyed life and people. So, one day he decided to do something special. He had a sign made. "Free compliments for anyone who needs or would enjoy one." He got permission to set at a table outside the grocery store. He was there when they unlocked the doors. Now people would walk by and read the sign, then look at him. Some smiled. Some looked with suspicion. Others full of curiosity. Finally, a lady stopped. "How much?" Free was the answer. Let's do this.

He gets up and looks at her from head to toe. Her dress, her jewelry. How she cut her hair. Her face. Then he was ready. He spoke to her.

"You are a caring individual. You took the time necessary to go out into the public and look nice doing it." (Others were starting to gather and hear his story) "Your makeup is flawless. And very well done. Your husband is a lucky man. I see your ring. Meeting you was my honor. Thank you for stopping."

She stood there totally stunned and somewhat embarrassed. "My, my, my. You just made my day. You should charge for this."

"You paid me with your smile." He looks around. "Who's next?"

Compliments cost nothing. They are free to those who receive them. Give them freely and be generous about it. Be sincere! You can brighten their day and lift their spirits. All for free. A gift from the heart.

Story 90
"Starting Over"

He stands on the beach. His toes in the sand. The sun is setting. "What a beautiful sight". The afternoon breeze moving softly. A perfect day to be standing here. And no he doesn't want to ruin the moment. He knows the sun doesn't rise or set. Terms used for thousands of years. Science stepped in to clear up the misunderstanding. But isn't it more romantic to watch a "sunset"?

He sees others watching. On the beach, on a deck having a drink, or looking out a window. A sight enjoyed by almost everyone. He wishes he had someone to share this with. You might say he's in-between girlfriends. Youth tends to place their career first. A relocation with a promotion is attractive. And if the partner isn't willing to follow, well, you end up watching a sunset alone. Phone calls will ensure a connection for a while. But with time…

Finally, you lose sight of the scattered colors. You make your way back home. Maybe have a glass of wine while browsing a singles sight. There is for sure more than one fish in the sea. And fishing can be fun. I think I'll send a message to this one. Wish me luck!!!

Story 91
"The Deepest Love"

A mother's love. The man has a moment of bliss. But the woman takes that moment and turns it into a child. Her body creates life literally out of thin air. She carries the unborn child for nine months. Each and every day, her child is a part of her life now. The father gets occupied with life and really doesn't know what the future mother is feeling. Sure, they talk. She tries to share her feelings of her changing body. But still, each and every moment, she thinks about being a mother to that child—her worries about what could happen, her insecurities about her relationship with her husband now. Does he still see her beauty? Does he understand what she is creating for them? Her emotions are scrambled, and her self-confidence is weak. Yet she continues. Then one day, she holds her baby.

She raises that child. The child one day says, "I love you, Mama." Her heart swells. Her eyes water. All the discomfort, all the crying, all the pain is gone now. All that is left is her love for her child.

She gives a kiss to the forehead and says, "Mama loves you too." That is a mother's love. And no man will fully grasp this.

Close but not the same. A mother's love trumps all. Treat them with the respect they deserve. They've earned it!

Story 92

"The Perfect Date"

He saw her at a table alone. An absolutely beautiful woman.

He sends over a drink. Has the lady ask her if he could join. She smiles but doesn't give an approval. After a while he walks to her table.

"I guess you want a dance now?"

"No. Just to sit and talk, I'm Joe."

She gives him a look over. Maybe for a minute or two.

It was a Friday night. The weather was clear and a great weekend was coming up. They had drinks and shared small talk. He walks her to her car and asks for her number.

"I'm not trying to be forward, just want to call later."

She hands a paper to him with her number and drives away.

Later at the hotel he calls. All kinds of questions asked. They learn more about each other. Interest shared. Common ground found.

"Would you enjoy going to the beach tomorrow?" he asks. And the date was set. He picks her up early and holds her hand while driving. She doesn't resist.

The day was perfect. They even kissed once. He didn't want to be too forward. But she was beautiful.

"May I pick you up for dinner later? I have a special place to show you. Is eight too late?"

"No, that would be fine. But don't think you will stay the night or anything."

He looks and smiles and thinks "a true lady."

"Not my intentions yet, but maybe someday." Her turn to smile and blush a little.

The weekend went too fast. They walked holding hands and shared very heartwarming time together. The weekend had only hours left.

"Drive and I'll follow. We both have work tomorrow." And they go home.

Having a romantic weekend with a wife you really adore strengthens the marriage. Dinner and dancing, acting like strangers, has a flair about it. First-time love is the best. Never let it become complacent and every so often try to re-create those first dates. Play the parts of strangers. But strangers falling in love.

Story 93
"How I Go"

Knowing full well I won't live forever, if I could choose my demise, what would I choose?

A peaceful ending in my sleep, I don't think so! A car crash with a careless driver? No interest there. So how? Maybe filing my dreams since youth. Skydiving would be interesting. Flying a plane? Saving a life? Being a hero has merit. We are exposed to so much. So many choices.

I have no desire to speed things up. I enjoy life. But my day will come. Of that I'm certain. The fantasy would be to take out our most evil people in this world. Speed up their fate. That one sounds good. Maybe living in a third world Nation helping the needy? Disease is so prevalent. What could I do before I go? I probably need more time to put more thought in this. What could I do starting now? Does it need to be a final act of life? So many choices!

I start out with a question about demise, and end up thinking about life. Strange really. We can do so much in life. But just filling our "slot" seems to be enough. So how do I want my ending to be? I want to slide into home plate throwing dust over everyone. A smile on my face, and money in my pocket. That sounds pretty good. I want people to talk about me when I'm gone. Good things. Maybe something no one knew. Yes my day will come, but until then I'll continue with my exaggerations, my slant on the truth. And trying to get that smile out of you.

Story 94
"My Quite Time"

She takes a break in her rocker. Very busy day. She reflects. She was dressed in yellow. Shoes so shiny. Her white bonnet with little flowers. She had an Easter basket on her arm. A prettier girl not seen. She saw that picture many times. A grandchild has it now. She looks over to her husband, sleeping in his recliner. Glasses hanging from his neck. The paper across his chest. What a handsome man he was. He still is but in a different way. She can remember their first kiss. Every detail of it still. He would be lucky to know the month. But she would agree no matter what he said and kiss his cheek.

That honeymoon so many years ago. She gave herself to him that night, so much love. The grandkids are in for a sleepover. A well-deserved break for the parents. They bring so much energy with them.

John and I move at a slower pace. Days like this are so cherished. Need to get moving again. I smell the pie in the oven, and the kids will be up from their nap. I promised them pie and ice cream if they took a good nap. It works every time. I enjoy my quiet time. I enjoy revisiting my life. I can still remember so much. I hear movement. That pie has to cool.

Story 95
"Just The Possibility of Losing Your Special Love"

He couldn't bring himself to release her hand.

The operation was her only chance at a longer life. But the operation carried a huge share of risk. Her age, her health. This could be his last goodbye. The thought of this made him tremble. The nurse says to him they must go. He just can't let go. He looks down at his wife of forty years. The injection brings on the sleep. She fights the path she knows she can't stop. One last weak "I love you" and she slips into the sleep. His tears flow freely. Gives a last kiss and it's the nurse that pulls their hands apart. She gives a promise to give him an update as soon as possible.

He sits for what seemed like long hours. What if she doesn't make this leap? She was his only love. She couldn't give him children and always regretted that. He didn't care. He loved her too much. Their lives were filled with love and happiness. They did volunteer work at a food kitchen after he retired. She always wanted to do for others. Her heart too big for her size. Just one of the things he loved about her. Her health took a change about a year ago. Didn't seem that big a deal at the time. Now he sits. Not knowing what the next few hours will bring. His heart was breaking.

He hears the footsteps approaching the door. The nurse enters the room. "She's very weak, but she'll be fine. You're a lucky man. Love gives strength. Go home for a while, she won't come back here till morning."

"No, I'll be here when she returns. I will always be there for her."

She smiles at him and says she must leave. Alone again he kneels. "Thank YOU for the additional time with my wife. I'd be so lost without her. I'm not perfect but YOU didn't hold that against me. Thank you, LORD."

Happiness filled their home for many more years. True love is very special. And mature love has no match! Not at any age.

Story 96

"Always Smiling"

She was a healthy bouncing little girl. Her parents were so proud.

As she grew she never really cried that much. She was better known for her big smile and loud laughter. That was her personality. Some people are just lucky that way. She stayed a happy woman all her life.

One day her grandson was in her lap and asked "mom says nothing upsets you, is that really true"? "Jason, you're still pretty young but for the most part it is true. We can control how we appear to others. It's not so wrong to hide your anger or disappointment. Why put it on the shoulders of the people you care about? A smile just makes everyone feel better."

And that is so true. Laughter is contagious. A smile relaxes. And it's hard to feel bad when you project a happy image. Keep your anger in check. Don't advertise your bad feelings. Make everyone think nothing upsets you. Many will envy you.

And when you do need that shoulder to lean on, don't hesitate.

Story 97
"This I will do"

There was a couple very much in love.

He did all he could do for her to show his love. She did the same. She would frequently ask him how she could be a better wife. His answer was always the same.

"Never allow our passion to wither. Always be there for me. You are the one I care for most. Never hesitate to ask for my help. And allow me to be the one you turn to in any situation. Hold my hand when we walk outside. Never stop wanting to date me. Wake up close to me. Always tell me how much you love me. Lay your head on my shoulder and whisper to me. Expect me to show my love for you every day. And in exchange, I'll do this."

"I'll love you forever. Nothing in my life will be more important. Everyone will envy the love you receive. I'll always try to look my best for you. When we walk holding hands, I'll swell with pride for others to see. You have always made me feel loved. Made me feel special. I must show you I feel the same. This I will always do."

"And coffee in bed is a given."

Story 98
"Protectors Come in Many Forms"

An old man takes his daily walk. The same as so many others. But this day turns out different.

On this day he finds an injured dog. His leg has a nasty cut. Probably been in a fight with another dog. He tries to approach but the dog will have none of it. So, he moves along. The next day he finds the dog still laid up. He knows he needs food and water. So, he turns around and goes back home. He returns with both for the dog. Still the dog is very aggressive. He moves as close as he feels safe and sits the gifts down. Then moves on his way.

The next morning, he brings food and water with him. Yesterday's food is gone. So, he moves close to add more. The dog growls very viciously. Not allowing him too close. He fills the bowls and moves on. This goes on for a few more days. Then one day the dog is gone. He's both sad and happy for his friend.

You see, as you age for the most part you spend time alone. And a friend, even a dog, is welcome. Then one day some young boys walk up to him. "Hey old man, you got money?" They quickly surround him. "Come on old man, just give it up. Don't make us hurt you." Suddenly he sees fear in their eyes. They back up. They no longer cared about the old-timer. One says "I thought you killed that dog. Look at his eyes. Let's get out of here." So, they run.

The old man turns to see the dog he helped walking away. That dog was a loner. He wanted no part of the man who helped him. But he did understand it was his turn to help. Animals understand more than we give them credit for. And a friend with a bad attitude and sharp teeth is not always a bad thing.

The old man smiled and went about his way. He never saw the dog again. He also was never bothered again. And to this day he leaves dog treats by the bench. They are always gone. But he knows he has a protector. A protector that likes dog cookies.

Story 99
"A Father Forever"

They were married for five years. She was a beautiful woman.

She had three children by three different fathers. That should have said something in itself. But love does blind you to the obvious. With time she grew tired of him, and wanted to move on again. Where did this leave him, and his relationship with his stepchildren? The boy was now 16 and needed a father figure in his life. The other two were much younger but had their needs also. The mother demanded her divorce.

It wasn't long before the boy got into real trouble. Now this is what made the stepfather a man. The mother didn't want him near her children. And even had a restraining order against him. Once you have a son or daughter, they carry that title for life. And he believed the same for stepchildren. So he went to speak to the judge. What he didn't know was his stepson was in the next room.

He told the judge of the hard life the boy had. The way he was raised. The mistakes of the mother. Please don't judge him so hard. He's a good boy inside. Give him the chance to turn things around. Jim heard it all. Never had anyone ever spoken up for him. He didn't really like the stepfather. He was far too strict. But he heard his words. And so did the judge.

The boy was given four months in jail. Once out, if there was no more trouble, his offenses would be sealed. An officer escorted him to his cell. Once there he stepped inside and the guard handed him six books. "Your father sent these" and left. He picked up each one and read the titles. "How to build character", "What it takes to be a man", "Responsibilities of being the man of the house", and so on.

He had the time so he read. He read them all. On the day of his release, he was met by an individual. A lawyer. He was hired to assist him in getting his family back. The mother abandoned the family and the children were wards of the state now. A legal adult. He had a job lined up. Transportation. And legal assistance.

"Who is paying for all of this? I have no money." "That is not your worry. Right now, we need to get your family back together. We need to move fast. All of my fees are covered. Your father has covered everything." "I've never even met my father. Why would he enter our lives now?" "I guess I should say your stepfather. We have work to do."

The battle was not easy. With time they were all reunited. Jim was the father now. And he was prepared.

Some men take their role as "father" more seriously than others. These are the men among us. Parenting is a major responsibility. Priority one. If you're going to be a parent, be mature enough to be responsible enough. Jim looked at the lawyer and said "let's address that restraining order!!!"

Story 100

"Leaving the Nest"

A young man is out jogging. He looks down and sees a very small bird. It has fallen from its nest. It has almost no feathers, and the tree is far too big to try to climb. So he takes the small bird home. He is going to college and still lives with his parents. His mother sees the bird and says it will never live. But the boy tries. He builds a nest with a heat lamp. He collects small insects and gets the bird to eat. The bird bounces back. He quickly learns how to care for the young bird. Weeks pass. Now the bird has its feathers. Its bond with its adopted parent grows strong. The mother is impressed with what her son has accomplished.

Soon the bird can fly around the house. When the boy returns from school, it sits on his shoulder and doesn't want to leave. But the boy sees the bird always returning to the window to look outside. He understands what he must do. So he gives the new friend extra attention, extra love.

Then he takes it outside. The mother sees her son release his bird to fly outside. It goes into a nearby tree and lands. And to his surprise, the bird sings. His heart swells and breaks at the same time.

After a few days, the bird moves on. Now it is he who sits and looks out the window, wanting his friend to visit. The mother comes up and puts her hand on his shoulder. "Why did you turn the bird loose?" she asks. "You loved that bird."

He looks up and says, "All birds must leave the nest one day. I have realized that includes me. School will be finished soon, and I'll be moving out myself. Thank both you and Dad for the support and care given to me. But it's time for me to go out on my own also. It was the bird that made me realize that I needed to leave the nest."

Boys do grow up to be men one day. The teachers can vary. They learn and grow. But they will stay in touch. They will give back the love given to them. Be proud the day your birds fly out on their own. It's the circle of life.

Story 101
"Never Allow Anger to be a Wedge"

A father and his daughter were always arguing. Nothing he told her seemed to please her. So, there was always an argument.

The mother has been gone for about two years now. Left with another man. The dad was trying his best. Even tried counseling. The daughter fought him the entire time. Then one afternoon the fight was harder than usual. The dad went to his truck and squealed his tires when leaving.

About two hours later she got the call. It was the hospital and she was told her father was hurt. She remembered the look he had when she told him he was a poor father at best. A weak man and that was why her mother left. She wanted to hurt him and she did. Words can do the same damage as blunt objects.

They led her to his bed. He was dying. Tubes were attached all over. He looked so helpless. Tears came to her eyes. She sat and held his hand. She began to talk.

"Dad, I'm angry. Mom left us and I blamed you. I know that isn't true. But my anger wouldn't release those feelings. I needed to blame someone and you were there. I have done you so wrong. Now you might leave this life and my last words were so hateful. I'm ashamed for what I said. Please come back to me. Don't leave me now. I need you."

As her tears fell, she felt a weak squeeze of his hand. He could hear her. She came back every day. She would always hold his hand. Always showing her love for him. She became a daughter any father would be proud of.

She was the same girl, but she no longer looked for reasons to be angry. Love and accepting her father was the answer to her change.

There are misdirected feelings all the time. To know what you think you know can be harmful. Our minds can create the story to fit our feelings. Question yourself. Especially if you believe with no proof. Misunderstandings can be repaired. Mistakes happen. It's just human. The "good" tries to reach the top. It doesn't always make it. Help it.

Story 102

"All the Reasons I Love You"

Out of all the lovely women in this world, you're the one I love.

And why? Let me see if I can speak such eloquent words: Your demeanor. Never hyped up on emotions. You seem to control your actions. You "check and balance" before you react. You seem so stable which helps me. The tender side of you. Beautiful smile, soft touch, eyes that speak to me constantly. I'm a very lucky man.

Do you ever get angry, sure. But you smooth out the offensive edges. You care about what you say. How you react. Slow drivers seem to punch a button or two. That just makes you more "every day" normal. When we're apart you call or text to just say "hi". Just to show you're thinking of me. So, I try to take your lead.

As I said, I'm a better man because of you. I'm thankful for our relationship.

I'm a lucky man.

Early love is always the most romantic!!!

Story 103
"The good in Life"

He was a gentle soul. This large man was so misunderstood.

He didn't pick his size, and he smiled a lot. Sometimes trouble would follow him. He didn't want it, but sometimes it just came to him. On those occasions, he handled it. Didn't enjoy how it went down, but he would stand his ground. Once settled, he would go back to who he really was. A kind man.

At the store, he would watch for who was buying what. He could see the stress on the older ones trying to get by till their next check arrived. So, often, he paid their bill. Wished them well and went on. They were ever so thankful. This went on for years. He stayed in the shadows but helped all he could, never asking for anything in return.

One day, he woke up in a hospital. He had blacked out in the store. He had a bad bump on his head. A doctor came to him and said they were running tests but were pretty sure it wasn't good. And sure enough, he was told he would never leave and should get his affairs in order while he could. He had no family but had lived a great life.

Later that day, people started showing up at his room. People he had helped along the way. The word about his health was out. So many came. His heart swelled, and his eyes teared up. And they kept coming. His room filled with flowers. A young girl around eight came in with her mother. She took his hand. "My mother told me I'm here because of a big man with a big heart who helped her out when she needed it most. I now know it was you. No, you don't remember my mom, but I love you for what you did for us. You were an angel to us."

And the stories continued. His last days were filled with the love and appreciation from so many. His funeral was so packed it filled the grounds. And most of the people there had only recently found out his name.

The good in people is shared daily. Things aren't really that bad. It's just the good is not always reported. The good in life often goes unnoticed.

Story 104
"We Never Know the Full Story"

It was a cold night, and he was running late. But he chose to stop and give money to a homeless person. Maybe she could get a room tonight.

The next evening on the local news they tell the story of a homeless lady who died from exposure while gripping a hundred-dollar bill. Unidentified, her body could be claimed at the morgue. This struck him hard. Could he have done more? Should he have done more? So, when she went unclaimed, he signed for and claimed her ashes himself. Then he hired a P.I. to find out her background.

Her name was Nancy. Nancy Thomas. Age 76, husband died nine years earlier. Had a son but lost him to street drugs. Her husband loved her and took care of all her needs. This turned out to be her downfall. She wasn't prepared to deal with the aggressive predators who came for her money. Within a short time, she was penniless. Lost her home, her car, and her dignity. She didn't understand government programs, aid facilities, she was lost. So, the streets became her home now. She begged for pocket change to eat. Huddled with other homeless when the rain fell. Winters were the worst. She learned all the tricks the streetwise knew to keep warm. But on that last night it wasn't enough. She had money but no way to get to a motel. And then she maybe didn't have enough? The weather turned very bitter that night and that was the end to her misery.

He looked at the report and then the Urn. He would have her laid to rest in a place under a big oak. Shaded from the heat. Protected from the rain. A marker with the inscription "here lies Nancy Thomas. A strong woman who finally met her match." Her husband was moved beside her. Reunited at last.

Yes, I should have done more that cold night. Maybe this small gesture will make up for it. She and her husband are together again.

Story 105

"From Kindness comes Beauty"

Titled by Kimberly Rooney

It was a bright sunny day. A perfect day to go to the park. And that's where they met.

She was noticed standing alone. This beautiful lady. And the girl was drawn to her. The girls personality was a little different than most. So she walked up and introduced herself. She would sit and talk. Enjoying her time together. But eventually she would have to leave, knowing she would return. And return she did. Many times. Talking to her escape for any stress she might be carrying.

Then one day she wanted her to come to her home with her. She gently walked with her to her home. She was given a place with a large window. A wonderful bed. All the light and warmth she could ask for. You could see she was happy. So happy that a single stem emerged. Over the next few day, the stem grew. And a bud appeared at the top. The girl was ecstatic. Her friend was maturing. So she talked even more than usual.

Then one morning a beautiful flower bloomed. Such a beautiful flower. The girl was a little taken back. Such a magnificent flower. The deepness of the colors, the shape. She now had a face to look at, to speak to.

Talking to your plants is good for you. Good for your plants. Plants feel your presence. You're caring. They have their own form of life. Respect that!!!

Story 106
"The Passage of Time"

People talk about the passing of time.

How fast their children grow. How soon it's a birthday again. Does a busy mind speed time? Or does time move at different speeds? A watched pot never boils. It took forever to finish this job. Is it the time or you? Everyone knows the answer. But why do we blame the clock? It's said the faster you move, the slower time passes. Science is not shy to give examples of that one. The measurement of time with a clock isn't that old really. It was just day or night.

Then we started to break that into chunks. Morning, evening, noon, afternoon. Suddenly, none of that was good enough. So, a tool to measure time was created. Now, instead of working daylight till dark, it's measured in hours. Lunch hour, overtime, eight-hour workday. Not a bad thing at all. A sign of the evolution of time. Science has divided a second into so many sections it takes a scientist to understand it.

So, when I say, "Catch you later," what time frame is that? Interesting to think about. Such an open-ended statement. A measure of time everyone clearly understands. Time rules our lives. Yet was time invented by man or discovered? You know there is a correct answer. Food for thought!

Story 107
"Complicated Love"

The term is out there that we of maturity share. Your EX

You don't marry your first love mostly. You fall in love but, with time or circumstance your love for each other drifts apart. I'm sure not all breakups are full of anger. You just both come to the understanding the ribbon that connects you both is undoing. So, you look again. You have a clearer picture of the one you want to be with. You fall in love again. This time it seems to be a better match. Or you're content to live single and just casual date. But in your private time you reflect on that "ex." At one time your heart was open to them. You don't have enough fingers and toes to list all the reasons that can break up a couple. It probably came down to a focused point. You no longer harbor anger or a broken heart. You and the other moved on. But you were in love with them at one time. Your love is held for that special someone. Things happen. There's not really a fault. It was a learning experience.

So, if you move too fast, love too quickly, choose poorly or any number of reasons, you find yourself looking again. You can wonder if a past love has changed. If you are still that person back then? It's a couple who shares in the success or failure of a relationship. Many times one more than the other. With the anger gone you can reflect with a small smile. Hope for the best for them. And love the one you're with now. Love with the passion of experience. Love is not between the sheets. That's the pleasure part. Love is the respect shown. Holding of hands. Eye to eye contact with a smile. The caring for each other. Do you not agree?

Story 108
"Tipping the Scale"

I stand alone. I'm smothered in a white light. And in front of me is a scale.

A dish on either side, connected by small chains. A pointer resting on zero. To the left are negative numbers. To the tight positive. Where am I? Then memories start to flow. I'm a small child. The way I acted, the actions I chose. The pointer would move. When it moved to the left the light would dim. Doing the right thing allowed the pointer to move to the right again. The brightness would return. I was standing accountable for my life. I was frozen there. Watching my life pass. These were all memories of truth. My life on display to me. There was nothing I could do to stop this.

I went up to my years as a teenager. I was losing ground. I was feeling very nervous. Then eighteen came. I volunteered to join the military. To go fight a war. To possibly die for strangers, I didn't know. To give them a better life at maybe the cost of my own. The pointer moved to the right. The light was bright again. My twenties, thirties, and forties not that much movement either way.

When I reached my fifties, things changed. Seems my life had improved in my kindness. I cared more for strangers. I wanted to help. Over the years I gained ground to the right. Then one day I saw the day I died. The memories I couldn't stop were ending. And I saw a focused point of light. I was drawn to it. I was going to a better place. I could now walk towards this new light.

We don't know how our day of judgement will be. But know we will stand accountable for our life. Be sure you can move to the light of focus, and not be swallowed up by the darkness.

Story 109
"I still Kiss him good night"

It was getting late. She was in bed for the night. Big day tomorrow. Christmas just hours away. The house was so quiet. Then she began to remember. This small girl who always wanted to sit on Daddy's lap. Her tiny world evolved around his big smile and his kisses on her cheeks. He'd been gone for years, but she still saw that big smile. She could still feel her mother brushing her hair. *So many hours of talking with Mom. I wish I had never grown up. I was able to take dance lessons. It was great. The lights were bright, but I knew Mom and Dad were watching. I always did my best.*

I remember school. That really cute boy in the back. I married him. After sixty-two years of marriage, he had to leave. We had a son together. Never did get that little girl; guess it just wasn't meant to be. Our son gave us two beautiful little girls, I'm glad to say. That's just as good. So every year, they come for Christmas. They don't want me to be alone. But in this old house full of memories, that could never be. So I must sleep. Tomorrow will be so busy. Both the girls will come in early and stay the day. The feelings are so good. I love Christmas. I kiss Tom good night. It's the back of my hand now. But I kiss him still every day. I sure miss him. Tomorrow will be full of love all day. I need to sleep.

Story 110
"A New Dawn"

The thunder wakes him. It's still dark outside.

He lies there a minute and gets his barring. His dog wants by his side. Thunder scares him. A very brave dog otherwise. The weather tells him it's not far away. Mentally he walks the yard. Will the rain harm anything? I'm sure many of you enjoy the sound of a soft rain, he sure does. Opening a few windows allows for better sound.

The plants needed water anyhow, so that's a job he won't have to do. The thunder moves closer. The dog shows his stress but also has comfort being close to you. He decides to start coffee. There are light things he can do during the rain. This gift from Mother Nature is a special time. A soft rain blanketing the house and yard. Cool breeze moving around. Yes, a very special gift.

He can hear the drops hit the roof. The sounds around him change. Daylight is just trying to start. Coffee is almost ready. He sets up a chair and table at the best location on the porch. He'll watch from a dry area. Coffee will be great this morning, as if it isn't on other mornings. He gets his cup and turns on music. A great day is ahead!

Story 111
"Happiness is never that far away"

It's been ten years now. But I still think of her. Why do my thoughts hold on? Why?

I hear she's married now. Lost track years ago. Just hope she's happy. She was a good person. For whatever reason my thoughts won't let go of the memories. We both agreed it was in our best interest to go our separate ways. At the time it was what I wanted also. What happened to me? Why can't I just move on? Maturity has its reality. Love seems always just out of reach. The ones I see finally grow tired of my lack to take the relationship to the next level. But I can't, my love just isn't strong enough yet.

So, I stay single. In my time of thought I drift back ten years. I remember "old times". I seem content with that. I know she's not the same. She could be a hundred pounds heavier. Maybe even more beautiful. Probably the latter. Either way she's a pleasant memory now. What I don't want is to be with someone who is like the one I loved. I would be still holding on to the past. I need that fresh start. The one I share love with deserves better.

One day I'll find love again. Happiness is never that far away. What is meant to be will happen. For now, my thoughts of the past do make me smile. And who knows, I might be a great catch for the right woman!

Story 112

"The Beauty of a Flower"

A flower bloomed in my life. More beautiful a flower never existed.

    As long as I give it the love and care it needs, it will flourish. I'm not its first caretaker. There has been others. But they never saw the beautiful flower my eyes see. Never did they want to care for it as I have!!! So, this flower with its fragrance so pure, grows in my garden now. An area to protect its Royal identity. So special is this flower that I would defend it with my life.

    This flower is My Universe. I really am in love with its beauty, its existence. With the way it's affecting my life. I find peace in that.

Story 113
"Marriage"

I see her walking in my direction. All eyes are on her. Such beauty. Hard to believe she found love in me…

But there she is. A proud smile on her face that I can barely see. Walking in my direction. A man walking by her side. Really not that sure I deserve her. But he trusts her judgement. With time I'll win him over. I must! He will be my Father-in-Law.

All dressed in white. A church full of people wishing us the best. Smiles fill the walls. The smell of flowers dominate the room. No one could have wished for a more magnificent day. Today she accepts my name as hers. I'm very proud. I drift to the first day we met. I was so impressed. I knew I must learn her name. And here I stand. Watching this gorgeous lady advancing towards me.

We now stand together. Her hand in mine. Her father seated. She speaks her words of commitment. And I say mine. Then I'm told I may kiss my bride. We are introduced to the crowd as Mr. and Mrs. My universe is complete. We now will travel together. Share our dreams.

But for now, we will break and run for the limo. Pelted with rice and flowers. A resort beach awaits us. A honeymoon suite and a bottle of champagne.

My first night with my wife.

Story 114
"My Special Person"

Her head rest on his shoulder. Sound asleep having dreams of innocents. He loves her so.

He remembers the first time he saw her. Such a beautiful girl. He knew they were meant for each other. Always looking for the time he had to spend with her. He wanted to be her protector. The one she ran to. But now she sleeps. Secure in his arms. Later they'll have a quite dinner together. Settle in for a little TV together. She doesn't care for his shows, so he'll pretty much give in to her. He just wants her happy.

He's planning a special gathering. Family and friends. Bought her a piece of jewelry. Nothing big. A small chain with a cross. He knows she'll like it. She'll be the center of attention. It will be her day. Everyone wanting their time with her. He'll have to share her. He knows she'll always return to him.

Being a single parent is not easy to start with. And having a daughter turning ten can have challenges. But he's up to the task. They lost her mother very early. He's done well. A very caring father. She's the sparkle in his eye. So for now he shares her time. Knowing full well she'll rest her head on his shoulder once more. You can be both a father and mother if those are the cards dealt. Or the other way around. And you can be very good at it.

Story 115

"Be Careful of What You Ask Your Grandkids to do"

Authored by Dick Speed

It's late January and the end of deer season is here. Our motorhome is set up in a location near the camp kitchen building. We have electrical power, but no sewer system. So, we rely on the holding tanks for our black and gray water waste. (For those none-campers, gray is your wash waters and black is your toilet waste.) It wasn't a problem to empty the gray tank, but to empty the black tank I would need to break camp and move to a location where it could safely be emptied. Since we only had about a week to go before the end of deer season and we would be taking the motorhome back home. I was watching my tank levels closely and minimizing what went in the tank.

Mary and I are at our hunting lease and have our two grandsons with us. Mason was 7 years old and Kayd was 4 years old. If you haven't ever seen young boys in the wide-open spaces, discovering all the new things, and adventures there are in nature, it is so heartwarming. Little things like cow patties (maybe not so little) are exciting, for boys living in the city. They were having so much fun discovering and investigating all kind of things. Not to mention walking around the concrete rim of the large water storage cistern.

On this particular Saturday afternoon, I'm watching UT Longhorns football game on the TV. I hear Kayd come in the motorhome. As he came by my chair, I asked "Where are you going boy?" "I need to go to the bathroom" he says. "Go outside and find a bush" I replied, thinking he just needs to pea. "OK Papa", and he leaves. In about ten minutes, Mason comes in as if in a hurry. "Where are you going boy" I asked? "Kayd needs some toilet paper"!

Not realizing at the time, I had just sent my 4-year-old grandson out to take his first dump in the wild.

Story 116

"Living Of Grid"

In today's day and age, why would anyone want to live off grid? A good question! Since I do, and as of the time of this writing, I've lived out here permanently for nine years now. This is my answer.

    I think I'm trying to hold on to the past. Not so far back, the technology has its advantages. I'm in my bed propped up by pillows, writing this. Turned off the air conditioner about two this morning as I do every summer morning. The house is cooled down and I save gas on the generator. Only need it during the hot summer months. June, July, August, and September. I burn around three gallons a night. Around three hundred a month. But only for those four months. Winter is very cheap. The heat is made with propane. The bathroom and kitchen. This brings the cost to probably a third of that. No house notes or land payments.

Have a well. So, no water bill. Anytime the generator runs the water is automatically pumped up. I have 200 gallons in holding tanks. That will last me around three days, if I don't run the generator to pump it back up. It's a 220-volt system. My electricity is solar. All generated with panels and fed to a battery bank. I can run my cabin with air conditioning all day to keep the house cool. Right now, I have an air cooler blowing on me. Even now I'll get cold enough to require a sheet to cover up with. So, my living requirements are taken care of.

I have 145 acres (all wooded) surrounded by closed in 13,000 wooded acres. And it's just me. I'm two miles from the closest home. No electrical service outside of my solar and generator. No roads other than a pipeline to get here. And I absolutely love it out here. I see all types of wild game almost every day. For that I have a real appreciation. You just don't know.

Loneliness is not an issue with me. Not my personality. I have dogs, cats, chickens, and ducks to care for. I stay busy. I'm outside almost all day every day. No TV, my choice. Have a stocked lake, grow a few veggies. I don't shoot my game. But my family and friends do. So they give me a share. Town is just a short hour away. I go in about every six days or so. It really is a great life to me. Maybe not for everyone, but for me, for sure. It allows me to write. I do carry a cell phone. I'm almost 75 years old. I think that's wise of me. But I have been challenged that it puts me back on the grid. Believe what you want. My safety trumps. I don't agree.

So, this is my off-grid life. No two days are the same. A simple life. Laid-back and adventurous. I'll have to leave one day. Go back to the city. Just think of the stories I'll have to tell. And I'm a story teller, so watch out!!!

Milton Keynes UK
Ingram Content Group UK Ltd.
UKHW021245191124
451300UK00007B/231